PAUL VANDORN

Diastole

First published by Cold Front Publishing 2022

First edition

ISBN: 978-1-7379662-5-8

This book was professionally typeset on Reedsy.
Find out more at reedsy.com

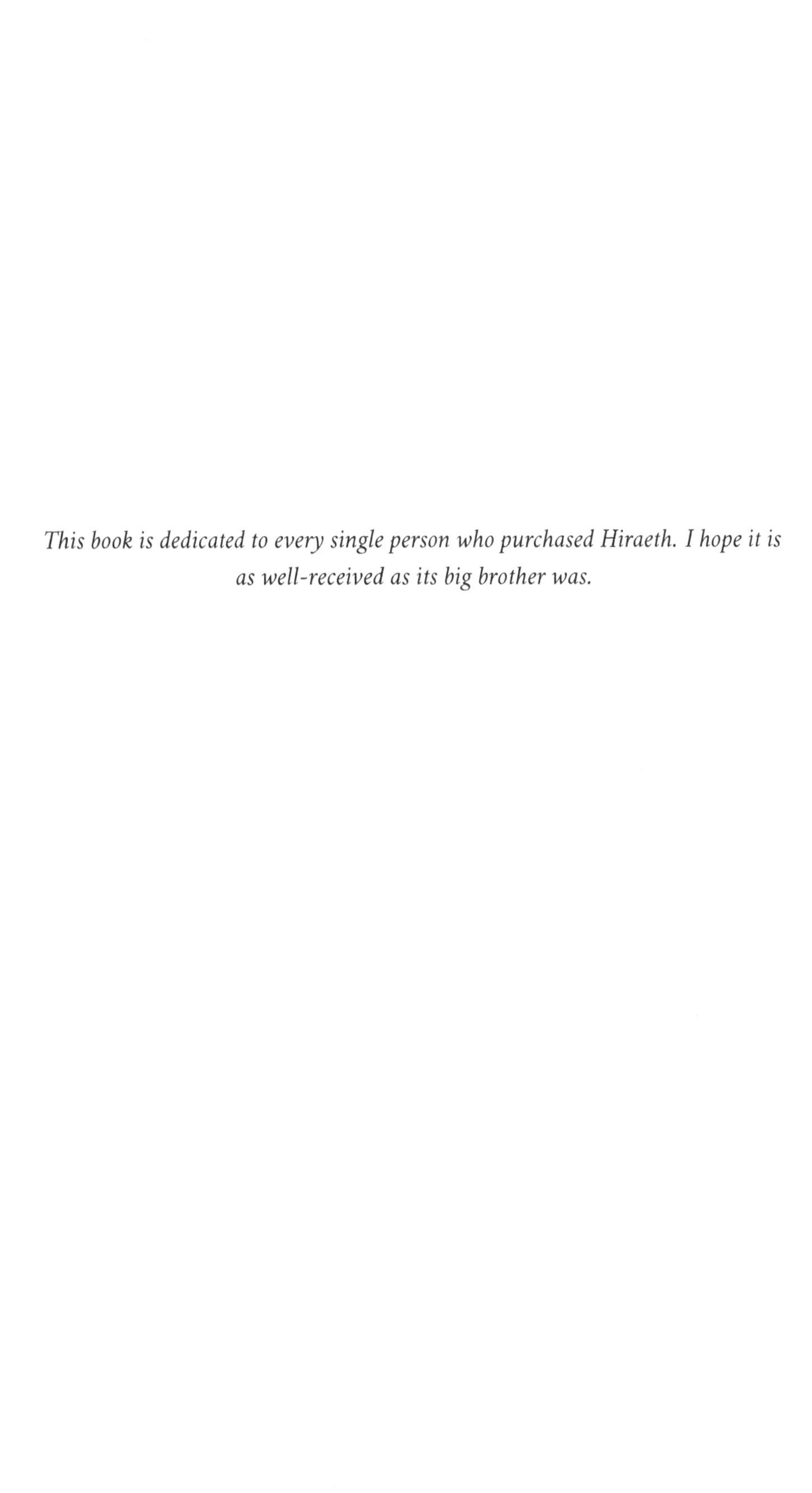

This book is dedicated to every single person who purchased Hiraeth. I hope it is as well-received as its big brother was.

"Einstein's Monsters," by the way, refers to
nuclear weapons, but also to ourselves. We
are Einstein's monsters, not fully human, not
for now."
— Martin Amis, Einstein's Monsters

Chapter 1

Monday, November 13th, 1995

Alistair Woodbridge accompanied Jedrek Ender on his morning perambulation around the grounds of Savista. The November air was cool, and Alistair drew it deep into his lungs. It felt good to expand his chest cavity again, though he still suffered occasionally from shortness of breath. Alistair pressed a hand against his stomach wound and braced for a cough.

"Is it getting any better, old friend?" Jedrek asked.

Alistair nodded. "It is; I owe you my life, Jedrek."

"Nonsense, it was Reka and Cage who saved you," Jedrek said with a dismissive wave of his hand. "Truth be told, I would have forbidden them had they asked my permission to take such a dangerous chance. Luckily for you, that Reka is a free spirit, and Cage suffers bouts of chivalry."

Alistair laughed and grimaced at the pain in his gut.

"You know, you'll have to take it easy. Our doctors couldn't remove the bullet from your stomach."

Three months had passed since Alistair and Joe Kott left Savista to search for Hayward Taft's corpse in the Barrens. What they found was anything but a corpse. Like a cockroach, Taft endured, and after getting the drop on him, shot Alistair in the belly. Alistair managed to return fire and sent him over the cliff with a lucky shot from his Dragoon, but not before Taft told him that he'd killed Joe.

Alistair shook his head at the thought. "I should have listened."

"Listened to who?"

"The progresinto, back at the Church of the Expiator. Joe and I stopped there a couple of days after we left Espero. He told Joe and me that only one of us would return," Alistair hung his head. "I honestly didn't think it would to be me?"

It was clear that Alistair was heartbroken at the loss of his friend. And to make matters worse, it was Reka who had come to his rescue.

"Most days, I wish she'd never come after me," Alistair said.

"I don't think it was you she was after," Jedrek said. It was a cold response, but they were living in cold times.

"Believe me, my friend, I am reminded of that every time I see her face. She always greets me with the same soft, sad smile."

"Don't take it to heart. I know Reka is happy that you survived."

"She may be, but I'm not. And I am haunted by it. And I'm haunted by not knowing that Taft is finally dead."

"Well, you can be of that. Cage said it was at least a hundred-foot drop from that overhang to the ravine below. No one could survive a fall like that."

"That's what I thought the last time, but here I am again, faced with uncertainty."

In his forty-plus years as a lawman, Alistair Woodbridge had shot more men than he cared to remember, and his big Colt Dragoons didn't leave any of them alive. But as far as Alistair was concerned, he wouldn't believe that Taft was dead until he saw his body quartered up and buried in the four corners of the Midwestern Territories. Alistair had underestimated Hayward Taft before, and it cost him dearly. And while there was nothing he could do to bring his friend back, he certainly intended to make sure Taft was dead and gone.

"Well, there's no point in troubling your mind with those kinds of thoughts. Not when we're facing another winter. Winter will bring her own worries. Still," Jedrek said as he drew in a deep breath of his own. "The air sure smells sweet today, old friend."

The air carried the soft fragrance of the jack pines, and all around Savista, the trees were ablaze with color, signaling winter's approach. Winter on the plains was especially brutal for the vagadi tribes. The vagadi faced harsher than normal conditions, food scarcity, and more frequent raids by the freebooters. Fortunately, Savista wasn't like the other vagadi. Savista was more like a small town than a camp and better suited to withstand the seasons. The *vagadi*, a word meaning wanderer in a mostly forgotten language, lived like the early Native Americans. They traveled the plains by foot, living in shelters made of pelts and wooden poles that they could tear down and move at a moment's notice. Savista, on the other hand, set their camp on a high plateau and built their structures of wood and stone. They grew crops, raised livestock, and hunted in the valley below. They collected water in cisterns, and in the acid season, when the burning rains fell and water was at a premium, they made juice using the fruits and vegetables from their gardens. Sustenance was plentiful, shelter substantial, and their position on the plateau highly defensible. Savista was still counted among the vagadi, though more by tradition than practice.

Just off the path, Jedrek and Alistair had been walking; a commotion arose as Agermonte and Barrister came upon a badger in its sett. A primarily nocturnal hunter, the animal had likely just returned home after a long night's work, only to be disturbed by the two massive beasts. Agermonte and Barrister meant no harm, tending more toward a much larger quarry; the giant spiders or the docco being their preference, but the badger was having none of it. Alistair could hear the little animal's hissing even over Agermonte and Barrister's barking, and he had to call to them several times to bring them to heel.

About a month into Alistair's recovery, Jedrek sent his people to Espero to retrieve Agermonte and Barrister. He said he thought it would do the old Ranger good to have his dogs with him, and he was right. Since their arrival, Alistair made it a point to join Jedrek on his morning walks and always brought the beasts along. They had been left in the care of Jedrek's father, Bolie Ender, back in Espero before Alistair and Joe had begun their quest. Bolie kept them fed and content as they awaited the return of their master, though fate had other plans. Reuniting with Agermonte and Barrister had been a great boon to Alistair, whose heart weighed heavy having lost Joe. He had come to think of Joe like a son and now understood with crystal clarity the sound logic behind the Rangers Council's decision to forbid family to anyone called to serve. Weakness and vulnerability were, in fact, the natural byproduct of love, and the Ranger's Counsel in Columbia had been wise to disallow the practice. Joe wasn't his flesh and blood, and he had only known the man for a short time, but their bond was deep. It had been forged in the fires of battle and quenched in blood, and the loss was crippling to Alistair. If he had it to do all over again, he would opt for keeping Joe safe over pursuing Taft, a known murderer, and for a Ranger, that was unthinkable, unforgivable.

Alistair knew he wasn't the only one who suffered the loss. Reka shared his pain. From the time Joe and Reka met until he dragged Joe off into the Barrens, the two had been inseparable. And it was easy to understand why. Both were brave, strong, and fierce but still caring. Like her, Joe didn't live for battle but rose eagerly to defend good against evil. Reka and Joe were kindred spirits, and she loved him, and because she loved him, she suffered. And like Alistair, her grief was compounded by the lack of closure. Not being able to turn his body over to the pastreco to be held in Diastole was terrible enough, but the thought of Joe as Rikolti, one more tortured soul imprisoned in the Barrens, was more than either of them could bear.

Both Alistair and Reka lobbied to lead a team into the Narrows to try and recover his body, but Jedrek had flatly denied their request. Emotionally detached from the situation, Jedrek saw the folly in chasing ghosts in the Barrens, and it was that thought, the thought of Joe being one of the ghosts of the Barrens that burrowed its way into Alistair's brain this morning.

"You realize, Jedrek, that with or without your blessing, I intend to return to the Barrens and find Joe's body."

Jedrek harrumphed.

"I would much rather go with your blessing and the aid of six good men," Alistair continued. "But one way or the other, I am going."

"Alistair, my dear friend," Jedrek pulled at his long beard and exhaled loudly. "I grow weary of this topic. There has never been, nor will there ever be, a successful recovery from the Barrens. You, of all people, should know that!"

"What do you call me?"

"Please, Alistair, for the sake of my sanity, I beg a reprieve from this topic."

Alistair threw his hands up in acquiescence, and upon nearing his quarters, bid Jedrek a temporary goodbye and reprieve. He would see him shortly for breakfast with the rest of the camp in the mess hall and perhaps broach the topic again. In the meantime, he would feed Agermonte and Barrister and wash up for breakfast. Alistair walked to one of the camp's root cellars, where he grabbed some carrots, potatoes, and a pound of venison and carried it back to his quarters. In his little kitchen area, he chopped up the vegetables, cut the meat into cubes, and put equal portions into two bowls. The dogs sat patiently, saliva dripping from their jowls until Alistair set their bowls down outside, signaling to them that breakfast was served. It was a sickening display. Snorting, grunting, and slobber flying through the air, but it did Alistair's heart good.

As the dogs devoured their food, a bell rang out, letting Savista know that breakfast was about to be served in the mess hall. Alistair cleaned his knife in his kitchen sink and washed his hands before heading over. As he neared the mess hall, children scampered about, and the smell of bacon pushed the fragrant aroma of the jack pines out of the air. Agermonte and Barrister walked ahead of their master sniffing happily. The sun was shining bright, and the whole of these parts brought him great joy. It's a good day to be alive, Alistair thought and then hung his head, feeling guilt at the sentiment.

"What's wrong, Mr. Alistair?"

Alistair looked down and saw a little girl with short brown hair and large almond-shaped brown eyes gazing up at him.

"I'm just missing a friend, child."

"Is she dead or just away?"

"It's a he, his name was Joe, and I'm afraid he's dead."

"My name is Thea, well Althea, but everyone just calls me Thea. I'll be your friend until you go to diastole to meet him if you would like."

Alistair smiled wanly. Thea's skin was still golden brown, her summer tan not yet faded, which made the whites of her eyes sparkle. It was the look of youth, the look of vitality, and it stood in stark contrast to the tired, weathered eyes that took her in.

"Well, that would be just grand, Althea, Thea for short," said Alistair.

He'd seen the little girl running around and playing with the other children but never bothered to learn any of their names.

"I'm very pleased to meet you," she said.

"Likewise," Alistair said, as Agermonte and Barrister seized the moment to garner some attention from the child licking her face and nudging her with their massive heads.

"These two monsters are my dogs, Ager—"

"Yes, I know," Thea giggled. "Agermonte and Barrister."

The more she shoved them away, the more they licked and nudged—and the more they licked and nudged, the more the child laughed.

"Well, it seems you know much more about me and mine than I know about you."

The child's laughter was contagious, and Alistair couldn't help but laugh himself.

"Momma said you were a fearless man. A Ranger. She said you chase the bad people away."

"Is that what she said?"

"Yes, and she said that you helped bring some of my new friends here and that you had to protect them from those nasty freebooters," her nose wrinkled as if smelling something terrible. "So you must be very brave."

"Well, Thea, I think you're very brave."

"Me? You think I'm brave?"

"I do indeed. I've seen grownups cry when Agermonte and Barrister got near them. But not you. You weren't scared for a minute."

Thea just giggled and continued to shove the dogs away.

"These guys? Come on; you're pulling on my leg."

"Pulling on your—"

Alistair was familiar with the phrase, though he'd never heard it put quite that way.

"That's what momma says when she thinks I'm telling a lie. Well," she said, closing one eye thoughtfully, "maybe not a lie; I get spanked for lies, but maybe just a tall-tale."

"I see," said Alistair. "Say, we'd better hurry over to the mess. You're gonna have to get cleaned up before breakfast."

In playing with Agermonte and Barrister, the girl's hands and face were covered in slobber.

"I'd like to meet your folks and tell them what a brave child they've raised."

"What's *foks*, Mr. Alistair?"

"Folks, with an L," he corrected. "Folks are your parents, your momma, and your poppa."

"Oh!" she exclaimed. "I don't have a poppa; it's just momma and me. My poppa was killed by the freebooters when they took our camp away."

"Well, Thea, I am very sorry for your loss. What say we go find your momma?"

"I say let's go!" Thea grabbed hold of Alistair's finger—giving him a static shock—and dragged him along to the mess hall.

"Ouch!" Alistair exclaimed. "What was that?"

"Oh, that happens all the time when I get excited."

***

Alistair knew Siobhan the moment he laid eyes on her. He remembered her taking shifts caring for him as he recovered from his time in the Barrens. He felt foolish. He should have seen the resemblance right away; he would have bet that she was the spitting image of her daughter at that age.

"Hello, Siobhan!" Alistair said, even before Thea could make the introduction. "Look what I found running around outside."

"Hello, Alistair. Still in the pink?"

"Sure am, and I have to tell you what a kind child you've raised."

"Is that right?" Siobhan said. "And what do we say, little lady?"

"You said I was brave!" challenged Thea.

"Thea!" Siobhan scolded.

"Thank you, Mr. Alistair," Thea said. It was sing-songy but genuine.

Alistair smiled at her. "You know Thea, it's better to be kind than brave, but you certainly are both."

Thea's face lit up and then scrunched again.

"But momma, why do I have to say thank you? I was the one who was being kind and brave. Mr. Alistair should say thank you."

"Thea!" Siobhan scolded again. "I'm so sorry, Alistair."

He gave a short, loud laugh. "Don't be. She's absolutely right."

"No, she is not right. Not if her mother says she's not," Siobhan snapped.

"Beg pardon, ma'am," Alistair tipped the brim of his Stetson.

Siobhan smiled at him, letting him know he was off the hook. "And I'm sure you'll be removing your hat."

Alistair pawed at his hat, pulling it from his head, his long gray hair flowing out from beneath.

"Perhaps you'll let me cut that for you," Siobhan said, her smile growing.

Alistair nervously smoothed his hair down.

"If you'll excuse me, our table is up," she said. "It's been nice talking with you."

"Of course," Alistair said as he gave a polite little bow, then he turned for his own table. "Goodbye, Mr. Alistair!"

"Goodbye, Thea."

As he walked away, he heard Siobhan telling Thea to wash her hands and face, or she would go hungry till lunch. Alistair chuckled to himself.

As he reached his table, he felt a tug at his sleeve. It was Thea.

"He's not dead, Mr. Alistair."

Alistair's jaw dropped. "Not dead; who's not dead?"

"Your friend Joe is alive; he's not dead. You were wrong when you said he was dead." And with that, she ran off to wash up for breakfast.

Chapter 2

John 'Fitz' Fitzpatrick leaned back in his chair and stared at the blinking green dot on his computer screen. Chief Vecchio had ordered him to take a little time off after the Kott incident, and the first case he caught when he returned was a simple one. A local farmer reported a stolen tank of anhydrous ammonia from his farm—no need to look any further than Horse, the latest motorcycle club to come roaring into town. It was far from the case of the century, but it felt good to be back in the world of the normal. Fitz's time spent in the realm of the paranormal had taken its toll, and the experience had impacted even something as mundane as writing a report. He'd written hundreds of police reports in his career and never had an issue. Start with the date and time, follow that with the offense, add the facts of the case and whether or not an arrest was made, and voila, you have a police report.

But now, facing that little blinking light sent shocks of stress through his fingertips. Like barreling full speed down a road with a flashing bridge out sign, the little blinking light was a visual reminder of that hot August day when they pulled Joe's lifeless body from the dark well deep in the forest in Northern Wisconsin. Writing the report regarding the disappearance and recovery of Officer Kott nearly drove him mad, but in the end, he'd managed to file his findings and avoid a psych evaluation, which, given all he'd been through, was the best he could have hoped for.

It had been three months since Hayward Taft murdered Detective Koen VanElzen in the Izhijiwan National Forest before escaping into the Barrens. Which, if you believed Lucas Travidi—the remote viewer who the Red

Hook Police Department had recruited to help with the case—existed in an alternate dimension. According to Lucas, Taft escaped after being knocked ass over teakettle into a well. But Fitz had been there in that forest when it all came to a head. Fitz would have bet the farm that Taft had to be down there because he sure as shit didn't climb back out. And yet search after search turned up nothing. Well, nothing, that is, except for Joe Kott, who disappeared without a trace from a field on the outskirts of town a few weeks prior. Red Hook was three hundred miles away from the bottom of that well, yet somehow, Officer Kott had ended up down there. If Fitz hadn't seen it with his own eyes, he never would have believed it. But he helped pull Joe's body out of that well. Fitz saw the black dust pour from Joe's mouth, nose, and from the stab wound in his gut—only to then vanish like vapor on a winter day.

Just thinking about it made the stress spread from his fingers to his whole body, and he was finding it hard to take a deep breath. He decided that he needed another cup of coffee, his third of the day, and it was only 9 a.m. The screech from his chair as he slid back from his desk was drowned out by the yelling that came from the lobby. Fitz knew that voice, though he hadn't heard it in years.

"Tree munts? Tree munts, and not one of you dummies thought to gimme a call?"

Fitz rolled his eyes. "Fucking Tague." Fitz should have seen this coming. Everyone was so busy looking for Joe that no one thought to call Bob, and maybe that was an excuse at the beginning, but it had been months since they'd found him. Bob Tague had been Joe's best friend since they met in grade school. Fitz knew he would have expected the same courtesy if it had been his best friend. That is if he had a best friend.

"Calm down, Tague!" boomed Sergeant Ronald Corliss.

"Calm down, my ass!"

It was a short reply, but Fitz thought it summed Bob up pretty well. Bob was a no-nonsense, get-right-to-the-point kind of guy. There was no soft sell and no gray area for Bob. In that respect, he reminded Fitz a lot of Joe's dad.

"You're going to calm down or get tossed out of here, Bob!"

"I ain't goin nowhere until I get some answers!"

Fitz set his coffee cup down on his desk and made a beeline for the lobby. Not many people had the stones to stand up to Corliss, but Bob did. The guy didn't seem to have a reverse gear or even a neutral, not that Fitz could recall anyway. Fitz knew that if Corliss so much as touched Bob's shoulder to move him toward the door, all hell would break loose. He dashed through the detective division, right past the report writing room, and burst through the door into the lobby. He needed to add some calm to the testosterone tsunami brewing before it came crashing down on the whole department.

"Bob! I am so sorry, I was the lead on the investigation, and I should have called."

"Jeez, Fitzy, no one called me or nuttin. Is he okay?"

"Yeah, he's fine. And again, I'm sorry, Bob. You should have been one of my first calls, but things took off so fast. One minute I was at home in bed, and the next, I was heading for Wisconsin."

"Wisconsin? What the hell does Wisconsin have to do with this?"

Fitz sighed. "Let me buy you a cup of coffee."

Fitz led, but Bob knew the way. They sat at a table in the break room. Fitz could sense that Bob was more worried than angry, and Fitz really did feel bad for not having called him. He knew that Bob would have done anything to help his friend. Once they had coffee in hand, Fitz told Bob the whole story, from start to finish, leaving nothing out. He told him about the murder at the Never Close, about the chase that ended with the offender's car wrecked and Joe Kott missing without a trace. He told him of the killer who escaped the hospital and the bodies left in his wake as he made his way to the Izhijiwan National Forest in northern Wisconsin, where he eventually escaped and where, somehow, they found Joe Kott barely clinging to life.

"You know you sound nuts, right?" Bob said.

"I know. I lived it, and sometimes I can't believe it myself, but it will have to do until I can find another explanation."

"Joe wasn't returning my calls, so I drove out. His house looked like nobody lived there. Mail and newspapers and shit piled up all over the place. I threw all the crap inside, came straight here, and I was talking to Cathy up front. She was telling me that Joe's in the hospital, and that's when Corliss stuck his big Irish beak in."

"Sorry about that, Bob," Fitz apologized, opting not to remind Bob that he too was Irish.

"But Joe's okay, yeah?"

"He's getting there," said Fitz. "When we found him, he'd been stabbed in the stomach, and he's still dealing with some complications."

Fitz could see Bob's fists clench up, but they weren't punching fists—they were bracing fists.

"What do you mean, complications?" Bob demanded.

"Joe's going to need another surgery. He developed an abscess in his stomach."

The chair shot across the floor and slammed into a wall as Bob bolted up from the table.

"Well, let's go! Which hospital is he at?"

Fitz still had a report to write. Horse had expanded beyond stove-top meth production into full-blown meth-labs. They'd been stealing tanks of anhydrous ammonia from local farms, and the county was crawling with DEA agents. He didn't have time for a hospital visit, but sending Corliss with Bob would be a colossal mistake—and after all, he kind of owed Bob the courtesy of a ride-along. He really should have called.

* * *

Joe woke up to see his best friend standing at the foot of his bed dressed head to toe in a white Tyvek suit. He could see Fitz through the windows in the observation room where flower bouquets in various states of decomposition had been put on display so that Joe could see them—but not risk infection from direct contact. All of the rooms in the ICU had observation areas, and Joe hated it. He felt like he was on display in some kind of medical zoo. Fitz was talking to a young lady at the nurse's station, and Joe noticed that he kept looking at his watch. The mid-day sun poured into the room from the bank of windows opposite the observation room, and Joe could see the beads of sweat forming on Bob's brow behind the goggles he was forced to wear.

"How many Tyveks did they have to kill to make that suit?" Joe joked.

"Ha ha, very funny."

"Seriously, you look like Dustin Hoffman in Outbreak."

"What the hell happened to you?" Bob asked, ignoring Joe's continued attempt at humor.

"You wouldn't believe me if I told you," Joe replied.

"So, all that crap Fitz was telling me was true? He said you went to, like, another world or something."

All expression fell away from Joe's face.

"Bob, there's a whole world out there that we can't see. It's just below us, or next to us, or—or something. I'm not really sure about that part, but it's there."

They'd been friends for so long, and knew each other so well, that Joe never considered for a moment that Bob wouldn't believe him. So, he started with the chase and ended with Corliss pulling his lifeless body out of the darkness. Joe was halfway through the telling when Fitz walked into the room wearing the same ridiculous getup as Bob. He'd already heard the story several times, so Joe didn't bother to stop and catch him up. When it was over, Bob stood in stunned silence. Joe presumed his mouth probably hung open, but he couldn't see it through Bob's particle mask.

"Eh-hem," Fitz cleared his throat. "So, we're going to have to get out of here. I spoke with the nurse out there, and she said they need to prep you for surgery. She said we could come back tomorrow."

"I'm gonna stay," said Bob.

"But the nurse..."

"Yeah, I know, but I'm still gonna stay."

Joe knew he wasn't being obstinate or disrespectful. He was just being Bob—loyal, dependable Bob.

"But the nurse..." tried Fitz a second time.

Like an actress hitting her cue, the charge nurse walked in.

"Boys, this is Terri. She runs this joint."

Both men acknowledged her with a nod of the head.

"Bet your ass I do, and it's time for you two to scram. I have to get your friend here ready for surgery."

"I'll be staying. Just point me in the direction of your waiting room."

"He's not going to be able to have visitors till tomorrow, and that's if he's lucky."

"That's okay, just tell me where the cafeteria is, and I'll be fine."

"I'll show him," offered Fitz, and the two walked toward the door.

"You'll come find me, right?" Bob asked the nurse as they left.

"Of course, um..."

"Bob, his name is Bob," Joe said with a smirk.

He watched as his friends shed their Tyvek skins and walked toward the elevators. Joe was jealous. Not of the little spark he thought he saw between Terri and Bob, but of anyone who could get up and walk out of this damned room. He hated the bed; he hated the walls, windows, and ceiling. He was hooked up to so many damned machines that he couldn't even get out of bed to take a piss, not that he figured his legs would work if he tried. He hadn't been out of bed in over a month, not since the abscess went to work on him. They had him lay on one side or the other throughout the day to avoid getting bedsores, but there was no walking. There were no televisions in the ICU, either. Joe asked if he could have someone bring his little black and white from home, but Terri told him that they weren't allowed because they interfered with the electronics in the room. He was stuck listening to beeping machines and the faint sound of the muzak coming through the overhead speakers in the hall.

Before the damned abscess formed, his doctor told him that he'd be home in time to enjoy Thanksgiving dinner with his family, but with Thanksgiving only a week away and this new complication, that seemed impossible. Not that he had anyone to spend it with anyway. His aunt passed away not long after his mother died, and his father had gone downhill fast in the last three months. On his last visit, Chief Vecchio told Joe that he'd visited his father at the nursing home to fill him in on his disappearance. Vecchio hung his head when he told him that his father didn't remember having a son. That had been two months ago, and from what he could gather, things had only gotten worse. But that wasn't the saddest part for Joe. He loved his father, and he hated knowing that he was confused and probably a little scared, but he took comfort in knowing that his father had forgotten about him. To Joe, that meant he wasn't worried about his son being laid up in the hospital, and it eased his guilt about wanting to leave Red Hook forever to be with Reka and Alistair. He'd give anything to be able to spend Thanksgiving in Espero or Savista or wherever Reka wanted to spend it, assuming they celebrated the holiday.

Lately, he'd been finding escape from boredom and loneliness through morphine, but that seemed to have come to an end. All he had to do was hit a button, and Terri or Chris, or one of his other nurses, would come in and send him off to dreamland with one simple shot. Joe would lie there and wait for the warmth to spread across his body like a blanket right out of the dryer, and quick as that, he was out. In his morphine dreams, Joe could fly, and the more he practiced, the better he got. He went from flying a few feet and crash landing to flying over the fields and watching the big combines harvesting the acres and acres of corn. He would fly down Main Street and watch the foot traffic in and out of the stores or over to Memorial Park to watch the kids playing ball. Joe had come to realize that the more he practiced, the farther he could fly. He'd made it as far east as Chicago's lakefront. Lake Michigan seemed so small to him now, having been on the Great Lake with Alistair and the Maristo. He'd flown as far north as the Izhijiwan National Forest, but finding the well was harder than he thought it would be. He'd told himself that the minute he saw it, he would fly down that well and back to Reka.

Chapter 3

When everyone was seated, Jedrek said grace. The believers bowed their heads; those who did not share his faith asked blessings of their gods or stood quietly until he finished. The camp cooks prepared eggs harvested from Savista's hen houses, bacon from their farm and bread, and fruits from Savista's fields, and all ate their fill. All but Alistair. Alistair had other things on his mind. He'd resigned himself to the belief that Joe was dead, and then, along came a child to plant a seed of hope.

"Don't tell me I'm going to have to make a plate for you too."

The soft voice stirred Alistair from his musing. "Beg pardon?"

"It's bad enough I have to make sure my sister eats. Am I going to have to worry about you too?" Eva Sokol asked.

"Mornin' miss, Eva," Alistair said. "I'm sorry, my mind was elsewhere. Care to join me?" Alistair slid over to make room.

"Thank you; I will," she said and set down the covered plate of food she had prepared.

"Is that for Reka?"

Eva frowned.

"I've noticed that you do that every day," Alistair nodded at the plate.

"And I'll keep doing it until she's ready to rejoin us for meals."

"She just needs time. They say it heals all wounds, you know."

"Time cannot heal hiraeth."

"I'm afraid I don't know that word."

"She's heart-sick, Ranger. There's a longing in her soul that can never be satisfied. Our grandmother Delyth said that it is called hiraeth. For her, it was her childhood home. Her soul longed to be in Wales again, but she could never return because of the split. For Reka, it's Joe."

Alistair knew he had nothing like that in his life, and he almost envied Reka for it.

"I've never had anything in my life that meant that much to me," Alistair said as his fingers ran over his forearm absentmindedly.

"I'm sorry for you," Eva said. "What's that?"

She asked, nodding at his arm.

When Alistair joined the Rangers as a young man, he visited a tattoo parlor and had the word *ROMANS* and the number *13* inked into his right forearm.

"It's something to remind me."

"Remind you of what?"

"Of what's important."

Eva smiled at him and got up. "Well, I need to bring this to Reka before it gets any colder."

"Of course," Alistair said. "Please give her my best."

"Why don't you come along?"

"I don't know if—"

"There's no need to avoid her, Alistair. She doesn't blame you. You had no more to do with Joe's decision than the man in the moon. Joe went because that is who he was."

Eva extended her hand, and Alistair took it, and together they walked out to the field where Reka was hard at work harvesting radishes and turnips beneath a gray autumn sky.

"Good morning, Reka."

"Hello, Alistair," she said as she got to her feet and hugged him. "It's nice to see you up and around."

Eva stepped forward with a tray. "Reka, we brought you some breakfast."

"Thank you, but I'm not hungry."

Eva set the plate on a nearby stool and adjusted the napkin she used to cover it. "Well, I'll just set it here in case you change your mind."

With that, Eva hugged her sister and excused herself to tend to her own chores. Alistair was glad she did. It saved him the uncomfortable task of asking her to leave so that he might speak privately with Reka.

"Reka, I want to return to the Barrens to look for Joe."

Reka didn't bother responding as she returned to her work. Alistair knew she was annoyed with him. And he couldn't blame her. Twice before, he had come to her with the promise of returning to the Barrens to look for Joe's body, and both times nothing came of it.

"I have had the same dream for three nights in a row. I see Joe walking near a river, unable to find his way home. I cannot shake the feeling that he is out there somewhere and needs our help."

Reka slammed her trowel on the ground and spun at Alistair. She was seething.

"You're saying that you think he's alive and has somehow survived three months alone in the Barrens? Are you mad?"

"I don't know what to think," Alistair said. "But I don't believe the Barrens has taken his soul."

"What are you talking about?" Reka screamed.

Alistair, but he remained calm. "There is something you don't know about Joe."

"Well, I know he's dead, and I know the Barrens has him. And I know that if you think the Barrens would give up a soul, you're as crazy as he is dead!"

"Reka, he wasn't from here."

"Are you saying he was from the Eastern Territories?"

"No. What I am saying is… Joe was not of this world."

The more he spoke, the more confused and angrier Reka became.

"Are you feverish? Maybe it's sepsis. You should see Siobhan."

"I know it sounds crazy. I didn't believe it myself, but it's true, and that's why the Barrens can't take his soul. That's how I know he can be brought out—or at least his body can be, and maybe his soul will follow."

She looked at him, and her anger turned to concern. When she saw him three days ago, he seemed fine. There was no mention of dreams or other worlds. She put her hand to his forehead.

"I'm not sick," he protested.

Reka's eyes glistened as tears pooled in them.

"Reka, Joe told me he was from a place called Red Hook, Illinois. My father showed me a book once. He called it an atlas and said that I was never to speak of it."

"Yes, it's a book of maps. The authorities in the Columbias outlawed them. They ordered us to round them up and burn them, said they were dangerous, but I also kept one."

"I studied that book, Alistair. It was wonderful," she said, smiling briefly, and then her smile turned sad. "There was a place called Illinois in the United States of America. I told myself that Joe must have seen the same book and just made up a story to tell me, though I couldn't imagine why."

"It was no story, Reka. It existed before the split—or maybe still exists, I don't know. But Joe was a policeman there."

Her breath caught in her throat, and she stepped back. Reka reached into her pocket and pulled out a small silver object, and held it tight in her fist.

"What is it, child?" Alistair asked.

She held her hand out and opened her palm.

"He gave this to me right before you both left for the Barrens. I asked him what the letters meant. He told me that the policemen wore them as part of their uniform. I didn't understand, but he said he would explain everything when he came back."

Her breathing quickened, and tears fell. The RHPD collar pin was scuffed, and Joe had snapped the tines off so they wouldn't poke her. She spoke through tears.

"He said it was a long story and that I wouldn't believe him."

Alistair wrapped her in his arms.

"There's something miraculous about that boy." He held her until the tears stopped. "Eat your breakfast and finish your chores. I'll expect you at breakfast tomorrow."

Chapter 4

Joe Kott was hovering over his own body as it lay dead on the operating table. *I thought they said this was a simple procedure,* he thought to himself. His arms had been strapped to boards perpendicular to the operating table, reminding him of Jesus on the cross, and his stomach was split and held wide open by spreaders of some kind. To the left of his body, there was a silver tray almost entirely covered in meaty-looking tubes that he assumed were his intestines, while to his right, the surgical team worked fast but without the slightest sign of panic. Surgical instruments passed from nurse to surgeon and back to nurse so quickly that it looked like a magic act. Above his head sat the anesthesiologist monitoring his gauges with occasional glances at the clock on the wall.

"No pulse, thirty seconds," the gauge guy said.

Softly, behind the mechanical sounds of the various machinery in the room, Joe could hear classical music. At first, he thought he might have been dreaming, but there was no way he would ever dream up classical music. For one thing, Joe hated classical music, and for another, he didn't know any, not well enough that he could conjure it in a dream anyway.

The gauge guy rechecked the clock. "No pulse, one minute."

And with that, Joe was ripped out of the room and plunged into total darkness. He might have been frightened, but he knew this darkness and welcomed it. Joe's un-beating heart soared as the darkness engulfed and constricted, forcing the air from his lungs. Joe opened his mouth eagerly to ingest the darkness and felt it rushing into his body, equalizing the pressure as it had done before. He was going home, home to Reka. Everything felt as it had before, there was no sound, no smell, and his eyes saw nothing but darkness. The only thing that was different this time was the feeling of loneliness—or rather the lack of it. He hoped it was because Reka would be there waiting for him. There was so much he wanted to tell her, so much he needed to explain. He felt the solid ground beneath his feet, and he began to run. He couldn't see a damned thing, but he knew he was heading in the right direction. Then, from somewhere in the distance, he heard a voice. It was reed-thin, but he heard it.

"No pulse, three minutes."

It was the gauge man's voice. Then another voice, followed by a pain sharper than anything he'd ever experienced.

"Cracking open the chest… Beginning internal cardiac massage."

Joe saw bright flashes. "What's *happening?" He screamed but couldn't hear his own voice. "They're trying to restart my heart. No!"* he cried again but still made no sound. *"Just let me go!"*

They were resuscitating him. He felt several chest compressions, and in an instant, he was back in the operating room strapped to the table, his body convulsing violently atop the table. The surgical team jumped away as black mist spewed from Joe's chest and stomach. The gauge guy nearly fell from his chair as the same black vapor poured from Joe's nose and mouth, filling his clear plastic breathing mask. Joe's eyes rolled back in his head, and he heard someone say, "What the hell is that?" And then he was out again.

Joe woke some hours later in the critical care unit in tremendous pain. A person in a Tyvek suit was tugging on him. He looked down to see three sections of rubber tubing holding the two halves of his stomach together and felt a wave of nausea roll over him. The nurse, at least that was his assumption, was lifting on the tubes and pulling blood-soaked gauze from the open wound.

"What the hell did you guys do to me?"

"Dr. Belter wanted to allow the incision to heal naturally to avoid further infections."

"Well, can you tug a little easier? Jeez!"

"I'm sorry, sweetie, I'll try and be gentler, but I have to change your gauze."

"Terri?"

"Yeah?"

"What happened to me in there?"

"In where?"

"In surgery."

"Dr. Belter will be in to see you in a bit; best you save your questions for him."

"What about the pain? Is there something I can get for the pain?"

"I'll check with Dr. Belter when he gets here."

"Bull shit! I need something now!"

Discomfort after major surgery was expected, but Terri knew Joe still had pain meds in his system. "That's not going to happen, Joe," she said matter-of-factly.

He'd tried the salty approach and got shot right down. "I'm sorry. Terri, I didn't mean to snap at you, but I'm in a lot of pain, and I'd really appreciate something to take the edge off."

"I know, and I'm just as sorry as I can be, but the doctor would have my hide if I gave you so much as an aspirin that he didn't order."

"Dammit, Terri! I'm the patient, and I want something for my pain!"

Terri's face, or what Joe could see of it behind the protective gear she wore, twisted into a look of confusion, and Joe knew what she was thinking. He was acting like a black-listed junkie begging pills from one doctor after another. But Joe didn't care. He just wanted to try and get back to Reka and thought that the drugs might help.

Terri smiled and fluffed his pillow. "I'll speak with Dr. Belter," she said and turned to leave the room.

It was clear to Joe that he wouldn't get anywhere with Nurse Terri, so he apologized again and closed his eyes. Sleep came quickly, even without the aid of pain medication, but it didn't do him any good. Regular sleep produced regular dreams, the kind he couldn't control and often made no sense. He'd woken a few times and lay staring at the ceiling, racking his brain on a way to get back, then it hit him. When he'd first woken in this damned room three months ago, Joe called into the Todd Zeelander radio show and spoke with a number of other listeners.

A few tried to tell him that he'd been abducted and likely probed by aliens, typical conspiracy nut jobs, but one guy may have hit the nail on the head. He said that the only way to slip between worlds was to do it between heartbeats. The trick, he said, was to extend the diastolic phase of the heartbeat long enough to make the journey but not so long as to kill the traveler. Joe hung up feeling less than hopeful but laying in his bed, recalling the events that led up to his—what would he call it, his departure? Suddenly it all made sense.

Joe knew exactly what he would do the moment he was released from his prison. There were no bars, just doors and windows and a bed that he couldn't get out of, but it was still a prison. A prison patrolled by women in white uniforms and run by a warden who shuffled his feet when he walked and kept tight control over the commissary. Need a shot? Sorry, gotta check with Warden Belter.

Joe closed his eyes and fell asleep. When he woke again, it was to the same tugging sensation that woke him the last time, though it was far less uncomfortable. He saw Bob standing next to him, watching Nurse Terri pull blood-soaked gauze from his wound and looking a little green around his gills.

"What's the matter, dickhead? Can't stand the sight of blood?"

Bob turned his head toward Joe, but his eyes remained transfixed on the bloody gauze being pulled from the raw-looking foot-long trench that ran from Joe's sternum to just past his belly button.

"How are you feeling, dipshit?"

"Like someone popped my stomach with a can opener."

They both laughed, and Joe winced in pain.

"Dr. Belter approved some pain meds for you, Joe," Terri said with a smile. "I'll be by later to check on you."

It was music to Joe's ears. His heart felt light and full of hope with the realization he'd made just before falling asleep.

"You okay, dude? You look kinda weird."

Joe became aware of the smile that stretched across his face at the mention of pain meds, and he felt self-conscious. "Me? Look at you! I see the way you keep checking Nurse Terri out," he said, changing topics.

"She's married, stupid, but Nurse Chris?" He waved a hand in the *hot* gesture.

"Yeah, I saw her," Joe said. "But you don't have a shot. You're a fleshy-headed-mutant, and she's an angel of mercy."

Bob laughed. "You don't think so?"

Their debate was interrupted by another person in a Tyvek suit. Only this one entered the room without so much as a knock.

"Hello Joe, I'm Dr. Belter. How are we feeling today?"

"Hey Doc, *we* are feeling like shit. What the hell happened in there?"

"What do you mean?"

"Doc, I got sucked out of my body or something," Joe said.

"Maybe we can talk about that later," Belter offered, with a quick dart of the eyes toward Bob. "You need your rest."

Joe disregarded the non-verbal cue. He wanted to make sure that what he thought happened in the operating room really happened. "I'm not tired, Doc. I want to discuss this now."

"Would you mind if I asked your guest to wait in the observation room? This is a—delicate matter."

Bob raised his hands. "Not a problem," he said and then stepped out of the room.

Once the door was closed, Dr. Belter lowered his voice and delivered the news. "Joe, we lost you for a few minutes."

What little color Joe had faded from his face. "What do you mean, *lost me?*"

"You flatlined. Your heart stopped."

The doctor's delivery matched the somber message.

"Wait, you're saying I died in there."

"Joe, there was more damage than we thought. There were some complications. It seems that your ureter was damaged and leaked causing an abscess in your stomach."

Joe waved his hand dismissively, "But I did die, right?"

"Well, no, not technically. Your heart stopped when the muscle had relaxed to allow the chambers to fill with blood. We were able to get it pumping again." Belter said, trying to cushion the impact. "The important thing is that you're young and healthy and you are going to make a full recovery."

Joe lay there not speaking, though his mind was going a mile a minute. He had his confirmation. What did the caller say? He said that the trick was to stop the heart long enough to make the trip but not long enough to kill the traveler.

"Joe, are you with me?" Belter asked. "Look, I can only imagine what a shock this must be, but I assure you—"

"How long was I dead?" Joe interrupted.

"You weren't dead, Joe. Your heart rested in the diastolic phase and needed our assistance to get it going again. As I said, you should make a full recovery, and that shouldn't be something you need to worry about."

A lump the size of a Granny Smith caught in Joe's throat. "Did you say diastolic phase?" It was the same term the caller used.

"Yes, it's the medical term for the space between heartbeats, when the chambers of the heart fill just before it pumps again." Belter looked at Joe. "Are you feeling okay, I mean aside from the obvious."

"Huh," Joe answered blankly. Somewhere in his brain a switch flipped and the connection was made. Joe thought of the big red barn, the place Alistair called diastole.

"I asked how you were feeling, Joe." Belter wrapped a blood pressure cuff around his arm. "You turned white as a sheet," he said as he listened through his stethoscope.

"What? Oh, no. I'm fine, Doc, thanks."

It seemed clear to the doctor that the news was a shock to Joe, but probably not for the reason he thought. It was natural to be shocked or disturbed by the unnatural. Once you're dead, that's supposed to be it, the end of the line—the promise of an afterlife notwithstanding. But suddenly, Joe knew different. He knew, for himself anyway, that there was a stopover in another world—the world of Reka and Alistair. Joe racked his brain, trying to reconcile the worlds he knew. Up until 1945, their worlds were the same. So that meant that...

"Joe, are you okay? Do you want me to prescribe something to help you rest?"

No, thought Joe, I want you to prescribe something to stop my heart again! But that's not what he said. "No, Doc, I just need to get my head around this whole thing."

"All the same, I'll put in an order for something to help you sleep if you should need it.?"

"Thanks,Doc," Joe said as he drifted back into thought.

"I'll give you a little time to sit with this. The rest of what I wanted to tell you can wait."

"Thanks Doc—say Doc, what about something for the pain?" Joe almost forgot to bring it up. He hadn't given up on the hope that he could cross over if he fell into a deep enough sleep. One he couldn't achieve on his own.

"You got it. Try and rest up." And with that, Dr. Belter shuffled out the door. Joe was in a hurry to return to flying—and looking for the well that he hoped would lead him back to Reka—but he couldn't just tell Bob to hit the road. Besides, if his plan worked, he might never see him again. Joe looked out past the observation room and could see that Bob had company. He was speaking with Chris and must have said something funny because Chris smiled a beautiful smile and tossed her hair back. Bob stood there grinning like an idiot, and it warmed Joe's heart. Still, if he wanted to get back to sleep and try to make it back to Reka, he had to get the show on the road.

"Hey dummy!" Joe yelled to make sure Bob heard him through the glass. Bob spun around; Chris just looked up at Joe with a *thanks for wrecking the moment*' kind of look. Joe loved that the two were hitting it off. It meant that Bob would have someone to talk to besides him, which in turn meant that he was free to take his shot of morphine and search the north woods for his way back home. Back to Reka and Alistair and the Midwestern

Territories, with whatever adventures they might hold. He might have been born in Red Hook, but his heart and soul were back there. Bob put his goofy-looking Tyvek suit back on and entered Joe's room.

"You look like crap. What'd the doc tell ya?"

"Get a load of this. He said I died on the operating table, but they brought me back. Can you believe that?"

Bob's jaw dropped wide open. "No shit?"

"Zero shit, buddy, that's what he said."

"Well did you see the light or anything?" Bob asked, followed quickly by, "What about your mom or my brother?"

The smile that was on Joe's face fell away. He'd heard stories of people having near-death experiences and being greeted by loved ones who'd preceded them into the afterlife, but for Joe, there was no bright light or welcoming faces. Quite the contrary. He'd been welcomed into that other realm by darkness, rain that burned his flesh, and giant spiders.

"No, man, all I saw was darkness." The words fell from his lips rather than being pushed out by the air in his lungs. "I don't understand it," Joe confided. "That world I told you about, that's what I was headed back to."

"You think that's Heaven?" Bob asked, not doubting one word his friend said.

"No, I think it's something else. Some world between here and Heaven. Either that or all the stories you hear are bullshit." Joe needed to get that next shot of morphine. He had to get back to the woods, but he needed a way back just in case he couldn't find it. Joe pushed his call button.

"Buddy, I need some rest. This wound is killing me," Joe said, pointing to his stomach.

"No problem, I'll grab a bite, and I'll be over in the waiting room if you need me." Bob slipped out of the room and out of his Tyvek suit.

Joe waited a couple of minutes before he pushed the plunger button that sent notification to the nurses' station again. What the hell was taking them so long? And why did Bob have to stick around? What good was he doing moping around here? Joe caught himself. Why was he being such an asshole? Joe pushed the button again, but he was pretty sure it was by accident.

"Hey! Easy does it with the button. We have fifteen other patients in this wing, and there are only four of us," Terri said as she came into the room. She delivered her remarks in a joking manner, but Joe could tell she meant every word.

"I'm sorry, Terri; I really need something for the pain."

Terri read the notes Belter made on Joe's chart. "Be right back, sweetie."

Joe knew he was moments away from liftoff, and he couldn't help but smile.

Chapter 5

The following day was much the same as any he'd experienced in Savista. Alistair joined Jedrek on his morning walk, with Agermonte and Barrister running reconnaissance just ahead of them. A blanket of thick gray clouds hung over the region like a blanket, and Alistair could almost make out the sound of the surf crashing the shoreline of the Great Lake several miles away.

"What's on your mind, old friend?" Jedrek asked. "You seem deeper in thought than usual."

"I suppose I am. What can you tell me about Thea?"

"She's a wondrous child. She was the one who sent us to get you. She told us that Mava was amassing a small contingent near your camp and that they were about to attack. She said that one of your people was meant for a greater purpose."

"What purpose might that have been?"

"She didn't say, just said that we had to save him."

"And that was good enough for you?"

"I should say. Thea has been touched by God."

Alistair snickered.

"Did I say something funny?" Jedrek asked.

"Yuri said that the girl came in answer to his prayers for his camp," Alistair said.

Jedrek rubbed his chin as if pondering the unasked question. "Who's to say? The Lord works in mysterious ways, brother. Maybe we should give thanks that He understands, even if we don't."

"Maybe," said Alistair, "but it wasn't Thea who came to find us."

"Thea?" Jedrek's voice boomed, holding back a laugh. "No, Thea never leaves camp. She's our seer. We could never risk that child's life. No telling what the freebooters might do if they got hold of her. It was my daughter Kallen that went for you."

"You sent your own daughter out to the Sokol camp in the middle of a battle?" Alistair asked.

"I know how that must sound, but Kallen is a master tracker, and when she doesn't want to be seen, not even Thea can find her. Besides, a child, especially a girl, is less likely to be mistaken for freebooters and killed. Kallen has her mother's disarming beauty."

Alistair remembered the lovely golden-faced child. "I see your point. Still, it seems dangerous."

"To live is to risk life, my friend."

"I suppose," Alistair said and then turned his attention back to gathering information about Thea. "You said Thea is a seer?" Alistair asked.

"That's right; she's gifted. Her mother Siobhan said she was born with it."

Alistair pressed further. "And without knowing Joe, she was able to single him out from the rest of the Sokol camp?"

"Why do you think it was Joe that she saw?"

Alistair wasn't ready to share Joe Kott's story with anyone other than Reka. Not just yet. "Or whomever," he said quickly.

Jedrek regarded Alistair for a moment, and Alistair thought he read suspicion in his eyes, but then Jedrek continued.

"Well, I don't know who or what she saw; and I don't know how she does it, but here you are. And it's not just you. Look around."

Jedrek gestured toward the camp. It was alive with activity. Some people were busy preparing the morning meal; others carried crops from the fields to the storage sheds. Children played in the open areas while their parents tended to their harvest.

"Almost every man, woman, and child you see owe their lives to Thea's visions."

"You mean she saw all these people's camps under attack?"

"Many of them, yes. We used to send out patrols on rescue missions, and we lost a lot of our brave fighters in battle. But once Thea began sharing her gift with us, all that changed. There are still occasions when we have to send fighters to rescue camps under attack, but far less often. With Thea's guidance, Kallen has been able to bring a lot of these people to Savista without risk to our numbers.

"Do they always follow her?"

"No, most don't," answered Jedrek. "I don't know; I think maybe God chose not to open their hearts to her message. It takes a strong leader to accept a child's help, especially in battle."

Alistair was embarrassed. If not for Yuri's leadership and humbleness, he'd have been one of the prideful. One of the lost.

"We owe her and Savista our lives. Thank you, Jedrek," said Alistair.

Jedrek placed his palm to his chest and gave a slight bow, "I'm blessed by your company, old friend."

Alistair returned the compliment with a warm smile and another question. "What about the camps that your fighters go out to save? Do they often join Savista?"

"Even fewer than the ones Kallen brings back. But it's not for us to force our ways on anyone. We are here to serve and offer protection when we can. We'll welcome anyone who chooses to join our family, but everyone has to earn their keep—the ones who come for a while and then choose to leave, go with our blessings, and if we can spare it, some supplies."

"Why would they leave?"

"I think some find our way of life a bit stifling. They are Vagadi; I think it's in their nature to wander."

"But there's safety here."

"Safety, but also rules, and to some people, that means giving up some of their freedom."

Just as Jedrek had finished speaking, a young boy ran to him with what seemed to Alistair to be a message of some urgency.

"Sorry, Alistair, there's something I have to take care of."

"Anything I can do to help?"

"Yes! If you can tell everyone that I will be late for breakfast," Jedrek yelled over his shoulder as he ran toward a small barn at the east end of the camp.

"There's a calf in breech!"

As Jedrek ran for the barn, Alistair turned back toward his quarters to prepare breakfast for Agermonte and Barrister. He'd only gone ten feet when Thea appeared at his side.

"Morning, Mr. Alistair," Thea said with a huge smile.

"And a good morning to you. Did you sleep well?"

"Momma said that I snored like a docco. Ever seen one of them, Mr. Alistair?"

"Sure have. One tried to make a meal out of Joe and me not so long ago. But Joe took care of him."

"That's good. If he didn't, we couldn't have become friends."

"I suppose not."

"It was better for Joe to do it than you."

"Do what?"

"Fight the docco!"

"Because I'm old?"

"No, because Joe can't die here."

"What did you say?" snapped Alistair.

"It's true. Your friend is from a different place, and he can't die if he's not in the right place."

Alistair studied the child. "You mean to tell me that if a docco ate Joe up, he wouldn't die?"

"He would be gone, but not dead, well not completely dead."

"You mean like a ghost?"

"Yeah, but he's in the right place now."

Alistair licked his lips; he could feel his mouth going dry. "How do you know that?"

"Cause I can see him."

Alistair looked around instinctively. "Can you see him now?"

"Maybe, let me try." Thea closed her eyes and concentrated. "Yep, he's in bed."

"In—" Alistair could hardly believe his ears. "So you can just close your eyes and see him whenever you want?"

"Most of the time, I can. But when I looked for him the day before yesterday, I couldn't find him for a while."

"Why's that?" Alistair asked.

Thea shrugged her shoulders.

"But you're sure he's alive?"

"Sure, I'm sure."

Just then, the breakfast bell rang. Alistair still had to feed Agermonte and Barrister, but he'd promised to deliver Jedrek's message.

"Thea, can you do something for me?"

"What?" Thea replied happily.

"I need for you to run to the mess hall and tell your mother to let everyone know that Jedrek will be late to morning prayer and breakfast."

"Why?" she pressed.

"He's delivering a calf is why. Now get going!"

"Okay, okay, you don't have to get pushy." Thea flashed her bright eyes, smiled her big smile, and ran off to deliver his message.

Alistair hurried off to feed Agermonte and Barrister and then wash up for breakfast. It seemed that every time he spoke with Thea, he learned something new, and now he was sure that Joe was alive. He hurried through the food prep, opting to toss large chunks of meat and uncut vegetables in his dog's bowls rather than cut them up the way he usually would. He didn't worry about them choking; they could swallow live cats whole if they had a mind to.

Dropping their bowls outside the door right off his kitchen, he quickened his pace down the path that ran from the cabins to the main road that would take him to the center of the camp where the mess hall, chapel, and medical center were located. He could barely wait to share the news with Reka, assuming that she'd taken his words to heart and came in for breakfast.

The explosion shook the ground under his feet. It came from the far east end of Savista, and Alistair knew at once that the camp was under attack.

Savista was no stranger to attacks, but most unprovoked attacks, those not spawned by a rescue, as in the case of the Sokol camp, came under cover of darkness. A second explosion followed quickly, and then a third. The chapel bell rang furiously, signaling the people of Savista to man their battle stations. Jedrek had recently assigned Alistair to a long-gun company. Although no attacker had ever made it far enough up the sheer mountain face to put the training into practice, the long guns were also trained as a repelling party. Alistair took off at a full sprint. There was some pain and discomfort, but he really wouldn't feel it till the next day—assuming he survived this one.

Reaching his battalion commander, a boy not half his age, Alistair received his orders to provide cover fire for the box-kite bombers. He reached the ridge just as the pilots launched their first kites—a natural updraft along the ridge made for easy launching of the large box-kites and their payloads. As the kites took to the air, mortar rounds screamed overhead and impacted the ground just a few yards behind the line, sending shrapnel and debris through the air. Alistair took aim over the edge and fired. He watched the mortar-man fall, but quick as he hit the ground, another was taking his place. Alistair sent a round through the replacement, and another mounted the weapon. Alistair made a quick count. Four large mortars capable of launching shells onto the ridge were foolishly placed in a cluster in a clearing about a hundred yards out. Alistair aimed and killed another mortar-man. It seemed they had an endless supply. He was dropping them as quickly as he could, but shells were still falling. He needed help, but the commander gave no order, and the riflemen seemed focused on picking off the random freebooters running toward the sheer rock wall.

It only took a quick look back for Alistair to register why no orders had been given. The young commander lay dead on the ground, missing the lower half of his body. The second in command stood a few feet away, trying to shove his own guts back into the hole torn into his stomach. He looked to Alistair, entirely perplexed by the fact that his intestines were coming out of his body.

Alistair assumed command of the battalion and directed the company. "Forget the foot soldiers; they can't get up here," Alistair shouted. "We need to concentrate our fire on the Mortars while the pilots get their kites in position!" The second company of long guns had arrived, and Alistair ordered them to direct fire onto the freebooters' gunmen as the pilots dropped their flechettes. The shelling ceased, and the coppery smell of the freebooter's blood wafted on the updraft. Assuming command allowed Alistair time to assess. It was a massive attack force. No less than five hundred fighters milled about below the ridge, and their lack of coordination made it clear to Alistair that several freebooter camps had joined forces to try and take the mountain home of Savista. With the long-range mortars out of commission, the battle would be over quickly—or so Alistair thought.

Out of the cover of the brush came a series of deep, earth-shaking thumps. It seemed the freebooters weren't as disorganized as Alistair thought. Mortar shells crashed onto the ridge, crumbling a portion of the mountain's face and spilling several box-kite teams over the edge. The anchormen on the ropes did their best to dig their heels in, but their efforts were futile. Whole crews, pilots, loaders, and anchormen plummeted off the ridge. A couple managed to fasten themselves to nearby trees, leaving their mates hanging over the ledge like human ornaments, which the freebooters used as targets. Alistair ordered his companies to adjust their aim just as a thunderous roar rose up from the north.

Chapter 6

Terri drew 125mg of Tramadol into the syringe, prepped the injection site with an alcohol wipe, and injected the powerful narcotic into Joe's shoulder. Joe had come to know that smell of the alcohol wipe and the sensation that followed. He waited expectantly for the warmth to travel through his body, followed by the blissful drift into deep sleep—but it didn't come. Joe shut his eyes tighter and concentrated, but neither warmth nor sleep came for him. *Something's wrong*, he thought. *The shot had always worked before, so what the hell was going on?*

"Terri," Joe yelled as she was about to leave the room. "What's going on? Why isn't it working?"

"Dr. Belter switched you from Demerol to Tramadol to help manage your pain. It's just as effective, but it won't stay in your system as long. He want's to wean you off."

"Well, it's not working," he responded.

"You have to give it a minute, sweetie. Is the pain getting worse?"

"Screw the pain!" He snapped. "I need it to…." He stopped himself. "I mean, the pain is, well, it's pretty bad, but I can live with it. I guess."

"Need it to what, Joe?" Terri asked.

"What?" he asked, pretending not to understand her question.

"You said that you need the meds to do something," Terri persisted. "To do what? What do you need them for if not for pain?"

"What are you talking about?" Joe challenged.

"Look, Joe, if you feel like you're becoming dependent on the drugs for reasons other than pain relief, I think you need to let Dr. Belter know."

The Tramadol was starting to kick in, and Joe's eyes were getting heavy. He let them shut, hoping she would drop the subject and leave him alone, and it worked. Terri pulled his covers up, fluffed his pillow as best she could with his head still on it, and slipped quietly out of the room. Joe could feel his respiration slowing and deepening. His mind was finally at ease. Soon he would drift off to the land of nod, and then he would look for a way back to Reka.

Joe stood at the mouth of the cave looking down at the river below when something fell from the cliff above his head. It was Hayward Taft, and as he watched the killer's body fall in slow motion, he could see the smile plastered on Taft's face. He reached for his Colt. If the fall didn't kill him, two rounds center-mass sure as hell would do the trick. He took aim, squeezed the trigger, and watched in disbelief as the weapon disintegrated into shimmering blue sand that spilled through his fingers. He made eye contact with Taft, and Taft's smile turned to laughter. Joe continued to watch, and he noticed that Taft had stopped falling. He just hung in mid-air, parallel to the ground as if he were lying comfortably on an invisible bed until he rose, stiff as a plank, to a standing position. Joe tried to move, but he was frozen in place. Taft moved his gaze from the rock wall back up to Joe's face and then launched like a screaming rocket straight at him. The paralysis broke, and Joe stumbled back into the cave, falling to the ground. Taft shot past him, mere inches from his face, and rocketed deep into the cave. Joe lay there on the cold, damp cave floor, trying to catch his breath and make heads or tails out of what was going on.

I'm in the Barrens, but something is wrong. There was no flying and no darkness welcoming him back—so how did he get back? As he wondered, he blinked, and suddenly he was in his grandfather's garage with Donna, his high school love. She was sitting on the workbench, legs spread just wide enough for him to fit between her thighs. He could smell the familiar oil-soaked wood smell and the gentle fragrance of her shampoo. He slammed his hands down on her legs.

"sonofabitch! It's just a fucking dream!"

"Ouch! You, asshole! That hurt," said Donna. "And I liked it."

Joe backed up to step out from between her legs, but she clamped down. "Just where the hell do you think you're going?" Donna said in a breathy voice. "You revved the engine, big boy, now you're gonna take me for a ride."

Joe pushed at her thighs, but they wouldn't budge. "Get the fuck off of me!" he demanded, but she just squeezed tighter.

Joe put his hands against her chest and pushed as hard as he could.

"Now we're talking, baby," Donna said as she sprouted two more arms on each side of her torso. The arms were spindly and barbed, tipped by spikes rather than fingers, and she drove them deep into his sides. Joe screamed in pain.

"Now give it to me like your father gave it to me!" Spit flew from her lips.

Joe blinked again, and now he was kneeling next to Donna, who was lying in an old pedestal-style bathtub. The water was tinted red by the blood that flowed from a wound in her neck and chest. Her blue eyes were clouded over and deflated like his mother's on the morning he found her dead, staring sightless at some imaginary point on the ceiling.

"Donna," the name slipped absentmindedly past his lips.

Her blue eyes flashed, and her wounds closed. The water cleared, and she was alive.

"Get undressed and climb in, Joey." He'd forgotten that she called him Joey. He hated that name unless it was coming from her. He loved being her Joey. She was so beautiful. Her blonde hair hung to the floor over the back of the tub. She didn't want to get it wet because it took so long to dry. She reached a hand out to Joe, and tears welled up in his eyes. He knew it was a stupid high school romance, but it reminded him that he'd failed at every relationship he'd ever been involved in. He had even broken his promise to Reka—or had he?

"No!" he shouted. Not at Donna's request, but at the thought of failing Reka. He would not let that happen. He put his hands on the edge of the tub to steady himself as he got up. Donna clamped her hands down on his wrists, and he could feel needles plunge into his skin.

"You ain't leaving me again, Joey," she said as she unhinged her lower jaw, revealing row upon row of pointed teeth.

The teeth were sharp and angled back toward her gullet like the Northern pike Grandpa Uno had mounted to the wall in his parlor. As a boy, Joe once stuck his hand up to his wrist into the thing's mouth. Uno had to break its jaw to free Joe's arm, but he seemed more worried than mad. He considered breaking Donna's jaw, or at least the thing that *was* Donna. She wiggled her tongue like a worm, and Joe heard her say, "Kiss me, Joey." The Donna monster pushed the needles through Joe's hands and straight through the cast-iron ridge of the tub and fused them on the other side. It raised its awful mouth toward him and gave a wiggle with its wormy tongue. The putrid smell of rotting death filled the room. Joe placed his feet against the side of the tub, leaned back, and pushed like a dead-lifter going for his max weight. The needles ripped through his hands as the Donna monster lunged toward him.

"Joe, stop! I need some help in here!" Terri yelled.

Chris came bursting into the room to find Terri using both hands to keep the IV line in Joe's vein. She held tight to the line as Chris pulled at his other hand, but she couldn't break his grip.

Both Chris and Terri began calling out for more help when Bob charged into the room.

"What's going on?"

"Bob," Chris said, "we have to get his hands apart before he pulls out his IV. He could rip his vein open."

Bob slid his hands under Chris' and pulled Joe's hands apart.

"Can you hold him?" Terri asked.

"I got him," Bob said as Terri and Chris raised the side rails on the bed and used straps to lash his wrists to the rails.

Joe thrashed around violently, and his stomach sutures began to bleed.

"Joe!" Bob screamed in his face, but he wouldn't respond. "What the hell is wrong with him?"

"You guys got him for a minute?" Terri asked.

Chris nodded, and Terri ran to the nurses' station and grabbed the mic for the hospital's emergency paging system. "Doctor Belter, code red, ICU,

Doctor Belter, code red, ICU." Terri slammed the mic onto the desk and ran back into Joe's room.

It took Belter a few minutes to make it back to the ICU, where he found Chris and Terri sitting on Joe's legs, Joe's friend Bob pinning his shoulders to the bed, and Terri raking her knuckles over Joe's sternum trying to wake him from whatever state he was in.

"What the hell are you doing?" Belter demanded.

"We can't wake him!"

"That's because he's having a convulsion! My god! What do they teach you in nursing school?"

"He's not convulsing doctor, he's actively fighting us, but he won't wake up," Terri corrected.

Belter stood back and ran a hand through his hair. "I—I don't," he stammered.

"Get your shit together, Doc. Do something!" Bob yelled.

Belter had to revive unresponsive patients and sedate violent patients, but he had never had a patient who was unconscious and actively resisting at the same time. He searched his memory and recalled the symptoms in victims of severe head injuries, but that wasn't the case with Joe.

"Doctor!" Chris shouted. "We need some help here!"

Belter's eyes darted around the room. "Terri, get me five milligrams of Naloxone."

Terri ran out of the room and returned with the loaded syringe. Belter pushed the needle into Joe's arm and pressed the plunger. In seconds, all of the tension in Joe's body slipped away, and he opened his eyes. Everyone in the room noticed the look of panic on his face, but they had other concerns that required their immediate attention. He'd soaked his sheets with blood from the sutures that had busted open during his thrashing. Bob retired to a chair in the corner of the room while the doctor and nurses tended to Joe. They used local anesthetics to manage the pain near the open wounds and began re-suturing them. The team worked as efficiently as a racer's pit crew, and before long, Joe was stitched up and lying on clean sheets. Terri checked his vitals. Joe was running a slight fever, and his blood pressure was through the roof, which was surprising considering the blood loss.

"I want eyes on him for the next twenty-four hours," said Belter. Get candy stripers up here if you need to, and call me directly if anything changes," he scribbled his pager number and home phone number on the information board in Joe's room. "He's not to be left alone, is that clear?"

"Yes, doctor," Terri replied. "Chris, you're on the first watch. I'll relieve you in two hours. Mr. Tague, I don't think it's a good idea—" Bob cocked his head and clenched his jaw. "See that he doesn't get in the way, Chris."

"Of course," Chris replied as the rest of the staff made their way out of the room.

Joe was resting comfortably. He closed his eyes, but he wasn't asleep. The pain wouldn't have let him sleep even if he wanted to. Chris placed a cool rag on his forehead. Belter ordered a halt to all of Joe's medications until he returned and was able to reevaluate him. Leaving the cloth on Joe's head, Chris sat down next to Bob and took his hand.

"You really love him, don't you?"

"He's like a brother to me. He's the best friend I've ever had."

"Well, you friend is in good hands. Dr. Belter is young, but he's brilliant. He'll get him through this."

They were only a couple of feet away, but Joe didn't hear a word they were saying. He couldn't shake the feeling that something had followed him back from the Barrens, but what? Eventually, the local anesthetic he'd been given eased his pain, and he drifted off to sleep.

Chapter 7

Like thunder rolling across the plain and drawn by the smell of blood and death, the docco bore down on the freebooters decimating their right flank. Leading the charge were three massive beasts. They were each the size of the largest docco Alistair had ever seen, plus a half. Rather than rounded battering ram heads like the rest, these had a shape that reminded him of the front end of his grandfather's 1934 Brewster Town Car. Round at the top, its face sloped to a fine point where a bone not unlike a bull's horn protruded from a tuft of coarse-looking black hair. Atop the animal's skulls sat an enormous rack of antlers that caused Alistair to wonder how the things could travel through wooded areas. His answer came as one of the mighty beasts plowed through the trunk of a tree no less than eight inches in diameter, snapping it in two without slowing its pace. In all his years in the territories, Alistair had never seen a herd of this size on the charge. And the three leading the way were entirely foreign to him.

"What the hell are they?" Alistair asked.

"King Bulls," yelled the man to his right.

Alistair had just assumed all docco looked the same, but he had been wrong. The three King Bulls gored their way through the freebooter's right flank tossing bodies in every direction while the other docco sank their teeth into flesh and crushed freebooter's bones. Like grizzlies, the docco didn't bother to wait for their prey to die before devouring it. Those who were able struck at the beasts' heads with fists, knives, and the butts of their rifles. Others, likely with their necks or spines snapped by the violent thrashing, hung moaning helplessly from their jaws, waiting for the pain and terror to pass.

One of Savista's long-guns fired, striking one of the helpless freebooters in the head, putting him out of his misery. Another took aim, but Alistair ordered them to hold their fire. He didn't want to waste precious ammunition on mercy killings. Jedrek, who arrived just as the doccos' carnage began, directed a questioning look at Alistair when the stay was given, but he did not contradict the order.

The freebooters redirected their fire into the herd. Several worked to lower the mortar's bipods to adjust for target height and fired. Even the mighty docco were no match for the mortar blasts, their bodies blown apart by the projectiles. Alistair ordered his long-guns to resume firing on the mortar-men. Several of his shooters dropped their guns and abandoned their posts rather than follow the order. Alistair understood their revulsion. He knew that they probably saw feeding the enemy to the herd as unnecessarily cruel, perhaps even as a war crime, though there were no rules of engagement in the territories. But the freebooters, at least, in this case, were their common enemy, and Alistair would use the docco to Savista's advantage.

Again, Jedrek did not contradict Alistair's order. Instead, he walked over to Alistair, whispered something to him, patted his friend on the shoulder, and walked away. The freebooter's long-guns continued to fire into the madness, but they lacked the blunt force necessary to halt the frenzied attack. The commanders of the freebooter forces, no doubt understanding their predicament, ordered a full retreat.

Alistair continued his attack on any freebooter that attempted to man the mortars, even if they intended to retrieve the weapon. Like every rifle abandoned, the mortars too would become part of Savista's arsenal. From his vantage point, Alistair could see the entire docco herd on the plain below. An undulating mass of black, gray, and brown fur, larger than any he'd ever seen. He could have allowed the freebooters to continue using the mortars on the docco with no fear of them stopping the herd, but he considered the destruction that would have been left in the wake. Ultimately it would fall to Savista to tend to the dead or risk the spread of disease from the rotting corpses. Alistair knew that tuberculosis, syphilis, cholera, and other diseases ran rampant through freebooter camps, let alone what the docco might be carrying. And the common concern, factual or not, was that disease could leach out of the bodies and into the soil as they decomposed or be spread by birds who stopped to feed on the carrion. And even with colder weather on the horizon, the stench would soon become unbearable, so Alistair opted to let the docco eat or drag off what they could, leaving far less work for Savista. As he watched, one of the King Bulls turned its head, viscera hanging from its antlers and over its face, toward Alistair as if to acknowledge his kindness.

After the docco had had their fill and wandered off, some from Savista went down to bury the dead. Other than the mortars and the fallen trees that Savista would use to heat their home this coming winter, the docco did a remarkable job cleaning up. Alistair posted a couple of his riflemen out with the sentries, just in case a freebooter or two came back to collect the mortars, and then made his way to Jedrek's quarters.

***

"You wanted to see me?"

"Alistair, my friend! Yes, please come in. Take a seat," he motioned toward a nearby chair. "I want to thank you for filling the role of commander when Captain Hutter and his second fell in battle. You were brilliant, and though I'm sure I know the answer, I would be doing Savista a disservice if I failed to ask."

Alistair had already begun shaking his head, but Jedrek asked anyway. "Would you consider staying on as a captain?"

"I have to find Joe," he replied.

"Joe is dead, Alistair!" Jedrek yelled in frustration. "Reka and Cage risked their lives to bring you back. Believe me, if there were any chance that Joe was alive, they would have brought him back too, but he's gone. Going back there now—three months later—it's madness. You have to know that! Even if you can't admit it to yourself."

Alistair bolted out of his chair. "He's not dead! He can't die here!"

"What are you talking about?" Plenty of people die here. Just take a look down in the valley."

Alistair rolled his eyes but didn't reply, so Jedrek continued. "And we both know that that search parties that go into the Barrens never find what they're looking for, and most don't make it back."

"They found me," Alistair said somberly.

"The exception that proves the rule!" Jedrek fired back.

"You? The undisputed lord of the land, quoting Cicero?"

"That's not fair, Alistair."

Alistair could see that his friend was becoming exasperated. "I don't mean to be difficult, Jedrek, but Reka and Cage went in looking and found me. They took a chance, and they brought me back, and I owe Joe nothing less. And they didn't know about the cave under the cliff."

"Not this again! Alistair, even if there is a cave under the cliff, no one could survive alone in the Barrens for three months."

"Taft did."

"And look at the monster he became."

"I beg to differ. I believe Taft survived *because* he was already a monster."

"More to my point. Look, Joe died in the Barrens, and now he's Rikolti, just like every other poor soul who has perished there. I'm sorry to be so harsh, old friend, but it's the truth, and I can't lose you or any from Savista hunting a ghost."

Alistair opened his mouth to speak, but Jedrek halted him with a raised hand. "And before you say it, I know I can't tell you or anyone else what you can or cannot do. But I will not support a foolhardy quest that will do nothing but add to the wretched legions of the Rikolti." Jedrek rested a hand on Alistair's shoulder. "If any part of him still exists there, it will not be a part you want to find, old friend."

"You'll have to excuse me, Jedrek. You have my answer, I will serve as captain until you can find a suitable replacement, and then I'll be on my way with nothing but gratitude for your kindness and benefaction."

Jedrek hung his head, having failed again to reach his friend. Alistair walked to the door and called back to him, "If we hurry, maybe there is still some breakfast to be had."

There were no hard feelings, no animosity. They saw things differently, and Alistair understood why. Alistair was bound by the Ranger's code, and there was freedom in that. No allegiance to anything but justice. And he saw searching for Joe as a part of that code. Jedrek, on the other hand, had all of Savista to consider. The good of the people and the land on which they lived. Any decision he made had to be made in the shadow of that great burden.

"Coming," Jedrek called and joined Alistair on the walk over to the mess. All but Savista's sentries, the wounded, and those tending to them had gathered in the dining hall for news of the battle. When Alistair and Jedrek entered, everyone stopped talking and gave their full attention.

Jedrek exhaled and shook his head. "This was a difficult morning, and there is still so much that needs doing," Jedrek said to the gathered crowd. "And we will all set about our duties when we leave this hall. But before anything else, we must give thanks to God for his grace. It is His grace that allows Savista to walk in His favor, and it is His favor that keeps us safe from our enemies. We can even be grateful for the docco. The docco ended our battle before we lost any more of our people. "Now, if there is food," Jedrek looked to the chefs, who responded by nodding, "let's eat and get to work."

The cooks did their best to keep the food warm and presentable, but most of it had lost its luster during the three-hour battle. Nonetheless, the good people of Savista ate without complaining. As Alistair sat and ate, he looked around, hoping to see Reka, but neither she nor Eva had made it to breakfast. As he sat absentmindedly, stabbing at his eggs and ham and scanning the room, he felt a tug at his jacket.

"They're in the medical tent with my mom."

Thea's face was sticky with what Alistair presumed was strawberry preserves.

"Looks like I'm going to have to call Agermonte and Barrister over to clean your face," Alistair said with a smile. "Did you eat anything for breakfast besides jam?"

"I had some apples. That's what I put the jam on."

"Well, I'm sure your momma will be pleased as punch to hear that."

"I'm making a plate for her. I'm gonna take it to her at the medical tent. I don't think she's had time to eat."

"Well," said Alistair as he dipped a rag into a glass of water and wiped at her face, "that's a fine idea, Thea. I think I'll prepare plates for Reka and Eva and join you."

Together they walked over to the medical tent, with Agermonte and Barrister trotting just ahead. Alistair was glad that he'd had time to feed them before the shooting started. All through the battle, the two dogs had stood watch over their master, and Alistair showed his appreciation by tossing a couple of slices of ham to them as they walked.

"How do they know where we are going, Mr. Alistair?"

"I don't know. I think maybe they're just smarter than we are."

"Why?" she asked.

"They know things that we don't."

"I know things that you don't know, Mr. Alastair. Does that mean I'm smarter than you?"

"I'm quite sure you are much smarter than I am."

Thea smiled her most satisfied smile. Alistair allowed the little girl her moment in the sun before continuing.

"Thea, have you been able to see my friend Joe recently?"

"Oh, sure!" she exclaimed. "He was here yesterday. Well, almost here, I mean."

"How so?" Alistair tried his best to sound nonchalant.

"Well, he made it into the darkness. He thinks it's the place between his world and ours; I heard him say so. But then some people pulled him back." Thea gave a little giggle. "He was so angry with them."

"The darkness," Alistair said in a voice just above a whisper. He was all in. Joe told him about the dark, but there was just no way Thea could know about it unless she could see it.

"So, my friend Joe is okay?"

"He's in a room full of white people," she said.

"You mean like ghosts?"

"I don't know, maybe," replied Thea with a shrug of her shoulders. "Look! There's my mom!" Thea lit up like a firefly and ran to her. "Momma! I made you breakfast!"

"That's funny," Siobhan said as she patted her body with her palms. "I don't feel like breakfast."

"Sorry, I meant I *made* breakfast for *you*."

Alistair had so many more questions, but they would have to wait. He stuck his head inside the tent and spotted Eva. She was busy helping bandage what looked like a minor wound on a young man's arm. The activity in the tent seemed to be winding down as the docco attack kept the Savista's injuries at a minimum.

"Hello, Alistair." The voice came from behind him, and he turned to see Reka wiping her hands on the only clean spot on her bloody smock. "Is that for us?"

Alistair glanced down at the plates. "That it is."

"Why, thank you. Eva and I are just finishing up here. We were hoping to make it to the mess before they put everything away."

"Looks like I saved you a few steps."

"You did at that," said Reka offering a slight smile as she walked off with Eva.

When she smiled, the corners of her eyes crinkled just the tiniest bit, and her full lips parted to show her bright white teeth. It was a lovely smile, but she hadn't shared it with anyone in over three months.

"Mr. Alistair," Thea called. "Look!"

Thea had managed to climb onto Barrister's back and was riding him like a pony.

"Thea! You get off of Barrister and stop bothering Mr. Alistair!" Siobhan said as she offered an apology to the Ranger. "I'm so sorry, Alistair. Sometimes I just don't know what to do with her."

"I'm glad for her company, as are the boys," Alistair replied as Agermonte and Barrister began shoving Thea around with their massive heads. "They've taken a shine to your little girl."

"I see that," Siobhan replied with a laugh. "She has always had a special connection with animals."

"Seems she has a special connection with everything. Jedrek says she's a seer."

"She is, Mr. Alistair. But it's a gift, not a parlor trick. In the future, I would appreciate you speaking with me before asking her to use it."

Alistair felt like he'd been scolded by his mother, but Siobhan was right to be protective. Alistair never once considered asking if she minded Thea using her gift to help him. "I'm sorry, I should have asked."

"Would you happen to have time for a visit tonight? Maybe after supper? Thea told me that she had seen my friend Joe. Mostly unsolicited, I assure you."

She studied him with a jaundiced eye and then called to her daughter. "Thea, would you like to help Mr. Alastair tonight after supper? He has some questions about his friend."

Thea was laughing so hard that Alistair worried she hadn't heard her mother's question, but eventually, she responded.

"Can he bring his dogs?"

"Well, Mr. Alistair?"

"They don't let me go *anywhere* without them," replied Alistair.

"Then it's settled. You and your furry friends may come for dinner."

"I didn't mean to invite myself to dinner!"

"I know, but I enjoy cooking, and it will be nice to prepare a meal for someone besides myself and Thea." Siobhan curtsied, mocking the formality of the proceedings.

"Agermonte! Barrister, to me!" bellowed Alistair. The two behemoths gave Thea a final nudge and bounded over to their master.

"See you later, Mr. Alistair," Thea said with an excited wave. "Momma?"

"Yes, baby?"

"Do you think he's going to ask me about the bad man?"

"Which bad man would that be?"

"The burned man. He's the one that pushed Mr. Alistair's friend down. I don't like looking at him."

"We don't judge people by their looks, young lady."

"I'm not momma, I see what he does, and he's bad, very bad. He tried to kill Mr. Joe with a knife, and he says he wants to kill Mr. Alistair."

Chapter 8

His body washed down the river and into a small cove shrouded by rocks and driftwood. Recovery had been difficult, but the Barrens saw to his needs. In the infancy of his convalescence, Hayward Taft subsisted on river leeches that, obedient to unseen forces, found their way into his mouth, which hung agape in his unconscious state. As the leeches attached to feed on the blood in his tongue, Taft would involuntarily chew them into a paste and swallow them.

In his dormancy, Hayward had a vision. He saw himself on the ground in a kneeling curled into a fetal position at the foot of a great mountain. He could feel his breathing quicken and cried out in anguish as new bone pushed through the flesh covering his scapulae. The pain seemed endless as each section of bone knitted itself into skeletal structures resembling bat's wings. Once the final finger of bone was in place, flesh grafted itself over his new appendages.

His evolution left him in a weakened state, but he was safe, shielded by his master, allowing him time to heal and regain his strength. After the incubation period, Hayward took some time learning to navigate the winds. Once mastered, he received his revelation in its totality. Hayward Taft, the once small, frightened son of Albert and Rose Taft, lifted himself into the air on his mighty wings. Soaring higher than any perch in the land, Hayward took in the vastness of his domain. The Midwestern Territories laid out in submission before him. Every creature in the land, alive only so long as it pleased him. Even at this dizzying height, Hayward could zero in on each blade of grass on the prairies if he so chose.

He spied a herd of docco charging across a prairie south of the Great Lake. Outside of the forces of nature, there was nothing more awe-inspiring than the docco thundering en masse across the plains. *How dare they display their might in my presence,* thought Hayward. He took it as an insult to his own power. Hayward raised his right hand to the heavens and struck at the beasts, but nothing happened. Perplexed, he stared at the herd. Then he watched with great pleasure as they charged into a phalanx of fighters gathered for battle and gorged themselves on their meat, and he understood why his father had stayed his hand.

Across the Dead Zone came a brilliant red ball of flame from the west. It was a thousand miles away, and yet he could feel its heat. It was his father. Not Albert Taft, that piece of shit. Albert was nothing more than the dropper that his *true* father used to sow his seed, a pitifully unworthy vessel if anyone were to ask him, but that was done and done. And now his father was calling him home. Hayward was to take his place on his father's throne. Across the Dead Zone, he would go west into the great unknown of the Western Territories to claim his birthright. The fire was his inheritance, his legacy, and Hayward would wield it as his sword to strike down upon the earth and cleanse it to his purpose. He flew at miraculous speed across the sky into the west. Hayward had just reached the outer edge of the Dead Zone when an unseen force blew him back east hundreds of miles. He was surprised but not angry. Hayward understood his task. There would be no easy tests for the son of the Fire King in the West. Hayward would make his pilgrimage by foot through the Dead Zone.

Now, months after his fall, wounds bound and healed by his malevolent benefactor, Hayward Taft, the revenant, would resume his holy work. Standing at the water's edge, he reached to his back, hoping to feel the wings of his revelation, but they were gone. *No matter,* he thought, *they will come to me in my father's time.* Time, the bitter enemy of life, was now nothing more than a concept to Hayward Taft. A yoke for others to bear, but not him. He was an immortal. Not in the traditional sense of the word—Hayward knew he could be killed; he just couldn't be kept by death. With the understanding of his wonderful new condition and having glimpsed his future, Hayward was filled with confidence and excitement for things to come. Still, mortal matters needed tending. Hunger, for instance.

Hayward plunged his hand into the water at his feet and pulled out a pale fish with a large mouth and bulbous eyes. He looked at it for a minute, considering its grotesque features, and then opened his mouth wide to bite off its head. Hayward hadn't opened his mouth more than a centimeter or two in the past three months. Doing so caused his lips and the corners of his mouth to tare. But that didn't bother Hayward in the least. He had come to appreciate pain, and he didn't mind the taste of blood, even if it was his own. He reached in several times and each time came back with a fish. *And why not,* he thought, *wasn't that their purpose?* Hayward splashed his face with cool river water and then straightened his back to a sickening chorus of snapping sinew and bone.

"Well, no time like the present," he said aloud to no one in particular. Benign as the sentiment was, it made him sad. Leaving the Barrens meant leaving Agnes again, and he hadn't even had the chance to lay with her. He needed that. He needed it so badly that he braved the crossing back over just to be with her. He decided he would take a day to lay near his sister before beginning his journey. Then he would leave to fulfill his destiny.

Hayward had a thought that spawned a devilish smile. *Maybe, in time, my father, The Fire King in the West, will grant me the power to bring her back fully? He thought.* With newfound joy, Hayward hiked up and out of the cove and made his way in the direction of Agnes' burial place. He felt stiffness in his bones, but considering all he'd been through, he thought he was doing rather well. As he walked, he considered how he might punish Alistair Woodbridge. The man had been a thorn in his side long enough. He fell upon the idea of staking him to the ground at the edge of the cliff where their two previous battles had ended. He would split his belly open with the beautiful karambit that his grandfather created. Albert Taft was an asshole, but his grandfather must have understood that his turd of a kid was destined for something great, even if it was only to be used as an eyedropper to deliver the seed that would become Hayward the Merciless.

"I will split your belly open," yelled Hayward, who was almost giddy at the thought. "Then I will pour hot coals into your gut and stitch you back up. I will watch you writhe in pain as your intestines and organs roast, and if my father wills it, I will keep you alive as I carve you open and feast on your heart." He delighted in the thought of seeing the terror in the fearless Ranger's eyes.

Chapter 9

When he woke, Joe felt surprisingly well-rested. Terri was sitting in a chair, thumbing through a magazine in her Tyvek suit.

"How long are you guys going to wear those stupid things?"

"You're awake," she said, smiling behind the plastic face shield."

"How long was I out?"

"You have been asleep for," she glanced at her watch, "let's see, about sixteen hours. How are you feeling?"

"I'm starving," Joe said. He tried to reach for his stomach, but his wrists were still lashed to the bedrails.

"What the hell?"

"Joe, you were combative when you came out of the effects of the Tramadol, and we had to keep you from ripping out your IVs. Dr. Belter thinks it has something to do with the residual effects of the anesthesia."

"Well, I'm fine now. Can you untie my fucking hands?"

"If you were my son, I would wash your mouth out with soap," she said, still maintaining a pleasant demeanor.

"Well, you're barely old enough to be my sister, so—"

"Be that as it may, Dr. Belter will be in to do his rounds in a little bit. I'm guessing he'll okay it, but it's not my call."

"Great," Joe said, sounding exasperated.

"I know Dr. Belter has cleared you for clear liquids if you're hungry."

"How about a burger?"

"I don't think burgers are going to be on the menu for a while, sweetie. How does Jell-o or broth sound?"

"Sounds like a piss poor replacement for a burger, but I can't exactly call for take-out, so Jell-O me up some broth!"

"Jell-O you up some—? Sit tight for me, and I'll see what I can do."

Terri walked to the door and called down the hall for a candy striper. The girl walked into the room and plopped down in Terri's chair. She was very pretty, perhaps seventeen years old, with long blonde hair lightened at the tips and bright blue eyes that reminded Joe of the girl dated in high school. The one he took to his grandfather's garage.

"So, you're a police officer?" she queried. "Is that how you got hurt?"

"Not exactly, I mean, I am a police officer, but how I got hurt is a long story," Joe said, "and you wouldn't believe me if I told you."

"My boyfriend wants to be a cop; I told him that it's too dangerous. I mean, jeez, just look at what happened to you. I heard you got hurt catching a murderer, the guy that killed all those poor people at the Never Close. Is that true?"

"Well, see I."

"I think you're like a real live hero." She talked a mile a minute and fired questions at him so fast that he couldn't process them, let alone answer them.

"And I heard there was a car chase and a big crash. I heard the guy shot at you, but you like dodged the bullets or something?"

"I what? No!" Joe tried to correct her, but she kept right on rolling. One question after another until Terri finally came back into the room.

"Okay, Donna, time to get back to your rounds. Thank you for keeping an eye on our fella."

The name sent a shiver up Joe's spine.

"Sorry about that. She's a sweet girl, but boy, oh boy can she talk," said Terri. "So, I spoke with the doctor, and he said he plans to remove your hyperalimentation line today."

"Hyper what?"

"The tube in your chest. That's what we've been feeding you through. It supplies your body with all the nutrients you need, but it doesn't do much for hunger. Belter said he was happy to hear that you got your appetite back."

"So, is that a yes or no on the burger?"

"Still a no, but broth and Jell-O are still on the menu," Terri said with a smile. "Now, do you feel up to some company?" She asked as she unbound his wrists. "Dr. Belter gave the okay."

Joe rubbed at his wrists. "Thanks and Bob's not exactly company."

"It's not Bob. Your buddy seems to have made a new friend."

"Let me guess, Chris?" It was apparent to anyone paying the slightest attention that he'd taken a shine to her.

"Yep, he took her out for an early supper."

"That dog!" Joe said with a smile. "Here I am, clinging to life, and my best friend is out skirt-chasing." Laughing hurt his stomach, but it was nice to have a reason to laugh.

"Anyway," continued Terri. "There's a Sergeant Corliss and Lucas Travidi at the nurses' station asking to see you."

"Send them in!" Joe said excitedly.

He hadn't seen his sergeant since the night this whole thing started. As for Travidi, Fitz said the kid was the one responsible for finding him and bringing him back. Terri brought the two men into the observation room and had them put on the protective gear. Joe had taken to calling them marshmallow suits. Corliss led the way, followed by Travidi and Terri.

"Core! Good to see you!"

"I've been here a few times, but you were always asleep," Ronald Corliss said. "There's someone I would like for you to meet. Joe, this is Lucas Travidi; he's the guy who found you."

"Well, I helped find you anyway."

Joe could tell he was going to like this guy. He offered his hand, and Lucas looked at Terri. She nodded an okay, and Lucas extended a neoprene gloved hand.

"It's really nice to meet you, Lucas."

"Same here," Lucas said.

"I'm going to step out. If you gentlemen need anything, just holler."

"I have so many questions," Joe said.

"*You* have questions? Man, I got a list of questions a mile long!" Lucas replied.

There was no tension or awkwardness between them. It was as if they'd known each other forever.

"I'll be happy to answer whatever I can," Joe said, but Lucas didn't know where to begin, so Joe started.

"How did you find me?"

"Well, it's kind of hard to explain, but I'm what is known as a remote viewer. I can lock in on a person and see around them."

"You mean like looking through their eyes?" Joe asked.

"Sort of, but sometimes it's more like standing next to them. I can see the person as well as their surroundings. I can't really explain it; it's just something I was born with, I think."

"Do you think you could do it now?"

"Sure, I can do it anytime. If you had a magazine, I could show you."

"No. I mean, could you look into that other world right now?"

"Yes," Lucas said, as all the happiness drained from his face. "Sometimes when I'm not even trying. I have nightmares about the things I see there. What happened there, Joe?"

That was Lucas' first question, and it was a doozy, but it would have to wait.

"What about Reka and Alistair? Can you see them?"

"Is one of them the man you were traveling with?"

"Yes! That's Alistair."

"I can remote view him," Lucas said. "He spends a lot of time with a dude that looks like he's in a motorcycle gang."

"Jedrek, his name is Jedrek. What about a woman?"

"There's a woman with dark hair; she looks too young to be his wife. Anyway, she went to this terrible place with a huge black man. That was where they found your friend."

"Reka and Cage, it has to be."

"Well, they found Alistair, but even after they found him, they stayed and kept looking. I think they were looking for you, but they couldn't stay for long, or Alistair would have died."

"Are they safe?" Joe pressed.

"I wouldn't say anyone is safe in that place. What the hell are those gigantic bear-looking things?"

"They're called docco, but I mean now, are they safe now?"

"I think so. They made it back to the camp with the biker guy."

Joe was relieved to know they were all back and safe at Savista. "There was another man."

"The tall thin guy?"

"Yes. His name is—"

"Hayward Taft," Corliss said. "We know all about that son of a bitch."

"How do you—"

"Lucas here. He identified him for us by remote-viewing you and your buddy."

"And before you ask," Lucas said. "I can see him too, and he's alive. He's the reason I have nightmares. Ever since I remote viewed him, he has shared his thoughts with me. I try to shut him out as much as I can, but so much still comes through. I swear, sometimes I feel like I'm going crazy."

"I'm sorry, Lucas, I really am, but do you think you could help me get back there?"

"What?" Corliss exploded. "You want to go back there? After all, we went through to bring you out?"

"I have to go back for my friends Cor.'"

"What the hell do you call us?"

"How far would you go for Rhonda?" he challenged.

He knew the question caught Corliss off guard. Ronald Corliss was a private man, and he knew he'd intended to keep his relationship private.

"Everyone knows Ron. You work with a bunch of cops. You think you can keep secrets?"

"Well, it's different." Corliss offered weakly.

"The only difference is that Rhonda is here, and Reka is there, in the Territories. If the roles were reversed, you would be willing to cross back over to get her, and you know it."

Joe knew that to anyone else, the conversation would have seemed nonsensical. At least anyone other than the contributors to the Todd Zeelander show. But these men had a very different understanding of the world than most. Lucas had seen it through his remote viewing, and Corliss had actually dipped his toes into the other realm. To them, the Midwestern Territories were as real as the Western Hemisphere.

"So, what do you think Lucas, is it possible for me to go there and bring them back here?"

"I don't know. You know way more about that place than I do."

"Yeah, but you're the one who brought me back."

"No!" He stopped Joe, "I didn't bring you back. I just led Ron to you once you were back in our world," he said and paused. "Well, halfway back anyway."

"Right! That's the part I need help with. The getting back there part. I'm sure I can find my way around once I get there. I have a map."

Corliss reached into his pocket and pulled out the beat-up old tri-fold wallet. "I think this belongs to you." He was about to hand it to Joe when Terri walked back into the room.

"Hey! No! Put that away. He can't have contact with anything from outside this room unless it's been sterilized! Why do you think you're wearing—" she waved her hand in his direction—"that?"

Joe reached for the wallet, but Corliss was already shoving it back into his pocket inside his Tyvek suit and offering his apologies.

"I think maybe Joe could use a little rest," Terri said.

"No, I'm fine," Joe protested. "Another hour, and we'll call it a day. I promise."

Terri set two hospital bowls down on the tray next to his bed. "See that he eats some of this," she said to Corliss.

"Will do, and again, sorry about that."

Terri smiled at the big man, "I've got my eye on you," she said and left the room again.

"Let me see that map," urged Joe.

"Are you nuts? That nurse will kick my ass. I'll keep the wallet safe for you, but the map is in there. What the hell is that supposed to be a map of anyway?"

Joe told them everything he'd learned from Alistair. The Trinity test, the flooding of the lakes and rivers and oceans breaching their banks. The lake fires, the spiders, and of course, the docco. When he was done, both Corliss and Lucas sat in stunned silence. Joe appreciated the opportunity to talk about his experiences with people who wouldn't think he needed to be fitted for a straight jacket.

"And there's something else," said Joe. "During my last surgery, the doc said that I flatlined."

"What the hell is that?" Corliss asked.

"It's like dead, but not completely dead," offered Joe. "Anyway, I made it back there, well, almost made it. I was right there, but they got my heart started again."

"So, you think you were dead or maybe half dead when you were there that whole time?" Corliss asked.

"No!" Lucas answered for Joe. "He couldn't have been dead, or I couldn't have seen him. I can't see the dead. Believe me; I've tried."

"I don't know," Joe said. "Maybe I was in some kind of limbo."

"So you think that place is like purgatory or something?" Corliss asked.

"No, I mean; I don't know. I mean, I was alive when I was there. But I think death, or maybe near death, is the door between the two worlds. I'm not sure."

"You're not listening to me," Lucas said. "I can't see the dead, and I certainly saw you. How else could we have found you?"

Both Joe and Corliss looked at Lucas as if they expected him to have an answer or some other helpful input.

"What are you looking at me for? All I'm saying is, whatever state you were in, you weren't dead. And neither are your friends."

"Lucas, can you see them now?" Joe asked hopefully.

"I would have to look for them. I mean, I can't see them the way I can see you."

"But you're sure you could find them if you tried?"

"Fairly certain, yeah."

"Can you show me how to do it?" Joe asked.

He thought he knew the answer, but he wanted so badly to see her face again. He wanted to see her in the worst way. And he wanted to see Alistair. He hadn't seen his father in months, but that didn't seem to bother him. Alistair, on the other hand, he really missed. He knew it would seem crazy to most people, but he also missed the danger. Joe had never felt more alive than when he was facing death. Joe never considered himself an adrenaline junkie, but maybe that was because he never had a good dosing.

He had been shot at on a few occasions, and it was scary. But nothing like his shootout with the Rokes or the battle with the freebooters. That was the real deal. Not just some drunk dickhead or shitbag felon not wanting to go back to jail, but men hell-bent on killing him. And the spiders and the docco, death waited around every corner, and God help him, Joe loved it.

"You're kidding, right? I mean, it's not like a card trick," Lucas said.

"I know," Joe said apologetically. "I didn't mean to sound like I don't think it's an amazing gift—if that's the right word."

"I'm not sure myself sometimes," Lucas replied. "Tell you what; I will try and find them later today, and I'll let Ron know how it goes, but don't expect too much. Some days I find them out working in the fields or eating dinner, and sometimes I find them sleeping. Not together! Just, you know, it's never anything exciting. But that other guy, Hayward Taft, he's another story."

"What do you mean?"

Lucas drew in a deep breath and exhaled hard, steaming up his facemask for a second. "It's like he knows I'm there, and he lets me hear his thoughts. I've never been able to hear anything before, and it comes through like all statically, you know, like when you almost have a radio station dialed in, but not quite, but he lets me—no, that's not right. He makes me listen. And sometimes I can see his—I don't know what to call them—visions, I guess. And they are fucking terrifying!"

Both Joe and Corliss listened intently as Lucas told him what he'd seen. He spared no detail. Lucas told them how Taft sprouted bat wings out of his back and about the great fireball in the west. Lucas explained that he could feel the heat radiating across the place that Taft called the Dead Zone. And he told them of the great evil force that seemed to call out to Hayward Taft like a siren song, beckoning him west beyond the Dead Zone.

"He seemed to feed on the energy it gave off. It made him stronger. It healed him. I'm telling you, Joe, I know you want to go back for Reka, but there is something evil there. An evil like nothing I could have ever imagined, and I've seen the Exorcist. He's on that island, and it's haunted by lost souls. I can't see them, but I can feel them."

"They're called the Rikolti," Joe said. "They are the souls of the people who died on the island. The island is called the Barrens, and I was almost one of them."

"Okay, gentlemen," Terri said as she came through the door. "Joe hasn't touched his dinner. It's time to call it a night. He has to eat and rest up. If you can hold food down for a few days, Joe, Dr. Belter will pull your hyperalimentation tube, and that's one step closer to hamburgers and going home."

"That would be great," Joe muttered.

"Well, I'm heading back to Indiana when I leave here," Travidi said. "If you need me, just have Ron get a hold of me."

"Yeah, sure," Joe replied, sounding a bit distant.

"See, he's had too much excitement for one day."

It was great news, and Joe would have had more of a reaction, but he was distracted by the little girl in the yellow dress standing in the corner of his room that no one else seemed to notice.

Chapter 10

The loud knock on the door came as no surprise to Thea, but it wasn't because of her unique ability. She had been watching for Alistair from the kitchen window for half an hour. Thea dashed ran to the door and flung it open to find Alistair standing there sopping wet. She looked around both sides of the ranger and frowned.

"Where's Agermonte? Where's Barrister?"

"I thought I might leave them home tonight," replied Alistair as he waved a hand in front of his nose. "Wet dogs."

A light but steady rain that had been falling all day soaked everyone and everything caught outside, and Alistair's dogs were no exception.

"But you said you were going to bring them." Thea protested, her face clouded with confusion.

"I did, but that was before they got all wet and smelly," Alistair said, offering a smile to soften Thea's disappointment.

Siobhan entered the room, wiping her hands on her apron. "I certainly hope you're not referring to my cooking."

"Whatever you're cooking smells wonderful. No, I was explaining to Thea that I didn't bring Agermonte and Barrister because they had been out all day and gotten wet."

"Alitheia!" Siobhan snapped.

"I'm sorry, Mr. Alistair." Thea puffed out her lower lip and hung her head.

"Did I miss something?"

"She knows better than to ask an adult to explain their actions."

"Well, I'm sure she didn't—" A stern look from Siobhan cut his response short. "You have a lovely home."

The living quarters Siobhan and Thea shared was a standard two-room slat-board cottage. One room doubled as a living room and bedroom, the other as a kitchen and dining room. Siobhan hung a curtain to create two separate spaces. The other was the kitchen, which doubled as a dining room. It was no different than Alistair's place, but the soft touch of a woman's hand made it feel warmer and more inviting.

"Your timing couldn't have been better, Mr. Alistair. I was just about to put supper on the table."

"It smells wonderful," said Alistair, removing his hat.

"Take Mr. Alistair's hat and coat and hang them by the fire to dry."

Thea held her arms out and smiled, perhaps to show there were no hard feelings. Alistair smiled in return and laid his heavy duster across her arms. Thea responded with a tiny grunt but bore up under the weight.

"You got it?" Alistair asked.

"I got it," she replied with a sharp nod.

Alistair set his hat on Thea's head. After she'd hung his things, Thea took Alistair by the hand and led him to his seat.

The table adorned by a small arrangement of wildflowers bundled and tied with a red ribbon had been set for three, and Alistair noticed that his plate and cup were free of chips and seemed brighter than Siobhan and Thea's. He assumed they had been Thea's fathers, which made him a little self-conscious.

"Do you like the flowers, Mr. Alistair? I picked them from the field."

"They're beautiful, Thea. Thank you."

"Thea, come help me," Siobhan called over her shoulder.

"I'll be right back, Mr. Alistair."

For dinner, Siobhan prepared fully dressed Cornish game hens and fresh vegetables. Alistair lived alone and never bothered with fancy dinners. He didn't even use a plate, most times opting to eat right out of the pot he'd used to prepare his meal. The three of them sat and ate and made light conversation, and it was the most pleasant evening Alistair could ever recall having. After supper, Siobhan brought out an apple pie and a roasted dandelion root tea served in the living room.

"This pie is divine, Ms. Siobhan, maybe the best I've ever tasted."

"I'm glad you like it. There's plenty, so don't be shy, and please, just call me Siobhan."

Alistair scooped a fork full into his mouth and, minding his manners, swallowed before responding. "I may just take you up on that—Siobhan, and, if you didn't mind, I would prefer Alistair. Mr. is so formal."

"Does that mean I can call you Alistair too?" Thea asked excitedly.

Alistair looked to Siobhan, and she smiled at his uncertainty.

"No, you may not."

Thea laughed, and Alistair helped himself to another piece of pie. The mood was light and fun, and Alistair was hesitant to bring it up, but Thea had yawned a couple of times, and he could see that his window was closing.

"Thea, do you think we can talk about my friend now?"

"Sure, Mr. Alistair. I was watching him before you got here. He was in bed again. He's always in bed." Her face scrunched up. "Is he always this boring, Mr. Alistair?"

"What do you mean, *always in bed*? What kind of bed?"

"Just a bed-bed. There are always people standing around him. They're dressed all in white, but I can never see their faces."

"Like ghosts?" Alistair asked nervously.

"No," Thea snorted. "They're just regular people. There's a lady; I think she's his mom because she was feeding him and wiping his mouth."

Joe told Alistair that his mother passed away when he was a boy, but Alistair saw no reason to bring it up.

"You wanna see him, Mr. Alistair?"

"What?" If he'd been standing, Alistair might have staggered back.

"Your friend, you wanna see him? Just take my hand."

Alistair took Thea's hand, and a pulse of energy passed between them. Alistair felt it from the tips of his fingers clear out to the ends of each hair on his head, and then the world before him splintered and fell away. It was as if he were an alien life form using his body as its vessel. Attached and yet detached, watching the world, as he knew it, through the portals of this organic ship tangled in a symbiotic relationship, neither being able to exist on its own but still separate.

As the old shards fell away, a new reality fell like pixels between two new sheets of glass. On some level, Alistair knew that he must still be in Siobhan's little cottage, but that was not the reality presented before his eyes. Before him, in a room of stark white and as clear and tangible as anything he'd ever know, lay Joe with a person in a white suit tending to him. It was no wonder Thea didn't recognize the bed as a hospital bed. The only hospital beds she'd ever known were in the medical tent where her mother worked. Stained in blood, occupied by patients crying out in pain, similar Alistair thought, to the images he'd seen in books of the medical tents in the American civil war. And like those tents, there was no convalescing in Savista's medical tent.

"Joe, it's me, Alistair."

Joe looked in his direction but didn't respond.

What's wrong with him? Alistair thought to himself.

"He can't see us, but I think he knows we're here," replied Thea.

Alistair reached out, letting Thea's hand fall away, and he was back in the little cabin staring blankly at Siobhan.

"What the hell just happened?"

"You wanted to see Joe," Thea said, matter-of-factly.

"I saw him, and I could hear you in my head!"

Without realizing it, Alistair had pushed himself against the back of his chair as far away from Thea as he could. "Were you reading my thoughts?"

"No, you were asking me a question. I could hear you," Thea replied.

"Are you okay, Alistair?" Siobhan asked.

"So that world, what we saw, that's real?"

"Sure, just like this one," Thea answered.

"Thea, fetch Mr. Alistair a glass of water. You look a little green around the gills, Alistair."

"That's the damnedest thing I've ever seen."

Siobhan took the cup of water from Thea and handed it to Alistair. "Here, drink this."

Alistair took a sip. "Got anything stronger?"

"I can make magnolia root tea. It's supposed to settle the nerves," Siobhan offered.

Alistair sipped his water. "I was thinking of something a little stronger than that." Alistair set his cup down. "Thea, that's a hospital bed you saw Joe laying in."

"Sure didn't look like a hospital bed."

"How long has Joe been there?"

"A long time, and it's so boring there," she whined. "The only time he does fun stuff is when he goes outside to fly. That's really fun! No one here can fly."

"He flies?" Alistair asked, wanting to make sure he'd heard her correctly.

"Yeah, sometimes he flies to a place with big glass buildings that go all the way up past the clouds!"

"Skyscrapers?" Alistair was astonished. "Has she ever been to a city?" He asked Siobhan.

"She's never been anywhere but Savista and our old camp out on the plain."

"Have you ever been to a city Mr. Alistair?" Thea asked.

"I have," he said.

"What was it like?" Thea asked excitedly. "Was it beautiful?"

"I don't know, as I would call it beautiful," said Alistair.

"Did you live there?"

"No, I passed through on my way to pick up a prisoner."

"What did he do?"

"He murdered a man in Espero and fled to a little town called White Church.

"Where's White Church?"

"You ask a lot of questions."

Siobhan smiled.

"It's in the southwestern part of Gerrings. The peacekeepers there caught him and turned him over to the jailer in White Church."

"What are peacekeepers?"

"I suppose they're like a posse," said Alistair.

Thea drew in a breath to ask another question, but Siobhan filled the gap. "She doesn't know much about how the law works, Alistair," Siobhan said.

His name sounded nice the way she said it, and it softened the lines on his face. "Well, let's see. First, you have the Judges. Now the Judges have the most power. They have jurisdiction over—" Alistair could see that he stirred another question in Thea. "That means they have authority or power everywhere in the Midwestern Territories. They can pass judgment and deliver—" the look of confusion settled deeper. "A judge can decide if a man is guilty or innocent. If the judge decides that he's guilty, the judge will decide their punishment. Does that make sense?"

The clouds lifted. "Yep," said Thea with a quick nod of her head.

"Good. Then you have the rangers, like me. Rangers have jurisdiction—"

"That means power and authority," Thea beamed.

"That's right!" Alistair said. "We have the power and authority to arrest bad guys anywhere in the territories. That means I can go clear up to Columbia and arrest a man if I have to."

"Only men?" Thea asked. Siobhan smiled.

"Well, no, anyone who needs arresting, I guess," replied Alistair. "Any more questions?" he asked with a playful glare.

Thea shook her head no, seemingly satisfied for the time being.

"Okay then," continued Alistair. "Once we arrest them, we take them to see a judge." Alistair looked at Thea and raised an eyebrow. Thea smiled and giggled.

"Alright then. Last you have the peacekeepers. The peacekeepers can arrest people, but only in the territory, they are sworn to protect. Then they turn them over to a jailer who holds them for a ranger or a judge, and that's about it."

Thea gave Alistair a thumbs up. "Got it."

"Okay, Thea, no more interrupting Mr. Alistair if you want to hear about the city."

"So, like I was saying, it was nightfall when I reached the outskirts of the city, and I needed to pass *through* the city to reach White Church. I had to abandon the Albatross earlier in the day because all of the roads had been overrun by the forest," Alistair could see that Thea wanted to ask but held her tongue. "The Albatross, that's my conveyance, my—truck as it were." Thea still looked confused. The thing I travel in. I believe Jedrek has it squirreled away for me, but I guess I could show it to you sometime," he said. "That is if your mother doesn't mind."

Alistair glanced at her, and Siobhan smiled and nodded her approval.

"Anyway, I made camp there for the night. Cities are dangerous places, especially when night falls. Lots of big buildings and dark corners where freebooters can hide," Alistair narrowed his gaze to drive the point. "So, I decided it best to wait till morning to head in. Well, I was sitting by my campfire that evening when I heard a noise from just beyond the glow it gave off. I almost didn't hear it because there was a docco out there somewhere roaring his fool head off."

He was sure his listeners had no problem imagining what that sounded like, having spent the morning listening to them attack the freebooters in the valley below. Thea seemed to be hanging on his every word, and Alistair leaned forward and lowered his voice for dramatic effect.

"I drew one of my Dragoons," he ran his hand over the grip of the gun on his right hip. "Then I lit the end of a hunk of firewood for a torch and started in the direction of the noise." He pantomimed the action without getting up from his chair. "As I neared the edge of my campfire's light, something jumped up and started running back into the woods. I gave chase, but my torch wasn't bright enough to light my way, and I tripped, twisted an ankle, and went sprawling to the ground."

Thea let out a gasp.

"My torch went out, and I was left in almost total darkness." Alistair paused, and Thea exhaled.

"As I waited for my eyes to adjust, I felt around on the ground for my gun and laid my hand on what felt like a boot. That was when I met good old Bodie. 'Name's Bodie Olaf Mr., you hurt?' He says to me. "Alistair raised the tone and rasp of his voice to mimic Bodie as best he could.

"I'd be lying if I said the man didn't startle me. I grabbed hold of his ankle to drag him to the ground. 'No reason for violence, Mr., I don't mean you no harm,' he says." Again, in his best Bodie voice. "Well, my eyes had adjusted just enough to the darkness that I could see that Bodie Olaf held something wrapped in a tattered rag in his hands. Bodie carefully peeled back the cloth exposing a bright white bioluminescent stone; Bodie called it his lightin' stone; it was about the size of an egg, and it cast its light in a huge arc around us. That was when I got my first good look at Bodie. He was about 5 feet tall, 105 pounds, and looked to be 100 years old. I still remember his threadbare blue and white bowling shirt." Alistair's face took on the soft glow of reminiscence.

"It said *Time To Spare* on the back and had his name *Bodie* stitched on the front left breast pocket." Alistair ran a finger in a loopy pattern over his breast. "Well, having gotten a look at him, I turned old Bodie loose and got to my feet. I was favoring my right ankle cause of the twist, and seeing that I was injured, Bodie offered to help me back to my camp. Then he bends down, picks up my gun, and hands it to me. He'd been standing on it the whole time, probably making sure he could trust me. I told him I was obliged and introduced myself. I asked him the name of the city up ahead. 'That's Bodieland!' "He said." "Used to be called New Gerrings, and before that, Kansas City.' "I asked him if he lived in Bodieland all by himself. Bodie told me that it was him and about a dozen others that called themselves 'The Show-Me's, like The Show-Me State, he says, get it?'

"What does that mean?" Thea asked.

"Well, near as I could figure, it meant, if you want me to believe what you're saying, you gotta show me," Alistair answered.

"So, Bodie helped me limp back to my camp, and since it was late, and for his kindness, I offered him a place at my fire. We talked a bit more, and then we decided to turn in for the night.

"The next morning, I awoke to birds chirping and Bodie yelling and throwing rocks into the trees. He's yelling at the birds at the top of his lungs, 'Shut up! You'll wake my friend!'" Alistair smiled and shook his head. "I told him that I was up and he could stop working so hard to keep the birds quiet."

Siobhan and Thea both giggled at the absurdity of it.

"We made breakfast, broke camp, and hiked into the city. My ankle felt pretty good, and it didn't slow us down none. The roads and walkways were all gone, overgrown with grass, plants, and moss. The earth will always take back what's hers. You mark my words, child. We're no more than fleas on her back, and when she's had enough of us, she'll scratch us right off." Alistair looked at Thea to make sure she was paying attention. She blinked her big brown almond-shaped eyes, and he went on.

"Some buildings in that city were forty stories tall. That's ten times higher than the rock face of Savista and near all of it covered by vegetation. Like mother earth was reaching up with grassy-viney fingers to pull it all back down."

"What does that mean, *stories tall*?" Thea asked.

"Well, let's see," replied Alistair. "Your house here is one story tall. If you put another house on top of yours, well, that would be two stories tall, and if you put another house on top of that house, it would be—" Alistair waited, and Thea did not disappoint.

"Three stories tall," she said.

"That's right."

"But, why would someone put houses on top of one another?"

"Well, they wouldn't out here, but in the cities, they need to make use of every inch of space. Cities were packed full of buildings like that. Didn't you say that you saw tall buildings like that when Joe was flying around?"

"Yeah, but they didn't look like houses, Mr. Alistair."

"Well, they weren't houses; you see, they were what they called offices."

"What's offices?"

"Places where people go to work."

"Like the fields?" she asked.

"Kind of, but inside and they don't grow things in them."

Siobhan laughed at the exchange, "Let's let Mr. Alistair finish his story," she said with a smile.

Alistair smiled back and continued. "A long time ago, way before you were born, cities were places full of people. In a city like Kansas City, more people lived in one building than all of the people in Savista combined."

"What happened to them?" Thea asked.

"Well, I'm getting to that, but it's kind of scary. Are you sure you want to hear it?" Alistair asked as he glanced at Siobhan for approval.

"It's okay with me if you think you want to hear it," Siobhan said to Thea.

Thea swallowed hard and nodded.

"Okay, but if it gets too scary, you just let me know."

"I will, I promise."

"Okay, so like I was saying, Bodie told me that most people tried to stay put after the split. You know what that is, right?"

"Momma told me that there were fires and earthquakes."

"That's right. And after the fires and earthquakes, a lot of people tried to go on with their normal lives; getting up in the morning, going to work, grocery shopping, and the like, and it all seemed to be going fine until the power failed."

"You mean the power and authority?"

"No, not the same kind of power. See Thea, there was a time when electric current flowed through lines into houses and buildings and delivered power, what they called electricity. You could turn on a light with the flip of a switch."

Thea's hand moved instinctively to her bottom.

"No, child. Not that kind of switch." Alistair took an oil lamp off the table and held it out. "There was a time before the split when we didn't use fire to light our way. Giant glowing streetlights lit the roads and walkways at night, and light bulbs lit homes and offices once darkness fell. There was a little button on the wall. They called it a light switch, and you just flipped it," Alistair pantomimed, flipping a light switch. "And the light went on. But when the power grid went down, that all stopped. The people began to panic, and some fled the cities."

"The school has a book about that!" said Thea excitedly. "Ben Franklin made light bulbs."

"Her school has three books. The Bible, The Hobbit, and Great American

Inventors," Siobhan said and then corrected her daughter. "No, Thea, he discovered electricity; Thomas Edison invented the light bulb. Isn't that right, Mr. Alistair?"

"I believe it is," Alistair said, with a smile, and continued.

"Most of the people who tried to hold out fell victim to animals. Before the split, animals like wolves and even bears were afraid of us, and they would stay away, but after the split, guns and bullets were hard to come by for a while, and without guns, predators quickly lost their fear of man. Wolves and wild boar hunted men, women, and children in the city streets. Poor Bodie's wife got eaten by boars. He said he tried to save her, and they turned on him. But the Lord spared Bodie. A docco near enough to hear the screams of Mrs. Olaf charged in and gorged itself on the fattened-up boars, and Bodie was able to escape." Alistair's eyes fell to the floor as he remembered his short-lived friendship with the curiously happy little man. "It haunted him till his last day," Alistair said and cleared his throat.

"Bodie told me that once the predators moved in, the people moved out. Some, like the Show-Me's, had survival skills, and they were prepared. Bodie's Show-Me's, and a few other groups, stockpiled supplies and weapons and trained for the dark days they saw coming. But most people were soft. They figured the government would save them, and they had no idea how to fend for themselves. Bodie said that most of them were nothing but food for the predators, and once that food supply ran out, the wolves and boar and the docco left. He told me that that was when things went from bad to worse. He said that was when the rats came."

Alistair stopped speaking momentarily. "Bodie said the rats were worse than the predators. One could be crawling above your head at any moment, and you wouldn't know it until it dropped on your shoulder."

Siobhan and Thea both looked up at their own ceiling.

"He said that he woke one night to that high-pitched mewing that some men make when they know they are going to die. Bodie bolted upright from his mat, pulled his lightin' stone, and saw them. Red-eyed rats in a feeding frenzy swarmed over the body of a fat man named Clover. Bodie said Clover's eyes were wide with fear, but he couldn't move, said the rats probably chewed through his spinal cord and paralyzed the poor bastard."

Alistair forgot his audience and went on. "Bodie said he watched as one of the rats plucked one of Clover's eyeballs from its socket while another chewed a hole through his neck and disappeared, whipping tail and all, into Clover's body. He said there were so many rats in the body that it moved even after Clover was dead." Alistair exhaled and shook his head. "So old Bodie set fire to the body and roasted it rats and all."

Thea and Siobhan sat staring at Alistair with eyes as big as saucers.

"Beg your pardon, ladies," he said and cleared his throat. "Shall I continue?"

"Will you be telling any more rat stories?" Siobhan asked.

"No ma'am, all done with that."

"Then please, proceed."

"Well, the sun was coming up, and even short little Bodie cast a shadow that made him look forty-feet tall. The shadows from the 40 or 50 story tall buildings were so tall that they disappeared over the horizon."

"Wow," Thea whispered.

"Wow, is right, little lady. Me and Bodie walked through the shadows of those buildings. All of 'em being crept up on by vines and moss. Made it look like the buildings were growing out of hills and mountains like the seedlings of stone and metal trees. The problem was when we stepped out of the shadow of one building, we couldn't make out too much in the shadow of the building ahead. See, when you're in the light, it's hard to see into the darkness. There might be something in there, something or someone in that shadow just ahead, just waiting to ambush you, but you couldn't see. And that's just what happened."

"What? What happened? What's ambush?" Thea asked excitedly.

"Now hush, and maybe you'll learn if you just listen." Siobhan corrected.

"It's sort of like getting snuck up on," Alistair said with a wink. "So, where was I? Oh, I remember. We had just gone from light into the shadow of another building when Bodie spotted it. I suspect it had been watching us for some time."

"What?" Thea asked excitedly. "What was watching you?" Thea seemed ready to burst.

"Thea," her mother scolded. "Please, Mr. Alistair, go on with your story."

"Right. There atop an old streetcar, stood a huge gray wolf. Bodie nudged me over toward one of the buildings. The front door was hidden by overgrowth, but Bodie knew a way in. We scrambled inside and ran straight for the back of the old department store, but the old wolf was already through the entrance and closing on us fast. I reached for my holster, but Bodie said not to shoot. He dragged me through a door at the back of the building, and we found ourselves in a stairwell. I pulled the door shut behind us just as the wolf slammed hard against it. The thing snarled and snapped and clawed at the door, but it was steel, and there was no way the wolf could get through it. We both sat on the floor with our backs against the door, catching our breath."

Siobhan and Thea seemed to need to catch theirs as well.

"When I got my wits about me, I asked Bodie why he didn't want me to shoot the damned thing. He told me it was because the docco would smell the blood. I'd forgotten all about the docco I heard the night before. Bodie was right; they could smell blood from miles away, but what choice did we have? If I killed the wolf, the docco might come, but if I didn't, we either had to hope the wolf would lose interest and leave; and that wasn't likely, or try to find another way out and run the risk of it tracking us down out in the open. So, I came up with a plan, a dangerous plan, but we had to try something. I thought that if I could open the door just enough for the wolf to get his head in and then pin it there, I could shoot it through the brain. That would stop the heart from pumping and maybe keep the blood to a minimum. But to do it, Bodie either had to be strong enough to keep the wolf from pushing through or steady enough to fire my Dragoon, which weighed more than his arm. We talked it over and decided that I would man the door, and Bodie would two-hand the revolver and shoot the wolf in the head."

Alistair had them spellbound. Thea swallowed hard and whispered, "what happened?"

"Well, I stood up to look through the little window in the upper part of the door. I wanted to see just exactly where the thing was. As I did, the little bit of light that made through one of the broken windows disappeared. I thought maybe clouds had covered the sun and waited a moment for it to pass. But it wasn't the sun. It was the docco. As loud as they are out on the plains, it curdles your blood when you hear one up-close in a building. Makes one sound like twenty. So, this thing let out a roar and dropped to all fours allowing the sunlight to creep back into the room. The wolf, big as it was, was still not half the size of the docco. It howled, and the sound echoed around the cavernous space. The docco charged the wolf, and it launched itself at the docco. It was hard to see what was happening, the room was dim and dusty, but the two animals smashed through display counters and empty metal racks. The docco was definitely the stronger of the two, but the wolf was fast. It jumped on the docco's back and tried to sink its teeth into the docco's spine, but the wolf was having more luck with the steel door than with the docco's thick hide." Alistair leaned back in his chair.

"The docco whirled and spun, trying to buck the wolf off its back, but the old wolf dug in and hung on. The docco ran full speed toward the door we were hiding behind. I grabbed Bodie by the collar and turned for the stairs, but it was too late. The docco slammed into the door crushing the wolf and tearing the door from its hinges. The weight of the heavy steel door and the 200-pound wolf had us pinned. The docco was snorting, and I could feel and smell its hot breath as it sniffed around the door. I could hardly breathe, and I was pretty sure Bodie was dead. The stairs behind us kept the door from crushing me, but my lungs couldn't expand enough to draw in much air. I would have lost consciousness, but the docco dragged the wolf's carcass off the door and back into the outer room to eat it. When it did, I was able to push the door up enough to suck some air into my lungs."

"What happened to Bodie Mr. Alistair?" Thea asked hopefully.

"Bodie was one tough little son-of-a…." he caught Siobhan's look, "gun."

Siobhan smiled, and Alistair continued.

"He was in better shape than I was, but we were still trapped. The docco would have been on us lickity split if we tried to escape. Our only hope was to wait for the docco to finish and be on his way, and hope it couldn't smell us over wolf's blood and spilled bowels. Piss, shit, and blood makes for a powerful smell."

"Alistair!"

"Beg pardon ma'am. I meant to say poop."

Thea wrinkled her nose.

"Anyway, when the sounds of crushing bones and slurping down meat stopped, I could hear the docco sniffing and snorting at the air again. For such a big animal, it moved quietly when it wanted to. The snorting was now nothing more than soft sniffs, and in the vastness of that room, I could not tell if the creature was coming closer or moving farther away. Bodie, who hadn't made as much as a peep this whole time, whispered to me. 'Is the docco gone?' he asked. And with that, the docco ripped the steel door away and flung it across the room like a child's toy. The docco rose up on its hind legs and bellowed. There were two wolves. One on its back, the other biting into its leg, trying to drag it down. Seemed our smell distracted the docco enough for the wolves to get close enough to attack. Bodie and I scrambled to our feet and ran up the stairs. Up and up, we climbed. The stairwell was black as a pit, and we fumbled in the darkness until we found another door. I tried to open it, but it wouldn't budge. Same with the next door. Finally, we found one that wasn't stuck. We pushed it open and found ourselves in another room. Similar to the one below, but with all the light of the day streaming in through the broken windows. We pushed the door closed behind us but could still hear the ferocious battle some two or three stories below. And it sounded like more wolves had joined the fight. After a while, I honestly can't say how long, but the snarling and snapping stopped. We sat wondering who'd won, and then we heard it. The mournful howl of a single wolf told the tale. Me and Bodie crept down the dark stairwell to find a single wolf lying injured among a pack of its seven dead brothers and sisters and one dead docco. I drew my pistol and shot it dead."

Both Thea and Siobhan gasped.

"Apologies, ladies.

"What happened to Bodie?" Thea asked.

"He accompanied me to the edge of the city, and that was the last I ever saw of good old Bodie."

"Would you like me to help you look for him?"

"No, can't see an upside to it, but I would sure like your help with Joe. Do you think you could check in on him from time to time?"

"Sure, I can!"

"Maybe we can look in on him again tomorrow?" Alistair asked.

"Yes! And maybe he will go flying again!" Thea yelled as she spun in a circle with outstretched arms seeming unaffected by the story of Bodie and Alistair's time in the city. "I love it when he flies! I feel just like a bird!" Thea stopped spinning, and Alistair noticed that her expression darkened.

"What's wrong, child?"

"When he goes flying, it's because he's trying to find his way back here," she said.

"Why does that worry you?" Siobhan asked.

"He has to pass through the darkness to get here."

"He told me about the dark," said Alistair. He said he had to pass through it when he first came here."

"The darkness is dangerous," Thea said.

"Why?" Alistair asked. "What's in the darkness?"

"Nothing," she answered, "but there are a lot of different places that the darkness can take him. He might not end up back here."

Chapter 11

Bright light streamed through his window and woke Joe from the first good night's sleep he'd had in as long as he could remember. His round-the-clock babysitters must have received the stand-down order because no one else was in his room. Not Bob, not a nurse, and not the little girl in the yellow dress. Joe watched dust particles dance on the sunbeams that streamed across his bed and thought about the little girl who had appeared on the periphery of his vision just before he fell asleep. He hadn't said anything to Terri when he saw the child. Telling his nurse that he was seeing things was sure to extend his hospital stay, and besides, he was sure she would have mentioned it if she'd seen the child. Joe checked his peripheral vision hoping to find her again, but she was gone.

He didn't know why, but he knew she was from the other world, Reka's world. The question was, who was she, and what did she want? He'd seen enough to know that she wasn't the same girl who led them to Savista. That kid was blonde. This girl had long brown hair. But why was she here? Was there something wrong? Did Reka need him? Joe could hear the steady beeping of his heart monitor pick up.

"How long has this been going on?" Dr. Belter asked, pointing to the monitor.

Joe hadn't noticed Belter walk in, but there he was in his Tyvek suit, snapping on his rubber gloves. The disruption of his thoughts brought his heart rate down. Belter walked over to the monitor and gave it a flick with his finger.

"Hmm, I wonder what's wrong with this thing?" Belter held Joe's wrist between his fingers and watched the clock on the wall. "Pulse is normal. How are you feeling, Joe?"

"I need some food, Doc, real food."

"Well, we're working on that. You haven't eaten solid food in three months, Joe, we have to ease you back into solids, but your appetite is a good sign. With any luck, we should be able to pull the feeding line out of your chest this week and have you back eating solid food in less than two weeks."

"Two weeks?" Joe Protested. "I thought I would be out of here by then. "

"Joe, you've been through a lot. You were stabbed in the chest, and that alone, well, to be honest, we're really not sure how you survived that. I would love to say that it was all us, but there had to be some divine intervention there. And on top of that, you developed an abscess that seemed immune to all of the antibiotics we tried, so we had to put in drainage tubes."

He pointed at the tubes running out of Joe's body.

"The abscess caused you to run a dangerously high fever that we couldn't seem to knock down even after draining it. It's a miracle that you haven't suffered any organ failure." Belter rapped his knuckles on the wooden top of Joe's dinner tray. "You can't rush your recovery, Joe; your body has just been through too much."

Belter disarmed Joe's anger and did it with so much compassion that it didn't hurt. And that was good because the next part sure as hell would.

"I'm going to have to change the dressing in your surgical wound."

Joe hated the process. For reasons unclear to Joe, Belter decided to leave his wound open and allow it to close by what Belter called *secondary intention healing*, and while the reason was unclear to Joe, the procedure was painfully clear.

"Nurse Terri just did it!" Joe protested.

Belter flipped open Joe's chart. "That was two days ago. Chris did it yesterday," Belter said as he soaked fresh white gauze pads in saline solution. "See, it's not so bad. You managed to sleep right through it. Say, would you mind?" Belter said, making a motion letting Joe know he wanted him to lift the front of his gown to expose his stomach. "Terri was going to help me, but she's prepping in the ER. There's a boy in the river." Belter placed his hands on the railings of Joe's bed and shook his head. "He's the second one since the beginning of the school year. We lost a boy back in August. The family name was Rivers; if that ain't some kind of irony, I don't know what is."

Joe lifted his gown, exposing a patch of blood-stained gauze laid over the V-shaped wound that ran from his breastbone down past his belly button. The doctor lifted off the gauze covering, and Joe could see the small sections of rubber tubing that hid the sutures that loosely held his stomach together. Tucked under the tubes and snaking its way through the trench carved into his flesh was more gauze, only this stuff was blood-soaked. He didn't have time to think about the little boy because Belter went to work removing the gauze, which dried to the raw wound in some places. Pealing it away was excruciating, but what Joe hated, even more, was the feeling of someone reaching into his body and tugging on things that were never meant to experience human contact. He could feel it all the way through his spine and up into his shoulders, and it made him nauseous.

"Tell me again why you didn't just stitch me up?" Joe asked through gritted teeth.

"The wound was so wide and so deep that if we stitched you up, the inside of the wound would have never healed. The tissue would have become necrotic and…."

"What's necrotic?" interrupted Joe, fighting to talk through the pain.

"Sorry, it means that the cells would die and rot. And then we would have to open you back up to clean it out, or the necrosis would spread."

"I see!" barked Joe, though he really didn't know what Belter was talking about.

"I'm sorry, Joe, I'll have your nurse give you something for the pain. We'll try a smaller dose of morphine and monitor you, but we're going to have to secure your arms just to be on the safe side. We don't want a repeat of what happened last time."

"That's fine," Joe said, finally being able to exhale now that the unpacking and repacking of the wound had been completed.

"I know it hurts Joe, but it's the only way to safely close your wound, and I know it probably doesn't feel like it, but it's coming along nicely."

If the payoff was morphine, Joe didn't care if they did it twice a day. Morphine seemed to be the key that unlocked his spirit from his body, and he needed that release to find his way back to Reka. Dr. Belter pushed Joe's call button, and a nurse that Joe hadn't seen before entered the observation room.

"I'm going to have your nurse prep the morphine for you, Joe. Try to rest up."

Belter walked out of his room and spoke with the nurse. Joe could see from his pantomime that he was instructing her to secure his wrists to the bed's side rails. The nurse nodded understanding, and the two walked out into the hall. Joe couldn't help but smile. He'd come so close on his last trip, and he felt like he might actually make it this time. The nurse returned with a gleaming silver syringe on a metal tray, and Joe's eyes widened.

"Hello, Mr. Kott. My name is Brooke. I'm going to be taking care of you until Terri gets back."

"I wish I could say it was nice to meet you, Brooke."

"Doctor says I have to secure your arms before I administer your morphine."

"Yeah, that's fine," said Joe, as he offered first his left and then his right wrist for strapping down.

"So, what, are you some kind of trouble maker?"

"No, ma'am, I'm actually a cop."

"Well, I've never known the two to be mutually exclusive," she said with a smirk.

Joe opened his mouth, but nothing came out.

"Say, maybe you know my husband Eric; he's a firefighter."

She secured his arms as instructed and administered the injection.

"Firefighter…" was all he managed to get out, only it came out 'firefire.'

Joe felt the welcoming warmth like a ripple in a pool from the injection site out. And then, like turning a key in a lock, the morphine set him free.

He floated above his body, like Ebenezer Scrooge being led around by the Christmas ghosts, and was mortified by what he saw. A thin, gray, sick-looking version of himself. Wrists strapped down to the bed rails, beads of sweat on his forehead and upper lip. He thought that he looked like a junkie on the nod, and why not, isn't that what he was? He thought it best to always be honest with himself. Grandpa Uno always said, 'Denial ain't just a river in Egypt, buddy boy.' But it was the only way he knew to get back to Reka, so who gave a shit what he looked like. 'Ya pays yer dime ya takes yer twirl.' Another of grandpa's sayings.

Being outside the confines of his body, Joe wasn't bound by the laws of physics. He passed through the glass in the windows of his room and out over the hospital parking lot. Rising into the air, Joe could see for miles in all directions. As he looked around, he noticed dozens of emergency vehicles with their overhead lights activated parked near the bottom of the dam. Floating in closer, Joe saw exhausted cops and firemen laboring against the unstoppable churning boil. He knew these men and women, soaked to the bone and risking their lives in what they had morbidly nicknamed *the drowning machine*. Red Hook saw one or two drownings a year in the river's boil. Usually, inexperienced kayakers who, despite all the posted warnings, ventured too close to the dam and got dragged into the boil's death roll. Just last year, Joe pulled a man from the boil after the water rolled his lifeless body to the surface. Joe grabbed hold of the man's life-vest just as his body was being sucked back under and dragged him to the shore where other first responders were waiting to administer CPR. That man lived, but he was an exception to the rule.

Joe moved in closer. Men and women in hip waders repeatedly reached long hooked poles into the boil, and they came back empty each time. Intermingled with the first responders, along the water's edge stood parents clinging to their own children, and one couple conspicuous in their number with only one another to hold on to. Joe could feel the weight of their loss; he had known that moment, that horrible moment when the frenzied atmosphere of a rescue is supplanted by the somber mood of a recovery. There was nothing for him to do here, and he was losing valuable time.

The dosage of morphine he'd been given would eventually wear off, and if he didn't make it back to Reka before he came out of his Morpheus state, there was no telling when he might get another chance to find his way back to her.

He would make one last pass over the boil before flying north to find the well. He'd gone about a hundred feet when he saw a hand reach up from the water. Joe darted to the surface and plunged his hand into the frigid waters of the Red Hook River, but he felt neither cold nor wet as his hand passed through the boy's wanting fingers. The young man looked up at him with pleading, terror-filled eyes. Joe dove headlong into the boil to grab hold of the boy but could do nothing. He was mist, vapor, a ghost with no more influence over the natural world than a thought or idea unacted upon.

Chapter 12

"What do you mean, lots of places?" Alistair asked.

"I don't know," replied Thea, "just a lot of different places, that's all."

"Have you seen these other places?" Siobhan asked her daughter.

"Sure, mom," she said matter-of-factly.

"Can you see," Siobhan's voice caught in her throat, almost afraid to ask her question, "your father?"

"No, daddy's in Heaven, I can't see Heaven, but I can see other places. I can see the other worlds before and after the great flood."

"You mean the Great Fire," Alistair corrected.

"No, Mr. Alistair, before the Great Fire. When the whole world was underwater. And I can even see the world before that when there were monsters."

"What kind of monsters?" Siobhan asked.

Thea grabbed her chalkboard and a piece of chalk worn down into a ball. Her tongue popped out at the corner of her mouth as she scratched out a picture of a dinosaur.

"Why, that's a fine-looking dinosaur, Thea," Alistair complimented.

"Thank you!" Thea smiled. "Mom! Mr. Alistair likes my; what did you call it?"

"It's called a dinosaur," he repeated.

"Where did you see that, Thea?" Siobhan in a tone that Alistair read as far too concerned for a child's rendering.

"In the other world, mom. The world with monsters."

"Has she ever seen a picture of a dinosaur?" Alistair whispered.

"No, I mean, I don't think so," Siobhan replied. "I'm certain we don't have any books on dinosaurs, but maybe at school or a friend's house."

"Have you ever seen pictures of those monsters?" Siobhan asked.

"Yes," she replied, raising a smile on her mother's face. "in the caves in the place where they live, but mine is better," she said with a prideful smile as she added a few trees and volcanoes.

And just as quickly as it rose, the smile on Siobhan's face fell.

"Would you like to see them?" Thea asked her mother and Alistair as she extended her hands.

Siobhan reached out hesitantly, and Alistair grabbed it before she could lock hands with her daughter. "It's pretty jarring. At least it was for me."

Siobhan nodded, and Alistair let her hand go.

"Are you coming, Mr. Alistair?"

Alistair took hold of Thea's other hand.

"Ready?" Thea asked.

Siobhan and Alistair nodded, and the little cabin faded away. Before them, where walls once stood, was a world of lush vegetation. The ground beneath their feet shook as a sauropod plodded from the tree line less than a hundred yards ahead.

"See? He's one of the nice monsters," they heard Thea say in their heads.

"He's my friend. I call him Max. Isn't he so big?" Thea said telepathically.

Forty feet above them, thick branches snapped like kindling as the giant dined.

Alistair and Siobhan stared in wonder. It had no trouble reaching the tops of trees taller than Espero's walls. And as large as the behemoth was, it seemed to take extra care not to trample the young saplings sprouting from the forest floor. They marveled at the giant, but their appreciation was short-lived.

From behind them, one passing right through Siobhan came three smaller dinosaurs. The travelers froze as the predators halted their advance and turned to face them. They were three or four feet tall, about six feet in length with dark green skin and darker green, almost black, tiger stripes running their entire length, stretched over coiled muscular bodies. Razor-sharp teeth festooned with hunks of flesh snapped blindly as the small predators sniffed wildly at the air. They stood on their hind legs and splayed their hooked claws menacingly in the air. The claws reminded Alistair of the fangs of the giant spiders that stalked the prairies.

Thea held fast to Alistair's right hand as her mother wrapped her in her arms. Alistair drew his weak side pistol and pulled the trigger in a flash, but the mighty Dragoon did not fire. Instead, the pistol crumbled in his hand and turned to dust. He went to release Thea's right hand, but the child held fast. Alistair drew the blade he'd always kept on his belt and braced for the attack, but it didn't come. The small predators turned their attention toward the sauropod feeding on the evergreens.

They spread out and attacked from three different angles, joined by three others of their kind from the other side of the giant. They sprung at their prey and sunk their dagger-like teeth and claws into its back, legs, and neck. The giant cried out in a deafening mournful wail.

Alistair looked at Thea, prepared to shield her eyes. Her face was red, her brow furrowed, and her scowl made his blood run cold. The child began to tremor and shake, and then it happened. Thea shrieked, and a pulse of light exploded from her body. Brilliant blue light that peeled the flesh from the dinosaur's bodies and turned them and everything else in its path to ash. The force of the blast caused Alistair and Siobhan to lose their grip on Thea, and they found themselves lying on their backs in the cabin. They scrambled to their feet in a panic, but panic turned to relief when they saw Thea standing unharmed before them. Then, as if overtaken by emotion, she sunk to the floor with her face in her hands, and she sobbed.

"What the hell just happened?" Alistair asked.

"I didn't mean it, mommy!" Thea wailed.

"I know you didn't, sweetheart. You're okay now." Siobhan clutched her daughter in her arms.

"I didn't mean it, mommy, I didn't," she cried.

"Shh baby, it's okay, everything is going to be okay."

"Why did God make things like that?" Thea asked.

"I don't know," Siobhan said as she rocked her daughter in her arms.

"What the hell just happened?" Alistair asked again.

Siobhan shot him a glance and shook her head. It was clear to Alistair that it was not the time to look for answers. Alistair got to his feet, dusted off his backside, and took a seat on the couch, silently running through a myriad of questions he would need to have answered at some point. *What the hell was that? Can she control it? Are there others like her out there? Can it be weaponized?* That one sent a chill down his spine.

Siobhan continued to rock Thea in her arms as the child shook and shuddered, trying to regain her composure. Siobhan ran her fingers over Thea's forehead and down her cheeks and smoothed her hair, and Thea responded. Her breath would catch and cause a shiver now and then, but Thea was calming down. And then Siobhan began to sing. Her first note pierced Alistair's heart, like a key unlocking a door to a chamber he never knew he had, and as she sang, the chamber filled.

He didn't understand a word; he wasn't familiar with the language, but it was the most beautiful thing he'd ever heard. And as he listened, he had to tilt his head back because he could feel his eyes welling up. He bit his lip and pinched his leg, but the tears came all the same. They streamed down the sides of his face and onto his neck. He couldn't let Siobhan see him this way and hoped the darkness would help keep his secret. The only light in the cabin came from the fireplace in the kitchen, and Alistair leaned back in the shadows. When Siobhan finished, she lifted Thea, who had fallen asleep, and carried her behind the curtain to their bed. Alistair took the opportunity to go into the kitchen and wipe his face. He sat at the table, not wanting to be rude and leave without saying goodbye.

After a few moments, Siobhan appeared at the edge of the wall that separated the two rooms. The firelight danced across her face and shined against her hair. Alistair thought she was as beautiful as her song, and he could not look away.

"She's asleep," Siobhan said, not seeming to notice the effect she'd had on him. "I had no idea she could do that."

"The time travel or the explosion thing?" Alistair asked with sincere concern for the latter.

"Both," replied Siobhan. "She has always been able to see other places, but I didn't know she could see other times."

"And the explosion?" Alistair asked, wishing he had a better word for it.

"I honestly don't know. I'm not sure she really knows." Siobhan said as she walked toward the table and let herself drop into the chair across from Alistair.

"She vaporized those things. Hell, she vaporized everything."

"I know, I was there," Siobhan snapped.

"I know, I'm sorry," Alistair offered his most sincere apology.

"I don't think she could help it," Siobhan replied. "She was so upset and so angry that it just came out."

"That's an incredibly dangerous—gift if that's what we're calling it."

"I agree," said Siobhan.

"And you say she's never done that before?" Alistair asked, still trying to wrap his head around what he'd witnessed.

"No, I don't think so," said Siobhan hesitantly. "I'm sure she would have told me if she had."

"Well, she didn't tell you about the time travel," added Alistair. "But you're right, as upset as she was; I'm sure she would have told you."

He said it in a way that offered food for thought without being accusatory or judgmental, and it was clear to him that Siobhan took it in the spirit in which it was intended. That came as quite a relief. He didn't want to make her angry, and he had chosen his words and tone carefully.

"Sometimes I wish she was like the other children who spend their days tending to their chores and playing without the added burden of her—gift."

"I'm sure it's difficult for her, but she bears it well," Alistair said.

She smiled an appreciative smile, and Alistair smiled back.

"After she's had a good night's sleep, we'll talk about what happened."

"I think that's a good idea, and I'll be glad to be here with you if you would like," Alistair said in support.

"Can I get you another piece of pie or cup of tea?" Siobhan asked, perhaps to return the evening to some semblance of normalcy.

"I would love another piece of pie, thank you."

Siobhan got up, poured two cups of tea, and cut a slice of pie for Alistair. The two moved their chairs over to the hearth and spoke in hushed tones so as not to wake Thea. They spoke of their childhoods and of their experiences, and slowly, the shock of the night's earlier events faded. They laughed and smiled, and Siobhan laid her hand on his. And even though it was only for a moment, the feeling of her hand on his lingered even after she had removed it.

The two of them carried on for hours, and it had gotten very late.

"Can I offer you anything else, Alistair?"

"Thank you, Siobhan, but I really should be going," he said as he got to his feet.

"It really has been quite an eventful evening," she said.

"That it has Ms. Siobhan," he replied.

"So, we're back to formalities, are we?"

"I should hope not Siobhan. I really had a very nice evening."

"That's more like it," she said. "Will we see you at breakfast, barring another sudden attack, that is?"

The morning's attack seemed so far off to him.

"You can most certainly count on it unless the good Lord comes for me in my sleep."

Siobhan handed Alistair his hat and coat and escorted him to the door. He stepped out onto the landing, and she stood leaning in the doorway.

"Siobhan, that song was beautiful," he said.

"Thank you," Siobhan replied. "My mother sang that to me when I was a child. She learned it from her mother when she was a little girl in Scotland. It's called Ba Mo Leanabh. It means hush, my little baby."

Even the words without the melody sounded like music to Alistair. "Well, it was as lovely as you are." The words slipped from his lips before he could stop them, and he noticed Siobhan's eyes widen.

"And your daughter," he added quickly. "And um, thank you for a lovely evening and a lovely dinner as well," he added for good measure, trying to minimize the word.

They both laughed softly at his feeble attempt.

"You and Thea are much better company than the two beasts waiting for me at home."

"You mean those two beasts?" Siobhan said, pointing behind him at Agermonte and Barrister, who had followed their master's scent to Siobhan's little cabin and waited outside for him.

"The very same," he said, tipping his hat. "Good night Siobhan."

"Good night Alistair," as she disappeared behind the door.

* * *

Alistair walked the path toward his cabin in the light of the full moon. The smell of pine and burning hardwood filled the night air, and he felt thirty years younger. Agermonte and Barrister plodded off the path as Alistair strolled and thought about Siobhan.

"You old fool," he said to himself as he laughed.

Then came another voice. "There's no fool like an old fool. Isn't that what they say?"

Alistair looked to his right. Reka was standing just off the path in the dark and staring up into the night sky.

"That *is* what they say. What are you looking at up there?" Alistair asked.

"The stars," she said softly.

Alistair smiled.

"They are beautiful, aren't they?"

"They're more than beautiful. They're a covenant."

"How so?" Alistair asked.

"Before he left, Joe promised me that he would come back to me. He said that until he did, every time I looked up at the stars, I should know that he was looking at the same stars. He said that would keep us connected until he returned. Every night since he left for the Barrens, I have come out here and stared up into the sky. I only hope he can see them from Heaven."

Alistair felt her words stir in his soul. She looked so fragile, standing in the moonlight, with her arms wrapped around herself in an embrace fending off the night's chill and comforting herself.

"So, move over, you old fool, because I say that there's no fool like a fool in love."

"I saw him tonight, Reka."

She smiled and exhaled loudly but did not take her eyes off the sky.

"Thea took me there, to his world, and I saw him."

Reka tore her eyes away from the sky, and he could see the moonlight reflected in them.

"It's true, Reka, Joe's alive, just like I told you. He's in a hospital. His injuries were more serious than mine, but he's alive."

"When, when did you see him?"

"Not three hours ago. Thea can time travel, or space travel or; hell, I don't know what to call it, but she took my hand, and I was there in the hospital with him, with Joe."

They stared at one another for a long moment.

"Well! What did he say?" Reka asked as if she couldn't believe she needed to.

"We couldn't hear him, and he couldn't hear us, but Thea said he's looking for a way back here."

Reka went weak in the knees, but Alistair caught her and held her until she composed herself. "Is that true? Is he really trying to get back here?"

"Yes, Reka."

Her face lit up brighter than the moon. "I knew it! God wouldn't keep us apart."

Alistair cleared his throat, "But you should know; Thea said that the trip back could be dangerous."

"What do you mean dangerous?" Reka asked.

He could almost see the brightness fall from her face like pieces of a broken mirror.

"She said that he has to come through darkness to get here, but that darkness can take him to other places, dangerous places."

"What can we do?"

"I'm not sure," Alistair said. "Thea had a tough night, but I will talk to her tomorrow after she's gotten some rest."

Chapter 13

Joe watched as the churning hydraulic of the Red Hook dam dragged the boy's body into the boil, where it spun helplessly. There was nothing he could do, but he couldn't just leave him. The boy bobbed up to the surface and hung there momentarily. He opened his eyes and blinked a few times before being pulled under again.

"You're still alive," Joe said, surprised.

Without a second thought, Joe dove deep into the water and made a grab for the boy's arm, but again it seemed to pass right through him. He lost sight of the boy and dove deeper but still couldn't find him. At that moment, Joe realized that he had been breathing underwater. The shock caused his airways to slam shut as he darted for the surface.

He clawed frantically at the water, reaching for the surface and life-giving air he would fine there. The tremendous churning backwash of the boil which spun the boy's body so violently had no effect on Joe. He passed as easily through it as if it were a soft mist. Still, he couldn't see the surface, and his lungs were burning. He pulled harder and finally saw it. Only a foot from his goal, but he couldn't hold his breath any longer and was forced to open his airway and breathe deep. The cold water rushed through his body with no effect. He burst through the top of the water and continued a few feet into the air. Joe tried to stretch his mind around the fact that he had been breathing underwater, but the concept was so foreign and contrary to the survival mechanism that he couldn't accept it. Still, he couldn't just leave the boy to drown. Joe decided to stay near the water and watch for the boy to resurface.

All around him, the first responders worked to recover the boy's body, and Joe had no way to reach them, to tell them that the boy was still clinging to life just a few yards away. Joe screamed in frustration, but he made no sound. Another huge churn and the boy popped back to the top. He was so young, so afraid, and so alone, and even though Joe knew he couldn't save him, he hoped that his presence provided him some level of comfort. As he watched, he saw the boy's mouth open as if he were calling to him. The effort made by the drowning boy ripped at Joe's heart, and he made one more effort to save him. The Red Hook was pulling its victim back below for perhaps the last time.

Joe took a deep breath, plunged into the water, and grabbed the boy's forearm. This time he felt his fingers press into the boy's flesh. Joe held tight, and the boy likewise gripped Joe's forearm. Joe looked at the boy and smiled as the boy's eyes rolled back into his head, and his mouth twisted into a ghoulish smile. Joe looked back at his arm as the boy's fingers turned into weeds that ensnared his arm as it would a boat prop. Joe felt the terror that the boy must have been feeling. He tried to shake free from the grasp, but it was hopeless. Joe tried to swim to the surface, but the boy only pulled him deeper. His lungs burning; Joe tried to breathe in the water like he had just moments ago, but now he felt the water rushing into his lungs, and though he knew it was cold, it felt like molten lead. Joe looked again at the boy and thought he looked sad. It was as though he understood that he was being used as bait to claim another victim for the ravenous river. Its appetite for the living, never satisfied.

Joe watched as his life played in reverse through his mind. The hospital, his friends, standing at his bedside. He thought of his time in the mine with Hayward Taft. Then he thought of Alistair and the Maristo; he thought of Reka and lingered there remembering the moment she wove her fingers in between his. He remembered the hike through the darkness that led him to the other world where he met Alistair and the night that started it all. He remembered visiting his father and Annie leaving him. He remembered driving to Michigan with Bob to buy his Mustang and Bob being his rock when his mom died. He remembered family vacations and fishing in the

Red Hook River with his dad. The same Red Hook that was now stealing it all away from him. He remembered hearing that drowning was a peaceful way to die; well, he thought to himself, *whoever told me that was a fucking liar.* The scene in his head faded to a cold and dingy gray.

* * *

Alone, in his hospital bed, Joe blurped up cold river water onto his sheets.

Chapter 14

Hayward's trip across the Great Lake wasn't easy, but it was uneventful. He went ashore in Falstead, under cover of darkness, aiming for the southern part of the territory, and near as he could tell, he made it. The area was heavily forested, and he would enjoy the concealment it provided until he reached the Alkali Flats. The forest would begin to dissipate there, giving way to miles of white alkali fields. Beyond the fields of alkali lay Glass Land. Ground superheated beyond 8,000 degrees by Gadget, the atomic bomb detonated fifty years prior that turned the sand to green glass called Trinitite; hence Glass Land was born. The entirety of Glass Land and the Alkali Flats had become known as the Dead Zone.

Hayward knew that once he hit the Alkali Flats, he would have no way to find food or water, and although Hayward believed that he was a deity of sorts, he knew he had to eat and drink. The trip from the Barrens to the mainland took almost two days, and Hayward Taft needed food. He'd hunted in Falstead and Kane before and had always had good luck. Several factions of freebooters used these woods as hide-a-ways, but tracking them down would likely take hours, and his aching belly demanded immediate attention. Wading back out into the water, he grabbed up lake weeds and reeds and used them to make a net. He stood, soaked to the bone in the cold water, and scooped out several small fish. He tossed them as far onto land as he could so they wouldn't be able to flop back into the water. Grabbing another in his net, Hayward shoved its head into his mouth, where it remained for several seconds before Hayward's teeth came together, crushing scales and bones. In no time, Hayward collected enough fish to hold him for a few days once properly smoked.

Having eaten and had his fill of water from the lake, Hayward built a small fire and constructed a tripod of fresh tree limbs he cut using his karambit. He hung his fish over the fire and peeled bark from trees to enclose the tripod creating a functional smoker. After smoking his fish, Hayward set off to look for signs of freebooters. He came to an unguarded but not abandoned camp and collected all the supplies he could. He was about to set fire to the rest of the freebooter's supplies when he heard a moaning sound coming from under a green tarp.

Hayward pulled on the tarp and revealed a wooden cage holding two young women and a young boy with hopeless, vacant eyes. He knew they'd suffered at the hands of their captors, and that made him smile. His first thought was to pull them out and slash their throats to deprive the freebooters of their fun, but when he reached for the cage door, the women rushed the bars and strained to reach him.

Startled, Hayward fell on his ass but quickly scrambled to his feet.

"To Hell with all of you then!" He screamed. "I'll just burn you with the rest of the camp."

Hayward laughed as he walked over to the smoldering campfire and stoked it back to life. As the fire grew, he grabbed a log that was burning on one end and began spreading the fire to the tents and supplies that he couldn't carry. Then he turned his attention to the captives. He jabbed the torch at them, but they didn't flinch. They weren't afraid.

"My name is Hayward Taft," he shouted. Still no reaction.

"Have you not heard of me?" Hayward asked, knowing full and well that he was infamous. His was the name parents used to scare bad behavior out of their children.

"We've heard of you; what of it?" Demanded one of the women, throwing her chest out and flinging her hair back in defiance.

How was this possible? He'd once caused a man almost twice his size to piss a puddle on the floor at his feet at the mention of his name. There was no point in killing them. He could take no pleasure without their fear.

He decided that he would release them. The freebooters would naturally assume their escaped prisoners were responsible for burning their camp and spend their time hunting them rather than interfering with Hayward's important work. He broke the lock off the cage and warned them not to follow him. The women grabbed the boy and shoved their way past him, causing Hayward to stumble back, knocking over a crate. Beneath the box was a small weapons cache. Several rifles, clubs, and edged weapons. Each woman grabbed a weapon and turned it over in her hands. What had he done? Certainly, they would turn their weapons on him, but they didn't. In fact, they paid him no mind at all. They simply took up positions away from the fire to await the return of their captors.

Hayward gathered his plunder and a few weapons and moved west through the forest. After walking about half a mile, he heard the first shot. That was followed by a volley of sporadic gunfire and then silence. Hayward kept walking, not the least bit interested in the fate that had befallen the captors or their captives. His father, the Fire King of the West, was expecting him.

After several hours, Hayward reached the Alkali Flats. The Flats were blanched white with a haze that hung in the air. Occasionally the haze would spiral into dust devils, stirred by a wandering breeze. The Alkali Flats were as foreign and desolate as the surface of Mars would have been. He wrapped a scarf that he took from the freebooter camp around his face and strapped on a pair of pilfered welding goggles. He flipped up the protective green lens in preference of the clear and stepped for only the second time in his life onto the Alkali Flats. He walked the rest of the day and well into the night, not surprised by the falling temperature that accompanied the setting of the sun.

Hayward set his pack down and broke out a canvas tent with wooden support poles, not unlike the tepees that once dotted the landscape in the days long before the split. Having erected his shelter, he selected a couple of pieces of wood and started a small fire with his flint. Hayward expected the crossing to take several days, though he had no way of knowing for sure, and decided it would be wise to conserve his supplies. He collected mainly food, water, and wood, knowing that the land would provide nothing until he emerged into the territories of the west. Hayward had never been to the Western Territories but placed his faith in the visions he'd been given by his father.

He made a meal of some nuts and dried fruit that he took from the freebooters' camp, and when his fire died, he turned in. It was pitch black and cold in his tent, and he remembered the blue bioluminescent stone he picked up back in the cave in the Barrens. He searched his pockets and found it. Hayward drew the stone, and it shone brightly in the small tent. He exhaled and watched his breath condense into vapor and then disappear as it was absorbed into the air. Laying back on some blankets and using his pack as a pillow, Hayward stared deeply into the stone. It was exquisite, and he thought of Agnes, and his heart ached. He felt it so deeply that the anguish escaped him in a sorrowful moan. A moan that was answered by a terrifying sound in the distance. Hayward knew that sound as well as any plainsman. Docco, *but how?* he thought. Nothing lived on the Alkali Flats. Everyone knew that. But he knew what he heard. Hayward slammed his fist shut, hiding his light shoving the stone deep into his pocket.

"I'm doing what you want," he whispered.

The docco roared again as if in response.

"I'm doing what you want," said Hayward, now in a voice above a whisper.

Again, the docco roared, sounding nearer.

"I'm doing what you want!" Hayward yelled into the darkness.

The ground shook, and a roar seemed to come from just outside his tent flap.

"I'm doing what you want!" He yelled at the top of his lungs.

Chapter 15

The announcement crackled over the hospital's public address system. Code blue room 306, code blue room 306. Chris slammed her coffee cup on the table and stood up quickly.

"What's that?" Bob asked. "What's code blue 306?"

"That's Joe's room. He's in cardiac arrest," she answered. There was urgency in her voice but not a trace of panic.

Bob's chair flew across the cafeteria as he shot out of his chair and hurried behind Chris to the elevator. Bob hit the call button. The number six lit up, showing the elevator's current location.

"Let's take the stairs," Chris said and darted off toward the stairwell.

Bob kept pace as best he could, but Chris was pushing through the door on the third floor before he cleared the second landing. She ran to Joe's room and jumped into the fray. Water was pouring from Joe's mouth and nose as Terri straddled his body, performing chest compressions.

"Chris, AED stat!" Belter barked.

She looked at the water pouring out of Joe and soaking the bed, "That's not advisable, doctor."

"Dammit, don't argue with me! Get the paddles!"

Terri looked at the water pooling around Joe's body. "She's right, doctor."

"When one of you graduate med school, you can advise on how to treat my patients, but right now, you get me the dammed AED!"

"He's lying in a puddle of water!" Terri yelled.

Belter's face turned red, the veins in his neck stood out like chords. Chris placed a hand on Belter's forearm and spoke softer. "Doctor, he's wet; the bed is wet. The AED may not be the best option."

Belter seemed to be responding to the gentler questioning of his authority just as Bob burst into the room.

"Joe! What are you doing? Wake up!"

Belter didn't seem to notice the intrusion, perhaps the realization that he'd almost electrocuted his patient was still sinking in. All activity in the room halted for a few seconds, though it must have seemed like minutes to Bob.

"Why are we standing around? What's the problem?"

"We need to use the defibrillator on Joe, but he's lying in a puddle. We need to move him to a dry bed," Chris answered.

Bob shoved Terri out of the way and scooped Joe up into his arms. He rushed into the hall with his friend's lifeless body in his arms, knocking over IV poles and monitoring machines and ripping one of the drainage tubes from Joe's side.

The first room he came to was occupied, but the second was empty. Bob dropped Joe on the bed and ripped the wet gown off his body. Terri followed behind with the AED while Chris wiped down Joe's chest with a towel.

Belter, his wits fully restored, grabbed the paddles. "Is he dry?"

Chris nodded. "Yes, doctor."

Belter gave the order. "Clear!" Everyone took their hands off of Joe, and his body convulsed as the three-thousand volts passed through him. Belter checked for a pulse and called for another application.

"Clear!"

"What's happening?" Bob asked. "Is it working?"

Belter checked for a pulse.

"We got him! I want him moved to CICU and get a quinidine drip started," Belter ordered and then added. "Chris, Terri, that was the right call. Thank you."

"Doctor," said Terri, pointing at the black matter pouring from Joe's mouth.

He looked and called for a basin. He held the basin under Joe's mouth to catch the black powdery substance flowing out of him and rechecked his carotid artery for a pulse. It was weak, but it was there. He looked back at the basin, but it was empty.

"What the hell was that?" Chris asked.

* * *

Rhonda picked up the receiver in the living room on the second ring. "Hello?"

"I'm looking for Ronald Corliss."

"May I tell him who's calling?"

"My name is Lucas Travidi, and it's kind of important that I speak with him."

"One second," Rhonda said and covered the mouthpiece, and yelled for Corliss, who was in their bedroom down the hall. "Ron, it's Lucas Travidi. He says it's important."

Corliss picked up the extension in the bedroom. "Hey, Lucas, what's up?

"Hi, Ron. It's Joe; he's gone again."

"What do you mean gone?"

"I was in my kitchen, and everything went black. I knew it was Joe, and when I tried to remote view him, all I saw was darkness."

"Are you telling me he's dead?"

"I don't know; I just can't find him. Could you call the hospital and then call me back?"

"Sure." Corliss hung up without another word.

"You look worried," Rhonda said as she stepped into the doorway. "What's wrong?"

"That was Lucas," said Corliss.

"Yes, Ron, I know; I answered the phone."

Ronald Corliss stared wide-eyed at the phone.

"You're scaring me, Ron."

"I'm sorry, he said that Joe is gone, that he can't find him."

"You mean he left the hospital?"

Corliss gave her the *one-minute* finger and dialed the number to the hospital. He knew it by heart. He had called it once a day for the last three months to check on Joe.

"Good evening, Saint Anthony's Hospital. How may I help you?" the receptionist greeted him.

"This is Ron Corliss, calling to check on Joe Kott."

"Good evening, Mr. Corliss; let me ring the floor for you."

Ron heard two faint buzzes and then the clunk of someone lifting a receiver from its cradle. "ICU, this is Terri; how can I…."

"Terri, this is Ron Corliss. How's Joe?"

Terri knew Corliss; everyone in the ICU knew Ronald Corliss. They'd been fielding almost daily calls from the sometimes impatient man for the past three months.

"Not good, Ron."

"What do you mean; not good?"

"Maybe you should talk to Dr. Belter."

"I don't need to talk to Dr. Belter, Terri; I'm asking you. What happened?"

She hemmed and hawed and then just said it. "Joe almost drowned."

"He almost—did you say drowned?"

"I know it sounds crazy. Somehow, Joe's lungs filled with water, and he went into cardiac arrest."

"In his hospital bed? How is that possible?"

"We're still not sure. Dr. Belter moved him to the critical intensive care unit. We've got him on a ventilator, Ron."

"So, he's alive?"

"Yes, but—"

"Thank you, Terri; I'll be up there in a bit," Corliss said and hung up the phone.

Rhonda was still standing in the doorway, arms folded. "What's going on, Ron?"

"They said he almost drowned," he answered blankly.

"How is that possible?"

Corliss just shook his head.

"Lucas said that he was gone. What did he mean by that?"

"He said he couldn't see him anymore," Ron Corliss said, staring blankly at the floor. "I think it's happening again, Rhonda."

"I'll grab my jacket and go with you," she said.

Corliss hugged Rhonda and rested his head against hers. "I don't know if I can do this again."

***

Bob sat with his head in his hands on a bench just outside the CICU. Chris, who had gone off duty two hours earlier, sat with him. She'd worked in the field too long to feel comfortable offering well-meaning but ineffectual platitudes. Instead, she rested a hand on his back in an attempt to comfort the worried man. When the door to Joe's room opened, they both stood up in eager anticipation of news as

Dr. Belter walked over and pulled up a chair.

"Please, sit."

Bob stood rigid until Chris gave him a gentle tug.

"Well, the good news is that Joe is breathing on his own."

"Good news? Hell, that's great news," Bob said, suddenly alive with hope.

"It is, but there's also some bad news. Joe's not responding to any stimuli."

As Belter spoke, Corliss stepped out of the elevator with Rhonda and walked over to them.

"Stimuli? What does that mean?" Bob demanded.

Belter paused to address the two new arrivals. "Can I help you?"

"Who are you?" Corliss barked.

"I'm Dr. Belter, and you?"

"Ron, this is Joe's doctor. Doc, this is Ron Corliss; he works with Joe. Now please, go on."

"There's no easy way to say it. Joe suffered a hypoxic brain injury."

"What the hell does that mean?" Bob demanded.

"It means he wasn't getting enough oxygen to his brain," Chris said.

"That's right," Belter said.

"Well, when can I see him?"

"It's going to be a while. Joe is comatose."

"Are you saying he's a vegetable?" Bob shouted and bolted back to his feet.

"Holy shit," Corliss said, rubbing his forehead.

"I didn't say that," Belter said. "We have him in a medically induced coma to see if we can slow the brain activity and give it a chance to reset, and hopefully bring the swelling down. It's far too early to even guess at a prognosis. There are still tests that we need to run, but there's no reason not to expect an acceptable return to normalcy."

Bob began pacing.

"Can someone please tell me what the fuck has happened from the time I left here?"

"Ron, honey," Rhonda placed a hand on his massive heaving chest. "Let's all sit down and hear the doctor out."

"Thank you," Belter said as they all took their seats. "As bizarre as it sounds, near as we can tell, Joe drowned."

"In his hospital bed?"

"Ron, I saw the water myself," Bob said.

"But that's impossible, right?" Corliss looked to the doctor for confirmation.

Belter dragged a tired hand over his face. "Well, it's rare, but not impossible. There are dry drownings and secondary drownings that occur out of the water. But this didn't look like either."

"What is that?" Bob demanded. "What is secondary drowning?"

"Secondary drowning, or dry drowning, happens after someone suffers a near-drowning experience. It could happen after the patient has reached the hospital. Dry drowning only requires that the victim takes in water through his nose or mouth that causes a spasm closing up the airway," Belter explained. "But that's not what we have here."

Bob raised up. "Why not? Why couldn't that be it? I mean, maybe some water got in his somehow—"

"We're not talking *some water*, Bob. We're talking about gallons of water."

Belter shook his head. "I've never seen anything like it, at least a gallon of water came out of him back in his room, and we just drew another two gallons from his lungs to keep him from drowning again."

Chris stared at the doctor, looking confused. "That's impossible."

Corliss looked at her. "Why? Why is it impossible?"

Belter cleared his throat. "Because vital capacity is only about 5 liters."

Corliss leaned in. "English Doc."

"Our lungs; our lungs have a capacity of about 5 liters." He looked at Corliss and then at Bob. They both had a corkscrewed look on their faces.

"5 liters is about 1.3 gallons, gentlemen. That means that when you inhale fully, you can draw in about 5 liters of air. If we replace Joe's air with water, that could account for the initial gallon, but not for the two additional gallons that we just drew out."

No sooner had he spoken when the CICU nurse burst out of the room.

"Doctor, it's back. The water is back!"

Belter exhaled, shook his head, and ran back into the CICU, leaving them to ponder the mystery.

Chapter 16

The gray was crushed into black as Joe felt himself being entombed by the darkness. It filled every molecule of space in his body so completely that it compressed the water into nothing. The darkness filled his body, rendering him unable to move. It forced its way into his ears, his nostrils, his lungs, and into every space in him. *Hello, darkness, my old friend. Maybe* Simon and Garfunkel knew something everyone else didn't, Joe thought. A moment ago, he was drowning. He could feel it. But in rode the darkness, like the hero in an old western rescuing him from the tracks mere seconds before the locomotive tore them to bits.

The crossing over was happening, but not at all the way he thought it would. *But who gives a shit?* He thought to himself. He was going back, and he couldn't have been happier. Again, just as before, he felt himself being pulled away from the world he was born into. The only difference was that there was no sense of dread or confusion this time. As he fell deeper and deeper into the darkness, the weight of it grew. It pressed in on him from all directions, and again he thought of being buried alive, but there was no fear. He couldn't breathe, but he didn't need to. And even if there was air, he could never have expanded his lungs to take it in. As he felt himself go deeper and deeper into the crossing over, a familiar feeling crept in and with it a sense of dread.

But why? He was going back to Reka and Alistair. Back to where he knew he belonged. Nevertheless, it was there, and like before, it was soul-crushing.

Joe tried to push it from his mind. Tried to focus on Reka. But the harder he tried, the more her face faded from his memory. He stopped trying for fear that he would lose the memory forever and surrendered to the loneliness. At that moment, the memory of Reka flashed to life in his mind, and he locked in on that image until he sensed that he had stopped falling.

It wasn't an abrupt stop like one might feel jumping off of a box, but when he went to put his foot down, there was something solid beneath him. Feeling much surer of himself than the last time he was in this place, Joe began walking. Like the last time Joe had visited this world, he couldn't see anything, and he didn't know which way he was going. So that was nothing new. What was new was that this time, he was wearing nothing but a hospital gown, a situation that he would remedy at his earliest opportunity. He only hoped that the acid rain wouldn't fall as he was woefully unequipped to protect himself against it. As he walked, he began to smell the soft fragrance of pine in the air. He breathed in deeply, and his memory was flooded with thoughts of Savista and the giant jack pines that grew there. He walked in happy oblivion, Reka's image growing clearer with each step until his left shoulder struck something hard. Instinctively, Joe put his hands out in front and slowed his pace as he felt his way carefully in the dark. He came upon a solid, round, rough surface. The trunk of a pine tree, he was sure of it. A few feet ahead, there was another, and then another, and soon he found himself pushing out of the darkness and into a grove of evergreens. He was expecting to find himself back in the barn, but he wasn't about to quibble. He was just happy to be back.

Wearing nothing more than his hospital gown, Shoeless Joe Kott felt the brisk air against his skin and the sharp pine needles beneath his feet. He continued on for more than an hour before he saw his first sign of life. A small, well-maintained farmhouse in a clearing about a hundred yards ahead. He doubted that freebooters would keep such a tidy little place, but having been surprised by how he crossed over and not ending up in the big red barn on his return had Joe feeling a little hesitant, and he approached cautiously. As he neared, he could hear a kind of moaning. The house sat in a clearing that provided almost no cover to conceal his movement.

Joe spotted clothes hanging from a line strung between a metal pole and a small shed at the back of the house and began his approach. As he got closer, the moaning grew louder and was joined by the sound of a woman singing an old folk song called "Follow the Drinking Gourd." He only knew it because he'd taken Annie to the Red Hook River Folk Festival a couple of years back and remembered the performer telling the song's story and its connection to the underground railroad. It shouldn't strike him as strange hearing it here, considering their worlds had run on the same track until the split in 1945, some 90 after the underground railroad ceased operation.

Thinking back on that day with Annie, unlike his other memories of her, warmed his heart. He quickened his pace; he was sure he could find help here. As he approached an opened window on the side of the house, he could smell something cooking. Joe was about to call out so as not to startle the old woman who had been singing so sweetly when he heard what sounded like a cleaver striking wood and a howl of anguish. Guttural and barely human, but still human enough to know it came from a man, the sound sent a shiver up his spine and pinned Joe against the wall just below the window.

"Awe hush now," he heard the old woman say. "It can't be as bad as all that."

Peering up over the windows ledge, Joe saw her. Her back was to him. She stood facing an old wood-burning cookstove. Directly behind her, lashed to a large wooden table, was a man; he was missing his left leg, and his head lolled from one side to the other as the old woman began singing again, perhaps to drown out the moaning. Joe dropped back to the ground so as not to be seen.

Maybe she's a doctor, a surgeon tending to a wounded man. There had to be some reasonable explanation, he thought as he summoned the courage to take another look. He rose up slowly, carefully as he looked over the window cill. The woman had moved from the stove down the table toward the man's feet. She still had her back toward Joe, allowing him to take another look around. Like his leg, the man was also missing his left arm. *Maybe there had been an accident.* Joe thought, but the notion was tenuous at best. A metal ring had been run through his left clavicle and scapula. A rope tied to the ring dangled loosely off the table. The man's jaw had been removed. Chopped, sawed, or broken off, Joe didn't know, but it was gone. It was no wonder he could only manage raw, guttural sounds. He caught the man's gaze and read the pleading in his eyes. It was the same look that the boy in the Red Hook River had, but rather than rescue, these eyes pled for death's release. The old woman, still singing, raised the cleaver and swung again. The crack of bone and the thud of steel biting into wood was quickly overpowered by the shriek of pain from the jawless man.

"That's better," she said as she walked toward a large rendering pot on the stove.

Blood poured from the stump where the man's right leg had been, and Joe fought back the bile in his throat. He watched the woman, who, aside from the blood-soaked apron, could have been his anyone's chunky old grandma. The blood-soaked apron and the red hot iron that she had just pulled from the fire in the belly of the old wood-burning stove. The hairs on the back of Joe's neck stood up as he dropped back out of sight. Sitting there, below the kitchen window, Joe heard the sizzle and pop of red hot steel on flesh as she presumably pressed the iron onto the bleeding stump to cauterize the wound.

Joe felt around for something to use as a weapon, and his hand fell upon a large rock. The man began to wail, and Joe heard a sound that reminded him of sliding a chair across a wood floor.

"Oh my," the old woman said. "We can't have you hopping around like that."

Hopping around? What the hell is she talking about? Joe thought as he forced himself to his feet to take another look and possibly smash the old lady's head in with the rock. The one-armed stump of a man writhed around on the table, and his eyes, like those of a frightened horse, rolled in his head. The woman walked over to a counter and removed a towel from a large cage containing a giant mouse, only it wasn't a mouse. It looked like a mouse but had a long snout rimmed with razor-sharp teeth. It smashed from side to side in its metal cage in anticipation of—of what? Joe only had to wait a moment to find out.

Looking closer, he noticed that the man's midsection had been chewed into a mass of red pulp that reminded him of uncooked hamburger. The woman placed the cage on the man's stomach, pulled the panel on the bottom, and the animal began its frenzied chewing and licking. The man's eyes rolled up, and tears rolled down his face as he became eerily still. After a few moments, the woman shoved the panel back in place, walked the cage back over to the counter, and commenced singing.

Joe turned and slid back to the ground. He retched a couple of times but was able to keep from vomiting.

"That poor sonofabitch, how could he just lay there?" Joe said to himself in a whisper.

Another memory, this one from his childhood, provided a possible answer that made his flesh crawl. In an animal behavior class, part of his high school's biology curriculum, he saw a film titled The Shrew, Nature's Anesthesiologist. In it, he learned that the shrew's saliva contained a paralyzing toxin that kept its prey alive but unable to escape. The guy in the film said that the shrew had to eat its own body weight in food every day because of its insanely high metabolism. Through the use of its paralyzing toxin, the shrew could eat its prey without killing it, thereby keeping the meat from spoiling as it consumed the animal sometimes over the course of several days.

While Joe knew that a normal-sized shrew could never inject enough of the toxin to affect a person, this one was larger than a well-fed house cat. As he sat and contemplated the living hell the man faced, the clothesline caught his eye again. Joe gathered himself, snuck over, and grabbed what he could off the line. He moved silently toward the shed and listened for several moments before he went in, but all he could hear was the moaning and the singing coming from the house.

Joe ducked inside the shed and pulled on the pair of jeans and a heavy cotton work shirt he'd stolen from the line. A hatchet with a gleaming silver head and a dark wooden handle caught his eye. It sat on a workbench next to a leather belt with an awl driven through it, perhaps to create a new hole for its owner's diminishing waistline. Joe pulled the awl from the belt, shoved the strap through the loops in the jeans, and buckled it. He weaved the tip of the awl through two of the punch holes, securing it in place, thinking it might come in handy. Then he picked up the hatchet and turned it in his hand; it felt good to be armed again. Sticking the handle behind the belt, Joe found some old rags and tied them around his feet. After making one last search around the shed for anything else he could use, Joe headed back outside.

"Follow the Drinking Gourd" was replaced by "Life Is Just a Bowl Of Cherries," a song his grandmother used to sing while she did housework. The thought turned his stomach. Joe knew there was nothing he could do for the man being butchered, but he hadn't ruled out killing the old woman. Though he would have to assess the risk before making a final decision.

Joe worked his way back toward the house. On the front stoop sat several pairs of worn boots. He would need something more than rags to cover his feet and decided to risk venturing toward the front of the tidy little house. He had no way of knowing how many—what could he call them? Were they cannibals? Joe thought it was likely. Whatever they were, he didn't know how many more there were in the house beside the old woman. Based on the clothing on the line and the shoes on the stoop, Joe guessed at least three grown men also lived in the house. He decided to grab a pair of boots and make a run for it. It made no sense to him to risk his life for someone who was as good as dead. Besides, he had Reka to consider, so he abandoned the idea of killing the old butcher.

Reaching the front stoop, he held the souls of the boots to his feet to decide on the best fit and left the rest sitting where they were. As he grabbed the mate to the shoe he had chosen, the front door began to open, and a long-fingered gnarled hand reached down to grab one of the pairs of boots. Joe ducked back around the corner of the house and watched as a tall, gaunt, large-headed troglodyte emerged from the house. He sat on the stoop, pulled on his boots, and closed the door.

"I'll fetch her pa, gimme a dang minute," whined the bizarre-looking man as he stomped off the stoop.

"Don't back sass me, boy!" barked someone from inside the house.

"Don't sass your pa!"

The second voice came from the window above Joe's head. In his hurry to get away from the front door, Joe planted himself back below the kitchen window. The old woman was leaning out to be sure her son heard her. Now she and Joe were face to upside-down face. The woman sucked in air to call out, and Joe swung the hatchet catching her right across the bridge of her nose. The heavy steel blade crushed her powdery old bones as its sharp edge sunk deep into her frontal lobe. Joe dragged her body out of the window and left her convulsing on the ground. Glancing back around the corner to see where the troglodyte had gone, he didn't want any more surprises; Joe watched as the son continued walking away from the house. Joe leaned back against the wall with the butcher's body still convulsing beside him and pulled the hatchet from her face just as the voice belonging to the one she'd called pa cried out.

"Where's dinner, woman?" But she was in no condition to answer.

"Now, where the hell did she get off to?" The pa voice said.

"I-o-know." Grunted someone else from another room in the house.

"Dammit, woman!" The Pa voice was getting closer, and Joe moved beside the window and stood up. Pa reached the window and placed his hands on the cill to lean out for a look. As he did, Joe plunged the awl into the men's temple and slid his quivering body, likewise to the ground, laying it carelessly on top of his wife's. Joe wiped the blood off the awl on the old man's hair and returned it to his belt. Pa stared unblinking into the sky above, and Joe peered around the corner again. The son emerged from a pit or cellar in the front yard dragging a girl on a makeshift leash behind. She cried and protested and pulled at the rope, but he was far too strong.

"Stop pullin! Pa wants you!" The troglodyte said.

When he turned to give another tug on the line, Joe sprung from cover and sprinted across the yard. He raised his hatchet in the air just as the alien-looking man turned back in his direction. He stood a full foot and a half taller than Joe, but Joe outweighed him by twenty-five pounds. Joe swung the hatchet and caught the surprised man between his wide-spaced staring eyes, but not before he was able to call out to his pa for help. Joe took two more whacks at the man's head as the girl crumpled to the ground and hid her face. Joe rose to his feet just as the front door opened and a dead ringer for the man he'd just killed stepped out holding knives in both hands.

"What the hell you yellin' about?"

Seeing Joe, the monster charged, and Joe flung his hatchet. The hatchet's blade caught the light and flashed as it tumbled through the air with all the grace of a flying cat. It struck the man on the bridge of the nose with the but end of the handle. Not the hit Joe was looking for, but enough to cause the twin to raise his hands to his face. Joe delivered a shoulder tackle that his high school football coach would have been proud of. The man dropped one of his knives as they tumbled to the ground, and Joe grabbed it. He buried the blade to the hilt in the man's chest, twisted it a few times, and took the other from the dying man's hand. He picked up his hatchet and stood ready to face his next assailant. The wait was short.

Chapter 17

The world fell silent. Even the wind died down for the moment. Hayward worked to keep his breathing under control but realized that a soft mewing was escaping his lips. He clamped his hands over his mouth and tried to sit motionlessly, but he couldn't stop shivering. Hayward knew he hadn't imagined what he'd heard, but now everything was still, and the stillness made it all that much more disconcerting. There was nothing subtle about the docco. They weren't stalkers of their prey because they didn't need the element of surprise. They weren't, at least to anyone's knowledge, hunters who relied on their sense of smell. If they could smell at all, which was doubtful, given the fact that they used their heads and faces as battering rams and didn't seem to even have noses at the ends of their snouts, their own unrelenting stench would likely blot out even the most pungent of prey. No, the docco were not subtle. They were destroyers and devourers attacking whatever crossed their paths. *So, what is this one doing? Could it have just passed me by?* Hayward wondered.

It had been almost an hour since he'd heard it, and he couldn't wait any longer. If he did, he would surely freeze to death. If, on the other hand, he took some kind of action, he would at least give himself a fifty-fifty chance at survival. Hayward reached into his pocket again and pulled his blue bioluminescent stone. Flipping open the flap of his tent, he plunged his arm into the darkness and opened his hand. He waited a moment, and when nothing tore his arm from his body, followed with his head. There on the ground, in the blue light of his stone, about three feet from his tent, lay the body of the beast. Hayward burst out laughing. His laughter breached the stillness and unleashed the whipping, stinging wind that slapped him once again into submission. He ducked back into his tent, but it was no good. The wind exploited every seam and tear in the canvass. It was already below zero, and the temperature would only drop before daybreak.

Hayward knew what he had to do if he hoped to survive the night. The docco was a gift from his father, and he would not let it go to waste. Hayward pulled his karambit, ran out to the docco, and split its belly open. He reached inside the warm body, dragged out the docco's intestines and organs to make room for himself, and crawled inside the beast. Once inside the warm body cavity, Hayward pulled the entrails in close as he could to insulate himself from the cold and settled in for the night. Hayward slept a dreamless sleep, like a man without a care in the world.

* * *

Hayward awoke feeling like he was sleeping in an oven. He emerged from the carcass, covered in the animal's blood and viscera. The thick coating of frost that formed overnight had been burned away by the blazing sun that had already begun baking the gore to Hayward's skin, hair and clothes. He opened his eyes and immediately regretted it. The glare from the sun and the crystallized alkali blinded him and almost dropped him to his knees. Hayward fumbled for the welder's goggles that were still on top of his head and pulled them over his eyes. He flipped the green welding lenses down and tried to open his eyes again. The afterimage from the blinding light burned onto his retina and hung like a specter in the middle of his vision. He blinked repeatedly, trying to clear it, but it seemed that it was there to stay, at least for the time being. The spatter on the goggles' lenses filled the remainder of his field of vision, and like a child playing blind man's bluff, Hayward felt around for his tent. After a few stumbles, he found his way inside and removed the goggles. Rubbing furiously at his eyes, Hayward eventually got the dark spots to fade, though his eyes still burned and teared. He searched through his plunder from the freebooter camp, found a cloth, and used it to wipe his lenses clean.

Hayward retrieved a cleaver, also courtesy of the freebooters, put the welder's goggles back on, and crawled out of his tent, which had already warmed to an uncomfortable temperature. The landscape sprawled out before him and was cast in an eerie green by his lenses. Aside from his little tent and the hulking form of the dead docco, whose body provided adequate shelter through the night, the terrain was flat and desolate. He glanced into the sky and offered an unspoken prayer of thanksgiving to his Fire King for the lifesaving gift of the docco but knew he couldn't expect another to drop dead outside his tent when night fell, and the cold returned. He also knew that he had, at the very least, one more frozen night to face before he hiked out of the Alkali Flats.

Hayward set about butchering and skinning the monster. He would take as much meat and hide as he could carry, along with his other provisions. He tried to lift his pack, but the hide alone weighed over a hundred pounds and was too much for Hayward to bear. He had to find a way to transport what he had, knowing that none of it was superfluous. Retrieving a bone saw that he found in the freebooter's camp from his pack, Hayward hacked off two of the docco's ribs and lashed them to two of his tent poles. He used his cleaver to separate the femur from the tibia and pelvis but quickly realized that the large bone was far too heavy to be of use. Instead, he used the smaller tibia for top cross support and one of his other tent poles for the lower. Lashing it all together, Hayward rigged up a macabre drag-sled of wood, sinew, and bone.

He had slept much later than he'd intended. The temperature was already nearing 100 degrees and would surely top 115 before the sun would begin its dissension into the west and bring with it the comforting cool of the evening, which would in turn surrender to the terrible night freeze. Hayward figured he had a couple hours of walking in him before he had to stop and let the heat pass, so he grabbed up the arms of his drag-sled and pulled west. He was hungry, he hadn't eaten since last night, but he had to make as many miles as possible before the sun reached its zenith. At that time, he would be forced to stop and construct a lean-to to protect himself from the blistering sun. After his shelter was up, he could take the time to prepare a meal. In the meantime, he would chew on some dried fish to keep up his strength.

After walking about seven miles, Hayward came upon a skeleton bleached white by the sun, though through his goggles, everything looked green. At its head was a marker stone that read.

"Here I lie and wait to die with one silver coin upon each eye. Nikola Sticky-fingers Steele, Born, April 3rd, 1966 - Died, December ~~12~~, ~~13~~, 14, 1990. Kiss my Ass."

Hayward thought the rhyme was stupid, but the epithet or was it an epitaph, he decided it was both, made him smile.

"Kiss my ass indeed, Mr. Steele."

Hayward looked around on the ground and frowned. Then he lifted the marker stone and smashed the skull to bits. He sifted through the shattered bones and found the two coins mentioned in the poem. It seemed that something had chewed through his eyes and into his skull to get at his rotting brain, and in doing so, caused the coins to drop into the dead man's empty head. Hayward pocketed the coins and decided Mr. Steel was the best company he would find in these parts, so he made camp to wait for the sun to begin its descent. He fashioned a lean-to used two of his tent poles and the docco hide and settled in. The hide was thick, and it made a perfect shelter. He twisted off the dead man's arms. The tendons were dry-rotted and offered no resistance. Then he snapped off the spine between the thoracic and lumbar vertebrae and dragged Steel's rib cage over near his lean-to. It would make the perfect grill to cook some of the meat. Docco was gamey, Hayward thought it tasted like shit, but he was in no position to be picky. He set the rest out in strips on another makeshift smoker. When he was good and starved, he knew he would be able to choke the meat down.

The green lenses made it impossible to tell when the meat was properly cooked, but he couldn't risk removing the goggles. It wasn't that raw meat chewed from the bone repulsed Hayward Taft. No, not in the least. But when the opportunity to cook the meat presented itself, he took it. Medium-rare being his preference. He continued to ration his water and kept his plastic jugs closed tight to prevent evaporation. He guessed he was still about 24 hours from Glass Land.

When Hayward was about ten years old, he and his best friend Alfred Gerard camped out in Gerard's backyard. They roasted hot dogs and marshmallows and sat up all night telling stories. One of the stories Alfred told was about a secret bomb project that his father once worked on. According to Alfred, the bomb was more powerful than anyone expected, and when it went off, it sucked tons of sand up into a giant fireball, and the heat turned the sand into liquid glass that rained down for thousands of miles scorching everything in its path. He told Hayward that the reason they called the land out west Glass Land. Hayward thought Alfred was full of shit, but now he would see for himself.

He sat in the shade of his lean-to and closed his eyes to catch a quick nap. As he slept, he dreamed a glorious dream. Again, he was flying, his large black wings catching the updraft and holding him there above the sands of the deserts of the southwest. He flapped several times and soared higher and higher before pulling his wings in a full dive toward the ground below. The speed was intoxicating, and the impact euphoric. He struck the ground and exploded into a towering pillar of flame erupting in a magnificent voluminous head of fire and fury, grander than anything he'd ever seen. At his base, he expanded violently in all directions laying waste to everything in his path. And as he drew back into himself, all manner of life was compressed into nothingness. Not the smallest blade of grass was overlooked. When he was done, he sat naked beneath his black bat wings, enraptured in his new creation devoid of life. He imagined the planet hurling lifeless in the void of space like a concrete ball, cold and dead. Every wrong righted, the planet's plague, stricken. Peace in his time.

Chapter 18

Bob sat, half asleep, his head bobbing back and forth in the pew in the hospital's chapel when he heard a voice and felt someone touch his hand. "You need to get undressed; I call you if he finds the rangers." Bob opened his eyes to find Chris sitting next to him, smiling sweetly.

"What? What did you say?"

"I said, you need to go and get some rest; I'll call you if anything changes," she repeated softly.

Bob shook the sleep-fog from his head and stretched in his seat. "How is he?"

"He's resting."

"Is he still in the—?"

"The medically induced coma, yes."

"When can I see him?"

"Bob, how long has it been since you've slept?" Chris asked, ignoring his question.

"What are you talking about? I was sleeping just now."

"That's not sleeping, Bob; that's barely even resting. Look," she placed her hand on his. Bob looked down and then back up at her. "Once the swelling comes down, Dr. Belter will bring him out, and I promise, you guys can visit for as long as you like. But for now, you need to take care of yourself. Otherwise, you're going to end up in a bed right next to him."

"I'm fine. I can sleep right here."

"You're not fine. Now, do what I said, or I will have security come and remove you from the hospital."

Bob tensed his shoulders for a moment, but Chris smiled, and he knew she was right.

"Do you have a place to go, a number where I can reach you?"

Bob felt the scruff on his face. "I suppose I could stay at Joe's house. I went straight there when I got into town, and the place looked abandoned. It might be good to show a presence there before some squatters claim it," he said, offering an awkward smile.

"I bet Joe would appreciate that." Chris smiled back. "Come walk with me," she said as she stood and offered her hand. Together they walked to the reception desk. Bob jotted down Joe's address and phone number on a piece of paper and handed it to her.

"You can reach me here. But if I don't hear from you tonight, I'll be back here in the morning." He admonished.

"Sounds like a deal," she said and pushed the call button for the elevator. "Joe is very lucky to have a friend like you."

"I think we're both kind of lucky," he said as the elevator door slid open.

"Shit, I forgot."

"What?"

"Fitz drove me here. My car is back at the PD."

Chris fished a set of keys out of her pocket and handed them to Bob. "It's the red Grand Am with the *"Donate blood"* sticker on it."

Chris smiled as she watched him get into the elevator, and Bob smiled back. He hit the button for the lobby, and the door slid shut. Bob was exhausted and pretty hungry, and with Joe's place a good forty-minute drive from the hospital, he decided he would grab a coffee from the cafeteria before he left. The elevator door slid open, and Bob stepped out, almost running right into Chief Vecchio.

"Bob! How good to see you," Vecchio said, sounding genuinely pleased.

"Chief, it's been a while," Bob said.

"How's Joe doing?"

"Not good; he's in a coma."

"I heard, Ron told me. I would have been here sooner, but—" Vecchio's eyes fell. "We lost another boy to the Red Hook. Our guys are still out there trying to recover the body."

"It's a bad day all around for Red Hook," Bob said.

"Do you have time for a cup of coffee, Bob?"

Bob was tired, but he was going to grab a cup of coffee anyway, and besides, he respected his old boss too much to turn down the friendly invite.

"Sure, as long as you're buying," he said with a smile.

The cafeteria was just down the hall from the bank of elevators.

"I'll grab the coffee; you grab some seats." Vecchio paused and looked at him. "You look tired, Bob."

"I'm fine," Bob said and walked over to a table near a window that faced the hospital's gift shop. He felt older than he had in years. His bones ached, his back was stiff, and his head was jumbled with all the happenings of the last couple of days. The gift shop across the hall was alive with shoppers streaming in empty-handed and coming out with floral arrangements, boxes of candy, or mylar balloons with sayings like, "Get Well Soon" stenciled across their colorful metallic faces. Some of the shoppers looked happy, while others seemed absolutely heartbroken as they shared the experiences of life and death that played out inside the walls of this building.

"Is black okay? I didn't know what you took in it," Vecchio said as he set a cup down in front of Bob.

"Thanks, Chief; black is fine."

"How you holding up, Bob?"

"I'm good boss, a little tired, but good."

"How are Maggie and the kids?"

Bob was a little surprised that his old boss remembered his sister-in-law's name. *How vested in a person do you have to be to remember that kind of detail?* Bob wondered.

"Maggie's good, but the kids ain't kids no more. Andrew, he's the youngest; he just graduated from college and took a job in Milwaukee. Some dot com computer bullshit, I don't know. They say it's here to stay."

"I think they're right," Vecchio interjected.

"Yeah, probably." Bob took a sip of his coffee. "Anyway, Matthew, the middle guy, is on with the fire department, and Johnny's been on the job for five years now. He's taking the detective's exam in March. Probably pass it on his first try. He got his mother's brains.'

Vecchio laughed. "And you said Maggie is doing good?"

"Yeah, I mean, you know, she worries, especially about Matthew and John."

"Who could blame her?" Vecchio offered.

"No shit. I tried to talk them both out of civil service, but this shit gets in your blood, ya know?"

"I do indeed," replied the Chief. "What about you, Bob? Girlfriend, fiancé, anything like that?"

"Hell, I never had time for nothin' like that. Raising the boys was full-time, ya know?"

"I'm sure. Well, that brings me to my next question, and I know the timing sucks, but I have to ask. Would you consider coming back to Red Hook?"

"Coming back? You mean to work here again?"

"We would work it out to buy your time from Chicago on your pension, and we'll match your time off. The pay is what it is, but the cost of living here is far less than living in the city."

The question caught him totally off guard. The truth was, being back in Red Hook, despite the circumstances, felt right. He grew up in Red Hook, met his best friend in Red Hook, and had it not been for his brother's accident, he would have never left Red Hook.

Maggie didn't need him anymore, and lately, he'd been feeling like he was holding her back. She'd gone on a couple of dates but always downplayed them, either because they were genuinely disappointing or because she didn't feel right about allowing herself to be happy with another man, especially with her dead husband's brother around.

Bob dated some himself but never really connected with anyone. The fact was, Vecchio's timing couldn't have been better. Being back in Red

Hook and seeing Joe again really made him feel grounded. It could also allow him to see where things might lead with Chris.

"You don't have to decide right now. Just give it some thought," Vecchio said.

"I'll do that, but I gotta ask; why?"

"Morgan and Koontz are pulling the plug next month, and between you me and the wall, we have one in the field training program who isn't going to make it," Vecchio paused a moment, "and we are still missing Joe. We're a small department, Bob, and that's a huge shortage in manpower. Besides, you're good police, and we'd love to have you back."

Bob sipped his coffee but didn't speak.

"Just promise you'll think it over, okay?" Vecchio said.

Bob nodded. "I will, boss."

"Excellent," Vecchio said as he stood up patted Bob's shoulder. "You'll have to excuse me; I have to get up there and check in on Joe."

Bob offered a sad smile.

"Thanks for the time, Bob."

"Sure, boss, and thanks for the coffee."

* * *

As he drove to Joe's house, he considered the Chief Vecchio's offer. He turned left onto Sumac, and the Red Hook River came into view. Bob could already see the hazy glow of the emergency lights near the dam about two blocks up and knew that somewhere in that cold gray water, the body of a little boy, the latest victim of the pitiless river, was being rolled and tossed about in the powerful boil.

Of all the things he missed about Red Hook, the river wasn't one of them. And it wasn't a fear of water. Living in Chicago, Lake Michigan didn't bother him in the least, but the Red Hook River was different. At least it seemed to be after the summer of 1979. The summer when the Red Hook River drowned a boy named Eddie Sanders.

Bob was riding his bike along the path next to the river on his way to

Joe's house when it happened. Eddie Sanders was paddling a boat down the river when he lost his oar. Eddie was five years older than Bob. He was a lifeguard at the Y and a member of Red Hook High's swim team, and there was no way he should have drowned. But he did, and eleven-year-old Bob Tague watched it happen.

The river wasn't running exceptionally fast that day. In fact, as it was happening, Bob could have sworn that it wasn't running at all, at least not until Eddie got close to the shoreline. Bob could recall every detail of every moment as if it had just happened. As Bob neared the bridge and the lights at the boil, he supposed it had just happened again. Not to Eddie Sanders, but to some other kid, some other poor family. Bob shook his head. "Fucking river."

He reached the bottom of the bridge and continued down Main Street past Sugar Maple Lane as he recalled the day back in 1979. He remembered Eddie trying to paddle with his hand after he lost the oar, but he couldn't seem to make any progress. That was when he stood up in the boat. He looked right at Bob and shrugged his shoulders as if to say; can you believe this shit? That was when, and to this day, he still couldn't say why, Bob stopped pedaling and watched it happen. Something rocked the rowboat sending Eddie over the side. Eddie didn't jump in; Bob was sure of it. And he was sure of something else. The rowboat sat motionless in the river. It should have continued on toward the dam, but it didn't. That was how Bob knew the river wasn't running.

Bob watched as Eddie swam toward him on the shore. He heard Eddie say something about the stupid boat when he was about two feet from the shoreline. That was when Bob saw the river run sideways. It ran from the west bank where he sat watching from his bike toward the east, and it slowed Eddie's progress to a standstill. That was when Bob saw the second thing that chilled his blood. Something in the river, or maybe it was the river itself, grabbed Eddie beneath the water and dragged him out toward the center. Eddie thrashed about for a few seconds and then began swimming frantically toward the west bank again. Bob looked out past Eddie and saw his rowboat sitting motionless in the center of the river with the rope used to tie it to the dock hanging over the side. Then the boat began to move toward the dam, as it should have from the very beginning. As it moved, it picked up speed, and that was when Bob saw the other end of the rope. Somehow it had become tangled around Eddie's ankle. Then the line went taught, and Eddie was sent speeding down the river toward the boil.

Bob slammed down on his pedal, calling out to anyone who could hear him as he hurried south following Eddie and his rowboat. A few people out in their yards seemed to take notice, but Bob couldn't stop. He just had to hope they were calling for help. Bob was pedaling as hard as he could to keep up with Eddie and his rowboat. He reached Main Street just in time to watch the boat go over the dam, dragging Eddie Sanders with it into the boil. As Bob sat on his bike, staring, unable to believe what he'd just seen, Eddie's head bobbed up a few times, and that was it.

In his time on the job, Bob had been on numerous calls for drownings on the river. Hell, it was good for at least one a year, as he recalled, but that was the only time he'd witnessed the Red Hook River drown someone.

He'd read somewhere that drowning was peaceful, but he knew that was bullshit. Aside from dying in his sleep, he couldn't imagine any death to be peaceful, but he couldn't think of one more terrifying than drowning.

Bob turned off Main Street onto Oak, drove a couple more blocks, and slipped into Joe's driveway. Making his way inside, Bob found his way to the couch and collapsed. Sleep came quickly, but it was a restless sleep, haunted by unsettling dreams. At 2 A.M., he woke to a pounding on the door.

Chapter 19

He ran at Joe, gibbering and jabbering in a language wholly foreign. No consonants and only the most rudimentary sounds of vowels could Joe make out. As impossible as it was to understand him, Joe found it equally difficult to estimate his age. He had the face of a rosy-cheeked child but the broad shoulders and strong build of a man who was no stranger to hard work. He was larger in height and mass than the man Joe had just killed, and he moved fast. If the guy could catch a football, Joe was confident that he would have made a fine wide receiver.

Joe knew that he wouldn't stand a chance against him in hand-to-hand combat, so Joe decided he would dodge the charge and try to catch him with the hatchet as he passed. Joe got on the balls of his feet and slid left, but his attacker anticipated the move and slammed full speed into Joe, sending them both crashing to the ground. The gibbering idiot's weight forced the air from Joe's lungs and caused his hands to fly together, bear-hugging his attacker and sinking the knife's blade into his broad back while the hatchet skittered off into the dust.

Joe managed to roll the large body off of himself and then laid there for a moment as he worked to draw breath. Joe felt the blade sink in and thought that the fight was over, but the man, Joe was sure now that his attacker was no mere boy, seemed not to notice the blade as he got back to his feet and lifted Joe off the ground by his stolen shirt. He pulled Joe's face close to his and sniffed at him, and Joe understood why the man couldn't speak. His mouth was an empty socket save the three broken teeth that clung yellow to blackened gums and the gnarled stump that was once his tongue. Joe felt saddened and repulsed at the same time as he pulled the awl from his belt and began sticking it into the man's side. The man seemed not to notice, so Joe swung for the side of his head, but he couldn't swing around the man's massive forearms.

He slammed Joe to the ground knocking the wind out of him again and then began choking him. Joe felt his airway close, and the drooling gibbering idiot began to smile and opened his mouth. The three jagged teeth moved toward Joe's face as his jaws stretched to their limit. Joe thrashed and stuck the man a few more times with the awl, but the man didn't stop, and Joe was losing consciousness.

Joe's eyes bulged, his ears started ringing, and he knew that he was about to blackout. He could feel hot breath on his face but couldn't smell it because he couldn't breathe. Warm saliva dripped onto Joe's face as the cannibal came in for his first bite. Joe's world began to go black, but the pain never came.

Through clouded vision and heavy brain fog, Joe watched as the girl on the leash stood over them, raised a large stone, and bashed the cannibal in the back of the head. The first blow got his attention. The second dazed him, and the third through tenth left his head a bloody mess. When she'd finished with the cannibal, she staggered toward Joe, raised her stone again, and then Joe's world went black.

* * *

Joe woke sometime later and stood up on unsteady legs. The western sky looked like a painting by a master who worked in watercolor, while the east resembled a wall washed in dirty gray. It was then that Joe realized he had not landed back in Espero. There was no doubt that Diastole would have been visible in the east if he had. The colossal red barn had a footprint roughly the size and shape of Tennessee and stood, at some points, higher than her tallest mountains.

"No, Joe, we're not in Espero anymore," he said to no one in particular.

The cannibal brothers lay dead at his feet, and the girl, who, for whatever reason, conked him on the head but decided not to kill him, was nowhere to be seen. Joe staggered back toward the kitchen window where the old woman and her husband remained stacked right where he had left them. After kicking at the old man, just to make sure he wasn't playing possum, Joe peered over the window sill at the half-eaten man lying dead on the butcher's table. A large blood-soaked stone sat in the middle of the man's head, where his face used to be, and Joe assumed that the girl had been at work here as well.

From there, Joe moved back around the front of the house. He sat on the stoop a minute to gather his thoughts and try to assess the damage to his head. He was reasonably sure she'd broken his nose, but that seemed to be the worst of it. So far, his return to the world of the territories had not been the homecoming he'd hoped for. Joe got back to his feet and walked out past the dead cannibal brothers to the door from which the leashed girl had emerged. It looked to Joe to be the door to a root cellar, but even before he set his foot on the first step, the smell of piss and shit and death filled his nostrils. It seemed the break wasn't as bad as Joe had thought.

Joe gagged at the stench and pressed his mouth and nose into the crook of his arm. With what little light made its way down into the hole, Joe could see a pile of bodies pushed into one corner of the room. Shallow holes were dug here and there, presumably used as latrines, and a matting of hay covered the floor. That was all Joe could gather before the smell forced him out.

Joe ran out of the cellar and clamped his hands on his knees as he bent over, drawing deep breaths and exhaling hard to blow the putrid smells from his blood-caked nostrils. When he composed himself, Joe picked his hatchet and pulled the knife from the gibbering idiot's back and then made his way toward the house. He was pretty sure everyone who lived there had been killed, but as he stepped back onto the stoop and prepared to go in, his stomach lurched, and he froze. It wasn't fear of finding more cannibals inside; he would enter carefully and dispatch whatever living things might attack. No, what frightened Joe was the horror show waiting for him on the other side of the door. The things that, once seen, can never be unseen. Bracing himself, he pushed through the threshold and into the little farmhouse.

The door opened, creaking softly on its hinges, into the living room. The small room was lit by two oil lamps, and what Joe saw surprised the hell out of him. The room was spotless. Not so much as a speck of dust anywhere. The furniture was covered in clear plastic, another reminder of his grandmother. Doilies rested below the few decorative objects on the coffee table and mantle above the fireplace. And the fireplace itself looked like it had recently been scrubbed clean. Stacked on the grate, three logs waited for a match to bring them to life.

Joe picked up one of the oil lamps and extinguished the other as he walked toward the dining room. The dining room was meticulously set for five with neatly folded napkins and chargers under the dinner plates. A smell reminiscent of stew wafted from behind a door that Joe assumed led to the kitchen. He'd seen the kitchen from the outside window, but now that he was inside, he had to clear it before he could move to the second floor. He swung the door open quickly and took the room armed only with a lantern and hatchet. The kitchen, as expected, was unoccupied except for the butchered man on the chopping table. The rest of the kitchen was well organized. All of the butcher's tools were hung neatly on the wall above a counter where spice jars, labeled and arranged alphabetically, stood in a perfect row waiting to be called into service.

There were things Joe thought he might be able to use, but he had to clear the rest of the house before he could worry about gathering supplies. Joe moved back into the living room and pulled the front door shut. There was no lock on the door; *cannibals probably encourage intruders*, Joe thought as he took a small green glass vase off the fireplace mantle and set it between the doorknob and the door frame as a makeshift alarm. With the front door booby trapped, Joe approached the wooden staircase. Even with the lantern held high, he could only see about halfway up the stairs; the rest was of the way was swallowed up by the darkness. As a cop, Joe hated staircases because the bad guy always had the upper hand. He planted his foot on the first step, which responded with a loud creak, advantage again to the bad guy. Joe worked his way up the creaking stairs to the second-floor, managing not to get himself killed in the process. At the top of the landing, he found four rooms with closed doors arranged motel style, all the rooms to one side. Connecting the rooms was a long corridor. Joe decided to start with the first door and work his way back to the last room.

Just as he had done when he breached the kitchen, Joe pushed the door open and entered quickly with the lantern held out in front and the hatchet drawn back and ready to strike. And just like the kitchen, he found it unoccupied. There was a large bed made up with pillows, a bedspread, and fresh flowers in a vase on the bureau. *This must be ma and pa's room,* he thought. Joe quickly ransacked the room, looking for anything of use and hopefully a better weapon. What he found were matches, candles, and a jackknife that he packed into a canvas valise he found in the closet. He moved down the hall to the next room. This room had one long bed and a simple chest of drawers, and again, no occupant. Joe searched the room and found a well-worn but patched jean jacket. He tried it on for size and, other than being a little long in the sleeves, the jacket fit him well.

The next room was much like the last, a bed and a dresser, but Joe discovered a surprise under the bed. If he recalled correctly, it was called a blunderbuss. Joe had seen a similar weapon before, back when he and Alistair sailed onboard the Ancora Imparo. With a barrel the same length as the stock and as big around as a billiard ball, Joe imagined it would probably knock him and his target both on their asses, but he took it anyway. The weapon looked primed and ready to fire, so Joe eased the hammer forward before stowing it in the valise. He moved down the hall to the next room and opened the door. Joe swallowed hard; two beds. He killed ma and pa; that was one bed, the twins, two more beds, and then there was the gibbering idiot that would have most certainly killed him if the leashed girl hadn't intervened. *So, who slept in the fifth bed?*

He doubted it was a guest room. He couldn't imagine that cannibals had a lot of visitors, at least none that would require accommodations. Mounted to the wall in this room was a rack designed to hold two guns. A carbine repeater hung on the top rack. The bottom was conspicuously vacant. Maybe that was reserved for the blunderbuss currently in his bag. He hoped that was the case because his question about who slept in the fifth bed had just been answered.

From outside the house came an anguished cry followed quickly by the crash of the vase he'd placed as an alarm.

From the bottom of the stairs, a voice cried out again, "Ma! Pa!"

But Joe knew they wouldn't be answering. He heard the door to the kitchen slam against the wall, and the voice called out again to Ma and Pa. Then Joe heard the heavy footsteps of a large man pounding up the stairs. Joe grabbed the old Evan's Repeating rifle off the rack and worked the lever to cycle a cartridge into the chamber, but there was no cartridge to cycle. The gun was empty. He reached for the loose shells scattered on the shelf just below the gun rack. His hands shook as he tried to load the bullets into the stock of the Evans. He almost had the first round in the port, but it fell from his trembling fingers. He shook another round from his palm to his fingers and tried again to hit the loading port.

The person who would claim bed five crested the staircase, and Joe saw him through the open bedroom door. His head was large and misshapen like the others, but it was different. A large nodule ran from his forehead onto his left cheek with a divot, presumably where his left eye should have been. The nodule spread over the bridge of his nose and partially over his right eye, leaving it barely visible under a skin flap. Having no discernible neck, his ears were no more than holes in the side of the flesh that spilled like lava from the top of his head and disappeared into his widened shirt collar. Despite the deformity, Joe could see the anguish on his face. Anguish that turned to rage when he saw Joe. The man howled, and spit flew from his lips. He bared his teeth and charged down the hall toward Joe.

Joe let the Evans fall from his hands as he fumbled to pull the blunderbuss from the valise, but he snagged the hammer on the interior of the bag. The deformed man tackled Joe and drove him into the dresser against the far wall. Joe's right hand had become entangled in the bag, and he was unable to pull it free to defend himself. The misshapen man clawed at Joe's eyes, and Joe was forced to bury his face in the man's soft neck-flesh to protect himself.

This man wasn't nearly as tall as his brothers, but what he lacked in height, he made up for in strength. He pushed Joe away and struck him in the side of his head. Joe saw stars. The deformed powerhouse reared back to strike again when Joe cocked the hammer back and fired the blunderbuss through the valise. The massive projectile exploded from the canvas bag and through his attacker's chest, sending him out of the room in a brilliant display of viscera.

As predicted, the blunderbuss kicked like a mule and slammed Joe back into the dresser. The roar of the weapon in the small room was deafening. Joe struggled to his feet. His ears were ringing, and he could taste the acrid black powder mixed with the blood at the back of his throat. Joe walked over to the body on the floor to ensure the blunderbuss had done its job. The weapon left a hole the size of a fist in the man's chest and tore out a bowling ball-sized hunk of flesh from his back. Looking at the heap on the floor, Joe felt a momentary sense of sympathy, but it passed quickly as he remembered the man being eaten alive in the kitchen and the woman dragged from the cellar for God only knew what reason.

Feeling sure that he had killed the last of this clan of cannibals, Joe finished searching the second floor of the house. He collected what provisions there were and packed them into a faded green canvas bag. The bag had a reinforced leather bottom and leather straps affixed by rivets. Joe thought it might have been an old letter carrier bag, but whatever it was, it looked up to the task.

Moving back downstairs, his oil lamp lighting the way, Joe returned to the kitchen and made a thorough search of the cupboards where he found carrots, green beans, and other assorted vegetables. There was an icebox that hadn't likely seen ice in over a decade. In the icebox sat part of a leg with the foot still attached, presumably belonging to the dead man on the butchering table. Joe left the meat, deciding on a vegetarian diet for the time being. Joe returned to the living room, grabbed a second vase, and replaced the broken door alarm. He also picked up the second oil lamp, which he'd extinguished earlier, to harvest the fuel and wick.

He searched the rest of the first floor, took everything he'd collected back upstairs, and barricaded himself in the back bedroom at the end of the hall. He placed the lamp on the nightstand between the two beds and loaded the Evans Repeater with far less shaky hands. He was familiar with the Evans and knew he had to load the cartridges one at a time, cycling the weapon once after each round. Something he never could have done under duress. It took him a couple minutes, and once he was done, he laid it across his lap. Then Joe turned the wick down in the lamp, blew out the flame, and leaned against the headboard for some shuteye. He woke some hours later to crashing glass shattering from the first floor.

Chapter 20

Hayward woke from his catnap and gave his limbs a good stretch. He ate a little, stowed his gear, and stepped off toward the west. The air was cool, and the sun had set just enough for Hayward to flip up the green lenses on his goggles without fear of burning his retinas. It was a beautiful night for a walk, and the colorful display in the western sky was breathtaking. As Hayward hiked, he whistled Rachmaninoff's Prelude in C-Sharp minor and imagined himself seated at his throne with all who had ever dared to cross him, dead at his feet.

Hayward had gone fifteen miles before he began shivering despite his quick pace and force exerted in pulling the drag-sled. Cold as he was, it was still too early and too light to consider stopping for the night. So rather than stop, Hayward opted to swap out his canvas cloak for the docco hide. He tossed the pelt over his shoulders, but despite the immediate relief from the cold, the weight was more than Hayward could bear. Pulling his razor-sharp karambit, Hayward began the difficult task of cutting through the thick hair and alligator-like flesh. He fashioned himself something of a poncho and stowed the trimmings into the pack on his drag-sled for later use.

Like the bison hunting Plains Indians that he read about, Hayward did his best to make full use of the animals, and in some cases, the humans that he killed. Though most of his run-ins with humans didn't allow him the luxury of time. Despite his lack of formal education beyond the seventh grade, Hayward considered himself a great intellect. Among his prized possessions was a vast library of books he had stolen over the years. In her short time with him, he and Agnes read every book he managed to steal, and his consumption of literature only increased with Agnes' passing. He was sure he'd read every book in the Midwestern Territories. Perhaps he'd find others to read in this new land.

After a few more hours, the sun had finally set, and the temperature, already freezing, seemed to drop by the minute. Hayward set down his drag-sled and began to disassemble it to turn its parts back into a shelter. By the time he'd untied the poles from the sled, he was losing feeling in his fingers. Even with the docco hide for warmth, his whole body had begun shivering so badly that Hayward could hardly control his hands. It was all he could do just to pick up the tent poles. The wind and alkali dust that it kicked up scratched at his face and stung his skin, and still, the temperature continued to fall. He could feel the stiffening in his joints, and his jaw throbbed from being clenched to keep his teeth from shattering. He struggled to keep his wits about him but was beginning to feel disoriented and confused. He wanted to puke, but he'd depleted his stomach of its reserves and had nothing left to purge. His fingers refused to obey his brain, and his hands felt like blocks of ice, and then the shivering stopped.

Hayward felt himself get lightheaded. He did his best to hold himself up by hanging his frozen arms over the top of the tenting canvas he'd hung between the first two poles, but his legs buckled, and he collapsed, pulling the whole thing down on top of himself. Hayward struggled to free himself from the pile, but the more he tried, the more ensnared he became. Cold, alone, and too weak to fight, he laid there in a heap and let his eyes shut.

* * *

Hayward slept well into the afternoon of the next day when panic's fingers cracked through his chest and gripped his heart and lungs and gave them a squeeze. His eyes flew open as the weight of the hide and the tent canvas crushed him, and the air around his face was too thick to breathe. Like in the tunnel that led him to that other world, he felt the powerful constriction beginning as the sweltering mid-day sun threatened to roast him alive in his fur and canvas oven.

In a panic, Hayward clawed and struggled against the pelt and the canvas, trying to free himself. But it seemed that the more he fought, the hotter and weaker he became. The irony was palpable. The docco skin and the tent-canvas that trapped enough heat to keep him from succumbing to hypothermia now threatened to roast him alive.

Hayward focused his energy on the material pressing against his face. If he couldn't draw in a breath, all would be lost. Digging with both hands, Hayward exploited a tear in the canvas. He pulled until he ripped through the material and got to the outside air. It was warm, but it was air, and he welcomed it. The panic that slithered its way up his spine and took root in his mind loosened its grip just enough to allow him to reset his brain. He reached for his karambit in the sheath on his belt and wrapped his fingers around the handle. Hayward expelled the last bit of strength in his body and plunged the sharp point through his pelt and canvas coffin.

The sharp curved blade passed from the stomach to the head, freeing his arms and shoulders. He peeled the coverings off of himself, taking some of his skin with it as the docco fur seemed to have baked into his bare skin where it made contact. Nevertheless, he tugged and tore, and at last, it gave way. Next, he took off his shirt, but that was even more difficult than removing the hide. Large plugs of flesh pulled free with the shirt. Blood dripped from the wounds sizzling on the hot ground. The alkali dust that swirled around stung the wounds, and like an airborne styptic powder, the dust contracted his tissue and stopped the bleeding.

Hayward continued the painful process of separating flesh from cloth until he was stripped naked, and once the stinging subsided, the breeze against his skin felt good. He looked himself over as best he could and felt a surge of bile rise from his gut. He was grotesque. His whole body had the look and texture of tripe. He rubbed at the purplish-gray honeycombed skin on his arm, but it wouldn't come off. He pulled at it and tried to rip it away, feeling sure that his normal pink skin lay just beneath, but it simply wouldn't come off.

"What's happening to me?" he said aloud.

"I am remaking you, my son."

It was just a whisper, but he heard it. It was his father's voice. The Fire King spoke, and with his words came a sense of calm. Hayward was beginning to think that his new father had forsaken him, but now he understood. The suffering was his father's way of readying him for the task ahead. He would be remade, from the frail, pathetic, piss reeking boy in the stained Howdy Doody pj's to his Fire King's agent of wrath. Oh, how he wished Albert Taft could see him when he came into his full glory. He pictured the scene.

Again, Hayward Taft saw himself seated on his throne at his *real* father's side. This time, he would order that Albert Taft, the pretender, the defiler, be brought before them. Then Hayward the Avenger would rise from his throne in his full glory, the grandeur bestowed on him by the Fire King, and Albert would fall prostrate and trembling on the ground before him. Then Hayward The Merciless; *oh, he liked the sound of that better than avenger,* would bring his foot down, smashing Albert's head as if it were a grape that rolled carelessly off of a plate and came to rest underfoot. Hayward could not repress the grin that crossed his face, not that he tried. Perhaps the king would resurrect Albert as a gift to him. He could hardly wait for the transformation to be complete. But that, in its own time. He still had to do his part, which meant making it to the Western Territories.

In the blistering heat of the day, Hayward walked, naked as the day he was born, except for his welder's goggles and a pair of boots he'd put on. He hiked across the alkali flats until finally, he came upon Glass Land. It had the same topographic properties as Blackfire back in the Barrens. Sort of misshapen and contorted as if the ground itself had blistered. It even sounded like it was in pain with the dissonant tones made by the wind over its rutted surface. Far in the distance, through his goggles, he saw men, little green men, and they were swinging something that looked like pickaxes through the air. He discarded the apparitions as figments of his exhausted and consequently over-active imagination, and he had no time for such nonsense.

If not for the uneven terrain, pulling the drag-sled would have been child's play over the glass-like surface. Like dragging a fork, tines down over a plate, uneven or not, the ground here offered little resistance. Travel here was much easier than it had been through the alkali flats, and Hayward made good time.

Bolstered by the progress he was making, Hayward hiked happily west as the sun dropped into the mountains now visible far off on the horizon. And as the sun dipped, the temperature followed, but nothing like the previous night. In fact, Hayward found it very comfortable. He removed his goggles because they were too dark to see through once the sun went down. The trinitite all around him glowed an ominous pale green, making his waffled skin look even more alien than it had earlier, and Hayward wondered what he would look like when his transformation was complete.

He thought of the magnificent wings he had in his vision. He pictured himself soaring majestically overhead as his subjects took to their knees so as not to offend their mighty Sky King. Surely what was happening to him was part of his glorious transformation into the winged ruler of the west. "Sky King!" Hayward shouted. "That will be my new name."

Hayward swiped at his brow and moved his hair out of his face. As he ran his hand back over his head, hair came out in a great clump. He looked at the hair in his hand and flung it to the ground. He ran his hand over his head once more and felt the same waffle-like texture on his now bald pate. He fingered the small divots just to be sure they were really there. His stomach churned, and he swallowed hard. He had to trust in his father's plan.

He paused to put his shirt and pants back on and then continued on his way. The past couple of days had really taken their toll on Hayward. His shirt hung like a loose-fitting rag, and he had to cinch his woven belt tight to keep his pants from falling off of his hips. If he stood still with his arms outstretched, he could pass for the world's thinnest scarecrow.

The Glass Lands were only three miles across where he was, and the Alkali Field on the west side of Glass Land was only a couple miles wide. Far shorter than on the east side. Across the alkali, he could see a forest, and with what he presumed to be the worst part of his journey behind him, Hayward pushed on. As hard as it was to pull the drag-sled through the alkali, it was far more difficult to manage once he hit the thick forest. Twice he'd considered carrying what he could and leaving the rest behind, but something told him not to. He was tired and hungry, and he'd been walking in total darkness through the woods for hours, but he'd finally reached a clearing.

Chapter 21

It was one of those times when you're not sure if the sound that woke you was real or just part of a dream, but Joe didn't have to wait long for his answer because the sound of shattering glass was followed by a loud bang like something heavy hitting the floor from somewhere downstairs. Joe glanced at the door to make sure that the chair was still wedged in place, and his hand fell naturally upon the Evan's Repeater he'd left on his lap.

He sat motionless for a few minutes and began to wonder if he'd actually heard anything when another sound came from downstairs, or at least he thought it was downstairs. This time it sounded like someone pushed a heavy chair across a wooden floor, and the screech ran up his spine. There was something unnerving about hearing someone else in a house when you thought you were alone, especially in the middle of nowhere with dead bodies scattered around.

If there had been any doubt that he was no longer alone, the loud crash and the sound of someone chewing erased all doubt. It seemed that every sound made in that quaint but hellish little farmhouse seemed to find its way up the stairs, down the hall, and through the one-inch space under the door into the room where Joe sat silently. More chewing, slurping, and popping sounds found their way to Joe's ear.

"That fucking shrew," he whispered to himself. *Of course*, he thought, it had to be the shrew. *The damned thing must have gotten out of its cage and started gorging itself on that poor bastard on the table.*

But as disturbing as that thought was, his next thought sent a shiver up his spine. *Shrews don't eat dead things.* At least not according to high school filmstrips. Images passed in parade fashion through his mind; wolves, bear, docco. His door would stop a wolf and might slow a bear down enough for him to empty his Evans into it, which should kill it or, at the very least, drive it off. But if that thing downstairs was a docco; well… the heavy oak door would be like paper and the shots from the Evans, little more than bee stings. His mind raced. *The blunderbuss,* he thought, *that might do the trick.* A shot placed just right might knock the monster on its ass and stun it long enough for Joe to make a run for it.

But there was a problem. He'd already fired it, and the blunderbuss was a one-and-done weapon. That meant that every time you fired it, it had to be reloaded before it could be fired again, and Joe didn't know the first thing about loading a blunderbuss; well, other than the fact that you could cram it full of anything that could fit down into the barrel. If he just had more time and more light, he was sure he could figure it out, but neither were on his side.

Rather than focusing on what he didn't have, Joe took stock of his options. He had the hatchet, a knife, an awl, the Evan's Repeater, and in a pinch, the blunderbuss could be used as a bludgeon. *Maybe I could slip silently down the stairs and make a run for it,* Joe thought but dismissed the idea as stupid. He'd seen the docco charge the Albatross, and as big as they were, they were a hell of a lot faster than he was. No, the best thing for him to do was to stay in place and remain as quiet as possible.

After a short time, the sickening eating sounds from the first floor stopped. *Maybe whatever it was ate its fill and would be on its way,* Joe thought. But he didn't have to wonder for long. The groan of the first step told him that his house guest was coming up for a look around. It scaled the stairs with what sounded to Joe like trepidation, and with that, docco was checked off the mental list. He'd seen the docco in action. There was no apprehension in the docco. *Bears aren't timid either,* Joe thought *unless perhaps a docco were nearby.* The creaking grew closer, pausing for shorter and shorter times between each step, and Joe knew he wouldn't be left to wait and wonder much longer.

Joe focused on the gap between the door and the floor. Any moment, he expected to see a pair of feet and hear the knob turn. As Joe watched, a strange blue light spilled in under the door in an arch stopping several feet short of Joe in his hiding spot. Joe could see the soles from a pair of boots and, as he predicted, watched as the doorknob turned.

His guest was human. The intruder gave the door a push, but the chair did its job, and the door wouldn't budge. The intruder let the knob snap back and stood silently just outside the door. Joe tightened his grip on the rifle. A strange scraping sound, slow and steady, began at the top of the door and continued down. In the glow of the strange light outside the door, Joe could see a hand and then a pair of knees in the gap. Joe's heart pounded in his throat as the arc of the light crept deeper into the room. Joe watched as the side of a man's face appeared in the gap. The face looked as if it had been chewed on by the shrew. The eye scanned the room but didn't seem to see him. His intruder's light seemed more of a hindrance.

Joe's grip tightened around his Evan's Repeater and slowed his breathing. He found his front sight and lowered his barrel slowly until it settled on the eyeball. Joe exhaled slowly, took the slack out of the trigger, and prepared to send the 300-grain bullet right through the intruder's eyeball. The shot was lined up, and the shooter was ready, but he hesitated. Joe felt a pinch in his chest and felt the remaining air in his lungs deplete. When he tried to draw a breath, he couldn't. Pain shot through his back, arms, and through his jaw, with a final stop in his chest. Sweat poured down his face, and nausea undulated in non-rhythmic waves through his body.

His concentration had been broken, and when he looked back, the eyeball was gone. Joe blinked hard and shook his head to clear his vision. It had watery, blurry. He stared at the space under the door, half expecting the intruder to kick the damn thing open and rush in, but as he watched and waited, his symptoms slowly began to subside, and he could hear footsteps moving away toward the stairs. Joe could hear the intruder laughing softly, almost sinisterly, as the stairs creaked and groaned as he descended back to the first floor. Joe couldn't move.

He thought of his body lying in the hospital bed. Something must have happened; the best bet was that he suffered another heart attack. *What did the doc call it? An infarction?* The doctors and nurses were probably doing what they could to save him. Was that how his life would be? Would he be forever tethered to that hospital bed, like Lieutenant Colonel White was tethered to the capsule on yet another filmstrip he'd seen in school? *Am I Major Tom?*

Joe closed his eyes and waited to be sucked back into that damned hospital bed. But that didn't happen. After a few moments, the symptoms passed, and he could breathe again. He inhaled and exhaled a few times before he tried to get up, still feeling a little lightheaded, but he was okay. Joe could hear the intruder walk out the front door, the screen door slamming behind him. Blood rushed into Joe's legs reawakening the nerves. The response came as a sensation of pins and needles in his feet. The window in Joe's room faced south toward the barn that he hadn't bothered to check. Joe rose on tingling feet, peered out the window, and watched as a gaunt, frail-looking old man shuffled along toward what Joe now realized was a beautifully maintained barn and probably a treasure trove of supplies. The barn had been painted emerald green with a prominent C the words, Callaghan Stables, and Farm stenciled above the door. The old man stood at the barn door, holding his blue light high above his head as he peered inside. Joe had a perfect shot.

The adrenaline surge that hit when he woke had since abated. That, coupled with the medical event he'd just experienced, left Joe feeling drained and foggy. He wanted so badly to go back to sleep, but he knew that if he did, it would be a hard sleep; and what would keep the old man from dragging a ladder over from the barn, climbing through his window, and killing him in his sleep? The answer was; nothing. He wished he'd been able to put a bullet through the old man's eye socket and been done with it. He didn't know the man, but in this place, odds were good that he'd have had it coming.

"No!" Joe scolded himself. "You are not a murderer."

Though, he supposed, the dead bodies strewn about the farm might have begged to differ if they could.

His "no" came out as a harsh whisper that cut through the stillness of the old farmhouse. Joe peeked out his window, sure that the old man heard him.

"Snap out of it, stupid," he ordered himself.

He knew there was no way the man in the barn could hear him, but he also knew he had to deal with him. If he didn't, he was sure he would fall asleep and lose every tactical advantage he had. Joe secured his hatchet in his belt and headed for the door with the Evan's carbine in his hands. He would find out who the man was and what he wanted. Then he would either send him on his way, secure him in a room or kill him. One way or another, Joe would have some closure and get some much-needed rest.

Joe removed the chair and opened the door. The hall was pitch black having no windows to allow outside light. Joe inched along in the darkness, almost tripping over the man he had shot dead. He found the stairs and picked up the glow coming from the moonlight that filtered through the screen door.

The top stair creaked and groaned in response to Joe's weight, and he stopped dead in his tracks.

"Fuck!"

He widened his stance and straddled the width of the stairs. Pressing his feet to the outside edges, he managed to eliminate the squeak, a trick he'd learned in his youth, though not through a high school film strip. Joe proceeded silently down to the first floor. Out the screen door, careful not to let it slam, he hurried across the yard. He stopped at the northwest corner of the farmhouse just in time to see one of the enormous green barn doors open. The old man exited the barn with his blue light held high in one hand and a leather lead in the other. A large black horse followed, pulling a short green buckboard. Once outside, the old man placed his light into a lantern hung on a shepherd's staff at the front of the wagon. The old man began walking toward Joe, leading the horse behind him. Joe sprinted for the root cellar and slid quietly into the opening. The smell hit him instantly, and Joe fought the urge to vomit.

The old man stepped forward and sniffed spasmodically at the air. His movements reminded Joe of a nervous pigeon. Joe hunkered lower into the hole and exhaled slowly through his nose to force out the stench. He watched as the old man pulled himself up onto the seat of the buckboard. Once settled, the old man snapped the reins, and the horse started off down the road with his blue light leading the way, sniffing as he went.

"Thank God," Joe said and let out with a small laugh.

It felt good to hear his own voice again. Hell, it felt good to smile again, he thought, but the smile ran away from his lips as he caught wind of what the old man had sniffed out. Joe had smelled it twice before. The first time was back in Espero, right after dealing with the Roke clan. The second time was when he and Alistair were attacked in the Albatross. Lightning crashed in the east above the forest, and the sickening smell of wet dog and rotting meat came in on the breeze. He had to get back to the house, grab his valise and the blunderbuss and make a run for it. If he moved fast, he might just make it. Joe started to climb out of the hole when the roar shook the ground under him. He braced himself and prepared to run for the house when something clamped onto his leg and dragged him down into the darkness.

Chapter 22

Agermonte and Barrister pawed at the door wanting to be let out, and Alistair obliged. Like giant clumsy puppies, the two crashed into each other and tripped over their own feet as they bounded out the door into the yard. Once in the yard, they tore down the path away from the house.

"What's gotten into them?" Alistair wondered aloud.

In answer to his question, Siobhan came walking up the path carrying a basket with Thea trailing behind. Agermonte and Barrister swirled and bounced around Thea, whose high-pitched laughter sounded sweet to Alistair's ear. Siobhan waved when she saw him, and Alistair waved back, feeling a quickening in his pulse.

"Good morning Alistair," she called.

"Morning, Siobhan," he replied as he walked down the path to meet her. "This is a pleasant surprise."

"I thought I might drop off some pie and escort you to breakfast; that is if you aren't too proud to be escorted by a woman."

Her beauty challenged the morning sun for radiance and her smile for its warmth. He'd heard that somewhere, or at least something like it, and thought that the author must have known someone like Siobhan.

"I would be honored, ma'am," he replied with an exaggerated bow.

She handed him the basket. "It's just leftovers, but Thea and I certainly won't finish them."

"We could so," challenged Thea. "Mom just didn't want to come by empty-handed."

"Please excuse her, Alistair. My daughter has much to learn about subtlety and feminine wiles."

"And how are you this morning, miss Thea?"Alistair asked.

"I'm great!" she said amid giggles and squeals as the two dogs licked her face and bumped her with their enormous heads.

"Let me put this in my cooling chest, and we'll be off to breakfast," he said as he disappeared into his cabin.

He caught a glimpse of himself in his shaving mirror, and the face looking back surprised him. He was smiling. He had been so melancholy and racked with guilt for the last few months and the face that greeted him in the mirror on the morning that he'd bothered to look reflected his emotions. He had been torturing himself with 'what ifs.' What if he hadn't let Joe go after Hayward? What if he'd listened to the warning from the Pastreco? What if he had stayed awake and gotten the drop on Hayward? He could have forced him to tell him where Joe was. The questions crawled over his brain like spiders and tugged his brow into a deep furrow, but Siobhan's smile broke the spell. It warmed his heart and started the healing in his soul, and his mirror reflected that. Siobhan made him happy, Thea made him happy, and his heart felt light for the first time in a long time. He could see himself being here, if only she felt the same, and of course, if she were older. *Just a few years older.*

He lifted the heavy stone top of the cooling box from the floor in his kitchen, set the pie inside, and set the lid back in place. He paused a moment and considered the last four months of his life. So much had changed since the middle of July, when he met the young man from a world he never knew existed. It seemed funny now that he'd accepted that reality so readily. But he had taken a real shine to the young man and could see no deceit in him. In fact, Alistair saw so much of what he once was in Joe. Clear-eyed and fearless, sure of himself and of what he believed in. Alistair seemed to have become less sure of what he believed in, giving a wider berth to the gray areas. He recalled their discussion about family and whether having a family was a strength or a weakness. Alistair argued that family was a weakness, and losing Joe, and the almost crippling effect it had on him, only reinforced his belief. But now, toying with the idea that he could have a family of his own with Siobhan and Thea, regardless of what form it took, he might need to reconsider Joe's point. Joe said that having people worth fighting for was more important than fighting for some code, and maybe he was right.

He knew he would do anything to protect Siobhan and Thea, and what better way than to enforce the law? He'd spent the majority of his life traipsing all around the territory of Espero chasing criminals, but maybe the time had come to take off the badge. Perhaps he could still serve the law without being a Ranger. Jedrek had offered him a position with Savista's guard. Maybe the work of ensuring the safety and security of Savista could be his new calling. With the death of the guard's captain, Savista would be vulnerable. Siobhan and Thea and the rest of the folks who called this place home would undoubtedly need protection. And while he didn't want to make things uncomfortable for Siobhan, he couldn't deny his feelings for her. So, he would hide them. Bury them deep and take whatever role Siobhan was willing to offer him just so he could be in the lives of these two extraordinary women.

"Alistair! What's taking you so long, old man?" called Siobhan.

"And there we have it," he said to himself, momentarily deflated.

They walked the path to the dining hall, following Thea, who took turns riding Agermonte and Barrister, giggling the whole time. The morning dew was still frozen on the grass, and it crackled and crunched under their steps.

"How is she, really?" Alistair asked.

"She's much better. We spoke about the burst; that's what she's calling it. She said she was angry and wanted to stop the little monsters from killing Max. She said that she hated the little monsters and the hate just exploded out of her like a burst of energy."

"If that's what her hatred can do, remind me to stay on her good side," Alistair said in as gentle a manner as he could.

"She asked if I have ever hated anyone."

"What did you tell her?"

"I told her that I wasn't sure, I mean, I hated the freebooters that killed my husband, but that was a faceless hate. I mean, I suppose that's hatred but kind of different, ya know?"

"I guess, but I've hated plenty and never exploded, or bursted, or whatever we are calling it."

"Are you sure?" Siobhan asked, casting her gaze at his pistols.

It came as a revelation to Alistair. Had he ever not killed a man in anger? Didn't he feel some degree of hatred for every man he'd killed? Or maybe it was the lawlessness that he hated, the behavior more so than the person. Certainly not the case with Maurice Roke; he absolutely hated that sonofabitch. But what about his sons? Alistair felt sorry for them. After all, what chance did they have with a father like that? Still, he had to kill them, and he supposed hatred crept into the picture as he fired his Dragoons. It was his hatred for Maurice, but whomever the target, hatred fueled his rage. If he was being completely honest, he had to admit, at least to himself, that he took guilty pleasure in hoping Maurice felt the sting as each of his sons was gunned down.

As they walked and Alistair pondered, he and Siobhan were joined by Reka and Eva.

"Well, this is a pleasant surprise," Siobhan said.

"Reka, will you be joining us for breakfast?"

"I will, Ms. Siobhan," Reka replied with a smile that hadn't left her face since her encounter with Alistair.

"Well, that *is* good news," Siobhan said as she put an arm around Reka's shoulders for a quick hug.

"Alistair tells me that Thea was able to find Joe."

Siobhan, whose skin was as white as alabaster, unlike her daughter's, took on a rose-colored hue, and Alistair caught the flash in her eyes. Feeling suddenly uneasy, thinking that perhaps he'd unwittingly betrayed her, Alistair began damage control.

"Well, she did, but the child had a rough night, and...."

"I can speak for my child, thank you," she reprimanded.

Alistair could feel whatever color he had fade away, and Siobhan must have noticed because her rebuke was followed by a gentle touch on his shoulder. He must have clenched his gut like a fighter bracing for a punch because when she touched him, he released his brace with an audible groan. Siobhan, Reka, and Eva shared a quick laugh at Alistair's expense, no doubt seeing the effect she'd had on him.

"Alistair is right, we had quite an eventful night, and she will need some rest before she does anymore *seeing.*"

"Of course," said Reka.

"What a beautiful morning," Eva offered as a change of topic.

"Isn't it?" Agreed, Siobhan, with a smile.

They discussed lighter things as they walked to the mess tent and carried the trend through breakfast, and Alistair was glad for the reprieve.

When they'd finished the morning meal, Eva and Reka accompanied them along the path until they reached their cabin. They wished each other good fortune until they were together again, as was the custom, and Alistair, Siobhan, and Thea continued down the path.

"Would you like to take my hand Alistair?" Siobhan smiled softly.

"I—"

"It's okay," she reassured, reaching her hand toward his.

Alistair extended his hand, and Siobhan laced her fingers through his. Neither said a word as they walked. But the question of age kept popping around in Alistair's head. How could he ask her age without being forward? Siobhan seemed to notice that he was struggling with something.

"Are you alright, Alistair?" She asked. "You look like someone trying to pick a lock with a blade of grass."

"How old is Thea?" He blurted.

"I see," said Siobhan. I'm 42 years old, Mr. Woodbridge. I'm old enough to know my mind and far too old to care about what others think of my decisions."

Alistair stopped walking and stood slack-jawed.

"But if you really were wondering, she's 12," Siobhan said with a smile.

"I—I was just—"

"I'm not looking to rush anything, Alistair, but I truly enjoy your company, and I would sure like to share more of your time."

Alistair smiled, "I'd like that."

Siobhan's smile widened. "And besides, you might even pass for handsome if you took that animal off of your face."

Alistair stroked self-consciously at his beard.

"You mean old Jasper here? Why I've been caring for him since he was a pup!

It was lighthearted ribbing, but she was right. It had been a while since he'd put a blade to his face, an oversite Alistair planned to remedy that at his earliest convenience, if not sooner. Siobhan laughed, and the lilt in that laugh caught the sweet spot in Alistair's ear. He knew then that he wanted to hear that sound at least once a day for as many as he had left.

He accompanied them home and promised a visit after the day's work had been done. Siobhan had her own work to attend to at the medical tent, and Thea had school and chores. Alistair called Agermonte and Barrister to his side and made a beeline for his cabin and his shaving kit.

* * *

Smoke billowed from chimneys, and the smell of burning wood wafted through Savista as it always did, but tonight it smelled sweeter to him. A neatly shaved Alistair Woodbridge walked the path toward Siobhan's place, with Agermonte and Barrister leading the way. Still, a few days shy of December and the first snow had fallen, albeit a light snow. The fresh snow blanketed everything in pristine soft white, and Alistair couldn't recall the last time he had stopped to appreciate the simple beauty of a clear winter's evening.

He made a mental note to speak with Jedrek about the job offer. Perhaps it was time to put down roots. It was far too early to think that Siobhan would be any more than a close friend, but Alistair could live with that. But maybe, just maybe, it could be something more. He'd always been a 'hope for the best but plan for the worst,' kind of guy, but now he found himself hoping and planning for the best.

What's happening to me? He asked the question even though he knew the answer.

Siobhan had gotten into his blood, and Alistair, thanked God, she had. Alistair knew his years as a lawman had taken their toll on him. He had grown suspicious, angry, and bitter, despite efforts to the contrary. And again, in all honesty, he hadn't realized how miserable he had become until he saw himself in Siobhan's light. He liked the thought of the new Alistair, the man she could help him become.

About twenty yards out, the dogs stopped dead in their tracks and raised their hackles. Then, as if called by a whistle Alistair couldn't hear, they broke for Siobhan's cabin. Alistair darted after them, but they were already slamming their massive bodies against the door before Alistair reached the walkway to her door. The door gave way under their relentless force, and Agermonte and Barrister charged into Siobhan's cabin. Alistair broke the plane of the door to see Siobhan clutching tightly to Thea as the two massive and terrifying animals menaced the women.

"Here! Now!" Alistair screamed, but the dogs would not heed their master's call. Instead, they stepped closer, heads lowered, hackles raised, snarling and whimpering and snapping their jaws at one another. Alistair thought immediately of Ranger Dalton's dogs Mercury and Mars, who, when overtaken by the evil in the Barrens, chose to destroy one another rather than turn their fury on their master. Alistair threw his body between Siobhan's and the dogs, but that only seemed to enrage them even more. Their jaws dripping and snapping. His hands found his pistols and came up, one on each dog, as he glanced back at Siobhan and Thea. What he saw frightened him as much as his dog's bizarre behavior. Thea's skin was pale blue, and her soft brown eyes had turned obsidian black, with a texture not much different from the shell of an egg.

The child, who laid stiff and unbreathing across her mother's lap, suddenly gasped and drew in a deep breath. Her skin regained its fading tan complexion, and her eyes returned to their warm natural brown. Agermonte and Barrister ceased their aggression and bounced over to Thea to lick her face; Siobhan pulled her away and struck Barrister's muzzle, not yet satisfied that the threat had passed. Alistair grabbed Siobhan and Thea into his arms and held them tightly. Siobhan struggled to break free, but he couldn't let her go. After a moment, she relaxed her body into his and trembled. Agermonte and Barrister lay looking bewildered at their master's feet.

"He knows he's there, mommy. He looked at him through my eyes. It's my fault, mommy!" cried Thea.

"Who's there, baby? Who is looking through your eyes?"

"The bad man, the man who hurt Mr. Alistair's friend. He was on the other side of the door, and Mr. Joe had a gun and blood all over him."

"What?" The word exploded involuntarily from Alistair. "Taft? Hayward Taft is back in Joe's world?"

"No, he's here."

"Here? What do you mean here? Here as in Savista or here as in Espero?"

"Neither Mr. Alistair, Mr. Joe's in the west, across the Dead Zone," replied Thea, finally getting her emotions in check. "I could hear the bad man's thoughts. He was going to kill Joe," she looked at her mother to see if she was going to get away with the informality. When Siobhan failed to correct her, Thea continued. "He was going to kill Joe, but the bad man decided to wait. He wants Joe to follow him."

"Follow him where?"

"West," she said and reached out to pet Barrister, but Siobhan pulled her away.

"No! Don't touch him."

"They're okay now, mommy; they just wanted to scare the bad man away."

Siobhan wasn't convinced, and neither was Alistair. "I've never seen them act that way before," Alistair said.

The December wind blew in through the doorway, and the cabin grew colder by the second.

"I'm freezing, mom," Thea said.

"Alistair, can you," she stopped and nodded at the door.

"Of course," he said and got to his feet.

"Luckily, the door jamb gave way before the dogs smashed the door itself to pieces." Alistair closed the door on its hinges and pushed a chair against it to hold it shut.

"I'll run to my place and get some tools."

"The door can wait. Just please, stay with us."

Alistair tossed a few more logs on the fire and wrapped them both in his arms. Agermonte and Barrister snuggled up against them to keep them warm. A hard pounding on the door woke them.

Chapter 23

The heavy finger on the doorbell and relentless pounding tore Bob from a dead sleep. He grabbed his 45 from the coffee table next to the couch, staggered to the door, and slid the curtain aside with the barrel of his gun. The man standing outside wore a baseball cap pulled tight onto his head and seemed to be staring down at his feet as he continued his attack on the door. Bob yanked the door open.

"Who the hell are you, and what do you want?"

"I called the hospital, but they said he couldn't have visitors. They wouldn't even go check on him for me. They said they were busy."

"I'm only going to ask once more," Bob said.

Lucas' eyes locked on the 45, and Bob didn't need to repeat his question. "I'm Lucas, Lucas Travidi," he said, his hands flying into the air.

"That supposed to mean something to me?"

"Any chance you could—" Lucas pointed at the gun.

Bob exhaled audibly, shook his head in disbelief, and tucked the 45 into his waistband.

"Thanks. This is his house, right? Joe's, I mean."

"Yeah," Bob said, not bothering to hide his annoyance at the intrusion.

"You're his friend, right?"

"What the hell do you want? I'm trying to grab a little shuteye."

"I'm sorry, I really am. It's just—"

"Wait a minute!" Bob interrupted. "You're the guy I saw at the hospital with Corliss."

"That's right, Ron; I was there with Ron."

"Yeah, well, Joe can't have visitors right now."

"I know, that's why I'm here. You have to get me in there."

"Just wait for visiting hours like a normal person," Bob said and began to close the door. Lucas put a hand on the door and pushed back. "Wait, you have to hear me out. It's important."

"Must be," Bob said. "Why else would you risk such a serious beating?"

Seemingly unfazed by the threat, Lucas went on. "Do you remember when Joe went missing?"

"Not really, no."

Lucas looked confused. "What do you mean, no?"

"It's not important. Get to your point," Bob snapped.

"Okay, well, Joe disappeared for a while. Like he was gone," Lucas paused, probably expecting questions that didn't come.

"And?"

"Well—anyway," Lucas began, still seeming puzzled. "I'm a remote viewer, and…."

"What the hell is a remote mirror?" Bob interrupted.

"Viewer, a remote viewer, I can see things in other places, in remote locations."

"Well, that's great. Now get lost so I can get some sleep."

"Look!" Lucas pushed harder on the closing door. "You don't understand! It's really important that we get to the hospital right away. I think he's gone missing again. I looked for him, but I couldn't find him. I think he might be gone again." Lucas was speaking a mile a minute. "I spoke with Ron earlier and asked him to go check on Joe, but he never called me back, and when I went to the police department and asked to see him, they told me he was off duty. I asked for his address, and they told me to get lost. The hospital kicked me out, I can't find Ron, and now Joe's gone, and no one seems to give a shit!"

Bob stared at the ranting little man. "Look, um…" Bob droned a moment.

"Lucas, Lucas Travidi!" He screamed in exasperation.

"Right, look, Lucas, I was at the hospital just a few hours ago, and trust me when I tell you; Joe is there, and he's not going anywhere for a while."

"What do you mean he's there?"

"He's in the hospital, the same place he's been for the past three fucking months, though no one bothered to tell me."

"He's not—" Lucas looked suddenly uncomfortable.

"What, dead? No, he is not fucking dead! What the hell's wrong with you?"

"I don't understand."

Bob's face scrunched in confusion. "What's not to understand? He's in the hospital, same place you're going to be if you don't get the hell out of here."

"Can I come in a minute, please?"

Bob shook his head. "You have one minute. Then, so help me, I'm bouncing you out on your ass."

Lucas nodded absently and stepped inside. He sat cross-legged on the floor, closed his eyes, and put his head in his hands.

"Look, kid—"

"Shh, I need you to shut up for a minute."

Bob was about to grab Lucas by the collar and drag him outside when Lucas' body shuddered. Bob stepped back.

"I see him again," Lucas said. "He's hiding, hiding from an old man on a buckboard—and something else. Joe's scared, real scared." Lucas moved his head like he was looking for something, but his eyes were still closed, and then his body, dragged by something unseen, slid three feet across the floor and slammed into the door."

"What the f—" Bob jumped back. "What the hell was that?"

Lucas came out of his trance and got to his feet. "We got to get to the hospital, right fucking now!"

Bob grabbed Lucas' shirt and pulled him out of the house. "Let's go! I'll drive," he said, pushing Lucas toward Chris' car. Bob started the engine and smashed the accelerator pedal to the floor.

Chapter 24

Siobhan opened the door to find a hooded figure standing silhouetted in silver moonlight.

"Good evening Siobhan," greeted the visitor.

His massive frame filled the doorway, and his voice boomed through the small cabin. Though he recognized the man as pastreco, Alistair stepped in front of Siobhan. "Welcome to Savista, Pastreco. What brings you here at this late hour?"

Agermonte and Barrister moved forward but remained close to Thea.

"We need your help, Ranger."

His voice was dry, and it croaked, which seemed appropriate considering the man likely hadn't uttered a word in over a decade. "You'll have to forgive me; I've never heard the pastreco speak."

"Be that as it may, you are needed."

"I'm retired; you'll have to find yourself another lawman," Alistair said.

"You are?" asked Siobhan.

He looked into her eyes, "I am."

"I have no interest in your laws. I came for your guns. They are needed west of here," the pastreco said.

"In Gerrings? Then you want Ranger Kenders. He's the law in Gerrings."

The Pastreco showed no sign of impatience or frustration with Alistair.

"As I have said, we have no interest in your laws and no need for a lawman. We need your help in finding and killing our brother. He calls himself Dioj Volos, and he must be stopped."

"The pastreco doesn't kill," Alistair said matter-of-factly. "Good night."

Alistair began pushing the door shut, but the pastreco didn't move.

"You are needed, Ranger."

"Momma, I'm cold."

Alistair was still dressed after falling asleep while watching over Siobhan and Thea, but she was right. It was getting cold in the little cabin. However, Alistair wasn't about to invite the stranger in, pastreco or not.

"Siobhan, please excuse us," Alistair said as he motioned for the pastreco to speak outside. "Block the door; I'll let you know when he's gone," said Alistair, not worried about offending the dark figure.

The men stepped outside and walked a few feet away. Alistair heard the chair against the door and felt a slight sense of relief.

"Look um…" Alistair waited for the pastreco to fill the space with his name, but he didn't make a sound.

"Well, whatever your name is," said Alistair.

"I don't have a name. I am pastreco."

"Right," said Alistair. "What use is a name to men who never speak? Well, whatever you want to call yourself, I'm not going to Gerrings with you to kill your brother. Besides, like I said, pastreco don't kill people, and I'm nobody's tool."

"My brother is in the Western Territories, across the Dead Zone. And you *will* come with me. It has been foretold by the elders."

"I don't care what they told you. I'm starting a new life here."

"You have other interests in the west Ranger. You have a young friend who requires your skills as well."

Alistair considered what Thea said about Joe and the bad man.

"You know where Joe is?"

"We do. He is with the Batalilo in the west."

"The what?"

"The Batalilo."

"What is the Batalilo?"

"You know. You have one there." The hooded pastreco raised a cloaked arm in the direction of Siobhan's cabin. "The child," he croaked.

"Thea?"

"She is Batalilo."

"Explain yourself pastreco, or leave." Alistair rested his palms on his pistols.

"You saw what she is capable of."

"You mean the burst?" The pieces were falling into place.

"There is another like her in the Western Territories. Your young friend has been chosen to guard her just as *you* have been chosen to guard this child."

"Chosen? Who chose us?"

"It is as it has always been meant to be."

"What are you talking about?' Joe isn't even from this world."

"And yet he is here."

Alistair exhaled loudly, expressing his frustration.

"If you don't knock off the cryptic bullshit and explain yourself, so help me God, I will blow you out of your shoes, pastreco or not!"

"The time is near Ranger. We must safeguard these children from my brother, who would use them to unleash their fury across the earth. Ranger, hear me. If we fail in this, there will be suffering like the world has never known, and there will most certainly be another reckoning, another split."

Siobhan, who had been listening at the door, stepped out into the night.

"What is he talking about, Alistair?"

"I think someone means to use Thea as a weapon, and I have to stop him."

Siobhan was neither frail nor weak-kneed, but she felt as if she were going to drop at that moment. She reached for Alistair, and he held her around the waist. "I've got you, Siobhan, and I won't let anyone harm Thea."

"We must go, Ranger; I have a ship waiting in Armada."

"But what about them? I can't just leave them, especially when you tell me that someone is coming for Thea."

"They will not come if we can stop my brother before he captures the child called Tine. If that happens, your friend will surely die, and you will need Thea's protection more than she needs yours. Thea will be tasked with defending the rest of the world from a living breathing weapon."

Alistair knew he had no choice but to join the pastreco on his quest.

"You're asking me to leave my family. This had better work."

"I assure you, Ranger, we will find him, and he will fall. Now please, say your goodbyes. We must go."

"I'll only be a moment."

Alistair escorted Siobhan back inside the cabin. They sat together on the couch, and their hands found each other. Siobhan did her best to hide the pleading in her eyes.

"Did you mean it, Alistair? Do you think of us as your family?"

Alistair hadn't realized that he had verbalized that sentiment. "I do, Siobhan."

Their grips tightened.

"Is his brother the bad man who wants to hurt Joe?" Thea asked.

"I don't know, I don't think so. I don't think Taft had a brother, and I certainly can't imagine that a Taft could become pastreco," he said, more trying to sort things out in his own head than answer the question.

"Thea, are you sure Joe is out there? Out in the Western Territories?"

"Yes, but…" she seemed unsure about finishing her thought.

"But what sweetie," Siobhan urged.

"Well, I can't see him anymore. I could see him before, but now everything is black. I tried to find him when Mr. Alistair was out talking to that man, but I couldn't find him."

Alistair's eyes found Siobhan's, "I have to try. If there's a chance, I have to try."

Siobhan took a deep breath and exhaled to push the quiver from her voice. "I understand. Just promise you'll come back to us."

"I shall do my very best," promised Alistair.

He wished he had the time to tell her how perfect being a part of her "us" sounded to him, but he had to go.

"Agermonte, Barrister," he called and saw Thea's eyes well up.

The dogs plodded over to him, ready to follow their master through the gates of Hell if necessary.

"Agermonte, Barrister," the dogs cocked their heads, studying Alistair, "you stay and protect our little family."

He patted their heads, and Barrister spun back and sat down next to Thea, giving a bark as if he understood. Agermonte lingered a minute, perhaps sensing that he might not see his friend again. Siobhan ran to Alistair and hugged him long and hard, "remember your promise," she whispered.

"I will," he assured her.

They exchanged warm, heartsick smiles, and Alistair turned and walked down the path with the man who visited in the night and brought unrest to Alistair's new life.

"Oh," called Alistair, "and you two stay at my place till I get back."

Siobhan didn't respond, but he was sure she heard him.

"I'll have to tell Jedrek and Reka before we leave. I'm sure she'll want to come along."

"We must go," the pastreco protested.

"Tell me what?" The voice came from the shadows.

"Don't you ever sleep, woman?"

"Not much these days. Tell me what?" repeated Reka.

"We're going out after Joe," Alistair said.

"I'll grab my things!"

Alistair looked at the pastreco with a *well, what can ya do* look. The pastreco didn't say a word.

She was back in a flash with a rucksack and a rifle.

"I have to get Cage, don't leave without us!"

"Meet us at Jedrek's place. We're heading there right after I grab my gear."

The pastreco followed Alistair to his cabin and waited while the Ranger went in and gathered what he needed.

Alistair reappeared wearing his duster jacket and hat and carrying his old rucksack over one shoulder and a rifle over the other.

"Any objections to Reka and Cage joining us?"

"None Ranger, we will need all the help we can get. But understand that not all will make it back."

Alistair froze dead in his tracks. The last time the pastreco made that prediction, he ignored it and lost Joe.

"Who told you that?" he demanded. "Did the elders tell you that too?

Like they told you that I would be joining you?"

"The odds tell me that Ranger," assured the pastreco.

Alistair was relieved to hear that only the odds were stacked against them. "Well, the odds be damned. We are all coming back! Joe, Reka, Cage… and the two of us. Mark my words, we are all coming back." Alistair punctuated *all coming back* to drive the point.

The pastreco simply bowed his head in an, as you wish, gesture, and the two of them continued on the path. As they approached Jedrek's quarters, Alistair was greeted by a sentry.

"Good evening Ranger."

"Evenin' Edwin. Would you please tell Jedrek that I need to speak with him?"

"Of course." The sentry nodded and another guard started up the hill toward Jedrek's place.

"Hey," said Alistair, "while we're waiting, let me ask; how the hell did you get inside Savista anyway?"

The pastreco stepped back several feet, opened his arms, and vanished from view. Alistair walked forward with hands outstretched. "Where did you go?"

The pastreco re-appeared behind him.

"I haven't gone anywhere."

"Well, that's some trick," said Alistair as he clapped his hands. "Could come in handy."

"It is no trick. Merely one ability of a mind slightly less hindered than yours.

"I wouldn't call it—"

"Alistair, who's your friend?" Jedrek called as he approached.

"He doesn't have a name. He's pastreco."

"I see," Jedrek said. "Welcome, pastreco. Your kind is always welcome in Savista."

"Thank you, Jedrek," croaked the hooded figure.

"You speak?" Jedrek said, sounding surprised.

"Yes, he does. I found it a bit off-putting myself. Anyway," Alistair interjected. "The pastreco says Joe is alive, and he's somewhere in the Western Territories, and we're going to get him."

When Reka and Cage joined them, they found Jedrek shaking his head back and forth in disagreement.

"It's a fool's errand, Alistair. The journey to the Western Territories is treacherous enough. If you make it, you will still have to deal with cannibals, poison air, and whatever other horrors that Godless place has to offer."

"It is after those other horrors that we go, Jedrek," offered the pastreco.

"Right, well, like I was saying, even if you survive all of that, you will have a second winter crossing over the ocean around the Dead Zone to get back home. I implore you, my friends. Please, reconsider."

Alistair knew Jedrek was sincere in his plea. He was concerned, and rightly so, but Alistair owed a debt, and it would not go unpaid. He also had to do whatever he could to keep Thea and Siobhan safe. As for Reka, Alistair knew that no one on God's green earth could have talked her out of going. Then there was the pastreco. He had his own reasons for going, *but why would Cage voluntarily join what looked to all like a suicide mission?* That answer would be made crystal clear to Alistair in its own time.

"Your concern is duly noted and much appreciated," said Alistair, "but we have to go. Agermonte and Barrister will stay behind to keep Siobhan and Thea company. They should be staying at my place. There was an incident at their place earlier."

Cage added that his boy would be watching the Straits and asked Jedrek to keep an eye on him.

Alistair lowered his voice so that only Jedrek could hear him. "Before I go, I have to ask two favors."

"Anything," said Jedrek, seemingly resigned to the fact that he wouldn't be able to dissuade his friend.

"I am going to try and get the Albatross going, and I'll need fuel."

"Done, and?"

"Siobhan and Thea, please watch over while I'm gone. And when I return, I would like to talk about the captain's position you offered."

"Also done," Jedrek couldn't help but smile, "and with great pleasure."

Jedrek extended a hand, and Alistair took it.

"Iru kun Dio. *Go with God,*" Jedrek said.

* * *

With the tanks full and their gear was loaded, Reka, Cage, the pasterco and Alistair boarded the Albatross bound for the docks in Armada.

Chapter 25

ob parked Chris' car close to the front door, and he and Lucas hurried into the hospital. The nurse at the desk was apologetic but told them they would need to come back during visiting hours. Bob flashed his badge, and she threw her hands up in a *hey, I ain't looking for trouble,* gesture. It didn't matter that it was a Chicago P.D. badge. It was silver and shiny and did the trick. They took the elevator up to CICU and found a team of tired-looking doctors and nurses standing in the hall.

"What happened? Is Joe okay?" Bob demanded, interrupting their conversation.

"Who are you, sir, and what are you doing up here? It's after visiting hours," one of the doctors barked back.

"Where's Joe?"

"Someone call security," the doctor said to no one in particular. "And the police," he added for good measure.

"Relax, Doc," Bob said, flipping his badge. "I am the police."

"Well, that's all fine and well, but you're still not supposed to be here after visiting hours." The doctor softened his tone and waved off the young intern headed for the phone at the nurse's station.

The hospital had begun taking security far more seriously in light of recent events, and who could blame them? Three nurses and a security guard were murdered, and everyone was on edge.

"My name is Bob, Bob Tague, and Joe Kott is my best friend."

"Well, I'm very sorry, Mr.—Tague, was it?"

Bob nodded, not wanting to waste time repeating himself.

"We can't give patient status to anyone but family."

"I'm the closest thing he has to family Doc. Joe's mother is dead, and his father suffers from Alzheimer's. His doctors say he doesn't have much time. I'm really all he has left, so please, tell me what the *hell* is going on!"

Bob was getting loud and animated.

"Perhaps you should come back in the morning and talk to his primary physician."

"Belter?" Bob asked. "You mean, he's not around? You're telling me he has a patient in a coma, and he fucking left?"

"Sir, there is really no—"

"Can you at least tell me if he's alive?"

"He is," the doctor answered, "But that is really all I can tell you."

"Thanks, Doc, we'll just sit tight here until day shift comes on," Bob said.

"What?" Lucas protested. "We have to—" Bob shot him a hard, knowing look, and Lucas quieted.

"I'm afraid you can't—" Bob clenched his jaw and tilted his head, his eyes drilling holes in the attending physician. "Never mind, enjoy your evening, gentlemen."

With that, the doctor and his team walked down the hall and disappeared through a door marked Hospital Staff Only. Bob sprung up out of his seat and made a beeline for Joe's room.

"Let's go. It's this way."

Lucas followed Bob to the door to Joe's room and reached for the doorknob, but Bob stopped him.

"Hang on, we can't go in."

"We need the suits?"

"Yeah, so let's just take a peek and make sure he's in there."

They cracked the door just wide enough to squeeze their heads inside and both exhaled. Joe was lying in bed. He wore a breathing mask and had numerous hoses and wires running into various machines.

"Might as well get comfortable," Bob said. "It's—" He looked at his watch. "Still a good four hours before dayshift comes on."

"But—" started Lucas.

"You were the one who wanted to come, buddy."

Lucas let out an exasperated huff and plopped himself down next to Bob.

* * *

Bob opened his eyes to the sound of busy people moving about and saw Dr. Belter standing near the nurse's station, thumbing through a folder. Bob got to his feet, stretched, and walked over to the doctor.

"What's the word Doc?"

"Morning Bob, I heard you caused quite a ruckus last night."

"That? Na, that was nothin'. See Luke here…."

"Lucas," called a sleepy voice from the bench.

"Sorry, Lucas said something happened to Joe like he was dead or dying or missing or something, so I came down here to find out what was going on."

"Well, Lucas was partially right. As you know, we had him in a medically induced coma to control the swelling in his brain, and when we tried to bring him back out, there were—complications."

"What do you mean? What kind of complications?" Bob asked, his level of concern rising again.

"There was a cardiac event, and he stopped breathing."

"A heart attack? He had another heart attack?"

"Not exactly, that is, it wasn't what we think of as a heart attack. More of an arrhythmia. Look, we're still running tests. We'll know more…"

"No offense, Doc, but do you guys know what the fuck you're doing here?"

Doctor Belter leaned in close to Bob, and in a whisper, like a kid not wanting his parents to hear, said, "Not a fucking clue Bob."

Stepping back and speaking in a normal tone once again, "Look, a lot of what Joe presents with are fairly normal run-of-the-mill symptoms. Not necessarily for a young man in his generally good physical condition, and I say generally because smoking isn't doing him any favors, but still, stuff we've seen before."

"So, what's the problem?" Bob pressed.

"The problem is the other stuff."

"What other stuff?"

"Well, for starters, I've never seen anyone cough up carbon-black powder that evaporated into the air like vapor. There is nothing in the human body that should produce something like that. Then there's the matter of Joe spewing up buckets of water while lying in a bed." Belter just shook his head. "There's just no precedent for that kind of stuff, Bob. So, no, we don't know what the fuck we're doing because we don't know what the fuck we're dealing with." Belter paused to let his words sink in.

"Now, that being said, I've put in calls to the Mayo Clinic, the University of Chicago, and Johns Hopkins. We are reaching out to some of the best and most prestigious research hospitals in the nation, hoping to find answers."

Bob could see that Belter wanted answers as badly as he did. "I'm really glad you're the one working on him."

"Thanks, Bob, and I'm going to add you to the family list so that you can get whatever information you need whenever you need it."

"Shit, Doc, I really appreciate it."

"Now, if you'll excuse me, I have to finish my rounds."

"See," said Lucas, "I told you something happened."

"Yeah, you told me, but we still don't know what the hell is going on."

"Your problem is that you don't listen. I tried to tell you. They can't pull Joe out of the coma because he's not really here. I mean, his body is, but not his, I don't know, call it his spirit or soul or whatever. That's in the other world."

"So, how do we get him back?"

"You just heard the Doc tell you that they don't know how to bring him back."

"Then how do I get there?"

"Get where?" Chris asked.

She'd just come on shift and was headed to the CICU to check on Joe when she saw them talking. Bob, not usually self-conscious, realized that he hadn't shaved or showered or even changed clothes since he last saw

Chris, and it seemed she noticed too.

"Please don't tell me you've been here the whole time," she scolded.

"No, see, I went to Joe's and slept for a couple hours, then Luke here."

"Lucas!" he corrected for a second time.

"Right, sorry, Lucas."

"Why is that so hard? My mom named me Lucas, not Luke." he pushed.

"What's wrong with Luke? Ever heard of Luke Skywalker?" Bob pushed back.

The conversation had gone entirely off-topic, and Bob was okay with that. He didn't exactly have a handle on the whole; where's Joe topic. He just knew that he was ready to do whatever it took to bring him back and out of the damned coma. But the feeble attempt at distraction failed.

"Good, now that the Luke versus Lucas debate is over. Get where?"

"Get where?" Bob stalled.

"Yes, Bob. You asked Lucas, 'how do I get there,' now I'm asking you, where *there* is?"

Bob hemmed and hawed. "No. What I meant was—"

She turned her attention to Lucas. "Can you shed some light on this, Lucas?"

Lucas crumbled. He began a long and confusing explanation about multiple planes of existence and the duality of man as both a physical and spiritual being. "Or call it the soul or whatever," he said.

"Are you supposed to be up on six?"

The hospital's sixth floor was home to the psych ward and the place they housed dangerous patients. It was also the scene of the grisly murders of the nurses and security guard.

"Bob, please tell me that you don't believe this nonsense," she added.

"You have to admit it, Chris. There is a lot of crap that no one seems to be able to explain."

"I'm sure people were pretty confused when Edison invented the light bulb, but that doesn't mean he got the idea from an alternate dimension."

There was a magazine on the coffee table near the bench where Bob and Lucas spent the night. Lucas Travidi dealt with skeptics in the past. He walked over to the table, picked up the magazine, and handed it to Chris. She held it in her hand and looked first at Lucas and then at Bob.

"Don't look at me; I don't know anything about this," Bob said.

The magazine's cover featured a chubby baby holding a globe in his lap. Reflections of the globe are seen in the child's piercing blue eyes. The copy under the image read "Treating the Earth Like Our Plaything."

"What am I supposed to do with this?"

"Just open it to any page, and I'll tell you what you're looking at."

"And what's that going to prove?"

"That—well, that—," he wasn't entirely sure what he hoped to prove. Chris hadn't questioned his abilities, only the existence of alternate dimensions, "It will prove that—um."

"I'm sorry, gentlemen, I have to check on Joe and see to my other patients."

Bob smiled, she was no shrinking violet, and he liked that.

Lucas, on the other hand, looked a little dejected.

"Bob, Lucas, are you two free for lunch? Say around 11:30?"

Wild horses couldn't keep Bob away. Lucas just shrugged his shoulders. Clutching her patient charts to her chest, Chris flashed Bob a smile and spun lightly on her heels toward Joe's room.

The way she moved reminded him of the girls in high school. Bob watched her walk away, momentarily unaware that Lucas was still there.

"Shit, sorry, man. What were we talking about?"

"Joe, we were talking about Joe. And whether your girlfriend believes it or not, Joe's body is the only part of him in that room right now."

Bob didn't correct him on the girlfriend comment, he liked the thought, but Chris was right. Joe's medical condition wasn't normal, but it wasn't supernatural either. And so what if Joe believed it. He had been through so much in the last six months. Who could blame him for snapping a little?

"Listen, Lucas, I need to get some rest. I'll give you a ride back to Joe's house so you can pick up your car."

Bob wasn't sure if he pissed Lucas off or hurt his feelings. The look on his face was somewhere between the two.

"What; your girlfriend," only it was more like guuuuurlfriend, "doesn't believe me, so now you don't believe me?"

There it was, more pissed off than hurt.

"Watch your ass Lucas," was the only warning he would get, but it worked.

"I'm sorry, but you have to believe me, we have to help him. I can see things, really."

Lucas sounded desperate as he shoved the magazine into Bob's hand. How was Bob to know that Lucas didn't give two shits whether he believed him or not? That all he wanted was to help Joe, and that was only so that he could talk to him about the disturbing and bizarre shit he'd witnessed trying to save him the first time. Bob didn't know any of that. He just heard the pleading desperation in his voice and took hold of the magazine.

"Okay, now what?" Bob asked.

"Just open it to any page, and I'll tell you what you're looking at."

Bob turned to the first image, an advertisement for a rather plain-looking 1995 Toyota Corolla.

Lucas shut his eyes and called it. "It's a car, a black Toyota Corolla. It says, *Corolla, Where Promises are Kept.*"

"No shit! Wow, Lucas, that was really good, but how do I know you didn't cheat?"

"Cheat? How could I cheat?"

Bob flipped to another picture. This time it was a field strewn with oil derricks, and again, Lucas nailed it. Bob shut his eyes, let the pages fall from his fingers, and jabbed a thumb on the page where he stopped. He opened his eyes and looked at Lucas.

"One more, and I'll believe it's not just some trick."

He looked down at the page and took in the image before looking back up at Lucas. Lucas' eyes fluttered, and he fell to the floor.

Chapter 26

In the pitch-black, Joe couldn't see the stairs but had no trouble feeling them as he was dragged down into the pit. Small bursts of light flashed behind his eyes each time his head made contact with one of the steps. When he finally reached the bottom, Joe grabbed for his hatchet, having let go of the carbine as he groped to stop his fall. The small bursts of light going down the stairs had been child's play compared to the pain and light he was about to experience.

His head exploded in a brilliant display of color, sparks, and pain as he felt something smash into the side of his head. The blow dizzied him and almost rendered him unconscious. Joe did his best to hold onto the hatchet, but he had all he could do to keep from passing out. Joe drew in a breath to object, but a hand fell across his mouth and nose to stifle his outburst.

Another roar, closer than the last and answered by several others, found its way into the pit, and Joe felt his blood run cold. Docco, a small herd, pounded the ground above them, half burying Joe and the stranger in dirt loosened from the cellar ceiling. Joe coughed and sputtered, trying to spit out the soil that landed in his mouth. He thought he remembered Alistair telling him that the docco didn't travel in herds, but he couldn't get his head around past conversations right then. Other, more pressing matters required his immediate attention. As his eyes adjusted to the dim light cast by a small oil lamp in one corner of the room, Joe could make out a gangly, human form clawing its way free from the cave in.

"Who are you?" he whispered dizzily.

"Shh," a harsh and hushed voice said. "Or so help me, God, I will cave your skull in for you!"

The musty earth and docco stench filled Joe's nostrils and mixed with the shit, and rotting death smells that permeated the cellar. Joe retched as silently as he could, believing wholeheartedly that his roommate would keep their word. As he got his stomach under control, Joe considered the the voice which he now thought belonged to a woman. It sounded vaguely feminine, he thought, but he couldn't reconcile that to the figure he saw clawing its way out of the dirt.

He supposed it didn't matter as he and his captor, or maybe rescuer; only time would tell, sat still in the darkness, listening to the herd ransack the farm. His roommate waited a good half hour after the last sound was heard before she raised the flame on the lantern. It was the girl he'd saved from the cannibals. She stood, carbine in one hand and hatchet in the other. "Get up. We're getting out of here," she said.

Joe did as he was told without argument. Together they moved up the wooden stairs and forced the heavy steel doors open. Sunlight cut in a two-foot-wide beam that washed over Joe's face. An instant splitting headache resulted, and Joe shut his eyes tight against the pain.

"Give it a few minutes. You'll adjust. My name is Tine."

"My head is killing me." Joe pressed the palms of his hands over his eyes.

"It's the light. Just give it a few minutes," she said.

"Yeah? Well, I'm sure you smashing me in the head has nothing to do with it."

Joe blinked and squinted until finally, he could tolerate the brightness. There before him stood the filthy little leash-girl. She was tall and thin, not yet a woman, though her voice certainly did not fit her age. On her head sat a long and tangled mess of red hair. Not a bright red, like a firetruck, more of a burnt orange. The freckles that sprayed across her cheeks and the bridge of her nose matched her hair. She smelled horrible, no doubt the result of living underground, and she no longer wore the rope collar around her neck, though the rope-burn marks remained.

"Well, Tine, was it?"

"Yes."

"Well, Tine, you saved my life; thank you."

"You saved mine, so I guess that makes us even. What's your name?"

"Joseph, but everyone calls me Joe. Were you down here the whole time?" Joe jutted his chin toward the pit. "I checked before, but I only saw a bunch of dead bodies stacked up."

"I was there. I hid under them when I heard you coming down the stairs. I didn't know what you planned on doing with me. You could have been as bad as—as bad as them."

"The cannibals?" Joe asked.

Tine shook her head.

"I'm pretty sure I killed all of them," Joe said.

"Good," said Tine with utter contempt. "Every night, I would pray that Dioj Volos would come and save me. You're not him, are you?"

"Pretty sure I'm not. Who is he?"

"What?"

Joe could tell he surprised the girl.

"Where do you live, under a rock?" The irony was not lost on either of them. "He's the one who is going to save us. Save us from the tickers and the rest of the evil out there."

"Is that what you call the cannibals, tickers?"

"Are you kidding? How have you never heard of the tickers?" She asked and then, in a more incredulous voice. "How have you never heard of Dioj Volos?"

"I dunno," Joe said, raising his hands defensively. "I just haven't, I guess."

Tine exhaled in exasperation. "Dioj Volos, he's the one who is going to save this world, Joe; save us!"

"If you say so, but I don't need saving, and I'm not him, but I am willing to see you safely back to your family."

"What family? The man on the table? That was my father, and those animals already killed my mother and my two brothers and sister. I don't have a family anymore, Joe."

They stood in the rising sun a stared. The house was leaning heavily to the left. Debris was scattered across the yard on the south side of the house. Glass, wood, broken furniture, strewn about the yard as if it had been picked up and dropped by a tornado.

"Good riddance," Tine said and spat on the ground. "You have no idea what they would have done to me." She shuddered. "But you came along, like an answer to a prayer and saved me, Joseph."

"It's Joe, just Joe. Did they butcher your whole family?" He asked as gently as he could.

"Just my dad and brothers. They used my mother and sister for bait, and I was next."

"What do you mean; used them for bait? What were they trying to catch?"

Joe thought he knew the answer. After all, what else would cannibals hunt besides people?

"They weren't trying to catch anything."

Joe was confused. "I thought you said they were hunting?"

"Who said anything about hunting? I said they used them for bait."

Joe shook his head, still not seeing the difference. "You lost me."

She exhaled loudly so Joe could see that he was frustrating her. Joe raised his hands apologetically.

"I'm sorry, please tell me what happened."

"They took my mother and my oldest brother first. They beat my father and my other brother half to death when they tried to stop them. My sister and I were too afraid to move. When I was ten years old, they dragged my mother and brother out of the cellar, and as soon as we were sure they were gone, my sister and I tended to our father and brother. Then we sat all night in the pit and listened to my brother's screams and my mother begging them to stop doing whatever they were doing."

Tine stopped visibly upset by the memory, and Joe placed his hand on her shoulder. Tine jerked her shoulder away from him, and Joe pulled his hand back. "I'm sorry, I was only—"

"I'm sorry, I don't like to be touched."

"Cool," Joe said. "Won't happen again. I was just trying to comfort you."

"No offense Joseph, but I don't need comforting. I need to *not* be afraid anymore. I need to feel safe, and I won't feel safe until I find Dioj Volos; no offense."

"None taken. I'll certainly do my best to keep you safe till we get you to him, okay?"

"Thank you, Joseph."

"It's Joe," he corrected again.

"I know, but I think I like Joseph better."

"Well, I don't. So, what happened to your mom…I mean, if you feel like talking about it."

"The old woman butchered my brother and hung his intestines all over my mother. Then those freaks dragged her away and staked her to a pole way out at the Y."

"What's the Y?"

"It's a fork in the road," she said, pointing to the north. "About two miles that way. They staked her to the post on the side that leads away from the farm here."

"You said you were ten when that happened?"

"Yes."

"How old are you now?"

"I'm twelve now," she said.

"And how do you know what happened to your mom and brother. Did they make you watch?"

"No, they kept us locked in the cellar," Tine said. "My father did."

"But you said you were locked in the cellar."

"I'm a watcher, Joseph," Joe studied her, remembering Lucas Travidi. "It means I can watch people, and that night my father told me to watch my mother. I saw them butcher my brother and drape his guts all over my mom. They did stuff to her before they dragged her out there, Joseph."

Tine cleared her throat and gave her head a quick shake, and her breath hitched before she continued.

"Anyway, the docco came charging at my mom. She couldn't even raise her hands to cover her eyes. That's when I…" she took two more quick hitching breaths, and her eyes welled up.

"I killed her, Joe, I killed the docco, and I killed my mother."

Tine burst into tears, and Joe, unthinking, knelt next to Tine where she was sitting and put his arms around her. She shoved him hard in the chest, almost knocking him over.

"What the hell! I'm sorry, Tine, but that's what normal people do when they see a little girl crying."

Tine clutched her bony knees to her chest.

"I'm sorry. I didn't mean to shove you so hard. Just please don't touch me."

Joe sat next to her but didn't touch her. "Sorry about that," he said. "That's on me. Anyway, I just don't see how you could have killed your mother if you were trapped in the cellar."

She closed her eyes and hung her head, her crazy red hair spilling everywhere.

"I flashed Joe. Well, the me that was standing at the Y with my mother did."

What does that mean, you flashed?"

I don't know what it is exactly, but when I get really scared or really angry, I can—I don't know, explode, I guess."

"But you're still here."

"I know that, Joe," she rolled her eyes. "I don't burn myself, but I turned everything, the docco, the ground, the post, and even my mother, into ash. And when I told my father what happened, he told me that I killed the only person he had ever loved, and from that day on, he never spoke again. I killed my mother and broke my father's heart. That was three years ago, Joe. When they came for my other brother and sister, he didn't even try to stop them. When they came for him, he walked willingly out of the cellar, and I was alone."

Joe sat silently as Tine told her story.

"That was a few days ago. I listened to my father scream for three days, Joe. Then you came. I would have been staked to the pole at the Y, wearing my father's guts, used as bait to draw the docco away from the farm just like my mother and sister."

"Nothing like that is going to happen to you, Tine, I promise."

Tine smiled a fragile smile.

"Who were the people in the cellar?"

"Just some other people like us. They brought them in a few weeks ago. A father and two daughters. He strangled them and then cut his wrist open with a sharp stone. Before us, there was another family. They told us that every year it was the same, the farmers would take some of their livestock out away from their farms and stake them to killing posts. Then they would split one of the animals open to sent the air, and the docco would spare their farms. They called it the blood offering. Well, animals are too valuable to sacrifice, so now they use people. And I was next Joe, but you saved me."

Despite her fear of being touched, the little girl gave him a quick hug, and her wild hair tickled his face.

"Hey, you said you didn't like being touched."

"You didn't touch me; I touched you."

"Fair enough," he said with a wan smile.

He thought of Reka and felt a sense of gratitude for her having a father who could provide for her safety until she was strong enough to protect herself and even return the favor. It made him sad to think of this child; how old did she say she was, 12? A child of twelve with no one to support her in a world that had gone so terribly wrong.

"Tine, would you like to come with me to Savista?"

"What's that?" she asked.

"It's a safe place," he assured her.

"There are no safe places, except with Dioj Volos," she said.

"Okay, but if we can't find your friend, would you consider coming with me? It's much safer than this place. It's north of Espero."

"I've never heard of Espero. Is it far away?"

"Well, what is this place called?" Joe asked.

"This is Dogtown, well, sort of the outskirts of Dogtown anyway, but I don't know why they call it that; I've never seen any here."

"Seen any what?" Joe asked.

"Dogs, stupid! It's called Dogtown, but there aren't any dogs! There was some back in Tomahawk; that's where we came from, well after Assumption.

I guess we moved around a lot. But there were so many dogs in Tomahawk! Hey, maybe they should trade names," the child babbled mindlessly.

He was only half-listening as he tried to recall any of those places on the map he had found in the wallet he took from Hayward Taft or on the map Alistair showed him while sitting at the table in the hold when they first met. That felt like a lifetime ago to Joe.

"Tine," she stopped her chattering. "What direction is the Great Lake from here?"

"I've never heard of it," said the girl, "but it sounds beautiful. I love water. Once when I was…"

Joe cut her off before she went on another babble, "Tine, are we in the Midwestern Territories?"

"What are you talking about?" she asked.

"Well shit," said Joe, "where the hell am I?"

"I told you, you're in Dogtown," Tine said.

"Okay, so let's figure this out. When I got here, wherever here is."

"Dogtown!" she interrupted.

"Right," he continued, "Dogtown, I came to, *Dogtown*," he exaggerated to concede the point, "from the east, and I know it was the east because I followed the setting sun in the western sky."

"You couldn't have come from the east," said Tine.

"What are you talking about? Don't tell me that the sun doesn't set in the west around here."

"No. Where do you think you are; the moon or something? The sun sets in the west, but there's nothing in the east but the Dead Zone. And you sure didn't come from the Dead Zone."

Dead Zone; that struck a chord. Joe remembered the swath of red that ran between the territories on the maps Alistair showed him.

"You know about the Dead Zone?"

"Of course, everybody knows about the Dead Zone. I really must have smashed your head good."

"First of all, let's just assume any amount of smashing on my head is *not* good. Second, if you're telling me that the Dead Zone is to our east, then we are in the Western Territories."

"If you say so Mr.."

"And if we're in the Western Territories, I have to get across the Dead Zone to get back home to Reka."

"I thought you said you were going to Savista."

"We are, Reka is in Savista."

"So, you live in Reka?"

"What?" Joe gave her a sour look. "No! Reka is a person."

"Reka? That's a funny name."

"Oh, is it *Tine*?" He said, mocking the kid with the odd name and burnt orange hair.

"Reka is the reason I came back here."

"Oh, so she's your girlfriend?" It was delivered in that sing-songy tone one might expect from a tween, and Joe ignored it.

"But Joe, you can't cross the Dead Zone. You'll die. Everyone knows that. My dad told me, well back when he was still talking to me, that if you even go near the Dead Zone, your skin will blister and fall off, and your hair and teeth will fall out." She pinched her fingers between her fingers and thumbs and stuck her tongue out. "He said your eyes would start to bleed, and then you...."

"Die," Joe finished her sentence. "I got it, thanks."

"Well, you will; you'll die, Joe, and I don't want you to die, I've lost everyone else, you're the only person I know in the whole world, and I don't want to be alone anymore."

She didn't cry, but her voice quivered. She was brave, there was no doubt about it, but she was still a child, and she was scared. Hell, Joe was an adult, and he was scared; who wouldn't be? It seemed like everything in this world wanted to kill you. People, animals, hell, even the rain could kill you in this Godforsaken place. He put his hand on Tine's head and gave it a quick pat. She didn't protest.

"I'm not going to die, and I'm not going to leave you. We'll find another way around the Dead Zone. Maybe we can sail south. Is there a seaport around here?"

"There's a town in Assumption called Reverie. My dad said the Maristo used to control it but not anymore."

"The Maristo!" Joe said excitedly. "The Maristo are here?"

"They used to be here, but my dad said that they all just left. He said that they ran like cowards. But he said that no one could really blame them. He said that Reverie is so dangerous that even Dioj Volos won't go there.

Joe knew the Maristo, and they were not cowards. It was more likely that the little girl's father was talking out of his ass or maybe making up for his own yellow streak. After all, hadn't he let his whole family get captured by the cannibals and then let them slaughter his wife and children? No, the Maristo would never turn tail. He was sure if they could make it to Reverie, they could find the Maristo. But he wasn't about to tell this kid that he thought her father was full of shit, especially in light of recent events.

"So, Tine, that's a really unique name. What does it mean?" he asked, changing the subject.

"My mother told me that it means fire."

Joe looked at her hair.

"Yes, Joseph, it's because of my hair." She rolled her eyes.

"Wow, that's some attitude for a twelve-year-old."

She stuck her tongue out at him.

"So, how did you end up here?" he asked.

"I already told you?"

"No, not here, as in the cellar, here in this part of the territories. Where were you headed?"

"We were trying to make our way north to Columbia when we were grabbed by the Tickers."

"I thought you said the Callaghans and the tickers were different," said Joe.

"What are you talking about?"

"The cannibals. Their name was Callaghan; it said so on the barn."

"Oh, that! Who knows what their name was? It could be the Callaghans, or it could be they ate the Callaghans. I'm talking about the tickers."

"Who are the Tickers?"

"God, Joe, how have you lived to be so old? Don't you know anything?"

"Well, I…" he began, but she cut him short.

"They're the ones who grabbed us and sold us to these… cab-a-nalls."

"Cannibals," he corrected.

"Whatever you call them, Joseph, they sold us for some horses. The tickers are bad people. They're killers and thieves and slavers. Everyone knows about the tickers. And they eat people too."

"Oh! You mean the Freebooters," Joe said.

"What are freebooters?" Tine asked.

"They're murderers and thieves, and I suppose slave traders too."

"Why do you call them freebooters?"

"I don't know," answered Joe. "Why do you call them tickers?"

Tine's face twisted into a question mark, "because they tick."

"What do you mean they tick? Like what? Like a clock?"

"No stupid, that's how they communicate, like we talk, well they tick. My dad said it was like the Morrisons code."

"You mean Morse code," he corrected.

"That's what I said."

"No, you said Morrison's code."

"Who gives a shit, Joseph? All I know is, I'm going to find Dioj Volos, and then we are going to kill every last one of them."

She obviously wasn't in the mood to be corrected, but he tried anyway. "It's Joe, not Joseph."

"Sorry—Joe," she said in a typical tween's mocking tone.

"Let's just focus on getting out of the Western Territories," Joe said dismissively.

"There's no way I am leaving them alive, Joe, not after what they did to us, to my family."

"Okay, we'll see what we can do, Tine."

Joe knew there was no point in arguing, but he had no intention of going after the tickers. Hell, all he had was a one-and-done blunderbuss and limited rounds for the Evans Repeater, which, come to think of it, he hadn't even tried out yet. Could be the thing didn't even work.

"Let's see what we can scrounge up around here and get moving," Joe said.

Tine hopped up and ran for the barn. She loved the horses. The Callaghans, though probably not the real Callaghans, used to drag her out of the pit to shovel their shit, but she didn't mind. She was just happy to be above ground and spending time with the horses. They were big, strong, and beautiful, all things she wanted to be.

Her captors fed her well, always vegetables from their garden or fruit from their trees, and she would always save apples and carrots for the horses. Tine would fantasize about escaping. About riding off with her father, brother, and sister; then later on about escaping with her father and finally, when she knew he was dead inside, on her own. And it looked like she was going to make it at last.

The barn's beautiful green doors were torn from their hinges, and there were holes you could drive a truck through in the barn's outer walls, but surprisingly, it was still standing. Joe followed behind, his headache finally subsiding, and he found Tine standing frozen just inside the blown-out doors. She didn't move, she didn't speak, and Joe understood why instantly. Shod hooves attached to portions of legs, smashed horse heads, and chest cavities of half a dozen horses were strewn around the blood-soaked barn. Entrails hung like macabre party streamers from the hayloft above them, and liquefied shit sprayed the few walls that remained standing. Scouring from the horses or docco shit, Joe could not say, and it certainly didn't matter. He took Tine by the shoulders and led her gently out of the barn. Again she didn't protest, perhaps too shocked by what she'd seen to worry about her own fears."

"I'm sorry you saw that. Are you okay?"

"I don't remember the last time I was okay, Joe," she sounded so grown up that it almost broke his heart.

They walked toward what was left of the main house and heard a soft moaning coming from inside. Unlike the barn, the door to the house remained hinged, and the screen door was closed, just like Joe left it. However, the wall of the house that faced the barn was a different story. It looked like a wrecking ball passed through it, and Joe understood how the furniture and the rest ended up in the side yard.

Joe stepped inside, but Tine froze.

"Are you sure they're all dead?"

Joe looked around. Wood and plaster covered the floor, and the furniture that once filled the living room was smashed to bits. The whole place reeked of docco.

"Yeah, Tine. I'm sure."

She stepped apprehensively through the door, looked around, and picked up a porcelain figurine that had somehow survived the stampede. "This was my mom's," she said.

Joe watched her turn it over carefully in her hand before smashing it to bits. "I don't want to remember her," she said.

When she said it, it didn't come out as a statement of sadness. Tine sounded strong, she sounded determined, and Joe understood. He understood, but it was still an uncomfortable moment, the kind of moments Joe had always hated.

"Well, I got a job for you."

The staircase that led to the second floor was collapsed, and Joe needed to retrieve the valise from the bedroom. He tried to jump, grab the ledge, and pull himself up, but he didn't even get close.

"If I give you a boost, do you think you can get up there?"

"Easy," Tine said.

Then Joe remembered the body he'd left on the landing. "You know what?"

"What?" She dais eagerly.

"I think it's better if you stay down here and keep an eye on things."

"Don't be stupid, Joe. I can do it, just boost me up."

"I said no, Tine."

"But just a minute ago…"

"You don't have to like my decisions or agree with them, but I need you to listen to me and do as you're told. Can you do that for me?"

"Sure," she sulked.

The groaning started up again in the kitchen. It was low and guttural and inhuman.

"I'm going in there to keep searching the house, and I need you to stay put. I don't want you to follow me in there under any circumstances, understand?"

Tine nodded her head. "Yes, Joe."

Joe unslung the repeater from his shoulder, holding it at the low ready position. He eased the door open, and a chill clawed its way up his spine.

Chapter 27

About a day outside Savista, they came upon a freebooter camp recognizable by the stockpiles of goods scattered around the compound. Except for Savista, no vagadi camp could amass such ample supply and weapons caches. Alistair slowed the Albatross and stopped near a nest of rifles stacked tee-pee style near a patch of blood-soaked ground.

"Looks like the docco herd came this way," Alistair said as he lowered the hatch. "Let's see if we can find anything useful.

The party disembarked and set out to scour the camp. Near the rifle stack, Alistair found part of an arm. Alistair imagined it being sheered off by powerful jaws and sharp teeth as its owner reached for his weapon. "The ash in this fire pit is cold," Reka called.

"Same with this one," Cage answered from across the camp.

Heavy iron stew-pots smashed flat under the weight of docco paws lay on the ground near the fire pits.

Alistair surveyed the landscape. "We're going to have to slow our advance a bit. I'd say the herd no more than a day ahead of us."

"But they hit our camp three days ago," Reka challenged.

"Unless they're on the charge, docco move slowly, especially on full stomachs.

"Time is of the essence, Ranger, and our mission, divine. There is no time to waste."

"Divine, or not, I'm not risking the lives of our crew to a herd of docco. You didn't see what these things are capable of, and I'll tell you another thing. This is no ordinary herd. This one is being led by three massive docco. And I mean massive by docco standards. Each with a rack no less than fifteen feet across."

"King Docco? Three running together?" The pastreco asked, a quiver in his voice.

Alistair had never heard the pastreco speak and certainly never knew them to be nervous or fearful of anything. "Is that supposed to mean something?"

"It means things are more dire than even we knew. We must go, Ranger. Now." The warble in his tone was gone, replaced by the force accompanying knowledge.

Alistair gathered his people and once again set off for Armada. They passed several more camps, simple vagadi camps, each one torn asunder by the herd. As they neared Armada two days later, the path cut by the herd turned west, and it took another full day to cross the width of it.

Just as dawn was breaking on the fifth day, the small band arrived in the port town of Armada. Alistair parked and struck a storage deal with a man who ran a dry-dock while Reka, Cage, and the pastreco gathered their gear. Though the sun had only begun its climb, Armada was fully alive. Fishing boats out for grouper and amberjack bobbed far offshore, and hundreds of poles spread for miles along the town's piers and shoreline. Daysailers with colorful jibs and mainsails floated carefree in the orange glow of the rising sun, and a group of young people aboard a twenty-footer called the Sans Souci moored just offshore, clasped hands and squealed with delight as they leaped into the water. Alistair noticed the look of wonderment on Reka's face.

"Your first visit to Armada?" He asked.

"It is." The words slipped softly past her lips.

"Have you ever seen the ocean before?"

"No, just the Great Lake."

"A drop in the bucket compared to this," said Alistair, sharing her sense of wonderment.

He thought he might bring Siobhan and Thea to this place one day, God willing.

"We should eat," Alistair said.

"There is no time."

They hadn't stopped for a decent meal since leaving Savista, having made do with the meager foodstuffs they brought along.

"When are we supposed to meet your ship?"

"Captain Sarros will find us when he is ready," assured the pastreco.

"Then there is no reason we can't stop for a good meal," Alistair decided. The travelers found a seaside restaurant and took an outside table facing the water. Bacon-wrapped shrimp, blue crab quiche, and hot coffee. Alistair could smell the ocean, but he couldn't appreciate it the way Cage could. He watched as Cage's nostrils flared and his chest expanded, drawing the sea air into his lungs. A smile crept across Cage's face as he exhaled and drew in another deep breath. Alistair smiled too, seeing the stoic black giant's child-like grin. After finishing his meal, Alistair leaned back in his chair closed his eyes as he basked in the warmth of the sun. Again thoughts of Siobhan filled his mind. *You really are an old fool Alistair Woodbridge,* he thought.

When they had finished eating, the pastreco removed a leather pouch from his belt and dumped several coins into the palm of his hand. The waiter, a tall, thin man with a sad face, rushed over and did his best to block the other patrons' view of the pastreco.

"Sir, please, some discretion," he said, looking about nervously.

But the pastreco paid him no mind as he sifted through the gold coins until he found one of sufficient size to cover every meal served in the restaurant for several days.

"Sir, I can't possibly make change for...."

But the pastreco placed the coin in his hand and closed the waiter's fingers over it, "no need."

The travelers slid their chairs out and began the mile-long walk to the docks following the shoreline path the whole way. A stroll would do them good after the long drive and big meal. Shopkeepers reclining in chairs or atop burlap sacks packed fat with various and sundry items called lazily offering everything from crocks of water to armaments capable of arming a private militia from beneath their colorful open-air yurts as Alistair and his company passed. Opium, the company of a woman, anything could be had in the streets of Armada, though the latter was far more prevalent and less expensive. The only thing outlawed in the territories was slavery, though the freebooters often enslaved their captives and bartered with and for them out on the plains.

"Should we buy some water, Alistair?" Reka asked.

"You'd be safer drinking seawater than anything that comes from those crocks. I've seen everything from lamp oil to cow's milk sold in those things, and I wouldn't trust any of these bastards to sanitize anything."

"Alistair is right," Cage said. "The shit in those jugs will give you the rot."

As they walked along the sun-warmed streets, Alistair noticed the six men who had been following since they left the restaurant. All of good size, the men followed at a safe distance but closed the nearer they got to the docks. Alistair casually folded the panels of his duster behind his pistols. Reka, seeming to notice, nudged Cage and unslung her rifle. Cage's bearded axes hung gunslinger style from rings on his belt, waiting only to be unleashed by the black giant. The pastreco carried no weapon, having sworn an oath never to take a life. But, even without the pastreco's assistance, Alistair felt confident as he thought of the story Jedrek told him about Cage and the men in the Barrens who tried to take his boy.

What are they waiting for? Alistair wondered. Each step favored Alistair and his group as they neared the dock and crew of the ship waiting to be paid for their transport.

"Ambush," he whispered to himself.

The area around the docks was far less open than the rest of the town. Crates stacked high in long rows waited just ahead as the dirt roads gave way to the worn wooden docks. Alistair was reminded of the rock walls in the canyons of Narrows. The crates would provide perfect cover for would-be assailants.

"We should address this before we step onto the docks," Alistair said, resting his hands on the Dragoons.

Cage's large hands dropped to his axes, and Reka fingered the trigger of her rifle.

"There is no need for you to spill blood here, friends," the pastreco croaked.

"Better theirs than ours," said Cage.

"Agreed, but you may rest easy."

The pastreco's words were of no comfort to Alistair as they continued on the path into the cargo yard and passed the first bank of crates. The bandits who had quickened their steps were now less than thirty feet behind and closing as they passed the second bank of containers.

"Enough," Cage spoke softly, but his growl reached Reka and Alistair's ears. The three spun on the six clueless pursuers with weapons drawn. The men halted and moved their hands toward their own weapons.

"Give us the gold priest!" Called one of the men.

He wore a patch over one eye and held a sawed-off side by side shotgun. The pastreco did not turn or comply.

"I am not a priest."

"I don't give a good shit what you are!" One-eye barked. "Give us the gold, or we'll drop you all where you stand."

"You want it? Come and get it!" Cage growled as he twirled his bearded axes.

"Boys!" cried One-eye.

Stopping short disrupted the ambush plan, and the four co-conspirators were forced out of their hiding spots and made to sprint the thirty yards down the dock toward the travelers.

Alistair glanced over his shoulder. "Four more coming," he said, turning his body sideways and holding his Dragoons in a crucifixion pose so that he could fire on both groups when the time came.

"Hold your fire, Ranger. You don't need to spill blood today," said the pastreco.

"I'm sorry, friend," said Alistair, with almost a tinge of sadness, "but you are wrong."

As if in response to Alistair's declaration, a shot rang out, exploding One-eye's head like a half-stick of dynamite set off in a pumpkin, his shotgun clanging harmlessly to the ground. Less steady gun hands might have fired in sympathetic response, but not Alistair and Reka. Alistair, the old warrior, was a veteran of more battles than he could count, and he held fast. Not so much as a finger twitched as the would-be ambushers darted their heads around like nervous fowl. Another shot rang out, popping yet another ones head and sending the remaining eight scattering among the crates and barrels spread along the docks.

"Greetings, pastreco!"

A stout barrel-chested man with white flowing hair and beard to match approached through the carnage, flanked by four larger men. The largest of them was a man equal in size to Cage.

"I'm Captain Sarros," announced the white-haired fireplug of a man.

Alistair and his travelers scanned and readied for the next attack, but Sarros put them at ease.

"They won't be back. Come! Serenity awaits my friends, and we are ready to set sail."

The captain extended a hand directing his guests toward his ship. Alistair paused and pulled a pack of cards from his vest pocket. They were the size and shape of standard playing cards, but instead of kings and queens, each card was stamped with the word Espero and the number 16. He slapped one on each of the two bodies as a calling card to let Armada's new Ranger know. Alistair bowed his head in remembrance of her old guardian, Ranger White, who he found trussed up and mutilated by Hayward Taft in the Barrens. The group allowed him a moment and then continued on, leaving the dead to be collected by the local pastreco.

"Guess we'll leave them for your brothers to clean up," Alistair said.

The man in the hood and robes nodded. "The pastreco will see to them."

As they walked, Sarros introduced his officers to his guests.

"May I present my officers?"

"By all means," Alistair said.

"I would like you all to meet Mr. Villwock, Chief Mate."

Villwock nodded.

"The Chief is my second in command," Sarros continued. "This bear of a man is the ship's Quartermaster, Mr. Ramsey.

Ramsey smiled an oddly disarming smile from a man so obviously capable of inflicting damage.

"Mr. Kohlhagen, here is Serenity's Sailing Master. This man possesses an almost uncomfortably intimate knowledge of the waters in the Great Southern Ocean," Sarros said. His officers, Kohlhagen included, erupted in thunderous laughter. "And the giant bald-headed black man there is the ship's surgeon, Doctor Walker. We just call him doc."

Doc Walker looked noting like the surgeon in Espero or any territory that Alistair could remember. He was perhaps four inches shorter than Cage but no less menacing.

"So, which of your men dispatched the bandits?" asked Alistair.

"The dock rats? They're the scourge of every port in every harbor town." The captain said and pointed skyward. There before them, soaring high above the crates and various shanties laid out in front of them, was a 170-foot-tall main top-mast flying the black M on the crimson field, the flag of the Maristo. Near the top of the mast was a man in the crow's nest. "That would be Mr. Ballazhi. Arben is one hell of a shot and one hell of a cook. The best on the open water if you ask me."

"Your cook took those shots?" Cage Abrams asked, not attempting to hide his surprise.

Cage better than anyone understood the difficulty in making headshots from that distance, let alone from the swaying mast of a ship.

"Sure did, that man has the eyes of an eagle and the steady hand of a surgeon—well, not our surgeon, but most."

Again the officers burst into laughter; Alistair, Cage, and Reka joined them this time. The pastreco didn't even smile. "And he's twice as good with the blade," Sarros added.

As they cleared the last row of crates and turned the corner, a large ship with Serenity emblazoned across the bow came into view.

"Serenity." It passed Reka's lips in a whisper.

"It is, ma'am," answered the man named Villwock. "She's a 100-foot Brigantine, carrying a crew of sixty. She's not heavily armed, twelve carronades in total, but she's light and fast and can easily outmaneuver the massive Man of War and Frigates used by the Corsair."

"Who are the Corsair?" Reka asked.

"The only other power on the water," Sarros answered as he was piped aboard.

Once the captain boarded Serenity, his guests were allowed to begin boarding, and he greeted each as they stepped onto the deck. The almost 3000-mile trip would take about fourteen days, with the first leg of the journey being the five-day sail to the island of Pico de Orizaba.

With all of the formalities out of the way, they made ready to sail.

"Put us underway, Mr. Villwock," called the captain.

"Aye!" he called back and began barking orders at the crew.

Directing his attention to his guests, Sarros said, "Mr. Ramsey will show you to your quarters; I'll greet you all back on deck in one hour."

The travelers followed Ramsey below deck to a cabin containing eight beds that would send a claustrophobic into a panic. Four on each side of the room, two on top and two below. Alistair and Reka would have their choice of the top bunks, but Cage and the pastreco would each need to use both bottom bunks to accommodate their massive frames. Ramsey lit the last of the half dozen oil lamps to help the deck prisms provide light to the room and excused himself. The four spent the remaining hour stowing their gear and using the small sink and water pump to clean up.

Alistair was first to finish. He made his way down the dimly lit corridor, passing bunks and cargo holds arranged in no particular order.

He reached the stairs and had to shield his eyes against the glaring afternoon sun. Armada was fading into the distance with nothing but open water in all other directions. He'd had the same middle of nowhere feeling before, most recently crossing the Great Lake on his way to the Barrens, but this was different. He had seen the ocean many times but never sailed on it. Floating on a piece of wood on a body this big made him feel small.

"Feeling kind of insignificant? I feel the same way every time we set sail. Like a grain of sand on the back of a Blue Whale," said Sarros.

"Yeah, something like that," Alistair answered. "Say, the Maristo are a pretty close-knit bunch, right?"

"I'd say so," Sarros replied.

"Well then, would you happen to know Tobias Enzo? He's the captain of…."

"Ancora Imparo," Sarros finished his sentence. "I know of Enzo, but we've never met. He sailed the Great Lake."

"What do you mean sailed? He's not—"

Again, Sarros ended Alistair's sentence, "dead? No, least not as I've heard."

Alistair sighed his relief.

"All I can tell you is what's been told to me," Sarros said, staring out at the sea. "The Ancora Imparo sailed out of the Great Lake through the Prosper Straits and docked in Armada about a month ago. Enzo said he was hunting a Corsair ghost ship called the Raven." Sarros spat as if the words left a bad taste in his mouth. "When he left Armada, Defender and Mystic sailed out with him."

Alistair closed his eyes for a moment. "I was with him when he started his hunt. I saw what they did at the Ramparts. The way things turned out, I wish I would have joined him then, but I was hunting my own ghost. I suppose I still am."

Reka, then Cage, and finally, the pastreco emerged from below deck to join Alistair and Captain Sarros in the hot afternoon sun. Like Alistair, Reka and Cage decided to shed their heavy topcoats, but not the pastreco. He still wore his robe, but he'd lowered his cowl revealing long tangles of brown hair and a face Alistair guessed to be about twenty-five years old. Clean-shaven and about as pale as one would expect a person who lived covered from head to toe in heavy robes would be. Ice blue eyes and a sharp-cut jaw, the very essence of a strong young man despite his pale complexion. Alistair was surprised; he'd expected an older, gruffer-looking face.

"Son," said Sarros to the pastreco, "you're going to want to lose the robes.

If you go overboard, you're gonna sink like a stone."

The young man looked down at his robes, "This is all I own."

"Mr. Ramsey will find you something more suitable."

Ramsey nodded and went below.

"Good, now. Just a few points of understanding while you're aboard Serenity. My cabin and the kitchen are off-limits. You may have the run of the rest of the ship, but my quarters are my quarters, and Arben would not take kindly to other hands in his kitchen. Is that clear?"

The four travelers acknowledged with head shakes and various forms of the word yes.

"In the event of an attack, you will all be expected to defend Serenity. She is all that stands between you and the crushing deep, and you *will* protect her. And that goes for you as well, pastreco."

The captain added the last part without acrimony and moved on quickly.

"Now, based on your destination, I am sure you are no strangers to violence, but close quarter combat onboard a ship is probably different than anything you are used to. So, you will spend time getting to know the crew. Learn their names, know their faces. I don't want to lose any of my men to mistaken identity. Reka, I saw that you carry the long gun. You will take to the crow's-nest with Arben. You will spend some of your time up there, so you know my men from that vantage point as well."

Ramsey re-appeared on deck carrying several items of clothing and handed them to the pastreco, who took them and stepped behind the mainmast to change. No one was ready for what stepped out from behind the mast. Clothed in cotton pants and an open linen shirt, the pastreco was ghostly white from head to toe, his body corded with muscle, scarred and welted by years of self-flagellation. The pastreco stood holding his robes.

"That's better," said Sarros, unfazed by the battered specter before him.

"You'll prefer those to the robes if you go overboard. Now, in the event of a storm, it will be your choice to either go below for shelter or stay on deck. If you stay topside, you will need to make yourself useful. We have a five-day sail to Pico de Orizaba, my friends."

Mr. Villwock saw to their training, not knowing they would need to call upon it so soon.

Chapter 28

Bob tossed the magazine, which landed open, on the table. The article titled The Ghosts of Hiroshima featured images that the writer claimed were blast shadows. Darkened images seared onto walls and pavement by the atomic energy released when the US dropped a bomb code-named Little Boy on Hiroshima. Shadows resembling a child, a bicycle, and another that looked like a man standing near a ladder, visible reminders of that terrible day.

"Doc, Chris! Somebody, I need help!"

Lucas was shaking and thrashing on the floor. Bob stood over him for a moment before dropping to one knee. He grabbed Lucas' shoulders, shook him, and yelled at him to wake up.

"What are you doing? Stop that!" yelled the doctor.

"What am I supposed to do with him?" Bob asked.

"Not shake him, for starters. Let's get him on his side."

"What for?" Bob asked.

"Because I'm the doctor, and I said so! How's that?"

"Sorry, Doc," Bob said and rolled Lucas onto his side.

"Grab a cushion off that couch," Belter ordered.

Bob flew to the couch and grabbed a cushion. Belter slid it under Lucas' head and began timing the seizure. It only lasted a couple of minutes, but it seemed like an eternity to Bob.

"What happened?" Lucas asked, his words coming out slurred.

"You had a seizure, son," replied Belter. "Have you had them before?"

"No, never," Lucas replied, only it sounded like newwa.

"What's wrong with him, Doc?" Bob was leaning over Belter, crowding him.

"He had a seizure."

"I know, but why does he sound drunk?"

"Sometimes seizures affect speech. It's a condition known as dysarthria. It's a symptom of a trans ischemic attack. Now, do you mind?" Belter said as he glanced back over his shoulder, sending a clear message.

Bob backed away, feeling uncomfortable and out of his element. "Sorry, doc."

Belter quickly ran through a battery of tests, asking Lucas to squeeze his hands and repeat simple sentences while Bob paced the floor like an expectant father.

"Lucas, are you diabetic or hypoglycemic?" Belter asked.

"No, I don't think so."

His speech was less slurred, a good sign.

"Can you smile for me and show me your teeth?"

Lucas complied.

"Very good. Any drug or alcohol use?"

"No, I don't smoke or dring." He meant to say drink, but it came out dring.

"How much sleep have you gotten over the last couple of days?" Asked the doctor.

"Not much, doctor, prolly like eight hours." This time, probably came out prolly.

"A night?"

"No, Doc, over the last couple of days."

"Well, I think we found the cause of your episode. Lack of sleep and stress. But we'll know more once we run a few tests.

Several nurses came to lend a hand, and in no time, they moved Lucas from the floor, onto a gurney, and into a room on the second floor, for observation. Bob followed the medical team, careful not to get in the way.

"Now you rest up, and I'll be back to check on you in a bit," Belter said.

Belter patted Lucas' hand and walked toward the door.

"We need to keep him calm, Bob."

"Got it, Doc," Bob nodded and stepped aside to let Belter pass. "You gave me a scare, buddy."

"So, we're buddies now?" Lucas said with a smirk.

"Sure, we are. Even though you are a pain in my ass," Bob smiled.

"You get some rest. I'm going to see if there's any news on Joe."

"Hey, on your way back, can you get me a PB and J?"

"I'll see what I can do, now shut up and get some rest."

Bob walked out of the room and down the hall and took the stairs up one flight to the third floor. He made his way past the couch where he and Lucas had spent the night and picked the magazine up off the table. There was something haunting about the images. Bob folded the magazine and stuck it in the back pocket of his jeans. The floor was alive with activity. Nurses, some Bob knew, most he did not, floated silently on white shoes in and out of patients' rooms. The floor was split into three wings, A, B, and C, with a centralized nurse's station that served as a hub for the three spokes. The first two floors were the original hospital built in the late 1800s. A simple rectangle with little thought given to functionality. Floors three through seven were added in 1982 and made much better use of space than the original design. Bob made his way past the nurse's station down to the C wing.

It took Bob several minutes before he found Chris. She was standing in a waiting area with her back to the hall. He approached quietly, intending to surprise her, but as he drew near, he heard a man's voice. He was speaking in harsh, hushed, broken sentences, and from her body language, he could tell that Chris was getting a dressing down. He heard the man say, "Do I make myself clear?"

"Yes, doctor," Chris replied softly.

"Bob darted into a room, not bothering to check to see if it was vacant just as Chris turned and made a beeline for the nurse's station. To his relief, the room was empty.

The doctor was young, probably fresh off of his residency. He went walking past the doorway where Bob had gone to hide, and he seemed to

Bob to look pretty pleased with himself. Bob slipped out of the room and hung a heavy arm over the doctor's shoulder.

"Say Doc, you got a minute?"

"No, I do not, have a…."

"Great, thanks," said Bob as he clamped his hand onto the back of the doctor's neck and steered him back toward and into the empty room.

Bob spun him around and closed the distance between them. The doctor instinctively backed into the wall.

"Listen!" The doctor said in a weak attempt to assert some kind of dominance.

"No, asshole, you listen."

The doctor made a lunge for the door, but Bob caught him by the front of his white doctor jacket and shoved him back into the wall.

"You ever talk to Chris or anyone else in this hospital like that again, and I get word of it; you're going to need a team of smug little motherfuckers like you to put the pieces back together. Are we clear?"

"You have no right…."

The quiver in his voice was music to Bob's ears as he stepped closer, invading more of the doctor's space.

"Are we clear?" Bob repeated the question through clenched teeth.

"Yeah," the doctor stammered. "Yeah, we're crystal clear."

"Good, now go apologize to Chris and make sure you work in how you behaved like an asshole, and it will never happen again."

"Of course, I really do owe her an apology; in fact, I was just going to apologize when you grabbed—I mean stopped to speak with me."

Bob stepped back, and the doctor scurried out of the room.

"What is it with these guys?" Bob said aloud.

He'd hoped to see Chris and get an update on Joe's condition, but the pompous little asshole of a doctor threw a monkey wrench into the works. Now, Bob had to get back down to the second floor before Chris saw him. He could work his way back down the hall to the stairs or risk waiting for the elevator near the nurses' station. He didn't want her to have to force a smile when she saw him, and he knew she would be busy reliving that demoralizing exchange repeatedly for a good long while. Bob certainly knew he would, and it wasn't even directed at him. He hoped the apology if delivered, would help. Bob really wanted to dot the good doctor's eye, but then Chris would have been suspicious of the apology; besides, he could always jackhammer him in the face at a later date if he failed to deliver.

Bob snuck out and made his way back to Lucas' room, where he found him sound asleep. There was a recliner in the corner, and Bob plopped down into it. The magazine he had shoved in his back pocket poked him in the ass, so he pulled it out and tossed it on the nightstand next to Lucas' bed. Then Bob grabbed the TV remote and flipped it on. The last thing he heard was Bob Barker asking for the final bid on a bumper pool table, and he was off to dreamland.

* * *

Hands jammed into the pockets of his lab coat, penny-loafers shuffling across the hard tile floor and glancing nervously over his shoulder; the young doctor approached Chris and several other nurses who had gathered near the nurses' station. Their heads snapped, and their eyes drilled into him as he cleared the phlegm from his throat.

"Um, excuse me, nurse, may I have a word?" The young doctor squeaked.

"Her name is Chris!" barked one.

"I think you've said enough!" snapped another.

"Yes, I um," he stammered.

"You um what?" another said.

Chris just stared at him. She could have called her comrades off, but she wasn't feeling particularly sympathetic. He was an asshole, and he needed a good raking over the coals. And what was her sin? He told her off because she dared to warn him about a potentially harmful interaction between the patient's medication and one he wanted to prescribe. A thank you was in order, but she would have been happy if he had just kept his mouth shut.

"Look, I'm sorry, okay!"

He raised his voice, and it was like chum in the water. Lucky for him,

205

they were in a hospital because if they hadn't been, he would have likely needed to be. But as it were, the nurses, now totaling six, not counting Chris, were forced by decorum and hospital policy to keep their voices down; and physical assault would have certainly been a violation.

It was clear to Chris that he was one of those people with parents who lacked the sense to ever tell their child no. More likely, he was fed a steady diet of trophies, ribbons, and atta-boys, whether he deserved them or not. On the other hand, Chris lived in hand-me-downs until she earned her first paycheck serving cones at Gert's in Red Hook.

"Chris, I'm really sorry. I acted like a jerk, and I had no right to speak to you the way I did. I hope you will accept my apology." He said, looking at his feet and wringing his hands.

Perhaps she'd misjudged the young man.

"And please tell your boyfriend or um, husband or whatever, that I'm really sorry." With that, he spun on his heels and walked away.

"*Nope*," she thought, "he is *an asshole.*"

The other nurses went from attack dogs to clucking hens. They all wanted to know about the boyfriend and what she thought he'd done to the smug little prick. Chris couldn't hide her smile. She was more than capable of fighting her own battles, but it was nice that he wanted to come to her rescue. But how and when did Bob cross paths with the young doctor? She hadn't seen him, and the whole Jekyll and Hyde act by the doctor couldn't have taken more than ten minutes.

Just as the excitement was reaching its zenith, the elevator doors opened, and Terri, the floor's head nurse, stepped out. One glance from her and the nurses scattered.

"What's all the excitement?" she asked Chris.

"The rarest of all things, a doctor apologized for his poor manners," Chris replied with a smile.

"Did you send him up to six?"

"Yeah, they diagnosed him with a god complex."

They both laughed.

"Is it something I need to address?" Terri asked.

"No, we'll let bygones be bygones."

"Fair enough," said Terri.

Terri walked into her office, and Chris made her way toward Joe's room to check on him. A cushion on the couch just past Joe's room was lying on the floor. Chris walked over, straightened it out, and had the strangest feeling that someone was watching her.

Chapter 29

The window he'd dragged the old woman's body through was gone. In fact, the wall that held the window was gone, as was the table and the chopped-up body of Tine's father. In its place, a docco lay helpless beneath a small, gnawing, pulsing brown mass. Joe guessed that the shrew mounted the docco as it fed on Tine's father. While the docco gorged itself on the man, the shrew climbed onto its back and began chewing through the docco's thick hide, injecting it with its venom, paralyzing the predator to feed on its living body.

The shrew shuddered and jerked as it moved its body to face the kitchen door. Joe stood motionless as the shrew emitted a high-pitched bark, its head twitching from left to right as if it knew he was there but couldn't see him. The docco made a sound like a man struggling to lift a far too heavy object as its head began to rise and Joe's eyes widened in terror. Just as he was about to turn and run, the shrew plunged its teeth back into the open wound it had chewed into the docco's back to administer more of its venom into the monster's circulatory system. And with that, the beast quieted back down. Joe closed the door slowly and moved some of the crushed furniture in front of it. The high-pitched barking continued from the other side of the door.

"Okay, change of plans." Joe put his back against the wall and crouched down. "But listen. There's a dead body up there. Don't look at it. It can't hurt you, so don't be scared."

Tine turned toward Joe with a look of exasperation.

"You're kidding, right?"

"Look, I just didn't want it to freak you out."

"I'll be fine. Just boost me up."

Joe laced his fingers together and held his hands low, so Tine could set her foot for a boost. She jumped to help, but Joe didn't need it. She was surprisingly light.

"The bag is in the backroom," Joe whispered. "It's heavy," *probably heavier than you*, he thought, "so be careful."

"Yeah, whatever," Tine called down to him.

* * *

The doors to the bedrooms were all open, spilling shafts of sunlight through their windows into the hall. The body of the mutant cannibal was cast in light and shadow, dead where it dropped. Lying on its back atop a gelatinous crimson paste, one unblinking eye staring sightlessly beyond the skin flap that obscured the top half of the eyeball at the ceiling. And her heart sank.

For all her bravado, she was still a child, and the sight of this lifeless mutated man upset her. She'd absorbed so much horror that she had almost become numb to death, but something about this dead brute made her sad.

"Snap out of it!" She scolded herself. "This is probably the animal who tied my mother to the post. The one who would have tied me out there."

But she still pitied the man. Even in her youth, she understood the violence inherent in her world, fueling the chugging, churning machine that, through death, sustained life. A necessary evil as accepted as the rising and setting of the sun. Rape, robbery, murder, even the disassembled horses in the barn all just par for the course in her world. And didn't that make this dead man as much a victim as she? She couldn't guess his age, but she was sure that he was younger than her parents, and even they were too young to remember the world before the split.

Before she passed, Tine's grandmother told her about the peace and joy of her youth before it was befouled by evil men. She said it wasn't man's

209

nature to destroy but that some men, perhaps they had been fed with sour milk, were hellbent on destruction.

She told her of the cold winter night in Poland when her family, along with thousands of other families, trudged through a dark train yard dragging along what possessions they could. How they were prodded up slick planks onto frozen train cars destined for a place called Belzec. She told her of the icy wind that cut through the open slats of her boxcar and the old couple who had frozen to death clinging to one another. Her grandmother told her that word made its way from the front of the train. They were headed to a death camp. Grandma said that some on the train cried, some screamed, and others prayed for mercy. Their mercy came in the form of an explosion that toppled the train and sent the cars piling into the snowy countryside. Tine learned that her grandfather suffered a broken neck and was left to die in that boxcar. Her grandmother, great-grandmother, and the other survivors walked through frozen fields and forests bound for areas controlled by the Soviet Union in the hope of finding sanctuary.

Her grandmother told her that they had to escape Poland or be slaughtered by the Nazis. She said that they eventually found their way to Denmark. There she boarded a ship bound for Great Britain. Her great-grandmother found work and eventually saved enough to book passage on a steamer from Europe to New York's Ellis Island. It was on that ship that she met Tine's grandfather. She remembered the tears that filled her grandmother's eyes as she remembered seeing the Statue of Liberty. Her message to Tine was simple. Hate burns hot and fast, but love endures.

Her reminiscence was disturbed when a cloud passed overhead, giving the illusion of movement to the corpse. Tine staggard backward and tumbled into one of the bedrooms striking the back of her head against a dresser, dislodging something wedged behind it.

"Tine! Are you okay?" Joe called up in a harsh whisper.

"I'm fine; I just tripped," she replied. She got to her feet and slid the dresser away from the wall to find a photo album. Tine thumbed through page after page of black and white photos. Early shots of the stables and a young girl riding a great black horse in a paddock. Tine was sure the girl's long flowing hair was as red as hers.

"Tine! What are you doing up there?" Joe called again, this time sounding a little angry.

"I'll be right down," she called back.

Tine wrapped both arms around the photo album and hurried to the back room where Joe told her she would find the satchel. She stuffed the book into the bag and returned to the landing.

"Got your bag," she said.

"That's great. Drop it down," Joe said as he held his arms out to catch.

Tine paused. She looked at the drop and then at Joe.

"How do I know you won't leave me?"

Joe smiled sadly. "You have my word, Tine."

She looked down, knowing she could make the jump but not sure that she wouldn't turn an ankle. She chewed her lower lip as she considered her options. It was clear that she didn't fully trust Joe.

"Leave the bag and jump down. I'll catch you," Joe said.

She stopped chewing and dropped the bag.

Joe caught it and set it down.

"Just sit your butt on the edge and drop. I won't let you fall."

She did as she was told and dropped into his waiting arms. He caught her, and she felt safe. She threw her arms around his neck and held tight.

"What are you doing?" Joe asked as he returned the hug.

"Nothing," she said. "Thanks for not dropping me."

* * *

Together they stood in the yard facing the cannibals' house. Joe hated wasting the oil and the second lamp, but if ever a place needed to be wiped off the map, this was that place. He lit the wick with a piece of flint and the steel blade of his hatchet. Drawing back his arm, he heaved the firebomb through the window into what was the living room. They stood side by side and watched the fire consume the grisly little farmhouse until nothing but the smoldering foundation remained. Joe wished they could cleanse their memories as easily. With the sun still hovering in the east, the two set off for Assumption, pushing them deeper into the western territories.

212

Chapter 30

Alistair climbed the stairs from the cabins below and was greeted by a blood-red sky and a nervous-looking crew.

"What's wrong with them?" he asked.

"We're in for a squall," replied Cage, who had already been standing on deck when Alistair came up. "And a bad one by the looks of it," he said, staring out at the open water.

It began as flashes of lightning that spider-webbed across the breadth of the sea. By midday, the wind had started to pick up and seemed to be coming from every direction. Still, Captain Sarros was able to steer Serenity toward Pico de Orizaba. The crew and the travelers ate a quick lunch of a pasty cereal not unlike oatmeal. Some of the crew complained. Arben laughed and told them they would thank him when it came back up.

The first raindrops, about the size of hen's eggs, landed with solid plops on Serenity's deck just around 1400 hours. Time had come for Alistair and his companions to put their training to the test. The sky darkened to a crimson-purple, and Serenity listed heavily to port as the winds increased. The bosun and topman climbed the rigging, up and over the futtock shrouds, disappearing into the darkness above. The rain began to beat the deck in a thunderous roar soaking everyone and everything topside.

"Mr. Villwock! Strike the Royals!" Sarros called as he lashed himself to the ship's wheel.

"Aye, captain!" The orders relayed up both masts until reaching the top where the royals were lowered and secured, and Serenity came partway back to true.

"Mr. Villwock! Maintain course and strike the top gallants!"

"Aye, captain!"

Again, the orders were relayed up the masts. Alistair watched as the top gallants fell and were secured.

Electric fingers reached down from the webbing above. Alistair waited, expecting discharges to vanish, but that didn't happen. The bolts attached themselves to the ocean and remained like strange bright barren trees. He could feel his eyes beginning to burn but couldn't look away.

Cage grabbed Alistair by the shoulders, spun him, and yelled so he could be heard over the sound of the thunder and the wind. "Don't look into the flashes, you old fool! Do you want to go blind?"

Alistair pressed his eyes shut and shook his head. "No, no, I don't."

"Gentlemen!" Sarros called. "This storm intends to drag Serenity down and us along with her. So unless you want your journey to end here, you best get to your stations!"

As if on cue, the wind picked up and pushed Serenity hard, listing her again to port. The pastreco, who had positioned himself in expectation of the order to reef the mainsail, lost his footing and went sliding helplessly from starboard to port across the deck. With one hand gripping rigging, Cage reached down, catching him at his wrist as he passed.

"Hang on!" cried the black giant.

Their skin was wet with rain and slippery, and Cage was struggling to keep his comrade from falling. Hearing Cage call out, Alistair began to move along the fife rail.

"Hold your position!" Cage screamed into the raging wind. "Better to lose one than to lose all!

Alistair moved back as he was told, as Cage and the pastreco locked onto one another's wrists. Knowing Cage was right, Alistair reluctantly rejoined Reka at the rigging. Less than thirty minutes into the fight, Alistair had never felt so exhausted in all his life. All he'd been doing was holding on, but that was no small task considering the torrents of water washed over Serenity's deck, pushing everything that had not been secured into the sea. Alistair looked out over the port-side rail seeing only blackness. Then the wind died, and for a moment, time stood still. *Could it be over?*

"Brace!" cried Captain Sarros.

Alistair turned just in time to see the sea, reaching for the heavens disappearing into the grim darkness above. The wall of water hung there for the briefest of moments before crashing down onto Serenity and her crew. Cage lost his hold on the pastreco, and he slipped away into the chaos.

Sarros stood drenched but resolute in the face of the storm. "Mr. Villwock! Strike the gallants and fore course. Reef the mainsail!"

Again, the order was repeated across the deck and up the masts.

"Ranger! Haul the mainsail down to reef!" Cage ordered.

"Aye!" Alistair replied.

The saltwater stung eyes and brined lips, but the small unit set about its tasks short one member.

"Ranger! Haul down on the luft kreigle line!"

"Aye!"

"Ranger! Hoist the mainsail! Reka! Re-tension-up the halyard!"

"Aye!" they both replied.

"Reka! Move to the clew and haul down on that line!"

"Aye!"

Despite the absence of the pastreco, not a beat was missed as the greenhorns reefed the mainsail to assure that Serenity would not lose her forward momentum. The captain ordered the raising of the storm jib, and Serenity was ready for battle.

With their work done, for the time being, Reka and Alistair moved toward the stern of the ship to make sure they were out of the way. The pastreco lay crumpled, unconscious, piled into the bulwark. Alistair and Reka worked until they revived him and then secured themselves and the pastreco to the stern rail. Serenity pitched high, crested a towering wave, and then began her plunge into the trough. Held fast by his tie-down rope, Alistair remained secured to the vessel, but his stomach lurched as his body lifted off the deck. Pain replaced nausea when Serenity reached the bottom of the trench, and he smashed back onto her deck.

There was tranquility in that moment. The peals of thunder muffled by the liquid walls of their aquatic amphitheater. Alistair looked up at the water stretching skyward in all directions, disappearing into the incredible mess that hung over their heads. It seemed to him that Serenity herself stopped to admire the sight. Alistair thought of Moses leading his people across the Red Sea. But the peace was short-lived.

"Tie off and brace men!" Sarros ordered.

The sea came crashing down on Serenity, dragging her and her crew deep below the surface.

Alistair blinked a few times, and the stinging went away. He could feel the water rush into his ears as he watched everyone and everything that had not been tied down float away into the cold water of the Southern Sea and then disappear into the black. He watched some of the men who were unable to hold their breath, or perhaps simply didn't have time to draw theirs deep enough, claw frantically at their own tie-down lines choosing to take their chances with their lost comrades in the hopes of finding precious air somewhere above them. Alistair knew that the men who had floated off were lost to the sea and that as long as he could stay tied to Serenity, there was still hope. And he was sure the men working feverishly to free themselves knew it too. But some other force, a force that must lie dormant until that moment, that brink of death moment, seemed to seize control and steal reason. Willing to do anything to protect itself from extermination, even to the detriment of the man it inhabited.

One of the sailors, Alistair, remembered him as one of the men who complained about Arben's pre-storm meal, pulled a knife from his boot, slid the blade between his chest and the rope, and slashed himself free of his bindings. When she was pulled under, Serenity rolled onto her side, and the man swam straight away from her deck, moving parallel to the ocean floor until Alistair could no longer see him. Others, not as disoriented as the complaining man but responding to the same strange force, unlashed themselves and reached hand over hand up invisible watery ladders until they too disappeared into the black water or simply stopped moving and hung like phantoms overhead.

Suddenly, as if possessed by her own unseen force, Serenity pointed her bowsprit skyward, rocketed upward, and breached the surface like a magnificent sea creature coming up for air.

Serenity had barely broken the waterline when Kohlhagen sounded the ship's bell calling the men to their rescue stations.

"Launch the longboats!" Captain Sarros called.

Two remained of Serenity's three longboats, and they were swiftly loaded and lowered into the water. Alistair ran to the rail, hoping to assist with the rescue efforts. It was too dark and the sea too tumultuous to see much of anything, but he had to try. He scanned back and forth across Serenity's starboard side, squinting against the ocean spray and pouring rain, and then he saw it. A single light dancing on the water. The men in the longboats could not see above the waves and had to rely on their mates aboard Serenity to spot for them.

"There!" Alistair yelled, pointing at the light just off the stern of the longboat.

The oarsman turned in the direction he was pointing and rowed hard. The light vanished beneath the surface and faded from view with rescue only a few feet away. Alistair's heart sank with the lost sailor, but he couldn't mourn him now. He had work to do. Off to the right, another light appeared.

"There!" Alistair called, pointing at the new light.

The longboat reached the man, pulled him aboard, and looked to Alistair for another rescue. Alistair scanned the water but saw nothing.

"Ranger!"

Alistair looked up. Reka had climbed the rigging for a better view.

She was pointing back to the area where he saw the first man. Alistair couldn't see a thing but put his faith in her and returned the longboat to look for the sailor. Soon he lost sight of the boat as it disappeared behind waves. Alistair looked to Reka, hoping she could direct them. Reka flailed her arms wildly and screamed into the storm, but he could see by her defeated posture that it was no use. The men in the rescue boat had no idea she was up in the rigging.

Alistair grabbed a lamp and tried to light it, but that too was hopeless. Being submerged had left the wick and the flint drenched. He looked around in frustration, felt a hand clamp onto his shoulder, and turned to see the pastreco. The pastreco held out his hand and opened it to reveal a bright white bioluminescent stone. Alistair seized it and scurried up the rigging behind Reka. He held the stone out to illuminate her from behind, and when the rescue boat looked back toward Serenity for direction, they saw her. She directed them to a second and then a third rescue. Then she signaled to the second longboat to rescue two additional sailors.

"Mr. Kohlhagen! Call the longboats back!" The captain ordered.

"Aye, captain!"

"What are they doing?" Alistair yelled to Cage from the rigging. "There are probably more men out there!"

"The captain cannot risk losing the whole boat to save a few. The sea will have them. Now get back down here! We must prepare to get underway." With the longboats secured, Sarros gave the order once again.

"Ranger! Reka! Reef the mainsail!"

Alistair and Reka reached the deck and got to work. The pastreco came along from behind Cage to lend a hand.

"Welcome back, priest!" yelled Cage.

"I'm not a priest!"

Alistair noticed the look of relief on Cage's dark stone face. It seemed that his group was growing closer. They accomplished their task, and Serenity had regained forward momentum.

"Mr. Kohlhagen, See to that storm jib!"

They battled through the dying breaths of the mighty storm well into the night, the sun never making another appearance that day.

A lesser ship and captain would surely have succumbed to the relentless beating, but Serenity was indomitable, her captain, fearless, and so the surviving Maristo would have another tail to tell.

* * *

Daybreak of the sixth day found Cage Abrams standing at the bowsprit as they reached the entrance to the harbor at Pico de Orizaba. Two towering, white monoliths marked the entryway and the point at which any ship entering was required to strike their colors. Carved into the white stone faces of the monoliths were the Twenty-Four Laws of Pico de Orizaba. Among them were warnings against killing, warnings against theft, against rape, cheating, providing false witness, bearing arms; the list went on and on. And while the list of crimes was extensive, the penalty for all twenty-four was the same. Death.

The method of carrying out the penalty was also brutally clear. Scattered about the entrance to the harbor was the guilty. Some long dead, others not so long, and a couple waiting for their punishment to be carried out by the rising tide. They cried out for help, but the law was also clear on aiding criminals, and Cage had no intention of joining them. Their hands, like those of the dead bobbing up and down around them, were bound. Their feet were tied to weighted stones with just enough rope to allow their heads above water. Orizaba's criminal element was kept afloat by small buoys affixed around their necks, on display as a warning to all. Gruesome, to be sure, but only a temporary distraction to Cage Abrams.

His eyes scanned the harbor for his one true love, The Andalusia. Cage wasn't a fool. He knew the odds were against him, but he hoped for a miracle. The mutineers wouldn't have stayed on the Great Lake. Cage was not Maristo. He was an independent, just one of many, but well known to the Maristo as was the Andalusia. Had the mutineers remained on the Great Lake, they would have run across the Maristo, and to a man would have all been hung. They had to sail out to sea, and with the Andalusia not being very large, they would have had to find safe harbor, especially in a storm like the one that almost took Serenity down. And if they remained in the South Sea, there was only one safe harbor that Cage knew of.

As Serenity cleared the floating cemetery and waited to be directed to their mooring by the harbor pilot, Cage used the spyglass he had borrowed from Kohlhagen and passed it over the water. The Andalusia was off to port, secured to a mooring, minus her skiffs. Her name had been changed, and she was now called Peccatum, but he knew his Andalusia. His eyes welled with tears. The truth was, Cage would have gone anywhere to protect Reka, but this was the real reason he had made the journey. The one in a million chance to see his beautiful Andalusia again. To see her and set right the past. He thought of the mutineers enjoying time ashore, unaware of the black storm headed their way.

Chapter 31

Tine sat humming a tune and warming herself in a shaft of sunlight that found its way through the leafy canopy above. Her tongue poked out from the corner of her mouth as she worked to fashion a slingshot from a Y-shaped branch and a section of inner tube she'd rescued from a disabled bicycle abandoned on the side of the road.

"Are you humming Burn by Deep Purple?" Joe asked.

Tine tilted her head and looked at him. "I don't know what any of that means, Joe."

"The song you're humming."

"It's Gershwin. It's called Fascinating Rhythm. My mother loved Gershwin."

Joe felt silly remembering that Tine's world had split from his about five years before the birth of Rock and Roll. "Oh, well, it sounds like another song I know. If you're good, maybe I'll tell you about something called Rock and Roll one of these days."

But Tine wasn't listening to Joe. "Shh," she said.

"What?" Joe asked, not lowering his voice.

Tine pressed her finger to her lips and gestured for Joe to be quiet.

"What is it?" Joe whispered.

"Tickers!" Tine whispered back, her eyes wide with terror.

Joe paused to listen. "I don't hear anything."

Tine tucked the slingshot into her back pocket and began grabbing up her gear. "Grab your shit, Joe; we have to move."

"But I don't—" A rapid-fire ticking sound rose and fell in the distance.

Joe slung his pack, carried his repeater low, and moved west from camp. The morning sun shone through the trees in jagged, blinding shafts. They'd only gone about two hundred feet when Tine stopped, placed a hand on Joe's forearm, and held a finger, first to her lips and then moved it to her ear. He took her meaning; be quiet and listen. Now, Joe heard what sounded like twigs snapping nearby and more ticking. As he listened more closely, he picked up a distinct pattern in the ticking sound. Some slow, some fast, some single ticks, and some sounded like a dozen in rapid succession, but all just above a whisper and expressed in a call and response cadence. The sounds were foreign and confusing to Joe, who had no idea what they meant or which direction they were coming from. Tine tugged his forearm, and they began moving again through the shafts of light. As they continued walking, the ticking rose to a fever pitch, followed by the sound of running feet.

"They're coming, Joe, run!"

Tine broke into a full sprint. Joe had all he could do to keep up. She had a lean runner's body and darted in and out of the trees like she had been born for just that purpose. Joe took more of the straight-ahead approach as the ticking sounds began to fall somewhere behind. Then Joe heard a heavy whomping sound, like a propeller blade cutting through the air. Tine must have heard it, too, because she ran toward Joe and pulled him off the path and in front of a tree. He watched as a bola wrapped itself around the trunk of a tree on the path ahead of them. He would have been ensnared and taken to the ground had she not moved him. Joe leveled the repeater and fired two shots blindly, in the direction the bola came from. No one cried out, but the ticking fell even farther behind. Joe and Tine took off again and continued to create distance between themselves and the tickers, and before long, it seemed that they had lost their pursuers.

* * *

The grinding of the cart's wooden wheels against the dirt and rocks on the trail almost covered the sharp report, but Hayward knew what he had heard. Two loud rifle cracks in the stillness of the morning. They came from southeast of his location, probably someone hunting up in the tree line of the mountain he'd just descended. But who was doing the shooting? The hunted or the hunter. In Hayward's experience, one couldn't be sure. He knew he left the Rangers…what could he call him? The Ranger's squire, his champion? He settled on boy. He'd left the Ranger's boy barricaded in the room at the farmhouse, of that much he was sure. His unseen and uninvited visitor provided the vision of the boy armed with the carbine holed up in that dark room just waiting to shoot him dead. Hayward was obliged to the third eye for that. Otherwise he might have pushed into that room and wound up dead. An unacceptable demise for the son of the king.

He considered burning the place down with the little sneak in it but, in the end, decided toe leave him for the docco. But for some reason the house was burning. That was an assumption based on the smoke he'd seen coming from that direction; that and the fact that he hadn't seen any other structures, homes or otherwise, since he had left with the horse and wagon upon which he currently traveled. As he saw it, there were only two possibilities. One was that the docco tore through the house knocking over a lantern which started the fire. Seemed he'd heard a story of a cow starting a fire back in the 1800s.

The other possibility was that the Ranger's boy started the fire, though Hayward couldn't fathom the reason. But if he had, then the boy would likely head west because east was out of the question, what with the Dead Zone being the only thing in that direction. North and south didn't seem likely either. He couldn't say why; they just didn't. No, the more he thought about it the more he felt that the sound he had heard came from the Ranger's boy's carbine, but he still couldn't venture a guess as to whether he was the hunter or the hunted.

No matter, there wasn't a carbine on the planet that could hit him, given the distance he had put between them. And he was sure they couldn't catch him because there were no other usable horses in the barn. He'd seen to that by cutting the remaining horses' Achilles tendons. An action that had two beneficial consequences. First, it prevented the Ranger's boy from catching him, and second, it would make it easier for the docco to catch and feed on the horses. The docco could probably catch them, hobbled or not, but this would ensure a meal for them and hopefully keep the monsters off his trail.

Thinking of the docco feeding was making Hayward hungry. He was considering dining on some of the meat he took from the man he found laid out for him in the kitchen when he noticed wisps of smoke just up ahead. As Hayward cleared a grove of trees, he came upon a small town called Perseverance. He approached the wall to the city but no one called to him to stop and identify himself. *No matter, the rusted metal structure would have offered little resistance to a god*, he thought.

Passing through the city gate, Hayward discovered a half-mile strip with a couple of roads that branched off the main drag. A saloon that doubled as a hostel where people who worked at a nearby mine could rent a room and a bath. There was a general store and a blacksmith shop, the latter reminding him of the stories he had heard about his grandfather.

Hayward halted his horse and tied him to a hitching post near a trough. Normally he wouldn't concern himself with such things as feeding an animal. Wasn't it free to graze as it walked? But since the trough was there and so convenient, he supposed he would tie it close enough to drink if it had a mind to. Hayward dismounted the cart and stretched his back which snapped and popped in appreciation. The long, lean figure walked into the empty saloon and strode up to the bar. Except for the miners, who were already up and gone, Perseverance was late to rise. With no one to serve him, Hayward walked behind the bar and helped himself to a bottle of whiskey and a jar of pickled eggs. When he had his fill, he walked over to the general store. Unlike the saloon, the general store was not vacant.

"Good morning—sir." The words caught in the shopkeeper's throat.

Hayward looked like something out of a fever dream. His pasty white honeycombed flesh forced bile into the man's throat, and he coughed up a bit of his stomach acid into a handkerchief he'd drawn from his pocket against the visitor's stench.

"Beg your pardon, sir."

But Hayward would not pardon the insolent, pudgy, myopic man. Instead, he lowered his head and allowed his most menacing grin to spread across his face. The shopkeeper was frozen with fear and didn't so much as budge when Hayward slipped behind him. Hayward leaned down and exhaled hot, sour, pickled egg breath on the man's neck. Piss ran down the shopkeeper's legs puddling on the floor at his feet. Hayward could smell the urine, and he felt powerful. Anyone could make a child piss in fear; make a little boy wet himself in his Howdy Doody pajama bottoms. But to make a grown man wet his grown-up pants, well, that took some doing. He could hardly wait for the Fire King to present good old Albert Taft to him and to see him soaked in his own piss, just like this silly bastard in front of him.

Hayward slid his karambit from its sheath and passed it in front of the shopkeeper's face. Sweat blistered across his brow and upper lip.

"Please, sir, take what you want; just don't kill me. I have a wife and child asleep upstairs."

"Are you giving me permission to take what I want?" Hayward whispered into his ear.

A little more piss dribbled out.

"Yes, sir, just please, don't kill me. I have a…"

"Do you think I need your permission to take what I want, you piss-ant?" Hayward roared.

"No, sir! Not at all, sir!" And he released his bowels.

The stench rose into Hayward's nostrils, and he raged. Hayward plunged the knife low into the shopkeeper's back and slid it almost effortlessly up his spine to his shoulders. The shopkeeper crumpled to the floor. Paralyzed and lying in his own droppings, the shopkeeper gulped at the air like a fish tossed onto dry land. Hayward brought his face close to the dying man.

"Now I'm going upstairs to rape your wife and eat your child."

Unwillingly, the man nodded his head in agreement and succumbed to his wounds. Hayward knew he couldn't rape the man's wife, not in the traditional sense anyway. He could hardly remember the last time he was able to get an erection. But the thought of eating a child connected with the pleasure center of his brain. He considered going upstairs and doing just that, but he was still full of eggs, and he knew he had to get back to the business of finding the Fire King. He grabbed supplies from the two shelves in the sparsely stocked general store and made his way back out to his horse and cart. He stowed his plunder and mounted the cart. A quick snap of the reins and the horse was off.

* * *

Joe and Tine reached the edge of the woods and found themselves at a precipice. The valley below was a sea of reds and browns and greens, the colors of America's great southwest. Joe could see a couple of small towns cut into clearings in the valley, and he would have loved to linger and appreciate their peaceful beauty, but they had to get off the mountain. They needed to reach the valley below, but there was no quick way down. Descending the face of the mountain was out of the question. A seasoned climber might not balk at the challenge, but Joe was no climber. Looking to his right, he saw a series of switchbacks that could lead them at least partway down, but it would be slow going. Thoughts pinballed around inside his head.

Should they risk the switchbacks or stand and fight? The switchbacks offered no place to take cover, at least not as far as Joe could tell, and there was no telling how far behind the tickers were. They would have to fight. If they hunkered down and waited, they would have the element of surprise. He was sure there were more than two of tickers, but if he and Tine could ambush them, maybe they could even the odds. One other option popped into Joe's head. They could try and hide, hoping that the tickers would just assume that they made their way down the mountain and move along.

"Tine, do you have any idea how many there were back there?"

"I don't know, unless you can see them and count them, you can never know. One tick sounds just like the next. You can't tell them apart."

Joe had to decide, and he had to decide fast. Enlisting Tine's help, Joe gathered leaves and broken branches of various lengths. He set the four longest branches down side by side with about eight inches of space between each branch. He weaved the shorter branches in between others, making a loose mat. Then he covered the mat with leaves and extended it over the edge on the precipice securing it in place using two large stones hidden by branches. He and Tine repeated the steps twice more, and once the trap was set, they took up positions twenty yards apart and waited. With the sun cutting into the mountain face and blinding anyone walking toward the edge, it might just work.

The ticking started. Joe made himself as small as he could, hiding behind a fallen tree. Two tickers entered the clearing and moved slowly toward the edge. They looked like wild mountain people. The man, bearded, the boy, too young to grow facial hair. They dressed in drab, tattered clothing, except for the yellow sashes worn right to left across their bodies. Their eyes darted around, and their heads cocked at peculiar angles trying to pick up sounds made by the two they were hunting. The young one sniffed at the air like a hound and twice seemed to be looking right at Tine. The adult moved closer and closer to the trap but stopped just short of it. The smaller one joined him, exchanged a few ticks, and called the others forward. It was a good-sized hunting party, seven altogether. The leader, or at least the one who seemed to be in charge, ticked and made a, *go take a look,* gesture with a pointed finger. The adult and the boy moved forward, peering over the edge. Inching farther and farther out, the large male stepped far enough out onto the trap to cause him to lose his balance. He reached back and grabbed hold of the boy's sash, and pulled him down over the edge. No ticks, just screams, as they plummeted to their deaths.

Tine rose up from cover, drew the pocket back on her slingshot, and fired a marble-sized rock. The rock buried itself in one of the men's eye sockets. He clamped a hand over the hole and howled in pain. She quickly rolled another stone from between her fingers, set it in the slingshot's pocket, and fired, snapping the pinky finger of the hand he'd raised over his wounded eye. Joe followed her lead and fired his carbine in rapid succession, dropping the other four tickers where they stood. The man with the shattered finger and the rock in his eye socket staggered sideways and joined his friends in the valley below.

To his surprise, Joe looked at Tine, who stood emotionless over the dead tickers. No joy, no remorse, like a carpenter having driven a nail into a board.

"Are you okay, Tine?"

"I'm fine," she said. Let's see what they've got."

The tickers all wore bolas on their belts and leather pouches on the yellow straps across their torsos. Tine squatted, pulled the pouch off one of the dead tickers, and began rifling through his pockets.

"Here, check this." She tossed a weathered leather pouch on the ground at Joe's feet.

Joe overturned the bag and dumped out its contents. Some dried meat wrapped in a piece of greasy paper, a flint, several little bundles of twigs wrapped in twine. There were three gloves, none a match for the others, and a length of rope. Joe stuffed the items back into the bag and helped Tine search the other dead tickers. Each man carried a knife and several bolas on his belt. Joe removed one of the bolas and examined it. Three sections of thin braided leather straps with rocks about the size of a child's fist tied onto the end of each strap, the other ends joined together. Joe swung it around overhead and threw it clumsily at a tree. The rocks all struck the trunk and dropped.

"No, stupid, that's not how you do it."

Tine grabbed a bola and separated the leather straps between her fingers. She twirled the weapon overhead and sent it sprawling through the air toward the same tree. The bola wrapped itself around the tree trunk.

"That's how it's done."

"Impressive."

She smirked and gave a quick, hard exhale through her nose. They finished searching the dead tickers and made their way down along the switchbacks. Loose gravel, exposed tree roots, and steep angles made for a slow descent. They both had their share of slips and slides, of skinned legs and bruised ass cheeks, but they made it down. It was well past lunchtime when they reached the base.

"You hungry?" Tine asked.

"I could eat," Joe said.

Tine pulled her slingshot, nestled a stone in the pocket, drew and took aim at a pair of ravens circling in the air just to their south, above the dead tickers. She released the stone. Joe could hear it cut through the air and watched as one of the large black birds dropped silently from the sky. Tine dropped another stone in place, fired again, and the second raven spiraled to the ground. Joe stood slack-jawed.

"Well?" Tine said with a raise of her shoulders.

"Oh! Nice job."

"Yeah, thanks. Now, how about you go get them before something runs off with our lunch?"

"Right, you start the fire; I'll grab the birds."

Joe hurried over to the fallen birds and worked his way through the spattered ticker remains. He couldn't help but stare. Two men and a boy, sprawled in crimson pools, left to bake under a merciless sun. Joe shook his head at the waste of life and left them undisturbed. He picked up the birds and carried them to the stream near their temporary camp. Joe was a hunter and made quick work of dressing the game. He grabbed one of the birds in one hand and gave its neck a quick twist pulling its head from its body. He tore the meat from the bones, dunked it into the water, and cleaned off the blood and feathers.

While Joe repeated the process with the second bird, Tine reached into one of the packs she collected from the tickers back up on the ridge and pulled out a twine-wrapped bundle. She kicked at the dirt, made a divot in the ground, and dropped the bundle in. She fished around in the pack again and pulled out a flint and struck it with a knife blade, also taken from the pack. The bundle sparked to life, and she nursed it into a good fire, adding twigs and hunks of broken tree limbs. They skewered the meat on sticks and roasted the bird over the fire. After lunch, Joe and Tine kicked out the fire and continued west toward a red stone wall on the horizon, unaware that they were being watched and followed.

Chapter 32

Chris dropped the pillow and spun around to find Lucas standing at Joe's door staring at her. He was dressed in his light blue hospital gown and matching socks.

"Lucas, you can't be up here! We have to get you back in bed."

She only took her eyes off of him for a second as she glanced down the hall toward the nurses' station to look for help, but everyone had been scared away by the head nurse.

"I'm going to need to grab a wheelch—" She turned back, and he was gone. "Lucas?" Chris hurried to Joe's room and opened the door.

"Lucas?"

She walked deeper into the room, checking corners and the open bathroom, but Joe was alone. She knew it was stupid, but she dropped to her knees to see if there was any way he might have managed to squeeze under the bed. A child couldn't fit under there, and she knew it, but she had to check. Chris fluffed Joe's pillow, checked his monitors, and slipped out of the room.

Stepping back into the hall, she checked both ways to ensure Lucas hadn't popped into the wrong room and then went down to the second floor. The second floor was active with the usual foot traffic, but there was no sign of Lucas. Chris walked toward his room, half afraid he would be there and half afraid he wouldn't. Slowly, she pushed the door open and peeked inside. Lucas was sound asleep in his bed, and Bob was sleeping in the chair next to him. Chris let the door close, and it gave off a tiny squeak.

"Hey," said Bob as he opened his eyes. "Is Joe okay?"

"Sorry, go back to sleep. Joe is just fine; I just checked on him."

"What brings you down here? You miss me?"

"I was just checking on Lucas," she smirked, "but of course, I missed you. It's been over an hour." She said it with a smile, but Bob could read the worry in her eyes.

"What's wrong?"

"Bob, has Lucas been here since we got him in bed?"

"Well, I dozed off for a bit, but yeah, I think so. Why?"

"I just saw him, Bob; I just saw Lucas. He was up on three."

He gave her a quizzical look.

"Yeah, he was standing by Joe's room."

"Just now?"

She nodded.

"Upstairs?"

"Yeah, I even spoke to him, and then he—he just vanished." She lowered her voice. "Bob, there's something spooky about that guy."

"That there is, babe."

The word slipped from his lips, but Chris didn't seem to notice.

They had been getting closer, but that was the first time a term of endearment had been used. Chris motioned for Bob to follow her out into the hall.

"Bob, it was so weird, ya know? I mean, I would have had to almost walk through him to get to the couch, and then—"

"Then what?"

"You know how you can tell when someone's watching you, right?"

"Sure," Bob nodded his agreement.

"Well, there he was. Standing there, staring at me."

"Chris, remember what we were talking about before? You asked me where '*there*' was?"

"Yes. You asked Lucas how you could get *there*."

"Well, Lucas is what they call a *remote viewer*." Bob made finger quotes.

"What's that?" She asked.

"He can look in on people in other places. And I know it sounds crazy, but—" he hesitated."

"What is it?" She prompted.

Bob ran his hands through his hair. "I don't know; he says he can even see into other worlds or something."

Chris didn't say a word, this was the most ridiculous conversation she'd ever been a part of, but then again, she had never worked psych.

"I'm not saying I'm totally sold, Chris, but if the remote viewing thing is even a little bit true, it would explain his being able to see you."

"Maybe, but it doesn't explain my being able to see him."

Bob gave his head another scratch.

"Well, let's wake his ass up and ask him."

Chris was not in the habit of waking sleeping patients. She didn't even like doing it for meds, but curiosity got the better of her.

"Fine, but let's make it quick."

Chris had meant to ask Bob about the asshole doctor, but it slipped her mind at the moment. They walked back into the room.

"Hey! Wake up."

"Bob, easy does it. We don't want to give the guy a heart attack."

Lucas was stirring but still not awake.

"Lucas, can you hear me?" Chris asked gently.

No response.

"Easy does it, my ass."

Bob grabbed his shoulder and gave Lucas a shake.

"Wake up, dipshit, we gotta talk."

Still no response, and that worried Chris.

"Bob, something's wrong."

She tapped him lightly on his cheeks, calling his name; nothing. She forced open his eyelids and shined her penlight into his pupils. The second her light hit his unresponsive pupils, the room went dark, and the emergency light in his room flickered to life.

"That was weird," she said as she checked to make sure the monitors attached to Lucas were still functioning correctly. Satisfied, she went back to trying to wake Lucas. Both of Lucas' eyes were wide open.

"Oh my gosh, Lucas, you had us worried."

But Lucas gave no indication that he'd heard her.

"Lucas?" Chris rechecked his pupils for dilation.

"Luke!" Bob stood up and yelled in his face.

Chris raked her knuckles over his sternum, a painful but effective way to arouse an unresponsive patient, but it didn't faze him.

"Holy shit, is he dead?" Bob asked.

She hit the emergency button and then checked his pulse. "No." His pulse was weak, and his breathing was shallow, but he was most certainly alive. Chris ran into the hall. The emergency lights cast a dim haze over the entire floor, and the call light above every room flashed in unison as if they were all connected to one button.

"Chris, what's going on?" Jenny, one of the floor nurses asked.

"I have no idea, but I need help down here, now!"

Jenny and the nurse standing with her when the lights went out started to run over to help.

"One of you page Doctor Belter and tell him to get his ass down here," Chris yelled as she pushed back into Lucas' room.

"Chris, what's going on?" Bob asked.

"You're going to have to wait in the hall."

She was already moving things around in the room to make space for the rest of the medical staff she summoned.

"But what's going on?"

"Please, Bob, just wait in the hall, and I'll come out and talk to you when I know something."

Bob's face dropped, and Chris felt it.

"I think he's gone catatonic, sweetie, now please, just give us room to work."

"Come on, we need you out of here," said one of the other nurses as she ushered him out of the room. He stepped out but peered in through the small window in the door as another nurse pushed past him and went in.

"They said it's like this on every floor," she said as the door closed behind her.

"Chris, his pulse is dropping!"

"Get the defibrillator in here in case his heart stops," Chris ordered. "And where the hell is Belter?"

Jenny ran back out and down the hall to grab the defibrillator, and when she returned, Dr. Belter was with her.

"What the shit is going on around here?"

"I don't know; I came in to check on Mr. Travidi and…."

"Not that!" bellowed the doctor. "The whole damned place has gone haywire."

"It's probably just a power outage," offered one of the other nurses.

"Screw the power outage. I was just up on six doing rounds with Doctor Morgan and Doctor Green. We have thirteen patients up there, and they all went catatonic right when the lights went out."

Belter went right to work on Lucas. "Then I come down here and…" He rubbed his forehead and exhaled in exasperation. "How long has he been like this?"

"Since the lights went out," Chris answered uneasily.

Belter scribbled something onto a notepad and handed it to one of the nurses. "Go fill this," he ordered. "We're going to try him on clonazepam and midodrine. And Chris, I'm going to need you to stay with him and call me if his blood pressure doesn't come up and stabilize." Chris nodded.

"In the meantime, I'm going up to three. They paged me right after you."

* * *

Bob stopped Belter as he exited Lucas' room. "Hey Doc, how's he doing?

"Well, Bob, it's really too soon to say. We are going to try and stabilize him for now, and then maybe we can see what we're up against."

"What happened?"

"Bob, with all due respect, I don't have time to walk you through this. We have at least fourteen patients in catatonic states and your friend Joe who is in a coma. We are going to have to run tests, check other hospitals in the area, and see if they have patients presenting like this."

It seemed to Bob that the doctor was talking more to himself. Belter paused, and Bob waited.

"You know, it's the damnedest thing."

"What's that, Doc?"

I've been with Saint Anthony's for twelve years, and I have only had one patient go catatonic in all that time."

"Really?" Bob asked.

"You're a cop, right?"

"Yeah, I'm a cop."

"So, you've seen some weird shit, right?"

"You could say that."

"So, listen to this and, ya know, tell me what you think."

"I'm all ears, Doc."

"So, the last time I had a catatonic patient, it was a little boy that they pulled from the Red Hook River. Now here we are, probably 10 years later, and we have another boy pulled from the river."

"I thought Vecchio said they couldn't find him," Bob interrupted.

"And that's another thing. The medics that brought him in said the guy that pulled him from the river saw a glowing ball hovering above the water, and when they made their way to it, the ball vanished, but the kid was right there reaching out of the water."

"Holy, shit," Bob was stunned.

"Holy shit is right. And then there's your buddy Joe, coughing up water and slipping into a coma, Lucas here. He slips into what is presenting as catatonia, and up on six, all thirteen patients went comatose as soon as the power failure hit. Now how do you figure that?"

"That's some weird shit, alright, but you don't know the half of it, Doc. And if I told you, you'd call the guys in the white coats to take me to the funny farm."

"Try me, Bob, 'cause I'm seriously baffled. I mean, fourteen patients all going catatonic at the same time? It's unheard of. It's like we're ground zero for some pandemic?"

"You lost me after baffled doc, but let me tell you what I've been told since I came back to Red Hook."

"Sure, but walk with me while we talk. I want to go check on Joe."

They walked to the stairwell; the elevators had gone into emergency use-only status. As they walked, Bob told Belter the whole story. Joe and his other world, Lucas and his remote viewing, and Bob was right. Belter looked at him like he was out of his mind.

"See, I told you," Bob said.

"Sorry Bob, I don't go in for ghost stories, but you did give me a thought. It's rare, and I mean very rare, but catatonia has been seen as a side effect of certain medications used to treat some patients suffering from mental illness. Maybe that's what we're dealing with here."

They arrived at Joe's room and went inside to check on him. Like the rest of the hospital, the call light above his door flashed, and the room was lit a single emergency light that flickered dimly above the bed where Joe lay seemingly unfazed by the goings-on.

Chapter 33

The bay at Orizaba was filled with ships, warships, cargo transports, fishing trollers, and not one flew their colors. Pico de Orizaba was a neutral zone, and hostilities were not allowed. Captain Sarros explained that, for the most part, the sailors policed themselves. But, when that failed, La Fuerza, Orizaba's heavily armed police force, would quickly, and at times, fatally restore peace.

"The offenders who survived were worse off than those killed by La Fuerza," Sarros said. "As a matter of formality, they would be taken before El Reconciliador, and after being found guilty, they would be sentenced to morto de maro, death at the will of the sea."

"Don't you mean *if* they were found guilty?" Reka asked.

Sarros laughed. "Dear lady, they are always found guilty."

Alistair, as a lawman, appreciated their swift form of justice, but Reka seemed apprehensive. "So if someone were to attack me, and I defended myself, I would be—"

Sarros shrugged his shoulders. "Perhaps it's best we don't find out."

Serenity followed the harbor pilot to her assigned dock, and in keeping with the law, the crew and travelers stowed their weapons before disembarking. Alistair was grateful to feel dry land under his feet as he and his fellow travelers stepped off the dock and onto the beach. They made their way into a lush tropical paradise of huge plants with leaves large enough for a man to use as a blanket and flowers more colorful than any Alistair had ever seen. Well-worn paths cut through the foliage led them from the beach into the little villages spread across the island. As they walked,

Alistair watched birds, more colorful than the plants, as they flew in and out of trees high overhead. Trees that were heavy with bananas, mangos, and fruits he'd never seen before. And all of it there for anyone to take and eat.

Sarros led his officers and Alistair's team to a cantina just off the beach, where they stopped for drinks and listened to local musicians playing mariachi and salsa music. Meanwhile, the rest of the crew went to work procuring the additional provisions needed for the next part of the trip. The men were free to take as much fruit as they thought they could use but had to bargain and pay for other things they needed. Things like rum, gunpowder, and fuel oil for the ship's lanterns. One contingent had been sent out to find a craftsman to repair the damage done to the storm jib. The crew would have time for recreation once their work was done, but paradise or not, work came first, even for the few sailors who had small families on the island.

Lodging on land for visitors was hard to come by and costly. Most sailors simply returned to their ships to sleep, but Alistair and his friends were landlubbers, and they needed a good night's rest on terra firma. Captain Sarros and his crew were well known and well-liked by Hernando Cristobal, the ruler of the island, though he preferred to be called El Presidente.

"Presidente! Como esta?"

"Capitan Sarros, it is good to see you, my friend."

Presidente Cristobal was a striking figure at almost six feet tall and broad across the shoulders. He wore a brilliant white suit festooned with medals and ribbons and chomped on a big black cigar.

"Welcome home!"

"You know Serenity is my home," Sarros said with a smile.

"Well then, welcome to your home away from home."

"Thank you, Presidente."

"If there is anything you need while in Pico de Orizaba, you have only to ask."

"Thank you, but we're only here for the night. We're bound for the Western Territories in the morning."

Cristobal's face contorted into a look of confusion. "No, you are joking. There is nothing good there. The sailors have abandoned the port towns. They say Assumption has been lost to the dead. Even your own Maristo have fled the mainland."

"The dead, how can that be?" Sarros questioned.

"I do not know, my friend, but I suggest you heed the warning. Look around you. Why would anyone choose to leave paraiso?"

Sarros jutted a thumb at the pastreco. "The priest here says it's a sacred mission."

"I am not a priest, I am pastreco."

Cristobal shook his head. "Well, I would not presume to tell a priest not to do God's work. I only know what the sailors have told me."

"I'm not a priest," the pastreco repeated, but it seemed he went unheard.

"Tell me more about this sacred quest," Cristobal asked.

"There is a man who calls himself Dioj Volos."

"God's will?"

"Yes; The priest tells me that he is a fallen brother who has turned against God."

The pastreco didn't bother correcting them again because Sarros got the only part that mattered correct. The pastreco joined in to explain that Dioj Volos was amassing an army and hunting for a weapon that would turn night into day and reduce every living thing in the territories to ash.

Cristobal listened intently and then spoke. "Again, I would not presume to contradict God. As long as you are here, you are welcome to use my cabanas, and my men will see that you have anything you need for your voyage."

The president's private ocean-side cabanas were as luxurious as anything the island had to offer.

"Thank you, Presidente, you are a good friend."

Hernando Cristobal held his hands up in a humble gesture. "Please, my friend! It is my pleasure and sacred duty as a man of God to see his agents are well rested for battle. I will have Rosa, my personal chef, prepare dinner for you and bring it to the cabanas."

Sarros bowed slightly with his hand over his heart. "You are too generous, Presidente."

"Nonsense. Now, I have much to do, my friend. Please enjoy your stay on Pico de Orizaba. Our island and her people are at your service."

Cristobal excused himself, and the crew from Serenity walked the path that opened to a beach with sand as fine as powder, sparsely dotted with white tents and several bonfires. Still not fully recovered from their battle with the storm and sapped by the midday heat, Alistair and Reka settled in for a siesta and later woke to music and the most wonderful smell ever to enter Alistair's olfactory. Rosa, a lovely woman native to the island, had prepared an excellent meal of fresh fruit and fish served on a bed of rice garnished with red salsa, corn, cilantro, and cheese. Alistair had never tasted anything like it and paid his compliments to Rosa by refilling his bowl several times. After dinner, they all drank rum and listened to tales spun by some of the island's elders. As enjoyable as it was, Alistair noticed that Reka looked sad.

"What's wrong?"

"Nothing," she replied, "it just reminds me of the last night I spent with Joe. You remember, don't you? We all had dinner and listened to the storytellers. Before the freebooters attacked our camp and drove us into the woods."

"And thankfully to Savista," Alistair added.

"Of course, and I am grateful to them," she said. "But I miss Joe so much."

"I know you do, child, and I remember it as if it were yesterday. And you can tell him all about the storm we faced when you see him."

Reka smiled and rested her head on Alistair's shoulder. "Do you really think we'll find him?"

"I know we will."

"And what about what the presidente said? He said that even the Maristo has fled the mainland. He said that it had fallen to the dead. What does that mean?"

"I don't think I wouldn't put much stock in sailor's stories."

Alistair sat with her in the soft light of the setting sun.

"Maybe when all of this is over, we can all come and live here." Alistair looked out to the sea. I could see settling here with Siobhan and Thea. We could live out our lives right here on this beach, free of worry. No more freebooters, docco, or whatever else might come."

Reka took a deep breath and exhaled slowly. "And we could bring Eva. I think she would love it here."

To Alistair, Pico de Orizaba was paradise. It was like heaven on earth. The islands only blemish, the floating graveyard, which he saw as proof that some men just have garbage souls. Men who could not be civil to one another and obey the law in a place of such beauty and abundance needed to be scrubbed from the face of the earth.

"Alistair, have you seen Cage?" Reka asked, snapping him from his private thoughts.

"No, maybe he met a senorita." Alistair said with a smile.

"Maybe," she said and rested her head against Alistair's shoulder again.

* * *

Cage slipped silently into the water from Serenity's deck and swam to the Andalusia. He entered on her starboard side, where the main mast cast a shadow in the bright moonlight. One sentry remained topside but was asleep on a bundle of coiled rope with a bottle clutched to his chest. Cage took his bearded axes and delivered simultaneous blows to both sides of the man's neck, freeing his head from his body and sending it tumbling.

Cage scanned the deck. Finding it vacant, he holstered his axes, dropped to one knee, kissed his first two fingers, pressed them hard into the wood, and rose to his feet. He walked to the bridge, where the worn wood of the ship's wheel welcomed him home with a flood of memories. Terrible, haunting memories of betrayal, murder, and of the boy. The boy he had to abandon to deliver retribution and wrath for the sins of the past. Cage tilted his head back, flared his nostrils, and drew in the thick, tropical air. Hands falling away from Andalusia's wheel and onto his axes. Gripping their handles, Cage made his way down into her black belly. He knew every inch of Andalusia and had no need for light to make his way. Twenty-two men remained sleeping aboard his ship.

Flashes of silver in the moonlight that peeked through the deck prisms glanced off Cage's blades. The bearded axes danced in his hands and quenched their thirst on mutineer blood. One after another, the men fell. They came with knives, maces, and hatchets, but not one landed a blow against Cage. Bodies were strewn from stem to stern by the great black avenger, darker than the night through which he moved. Reaching the captain's quarters, a musket ball smashed through the door, striking Cage in the right shoulder. He raised a foot and splintered the old wooden door. On the bed, a quivering boy of thirteen or fourteen pinned himself against the headboard as he pushed wildly with his feet against the soiled bed covers.

"Please, don't kill me!" Tears streaming down his face, hands pressed out in front as if he was pushing against an invisible wall.

"Where's your captain?" Cage roared.

"Captain Rancor is gone. Please don't kill…"

"Who the fuck is Captain Rancor?"

"Captain Rancor Simms, Captain of the Peccatum?"

"The bilge rat's name is Rico Simms, and this ship is the Andalusia! And I am her captain!" His bellow shook the room.

"Of course, sir, anything you say, just please, let me live."

"Where is Simms?"

The boy raised a trembling finger, pointing at an open portal.

"Please, sir, let me live, and I will serve only you."

The axe caught the boy between the eyes, silencing his whimpering pleas.

Cage worked it free from the young man's skull and walked back through the dead and dying, dumping lamp oil along the way. He climbed from below and smashed the ship's stern lamp onto the deck. Drenched in blood, Cage dove back into the harbor and swam after the coward. Simms reached the shore and ran up the beach towards the jungle. With the glow of his burning ship behind him, Cage emerged, cleansed of the blood of his victims by the water, and gave chase.

"Simms, I have come for you!"

Rico Simms had grown fat as the captain of the mutineers, and Cage was upon him quickly. Simms turned to fire his musket, but having been submerged, the musket failed. Cage lopped his right arm off at the elbow.

Eyes wide with terror and shock, Simms glanced in disbelief at his arm lying at his feet and then at Cage.

"You're, you're dead."

"I am. I have been dead since the day you took my Andalusia, and now, I've come to bring you back to hell with me."

Cage sunk an axe blade into his hip, shattering bone and dropping Simms to the ground. Simms raised his left hand in a pathetic attempt to shield his head, and Cage took that too. Cage remembered the day this man stood over him and pissed in his face to the laughter and applause of the other mutineers. Simms had been his second in command, and as such, was given authority to replace men who fell in battle. In time Simms managed to swell his loyalists to just over two-thirds of the sailors on board the Andalusia. They murdered the rest of the crew as they slept and then went for Cage.

Cage smashed Simms' jaw with the butt of his axe and pulled his tongue from behind the dangling mandible. The axe came down, slicing off his tongue and shaving away part of his jaw, but Cage still was not content to let him die. Simms made guttural noises, his head lolled back and forth on the edge of consciousness. Cage leaned close to what remained of his face, whispered "Andalusia," and struck him dead.

He dropped his axes and turned to face La Fuerza.

Chapter 34

The red stone wall that Joe had spotted in the distance wasn't stone at all, but rather rusted-out cars stacked about three high and curving off in either direction. Joe couldn't imagine where the town had gotten enough cars to construct the peculiar rampart. They walked through the opening in the wall and were greeted by another wall of rusted vehicles about ten feet ahead. Unsure which way to go, Joe looked to Tine, who responded with a shrug of her shoulders.

"Right?"

"Sure, I guess," Tine said, and the went right.

As they followed the curve, the entrance disappeared, and eventually, they walked themselves into a dead end.

"I guess we should head back the other way," Joe suggested.

Tine rolled her eyes and shook her head. "Good idea, Joe."

"No one likes a smart ass, Tine."

They walked back past the opening and followed the curve to the right, where they found another opening and another wall.

"You have got to be kidding me," Joe said. "You pick this time."

Tine picked left, and they found the third and final opening in the concentric circles that guarded the city. They cleared the last wall, saw the town still a half-mile away, and began walking. As they walked, they passed blocks and blocks of concrete foundations. No lumber, piping, or anything else remained, only the footprints of what were once family homes.

It was past suppertime when they reached the first house in the town of Perseverance. Like most places Joe had seen in this world, it had that stuck in the past look. A modest single-story slat board building, its once bright mint green paint faded dull and flat by time and neglect. Joe stopped to admire the 1940 International pick-up truck with words painted on the door.

"What does it say?" Tine asked.

"It says, Amari and Son's Lumber. Mr. Burton had a truck like this back home, only it had BGS painted on the door."

"BGS?" Tine asked.

"Yeah, sorry. Burton's Grocery Store. It was the only grocery store in Red Hook."

"What's Red Hook?"

"It's where I'm from."

"I thought you said you were from Savista."

"I am; look, I'll explain later. Right now, we have to see if anyone's home."

Joe walked up the walkway to the front door and knocked. There was no answer, so he tried again.

"I don't think anyone is in there. Boost me up to the window, and I'll climb in and unlock the door."

"First of all, I don't know that the door is locked," Joe said.

"Well, turn the knob," Tine said as she tried to push past him.

Joe grabbed her by the shoulder, and she pulled away. "And second, we are not breaking into someone's home."

"But there could be supplies in there, Joe! Stuff we need."

"And if there is, we'll find the owner and trade or work for it."

Tine took a step back and put her hand on the hilt of her blade. "You're not trading me for anything, Joe."

Joe took a step toward her, and she withdrew further. "I wouldn't trade you for anything in the world, Tine. I mean, not that I could, I mean you're a person and—this is stupid. You're not property that someone can trade. "I meant that we would trade stuff, like the knives we took from the tickers or," he was at a loss; they really had nothing worth trading. The fearful look on Tine's face began to soften.

"Look," Joe said. "How about if we restart? Did you happen to read the sign as we walked into town?"

Tine shook her head. "I can't read, Joe."

"Well, it said Welcome to Perseverance, Population 60. So there has to be someone around here."

"But what if they're bad people, Joe?"

Joe checked his repeater and loaded a few more bullets into it. "Then we'll deal with them," he said.

Together they walked down the center of what Joe could only assume was Main Street; neither saw a soul. Joe thought of Revelation, the town where he and Alistair stopped hoping to find people and supplies but found instead the church locked tight with the town's supplicants inside. Like this town, Revelation had homes, some with smoke billowing from their chimneys, and Joe stopped and knocked at those doors, but no one answered.

They continued past the first intersection and crossed onto the second block. More of the same; no one answering Joe's knocks. They stopped in front of a building in the middle of the second block. The place looked like every other house on the block, except for the sign out front that read SALOON. Joe knocked. Sign, or no sign, it still looked like a house, and he felt odd about walking right in. But this door gave way to his knocking, so they stepped inside. Windows open, oil lamps burning; the place looked open for business, but it was vacant.

"I don't like it here, Joe. Let's go, let's get out of this place. We can find supplies somewhere else."

"Maybe you're right," Joe said. "Let's keep moving."

They continued down Main Street, almost at the end of the second block, when they heard the faint sounds of people arguing. Again, the place looked like the rest of the houses, but this house had a sign that read General Store. Joe stepped toward the door, and Tine grabbed his arm. "Please, Joe, no."

"It's okay, Tine, you've got my back, and I've got yours. We'll be okay."

He hoped he sounded convincing, but it was hard since he wasn't convinced. He pushed the door open and slid inside with Tine clutching his arm.

"Suppose these hoodlums come back while we're out looking for them…

what then?" One of the men in the crowd asked, addressing a short fat man wearing a black hat with a brilliant brass buckle keeping a black band in place. Joe thought he looked like a pilgrim.

"We understand your concern Olon, but we have to do something."

Voices rose and fell, and there was much murmuring, but slowly the arguing stopped as everyone turned to look at the two strangers.

"Good evening folks, my um… sister and I were hoping to find some food and lodging for the night."

It seemed to Joe that the town's whole population had all crammed into the little store.

"What's your name, boy?" asked the man in the hat.

"Joe, Joe Kott, sir, and this here is my sister Tine."

Tine looked at him with a raised eyebrow.

"Well, Mr. and Ms. Kott, you'll have to run along. We are in the middle of a rather urgent matter; town's business."

"I see," Joe cleared his throat. "We were hoping to stay the night. We'll pay; we aren't asking for something for nothing."

"Young man, if you don't leave…."

"Randall, where are your manners," scolded a woman standing near Joe and Tine. "I'll take them in for the night. Let's go, children."

"You'll what? Now see here!" Randall protested.

"Don't fight me on this, Randall." She was a little shorter than the man with the hat but not nearly as wide.

"But…but, we ain't done yet?"

"But me no buts. We've been here jawing for the better part of the day, and I still ain't heard nothin' worth listening to."

She walked out, leading Joe and Tine away from the general store against a smattering of harrumphs, and hear hear.

"My name is Devlin, the old blowhard up there'd be our Mayor, the honorable Randall Amari."

"Like on the truck," Tine said excitedly.

"That's right! Nice enough fellow, but he likes things, just so, and when they go off-kilter, well, let's just say it throws him."

"What's going on?" Joe asked.

"Well, dear, someone murdered Sam Halverson, the owner of the general store."

"Was it a robbery?" Joe felt his police senses tingling.

"Not really sure. The money was left in the till, but some shelves were cleaned out. The problem is, no one can say if the shelves were full, to begin with."

"Did Sam have any fallings out with anyone?"

"Oh, I doubt it. Sam was a nice man; let you run a tab for better than a month if you needed. No, I can't imagine anyone in Perseverance wanting to do Sam Halverson any harm."

"Was he in debt to any of his vendors?"

"His what?" Devlin asked.

"His vendors, the people who sold him the stuff he put on his shelves."

"Well, I couldn't say. You sure do ask a lot of questions."

"It's a force of habit. I used to be a policeman."

"Oh." Devlin smiled and turned at the 1940 International's back bumper and up the path to the faded mint green house.

"Here we are." She opened the door and invited Joe and Tine in.

"This is your house?" Tine asked.

"For the past forty-two years, dear."

They followed Devlin through a living room that reminded Joe of the Callaghan place; neat and orderly and everything *just so*.

"Then you're married to the town's mayor," Joe said, stating the obvious, and again, Tine rolled her eyes at him.

They passed through a doorway and into a comfortable kitchen that, not so oddly, looked more lived-in than the living room. On the table sat two cups on saucers. Next to one cup and saucer sat an empty plate, presumably from breakfast. Next to the other, a book opened and face down.

"Just as soon as I pick up a little, I was gonna fix supper. Either of you hungry?"

"We sure are," Joe answered for both of them.

"You can wash up in there," Devlin motioned toward a small door off the kitchen. "There's some lye soap on the sink."

Tine went first and came out with a clean face and hands. She even managed to pull her hair into a ponytail that exploded out of the back of her head. It was the first time Joe managed to get a good look at her face, and he was surprised by how pretty she was. Before cleaning up, she looked like some feral child raised by wolves. Now before him stood a perfectly presentable young lady. Upturned emerald green eyes, a soft petite nose, and full lips, all set in a pale, heart-shaped face. The soap also did a number on Tines freckles. The majority being dirt and but blood spatter, washed away.

"What are you looking at?"

"I'm not sure," Joe joked, "but I think it's a girl."

"Ha ha, very funny. Your turn."

"Never mind the teasing," Devlin sounded like a mother. "You look lovely…Tine was it?"

"Yes, ma'am, and thank you."

"Now Joseph, you leave your sister be and let's see if you clean up nearly as well."

Tine snickered, knowing how Joe felt about being called Joseph, and Joe was about to protest but thought better of it. The room was small, maybe 3 feet by 4 feet. The floral pattern wallpaper yellowed with age. Plumbing showed where the toilet once sat, the hole in the floor covered with linoleum that did not match. In place of the faucet, a small hand pump sat on the sink. Joe pumped the handle, and water splashed out. Looking up, he caught a glimpse of himself in the mirror. "I'm one to talk," he said to himself. He soaped up, washed his hands and face, and dried off on a towel hung on the wall. He stepped back into the kitchen to find Tine helping Devlin prepare lunch.

"Take a seat, Joseph," Tine called over her shoulder with a smirk. "Me and Mrs.., umm…."

"Amari dear, and it's Mrs. Amari and I."

"Well, Mrs. Amari and I," Tine said and smiled at her host.

Joe saw Mrs. Amari smile back, and he saw Tine's face light up.

"Almost have lunch ready," Tine continued. "So, you sit down." She leaned over toward Devlin and whispered. "Sometimes I think I'm the adult, and he's the child."

"I heard that!"

Tine and Devlin burst out laughing, and Joe joined in.

"You two don't look a bit alike, but you sure do bicker like a brother and sister."

Joe and Tine exchanged a look.

"It sure is nice to hear laughter in this house again."

"Don't you have any children, Mrs. Amari?"

"Our children are all grown, sweetie. We have two boys. One's living up in Columbia, and the other took on with the Maristo. We don't see either of them but once every couple of years." Her eyes cast downward as she spoke, and the room felt somber.

"Well, I hope you see them again soon." Tine smiled.

"Randall and I are planning a trip to Columbia in the Spring," Devlin replied, and the smile returned to her face. "You two are welcome to stay here as long as you like. I'm sure Randall won't mind."

"Thanks all the same, but we have to get to the seaport in Assumption."

Devlin furrowed her brow and looked at Joe. "Reverie? You're talking about Reverie? Are you telling me that you… you and this child are going to Reverie?"

"Well, we're trying."

"No!" she interrupted; her face suddenly blanched white. "You stay away from that place. It's too dangerous."

"That's what I told him!" Tine said, pointing triumphantly at Joe. "See stupid? It's too dangerous, just like I said."

"Joe, you have to listen to your sister. Reverie is no place for nice folks like you. You wouldn't last an hour in that godforsaken place."

The front door opened.

"Devy, I'm home. Thanks for cocking up the meeting. I just about had a posse ready to…." He stopped dead in his tracks. The two strangers from the meeting were in his kitchen, and Devlin looked like she was about to cry.

"What's wrong, Devy?"

"These two are talking about going to Reverie."

"Reverie?" His voice was rich with incredulity. "In Assumption?"

"Yes, sir Mr. Mayor."

"Don't you; *Mr. Mayor* me, boy! You need to have your head examined!"

Tine narrowed her gaze. "Hey! Leave him alone. Joe's not from around here."

"Where's he from, the moon?" Randall Amari was damned if he would take guff from a little girl in his own home.

"He's from Reka!"

Joe threw her a look. "Savista, well by way of Red Hook."

"Where the heck is Savista?" Randall demanded.

"It's…" Tine started, but Joe took over.

"Savista is in the Midwestern Territories, in the state, or province, or, well whatever, it's in Gerrings."

"Gerrings is a territory son. You sure that's where you're from?"

"Mr., if I told you where I was from, you wouldn't believe me."

"Well, wherever you're from, you ain't going to Reverie."

"I'm sorry to argue, Randall, but we are."

"Hot-dang-it! Mother—I, I mean, Devy and I have spoken!"

With that, Devlin broke down, and Tine ran to comfort her.

"Now you've gone and got my Mrs. all upset."

"I'm sorry, I…."

"It's okay, Devy, they ain't going to Reverie. Only a complete idiot would go near that place."

That made Devlin cry even harder.

"Hot-dang-it!" Randall took off his tall mayor's cap and set it down on the table.

"Will you two get out of here?" Tine yelled.

Joe and Randall scurried out of the kitchen, through the living room, and onto the front porch. Joe wondered if he looked as dazed as Randall. Why hadn't he just shut his mouth? Come the morning, he and Tine would be on the road, never seeing the Amaris again. He should have kept his mouth shut, and he knew it.

"Randall, I'm really sorry about that."

"It ain't entirely your fault. See, about twelve years ago, our son Charles left home; against our will, you understand. Anyway, he joined up with the Maristo in Reverie. We never saw him again, but we heard the stories."

"What kind of stories?"

"Terrible stories, son. Human sacrifice, cannibalism, rapes in the streets; in broad daylight! Every kind of debauchery one could imagine, and plenty one couldn't. I heard they dragged a parson from his church, hacked him to pieces, and roasted his flesh over a fire made with Bibles, hymnals, and the crucifix torn from the alter. Devy and I, well we wanted to go see for ourselves, see if we could find our boy, but we had Benjamin to care for, and frankly, I could never take Devy to a place like that."

"I'm so sorry, Randall."

"That's why we were relieved when Benjamin said he wanted to move to Columbia."

"Is it safer there?"

"Oh, my yes. The city is fortified and protected by the Casavio and four Rangers."

"Where is your Ranger?"

"Our Ranger?" Randall blew air out between his lips and teeth. "Pffff, we ain't seen a Ranger in over a decade."

"But wait, Devlin said you see your sons every couple of years."

"Yeah, I know, but the truth is, we haven't seen Charles since the day he left. I tried to talk Devy into moving to Columbia, near Benji, but she won't go. This is the only place Charles would know to look for us."

"Couldn't you leave word for him here in town?"

"Suggested that son, Devy won't bite. She already told the whole town that we visited him and that he's doing fine. She doesn't want anyone's pity. She's a proud woman."

"Well, like I said, I sure am sorry. Is there anything I can do?"

"You could tell her you changed your mind and you're going to New

Post."

"Where is that?"

"North of the western end of Tomahawk."

"Where's Tomahawk?"

"You're in Tomahawk, son. Are you sure you're okay? You didn't take a hit to the head, did ya?"

"No, like I said, I'm not from around here."

"You have made that abundantly clear, son."

"I thought we were in Dogtown."

"See that mountain ridge out there?"

He pointed east, over the rusting wall, to the barely visible series of switchbacks he and Tine descended, back where they left the dead tickers.

"That's the start of Dogtown. This is the eastern part of Tomahawk. And Tomahawk runs clear out to the sea."

Joe considered the distance, and then another question came to mind.

"Say, Randall; ever heard of Dioj Volos?"

Randall let out a loud ha! "Hogwash son, pure nonsense."

"So, you've heard of him but don't believe in him?"

"No more than I believe in Santa Clause."

The front door swung open Tine stood in the doorway.

"You two," she cleared her throat, "*gentlemen* can come in now."

They got up, brushed the seats of their pants, and entered timidly. Randall with his great buckled hat in hand and Joe staring at the floor.

"I'm sorry, boys," Devlin offered.

"We're the ones who are sorry," they both said, tripping over their apologies.

"I'm sure Randall told you, we haven't seen our son Charles in twelve years."

"He said it has been some time, yes. And I am truly sorry."

Devlin smiled.

"Randall tells me we can reach a port town in New Post; I think maybe we'll head there instead."

"Oh," Devlin's eyes widened. "That is a wonderful idea. I'm so glad

Randall talked some sense into you." She wrapped her arms around Joe and squeezed. "Now sit and eat. Tine worked hard on this meal."

Supper consisted of grilled cheese on what Joe thought tasted like sourdough and tomato soup. It was simple, but it was wonderful, and Tine was grinning from ear to ear. After supper, they all sat on the front porch. Devlin made coffee for the grownups and warm buttermilk for Tine.

"Normally, I like to make a bigger spread at suppertime, but with that fool meeting today, the time just slipped away."

"That's right, Devlin said the shopkeeper was murdered," Joe said in a way that was more of a question than a statement.

"Sam Halverson was his name, salt of the earth." Randall hung his head again, "He sure didn't deserve to go out like that," and sipped pensively at his coffee.

"What way?" Joe asked.

"Not for mixed company, Joe." Randall glanced quickly over at Devlin and Tine.

"Let's see to the dishes, sweetie." Devlin got up, and Tine followed her into the house.

"The bastards knifed him in the back and cut him open, Joe. Poor Sam pissed and shit all over the floor."

"Tickers?

"Hell no, tickers never come into town. They're highwaymen. This had to be some traveler, like—well, like—"

"Like me," Joe said, finishing his thought for him.

"Well, yeah, sorry to say."

"Where exactly was he killed?"

"Right where I was standing. Thought it seemed appropriate that we form a posse right where Sam was killed."

"Who processed the crime scene?"

"Who what now?"

"You know, took pictures, dusted for prints, collected the evidence."

"What are you talking about? We ain't got nothing like that in Perseverance, heck we don't even have a sheriff."

"Then who makes arrests and keeps the peace?"

"We all do. Punishment falls to me as the mayor, but we all serve as our brother's keepers here."

"So, did anyone see anything? I mean, in a town of sixty that spreads what, three or four blocks? Someone had to see something."

"Well, a couple of the town's women on their way back from the farm; they go out to gather the eggs every morning, they saw a man on a cart riding out of town headed west. Said it was a green cart with gold letters."

Joe's jaw dropped.

"Something wrong, son?"

"That's the man from the Callaghan's place."

"You know him?" Randall pushed his seat away."

"I think he was trying to kill me. I barricaded myself in a room, and he was trying to get in."

"What room? Where?" Randall was standing with his fists clenched."

Joe pointed toward the mountain in the distance. "Up there."

Randall was red-faced. "I think you better explain."

"There was a house up in those mountains, The Callaghan's Place. They were cannibals. I rescued Tine from them. They had her locked in a cellar." Eventually, Joe told Randall the whole story, leaving the fat little man looking and feeling quite ill.

The screen door opened again, and Devlin stepped out onto the porch.

"Joe, I fixed you a place on the couch, Tine can have—What is it? What's wrong?"

"Oh Devy, these children have been through so much."

"What's he talking about, Joe?"

"It's a long story, but I think I might know who killed your shopkeeper."

"How's that?" Devlin asked.

"I think Tine and I came across him."

As if on cue, Tine came back out onto the porch.

"What are you guys talking about?"

"Tine, remember the old man from the Callaghan's place?"

She shivered, "I don't think I could ever forget him."

"Well, I'm pretty sure he's the one who killed the shopkeeper. Someone in town said they saw a stranger leaving town on a green cart with gold letters."

"The cart he stole from the barn!" Tine made the connection.

He couldn't say why, but Joe felt he had a score to settle with that old man.

"Tine, grab your gear. We have to get after him."

Tine turned to head into the house when Devlin stopped her. A sudden chill in the air and the distant crack of thunder caused Joe to turn his face to the wind, which carried on it the faint smell of the sea.

"You'll do nothing of the sort." Devlin took on a stern motherly tone. "You will both spend the night here, and after breakfast, you will be free to do whatever you like, but tonight, you will stay here with us. You wouldn't last half the night on the road with those damn tickers out there, and besides, there's a storm coming."

Joe considered arguing, but he knew she was right. Devlin made a *come with me* motion, and Joe and Tine followed her inside.

Devlin pointed to the couch. "I left an extra blanket on the end table. Tine, you may have the boy's room." Joe stopped at the couch; Tine continued following Devlin. "Randall, you coming?" She called to the stunned little mayor, still standing on the front porch.

Randall turned his head toward the approaching storm.

"Joe, can you give me a hand, son?"

Joe hurried out to the porch to find Randall closing the shutters over the windows.

"What's going on?"

"It's going to be a big one. Do you smell that?" Randall sniffed at the air, and Joe followed suit.

"Yeah, I smelled it before. It smells like the sea."

"That's right."

"Are we close?"

"Over a thousand miles away. Give me a hand, would ya?"

Overhead the clouds were already churning. Joe and Randall finished closing the shutters and walked into the house just as the first raindrops fell.

Randall pulled the door shut. "Well, we're buttoned up pretty good. Let's try and get some shuteye."

They all said their goodnights from their parts of the house, and Joe lowered the wick on the table lamp. Tired as he was, he couldn't sleep. He had so much on his mind. Caring for Tine, getting to Reverie, finding a ship willing to take him and the girl all the way out and around the dead zone, and for what? What did he have to offer in the way of payment? All he had was worthless to the Maristo. They already had guns; food was probably out of the question. He had no way to hunt anything worth eating and no way of transporting it even if he did. He could offer to work his way across as a ship's hand; he was sure he and Tine could make themselves useful, but that was a long shot.

Joe had been asleep for several hours when a crack of thunder shook the house and woke him. As he lay in the dark trying to fall back asleep and listening to the wind as it tried to rip the shutters off of the Amari's tiny home, a flash of lightning exploited the gaps in the shutters and bathed the room in silver light. The flash faded, and Joe began counting the seconds and waiting for the peal of thunder, but it never came. Instead, from somewhere out there in the darkness, in the storm that was threatening to tear Devlin and Randall Amari's home to pieces, he heard it.

"Docco," he said out loud.

"You heard it too?"

Joe turned to see Tine clutching a pillow in the dim light of the oil lamp.

"Joe! Gonna need your help, son."

Randall Amari startled both of them. The fat little man was pulling his suspenders up over his shoulders.

"You heard it didn't you?"

"The docco?"

"Hell yes, the docco. I'm gonna need your help, Joe."

Randall pushed past Joe and went out the front door. Joe followed him and was almost blown off the porch by the wind.

Randall grabbed his arm and pushed him back into the house. As soon as Joe was safe. Randall took hold of a handle and cranked away. Just above the din of the storm, the siren screamed its warning into the night.

"There, that ought to do it."

"Do what?"

"Let everyone know to get to the bank building. Tine, you get Mrs. Amari to the bank building and stay with her."

"But I don't know where that is."

"She'll show you, child."

Tine's face lit up. "You can count on me."

"I know I can Tine."

"And what are we doing?" Joe asked.

"We gonna get Sherman!"

Chapter 35

Hayward pulled the last of his gear into the small cave opening at the base of the foothills. The canyon pass he was about to enter looked an awful lot like the Narrows, and he wasn't about to risk venturing in in the dead of night, especially with the threat of bad weather. Hayward was cold and tired and felt fortunate to have found shelter from the storm. He would get some rest and start up the steep-looking pass in the morning. Hayward set the horse's reins under a large rock to keep it from running off if it got spooked in the storm.

Hayward entered the cave, rested his back against the wall, and listened to the approaching storm. As he sat, he recalled the time; it felt like two lifetimes ago when he and Agnes took shelter in a similar fashion in a cave in the Barrens. It had been dark that time as well, and there was a storm, but that wasn't the memory that haunted him. What terrified Hayward was watching and listening to the Rikolti as they paraded past the entrance to their tiny shelter.

Even now, all these years later, Hayward felt a tingle run up his neck and couldn't fight the urge to look outside for the dead miners. Hayward walked to the mouth of the cave and squatted down to look outside. No ghost miners stalked the night, but when he looked over at his rig, he saw the blue light blazing in the lantern hung on the shepherd's crook mounted to the buckboard. The rain was coming down in fits and starts, and if he hurried, he could reach his light and make it back into the cave without getting drenched.

Hayward darted out of the cave and pulled the lantern, crook and all, down from the buckboard. As he turned back for the cave, something caught his eye. Several men darted inside and disappeared from view. Hayward wanted to get back into the cave to protect his property and to take shelter from the storm, but he had to be smart about it. He knew the jackals would be waiting to ambush him the moment he poked his head into the darkened cave. Removing the stone from the lantern, he hooked the lantern to his belt, allowed his eyes to adjust to the brightness, and tossed the stone into the cave. With his karambit in one hand and his staff in the other, Hayward hurried into the cave. The tickers, momentarily blinded, raised their hands to shield their eyes from the light of the blue stone. Hayward picked out two tickers standing close together, closed his eyes, and slit their throats. With his eyes still closed, he caught the second ticker as he was falling and tossed his body atop the stone, plunging the space back into darkness. The tickers' eyes had just enough time to adjust to the light when they were plunged back into total darkness. Hayward hooked the next ticker by the back of the neck with the crook in his staff and pulled him in close enough to smell the man's rancid breath. The karambit sunk into the man's gut and slid effortlessly across his belly, spilling his innards on the cave floor.

With his last move, Hayward had lost his advantage. Uncovering the stone would blind the tickers whose eyes had, by now, adjusted to the darkness, but it would also blind him, so he opted to fight in the dark. Hayward listened for any clue to their location and heard something slice through the air just inches from his face. He crouched down, extended the staff up and out front, and felt something grab onto and coil around the staff. Tightening his grip on the shaft and pulling himself forward in the darkness, Hayward extended his blade, sliding it into some fleshy part of a living thing that answered with a sound reminiscent of a gut punch.

Hayward jabbed the blade into the flesh several more times when he heard a rapid ticking coming from somewhere to his right in the dark. He spun and slashed, but his blade did not land. Hayward sunk low again and swung his staff in a slow circle around his body. He held the staff at ankle level and made contact with something behind him. He lunged at the body and realized that he'd already dealt with that one. Raising the height of the staff, Hayward tried his search method again. This time the ticking came from just ahead. Hayward inched toward the sound. Another pass with the staff found his target. Hayward lunged forward and felt something heavy strike him between his shoulder blades. The blow knocked the air out of his lungs and dropped him to one knee. Hayward spun and struck out with his blade. The karambit sunk into soft flesh, and then all went black for Hayward as the man responded with another crushing blow to the top of Hayward's head.

* * *

Hayward Taft opened his eyes to a swirling and buzzing cacophony of black flies swarming around him. As the mass moved, some of the flies landed in his honeycombed skin and fed. Even over the discordant whirring and buzzing of the beating of their wings, Hayward could hear the regurgitating and slurping of the feeding insects. Waves of nausea undulated through his body till he began to dry heave when mercifully everything stopped. The flies hung motionless, soundless in midair, and then parted like a black curtain. There before him, sitting atop a throne of fire, was a man in a hooded black sackcloth robe. The hooded figure motioned for Hayward to take a seat at his feet, and Hayward obeyed. The man dropped his hood. He looked to Hayward to be in his mid to late sixties. His skin was tanned and weathered, his head shaved on the sides with long white hair braided tightly from his forehead down his back. He had deep-set blue eyes in a rugged and heavily scarred face. Hayward had never seen such a menacing-looking person, but somehow Hayward felt safe.

"You have heeded your father's call, and I am pleased."

Hayward bowed his head as if receiving a blessing.

"But your work is just beginning, my son."

Hayward buried his face in the man's feet. "Command me, father."

The old man leaned forward, placing his elbow on his knee, bringing himself closer to Hayward's level.

"Your journey has been long and difficult, but I have been watching and providing. Now you must return home."

Hayward balked at the request, and the flies swarmed furiously, slamming their weightless bodies harmlessly into Hayward's face. The old man slammed a fist onto his knee, and the flies fell dead to the ground.

"You will go to the territory called Gerrings to a village called Savista. There you will find a child named Althea. You will collect her and take her to the Barrens."

"But how will I know her?"

"You will feel her; you are already connected. You have seen through one another."

"I will do as you say, but might I beg one favor?" Hayward wanted two; he wanted his sister Agnes back, and he wanted his father Albert to suffer at his hand, but he didn't want to incur the Fire King's wrath, so he would just ask for the more important of the two.

"If I am successful, would you return Agnes to me?"

"My child, when we are done, you need only remain in my favor to have anything you desire. Together we shall devour our enemies. But be warned, the child you are to take is a weapon more dangerous than any mankind has ever known. She is a world ravager, a destroyer, and we must have her." The old man's fists clenched, and his jaw tightened.

"I won't fail you, father."

The old man softened. "I know, my son. There is one more thing."

Hayward leaned forward in anticipation.

"The man you left behind in the cave, the one you saw beyond the door in the farmhouse. You are to avoid him. If your paths cross and one must die, you are to lay your life down."

Hayward's eyes widened, "but father…."

"Silence, my son," the old man said gently. "He is delivering a weapon to me, just as I am offering Althea to you. Once I have the weapon, I will erase him from existence, but you are to avoid him at all costs."

"I understand, father, and I will do as you ask."

The old man smiled, and his blue eyes flashed and lit the room. The flies reanimated and clouded around Hayward's head, lightly brushing past his face and stirring Hayward from his stupor.

* * *

He became increasingly aware of the spray hitting his face. The storm was upon him, and rainwater spilled into the cave opening. A lightning flash illuminated the space just long enough for Hayward to locate the body that he'd thrown on top of the stone. He pushed the dead man aside, and the stone filled the space with bright blue light. Water was rushing into the cave and threatening his possessions, so Hayward grabbed the bodies of the five dead tickers and stacked them sandbag style at the mouth.

Hayward was excited. Clear direction had come at last. He thought about what the man on the throne said, about how he had been watching over him, and it made Hayward feel good, feel loved, feel like he belonged. Whatever challenges lay ahead, he was ready, but unfortunately, he would have to wait to face them. In the meantime, he would see to more immediate needs. The falling rain sounded like bacon frying, and it made Hayward hungry.

Chapter 36

La Fuerza rushed in and drove Cage to the ground smashing him in the head and back with boots and rifle butts. He could have fought, but Cage offered no resistance. When they had beaten him unconscious, four officers dragged him off to the pillories to await judgment. Pico de Orizaba had no jail because none was needed. Suspected violators of the 24 Laws were taken to El Foro, Orizaba's open-air forum, on the east side of the island, where they would wait, sometimes days, weeks, or even months, for the arrival of El Reconciliador, The Reconciler.

The accused were placed in one of twelve wooden apparatus with no protection from the elements. The islanders believed that it was simply God's will if a prisoner died due to being left for days beneath the blazing sun. Once his neck and wrists were secured, the guard doused Cage with a bucket of water drawn from the nearby harbor. The saltwater burned in his many cuts and abrasions, but Cage never cried out. From his position in El Foro, Cage could see flames lick across the deck of his old ship, and he felt a sense of peace.

As the blaze grew in the harbor, it drew many onlookers, including Alistair, Reka, and the pastreco. Smoke billowed, and fire filled the night sky as the onlookers watched the flames raced up Peccatum's masts. Cries of anguish rose up over the crackling blaze as it consumed those left clinging to life aboard the ship.

"What happened here?" Alistair asked a fellow onlooker.

"It was the black giant! He burned the ship and murdered her captain!"

The man's accent was thick, but Alistair understood, and his gut twisted.

"Where did he go?"

"Nowhere, señor. La Fuerza took him."

"Took him where?"

"El Foro," the man said, pointing toward the top of a tall dune.

Alistair grabbed Reka and the pastreco and ducked back into the crowd. "It was Cage," Alistair said.

"Cage? Are you sure?" Reka asked.

"I'm almost positive. A man I spoke with said that a black giant burned the ship and murdered the captain."

The pastreco was conspicuous in his silence.

"You," Alistair said. "You sonofabitch, you knew this would happen."

The pastreco lowered his head. "No, Ranger, I did not. I only said that we would not all make it back. It is not for me to know who will not return or how they will meet their end."

"We haven't lost him yet," Alistair snapped.

"Yes, Ranger, we have."

"Bullshit," Alistair said and started toward the dune.

The three hurried across the beach and began the climb. They reached El Foro, and Alistair rushed toward Cage. The pillory which held Cage was made for a man of average height, and Cage was forced to bend his body to accommodate the medieval structure. In the sand in front of him lay his bloodied axes. Exhibit one in the prosecution's case. As Alistair neared Cage, he took a rifle butt to the gut, dropping him to his knees. Reka lunged for him but was stopped by the pastreco.

"You mustn't," he cautioned her and held his hands out to show that he meant no harm.

The pastreco walked with his hands raised toward Alistair, and the guard raised his rifle to fire. Sarros and his officers came at a run, and six more of La Fuerza's guards closed ranks, ready to turn back any attempt to free their captive.

"Alto, alto!" Sarros bellowed as he approached.

Sarros put himself between La Forto and the Ranger and spoke to the policemen in their native tongue.

"Observamos y acatamos las veinticuatro leyes. Permíteme hablar con mis amigos. Él es un hombre de la ley como ustedes. No quiso faltarle el respeto."

"What did you tell him?" Alistair asked, holding his stomach and staring fiercely at the guard.

"I told him that you were a lawman like him and that we observe and abide by the twenty-four laws. And I assured him that you meant no disrespect. Now tell me, What the hell is going on here?"

"That's what I was trying to find out before that sonofabitch hit me."

"Okay, just stay calm," Sarros said. "Let me see what I can find out."

Sarros spoke with the guard in Spanish, and Alistair couldn't understand a single word. Sarros handed the guard a coin when he finished and shook his hand.

"Did you get it all straightened out?" Reka asked hopefully.

Sarros looked somewhere between furious and sad. "No, Reka. They say that they don't know if he started the fire aboard the Peccatum or not, but they watched him hack a man to pieces in the jungle." Sarros pointed at the bloodied hatchets lying in the sand in front of Cage. "He will be judged and put to death."

Reka screamed, "No!" as she rushed toward Cage. Villwock grabbed her around the waist and held her back.

Sarros was right, Alistair was a lawman, and as a lawman, he understood crime and punishment.

"Can we speak with him?" Reka asked.

"I'm sorry, no. The commander wants us all away from the stockades."

"But we have to do something!"

"We will do nothing!" Sarros snapped.

Reka fired right back. "We have to get him and get off this island!"

"If there is a legal way out of this, we will find it. If not, your friend will be put to death. And I truly am sorry, but he knew the consequences."

"We can't just leave him!" She protested.

"The rules in Pico de Orizaba are very clear!" Sarros said. "They were written on the monoliths as we sailed into the harbor! We saw the two criminals paying the penalty for violating the law! Your friend did what he did, knowing the consequences he faced. So, hear me, and hear me well! This island is home to some of my crew and a second home for Serenity. Hernando Cristobal has always welcomed us here, and neither I nor my crew will violate the friendship we have forged over the years or the laws of Pico de Orizaba."

"But…," Reka tried to interject.

Sarros ignored her and continued, "Now, nothing will happen tonight so let's get some rest and try to figure this out in the morning. I will speak with Presidente Cristobal first thing."

Reka was breathing hard through clenched teeth as Alistair led her away back to the cabanas.

* * *

Through swollen eyes, Cage watched his friends leave. Moonlight glinted off one of the axe blades and caught his attention. As he looked at the bloodstained weapons, he felt a lightness in his heart, and he smiled.

"What the hell are you smiling about?"

There were two other men in the stockade, one in a pillory like Cage and the other, the one talking, in a stock. Several bottles of rum sat on the ground next to him. Cage paid him no mind.

"I said, what the hell are you smiling about, imbecile!"

Still, Cage did not speak. The same could not be said for the other man in the pillory.

"Shut up, asshole! He probably has a fractured skull and a broken jaw, and he can't answer you."

"Is that right? Do you have a broken jaw, dummy?"

Cage remained silent and closed his eyes.

"Maybe he's deaf too!"

"I wish I was deaf, now shut the hell up!"

The man in the stock craned his head up as far as he could to get a look at Cage.

"Say, you're a big sumbitch. How many of them little Mexican fellers did it take to bring you down?" He paused a moment. "Still not talkin' eh? Well, it took three of em to bring me in. I'll tell you what, they ain't never gonna forget they were in a fight. Why I bloodied the hell out of them three Mexicans."

"Sonofabitch! Would you shut the hell up already? I'm trying to get some sleep. I've been in this damn thing for three days! I've pissed and shit myself and haven't eaten anything but that slop they give us, but the worst part of it all is listening to you yammer on! Now shut your mouth!"

"Don't you worry, the Reconciler will be by soon enough, and you won't have to worry about nothin' after that, cept for drowning!"

And with that, the man in the stock burst out laughing.

One of the guards sitting near the fire in the center of the ring of devices shouted, "Cierra la boca antes de que yo la cierre por ti!"

"What'd he say? the talking man asked."

"He said that if you don't shut your damned mouth, he's gonna come over here and shut it for you. Now shut the hell up!"

Cage drifted off to sleep, unsure if he would ever open his eyes again.

* * *

Alistair and Reka sat near the fire outside their cabana. Everyone else had turned in.

"What are we going to do, Alistair?"

"I don't know if there *is* anything we can do."

Reka's eager eyes fell, and Alistair saw the disappointment in her face.

"I'm sorry, Reka."

"You're sorry? That man risked his life to bring you back from the Barrens, and all you can say is sorry?"

"I didn't ask you or anyone else to come and get me! Most days, I wish you hadn't, so don't try and guilt me, woman! Cage is a grown man, and Captain Sarros is right. He understood the consequences."

It was clear that Reka had touched a nerve.

"I'm sorry, Alistair, I just don't know what to do."

"I don't know what to do either, Reka."

They sat against one another, staring into the fire until they both fell asleep. The following morning, the hot sun rose and began baking Pico de Orizaba. The heat woke Reka from a heavy, troubled slumber. Grinding the sleep from her eyes and feeling quite nauseous, Reka sat up and worked the stiffness from her neck. She leaned over and shoved Alistair.

"Wake up."

Alistair stirred, but that was all, so she shoved harder.

"Wake up, Alistair!"

"I'm up, I'm up."

Alistair pushed himself up on one elbow and dragged a hand down over his yawning face. Reka was already up on her feet, drawing deep breaths, trying to shake the nausea. She had much to do and refused to let an upset stomach sideline her. She bent over, hands on knees, and resumed her deep breathing.

"What's wrong with you?"

"I don't know."

"Let's get back to Serenity and talk to Doc," Alistair said as he got to his feet, brushing the sand off of his backside.

He put an arm around her lower back and placed his hand on her elbow, trying to help her stand upright when she pulled violently away.

"Are you insane? There's no time for that. We have to help Cage."

"Shit, I was hoping that was all just a dream."

They'd both hit the rum pretty hard before the fire in the harbor drew them away from the bottle. Alistair placed a hand on his chin for a moment and then reached for one of the bottles lying strewn about them. He shook it and tossed it aside. Picking up another and another until one finally responded to the shaking with a slosh.

"Here, drink this," he said, pushing the bottle toward her.

"Are you crazy? That's probably what got me feeling so shh…." She paused to dry heave.

"Come on, bottoms up. Hair of the dog."

Her hair covered one eye while the other glared at him. He shoved the bottle at her again.

"Let's go. It's this or Doc."

She grabbed the bottle, tossed her head back, and poured the warm, backwashed spirits down her throat. Her stomach lurched, and vomit rocketed out of her like a demon expelled in an exorcism.

"Asshole!"

She threw the bottle at Alistair, who managed to duck out of its path, and she upchucked again. When the retching finally stopped, Reka dragged the back of her hand across her mouth and stood up.

After a few deep breaths, "Well, I'll be damned; I think it's working."

"Good," Alistair said with a smile, "Let's get to the stockades."

They walked across the hot sand to the path. The path was shaded by palm trees and ten degrees cooler, but Reka could smell the rum sweating out through her pores. They stayed on the trail as long as they could before making the climb up to El Foro. Reka hadn't noticed the other men last night but now saw them in full blistered clarity. Their eyes puffed almost shut, not from a beating but rather the result of sun poisoning. Large blisters on their exposed skin, some leaking puss, others looking red and painful and ready to pop. By comparison, she thought Cage looked well. His head looked swollen, and he was bruised from the beating he suffered at the hands of La Fuerza, but the absence of puss-filled heat blisters gave him an edge over the other man in the pillory and the man in the stock.

A half dozen guards stood watch over the prisoners, with a dozen more resting in the shade of several palm trees. The guards on duty noticed their approach and stopped them as they made their way toward Cage.

"Alto!"

"We're here to see our friend. We were told that we could see him in the morning."

"You have been misinformed señor."

"Your captain told us…."

"But señora, I am the captain, and I can assure you; no one speaks to the prisoners before they are seen by El Reconciliador. If someone told you otherwise, they were mistaken.

"But…",

"No señora, no buts, it has always been this way."

Reka was not feeling well, and she was in no mood for bureaucracy or diplomacy; and gave Alistair a look that communicated her feelings. Alistair held up a hand.

"Captain, our ship's captain, Captain Sarros, is good friends with Presidente Cristobal. Is there any way we can just speak with our friend?"

"I am sorry, my friend. We love our presidente, but he does not involve himself in the affairs of El Reconciliador, just as El Reconciliador does not involve himself in politics. It has always been this way."

Reka had heard enough. She shouldered past Alistair.

"We are going to talk to our friend, and there is nothing you can do to stop us!"

The captain of the guard whistled and was immediately flanked by his men. The twelve resting under the palm trees bolted to their feet and came running. The captain remained calm and respectful, and Alistair could see that it was really pissing Reka off.

"Señora, por favor. We have room in the stocks."

He motioned with one hand toward the nine empty devices.

"Attempting to free a prisoner is a violation of las veinticuatro leyes; cómo se dice, the twenty-four laws, and is punishable by morto de maro."

Two Dozen armed, powerfully built policemen now stood between Reka and Alistair and their friend.

"Por favor señora, do not force me to have any part in your death."

"When is the hearing?" Reka demanded.

"We do not know señora, but when El Reconciliador arrives, the bells will sound," he pointed to two large bronze church bells visible in the towers of La Iglesia de Cristo Redentor. The church sat atop the highest point on the island. Its bells could be heard clear out to sea.

"When the bells ring, you will have one hour to come to the church for the hearing."

"We'll be waiting. Do you hear me? We'll be waiting at the church for our friend!" Reka yelled to be sure Cage could hear her.

"I need a friend. You want to be my friend, beautiful lady?"

The guard nearest the man in the stock delivered a light tap of his rifle butt to the back of his head.

"Cállate, cabrón!"

Chapter 37

Tine followed Devlin into the tiny powder room off the kitchen and closed the door behind them. Devlin gave a quick tug on the old water line and the space where the toilet used to be dropped open.

"You first, sweetie."

Devlin's smile was warm and reassuring, but Tine took a step back, feeling uneasy about climbing down into a hole.

"What's wrong, afraid of the dark?"

The dark, she thought, *the dark ain't shit*. It was people that she feared.

"No, ma'am, it ain't the dark that bothers me."

"Well, then down you go, we can talk about what's troubling you at the bank building."

Still, Tine wouldn't budge. Glass from a window in the kitchen shattered and the door to the powder room shook violently, startling Tine.

"I'll tell you what," Devlin said in her most calming voice. "I'll go first; how does that sound?"

Tine nodded in agreement but did not speak. Devlin, wearing a long loose skirt, reached down between her legs, grabbed the bottom of her skirt, and tucked it in her waistband.

"Always time to be a lady."

Devlin grabbed the lantern from the sink, and down she went. Tine stood at the top of the hole, peering back and forth from the dim light below to the failing door. Finally, a loud crack from the door frame sent Tine in motion. She climbed down into the darkness and heard a scream from just ahead. Tine watched in horror as Devlin pushed past her and scurried back up the ladder.

* * *

Outside, the storm raged. The rain came down in sheets mixed with hail battering the tiny house while the wind threatened to tear it from its foundation. Randall Amari pulled a rope from a small chest near the backdoor just off the kitchen and handed one end to Joe. He had to yell to be heard over the wind.

"Tie this end around your waste." Randall tied the other end around his own waist and then checked Joe's knot. "Here, you're gonna need this," Randall shouted and handed Joe a pickaxe.

Joe took the pickaxe but had no idea what to do with it.

"What's this for?"

Randall was a stout, powerful man with a low center of gravity and, as such, was far less likely to be blown about by the wind.

"If you feel yourself being taken by the wind, sink the pickaxe into the ground and hold tight." Randall held the rope out so Joe could see it. "I'll follow the rope back to you and help you up. We just have to make it to the pole barn." He pointed out the window on the back door at a barely perceivable structure about thirty yards away.

"Got it!" Joe yelled back. "Who's Sherman?"

"What?"

"You said we have to get to Sherman; who is Sherman?"

"Sherman's a what, not a who, son. A thirty-ton, World War 2, death machine. Devlin's brother Jack sent it over piece by piece during the war. He was stationed in Detroit, Michigan, well, what used to be called Detroit, but that was long before your time," Randall said.

"Not so long as you might think," Joe said.

"What?"

"Nothing. You were talking about Detroit."

"Oh, right. So, like I was saying, it's long gone now, but Jack oversaw production of the Sherman Tanks. We weren't sure what the hell we were gonna do with it, Devy and me, but the thing sure has come in handy. Really does a number on the docco! You ready?"

Joe nodded in the affirmative and tapped Randall's shoulder twice. It was a trained reaction to preparing to go through a door with a partner. Randall smiled at him, taking it as more of an *atta boy,* and pushed hard against the pressure that had built up in the house. He shoved with his shoulder and got the door to budge, and the wind took it from there. The door ripped from its hinges, smashed the kitchen window, and sailed off into the night.

Randall lowered his already low body and dug into the storm. Joe followed right behind him and immediately lost his footing. He tumbled like a log, rolling along the ground until his body was parallel to the direction of the wind. Like a human windsock on an airfield, he flapped a few inches above the grass. Regaining his wits, Joe swung the pickaxe and sunk it into the wet ground. Randall stopped and looked back, but Joe waved him on. It was slow going, but Joe inched along on the ground like he was climbing the face of a mountain. As he worked his way across the yard, the docco roared somewhere in the darkness. About ten yards from the pole barn, a hunk of wood came cartwheeling by and hit Randall in the head. The blow dazed him and knocked him on his ass. Joe clawed his way to him and dragged Randall the last thirty feet into the barn.

Again, the docco roared. Joe shook Randall by the shoulders.

"Wake up!"

Randall stirred, clearing the cobwebs while Joe marveled at the World War 2 Sherman Tank parked in front of him.

"Holy shit."

"Don't blaspheme, boy."

"I'm sorry, but, I mean, that's a Sherman tank!"

"I told you it was. Now give me a hand."

Randall hoisted his bulk onto the tank, up to the commander's hatch, and lowered himself down through the opening. Joe tried to follow behind.

"No, son, you hop in the driver's hatch," he poked his head out and motioned toward a smaller hatch just below the turret.

"I need you to drive; I'm too fat to make the squeeze."

"I can't drive a tank!" Joe protested.

"Well, Sam Halverson's dead, and right now, you're all we got. So, what do you say?"

"I guess I could try."

"That's the spirit boyo! Now don't you worry, it's as easy as falling off a log."

Joe thought it was funny that the last time he had heard that expression was when Alistair taught him to drive the Albatross.

"Besides, it's easier than operating the gun."

Joe lifted the heavy hatch and dropped in, closing the hatch on his way down. It was black as night in the belly of the tank, and Joe couldn't see his hand in front of his face.

"Reach over your right shoulder. You're gonna feel two knobs." Randall called in the darkness.

Joe reached and felt the knobs.

"Got it."

"Good, now turn them both to the right.

Red light filled the claustrophobic interior. Randall held up a headset and pointed to a similar unit hanging just above Joe's head. Randall put the headset on, and Joe followed suit.

"Joe, can you copy?"

The voice crackled through the speaker in Joe's headset.

"Copy."

"Good, now I'm going to make this as easy as possible."

Joe liked the sound of that.

"Now, you can't drive if you can't see, so grab that box next to where your headset was."

Joe reached up and plucked the box from its holder.

"That's your periscope. Pop that in the fitting overhead."

Joe plugged the box into the port and pressed his eyes to the viewer, just as lightning flashed, leaving floating shadows in his vision.

"Okay, now you see the two pedals at your feet?"

Joe looked down, trying to blink the dark spots from his eyes.

"Sure."

He pinched the bridge of his nose between his thumb and forefinger and rubbed.

"Left is the clutch, right is the gas. Ever drive a stick shift?"

"Sure! Back home, I have a 68 Mustang."

"A what?"

"Like in Bullitt, a Mus—, yeah, I can drive a stick."

"Good. To your right is the gear shifter."

Joe put his hand on the shifter, "okay."

"If you thumb that button down and move it left and up, you'll be in first, left down is reverse, one to the right and up is second, and so on, but remember, you can't get first or reverse unless you press that button."

"Got it. Now, how do I start this thing?"

"See that long lever hanging down to the right of the tread control levers?"

Joe found the lever.

"That's the one. That's your fuel cut-off. Go ahead and push that forward. That'll supply fuel to the engines. "

The lever moved easily forward.

"Good, now we're ready."

"Is there a key or something?"

"No, you just push the two buttons lower right on the instrument panel, and we're off to the races."

"Great! Ready when you are." Joe knew he should be nervous, but he was just too excited to be scared.

"Right! Now we just have to wait for our loader."

"Our loader?"

The loader's hatch popped open, and a man who Randall introduced as Colin Mirkwood dropped in, settled into the loader's seat, and strapped on his headset.

"Whatcha say, Mirk?"

"Yo Randall," Mirkwood greeted. "I say we kill us some docco!"

"You heard the man Joe, push the start buttons, and let's get rolling."

Joe pushed the buttons, and the Sherman's twin GM 671 diesels rattled to life.

"I do love that sound," the less familiar voice crackled.

"Okay, Joe, give 'er the gas."

Joe pushed in the clutch and slipped the Sherman into first. The gears moved as smooth as silk, which came as a surprise to Joe. Thirty-three tons of fifty-year-old steel and gears, one might expect some rough shifting, but not on this thing. The Sherman crawled out of the barn into the storm. Joe pressed his eyes harder into the viewfinder as if that might help him see better. The tank's headlights cut into the darkness but reflected mercilessly off the driving rain.

"Ease her to the left, Joe."

Randall guided Joe out of the barn and between his house and his neighbor's. The Sherman trundled onto Main Street and turned right on Randall's command.

"Mirk, unlock the turret."

"Roger," Mirkwood pulled the locking lever and gave it a turn, freeing up the tank's turret.

"Load the 76," Randall ordered.

"The what?"

"Sorry, Joe, that was for Mirk."

Collin Mirkwood levered open the breach, pulled a shell from wet storage, and angled it into the 76. He slammed it forward, tripping the ejectors, which caused the breach to shut. They rolled on just past the Welcome to Perseverance sign.

"Hold her steady right here, Joe. Mirk, you call out if you see anything!"

"Roger."

Joe pulled back on the levers, pushed in the clutch, and dropped the tank back into neutral, letting the Sherman idle. The storm beat relentlessly on the tank's metal skin, creating an almost relaxing din.

"There he is, forty yards ahead, six degrees east."

Not an ounce of tension or excitement did Colin Mirkwood give away.

Like the whole thing was a matter of routine. Randall adjusted the traverse and ordered Mirkwood to set the elevation.

"Joe, there's a switch over your right shoulder. Give that a flip."

Joe found the switch and flipped it as he was told.

"Nothing happened," called Joe over the headsets.

"That's what you think. Take a look out your periscope."

Outside Joe could see brilliant white lights flashing across the front of the tank.

"That's going to draw him right toward us," explained Randall.

"Thirty yards and closing. The elevation is set," Mirkwood said calmly.

"Prepare to fire Mirk."

Colin Mirkwood moved his foot over to the firing pedal. Joe watched through his viewer as Randall gave the command to fire. The tank rocked back as the shell exploded out of the barrel of the big 76. When the smoke cleared, the docco lay dead in the road. The breach opened, the spent casing dropped out into a catch net, and Mirkwood re-loaded the big gun.

"There's another one!" Joe yelled, unable to contain his excitement.

"Where is it, Joe? I can't see it."

In looking back at Randall to report his finding, Joe pulled his eyes away from his periscope and lost sight of the docco. He searched frantically for the giant bear-like creature and found that there were now three huge docco bearing down full speed on the Sherman.

"Three, up ahead on the left. They're coming fast!"

"Dial em in and fire at will Mirk. I'm gonna suppress with the 50."

Randall threw open his hatch, pulled the 50-caliber machine gun from its bracket, and mounted it to the traveling clip. His hands moved with the speed and precision of a concert pianist as he loaded and fired the belt-fed machine gun. Joe felt the temperature drop in the interior of the tank and watched as tracer rounds shot like lasers into the night. One burst struck heavily into one of the monsters and produced a fine red mist in the rain. The docco was cut in two by the weapon, but the other two charged on having only been grazed.

Mirkwood picked up one of the creatures in his periscope, "firing!"

Randall dropped back into the tank, and Mirkwood fired. Joe felt the concussion through his chest and watched the animal drag what was left of its body through the mud for a few feet before it bled out and died.

"Great shot Mirk," Randall's voice scratched through the headset. "Joe, reverse, twenty yards."

Joe shoved the clutch to the floor with his foot and slammed the gear shifter to the left and down. He let up on the clutch, and the Sherman lurched forward and died.

"Shit!"

"It's okay, son," Randall said calmly. Clutch, start buttons, and thumb the shifter."

Joe went to work correcting his error just as another docco slammed into the Sherman. If not for the soft audible thud, no one inside would have had a clue that the beast had crashed into the tank's hull. A second docco scrambled up its fallen mate tearing the fifty-cal from its mounting and sending it, belt box and all skittering off into the darkness.

There was something different about this docco, Joe thought. The docco back in the Midwestern Territories seemed—what was the word? Less human. How did this one know to attack the 50 cal? How could a docco be capable of that kind of reasoning?

"Mirk, grease gun," Randall called, driving Joe from his thoughts.

Mirkwood grabbed the sub machine gun and handed it to Randall, who pressed his body down into his seat and fired into the muzzle of the howling docco. Razor-sharp teeth snapped in the jaws of a head too large to fit through the hatch. Blood sprayed the interior of the tank as the docco continued to snap and snarl as if the bullets were no more than bee stings to this brute. A second burst from the grease gun did the trick, and the beast pulled his head from the hatch. Randall reached up to close the hatch as the docco reared up to jam its clawed paw into the hole. As it stood ready to tear into the compartment, Joe slammed the tank into reverse and pushed hard on the gas. The Sherman launched in reverse, sending the docco toppling off the turret. Randall pulled the hatch shut and locked it. A slurry of docco blood and water sloshed around the floor at their feet as they readied themselves for the next attack.

Chapter 38

The twin bells stared down like bronzed eyes from the domed terracotta towers of La Iglesia de Cristo Redentor. Alistair could smell the sun-warmed wood as it baked the arched double doors. Heat radiated from them and bit his hand as he pulled on the wrought iron rings to open the door. Stepping over the threshold, the church's interior felt cool and damp, a welcomed relief from the heat of the morning sun. It took a few moments for their eyes to adjust to the soft glow given off by the hundreds of candles placed around the sanctuary, but when they did, the group found that they were not alone. To the right and left of the altar, old women draped in black faced the back of the church, murmuring softly as they passed beads through bony fingers. The pastreco pulled the door shut and knelt in the aisle at the back of the church with his head bowed. Reka and Alistair walked to the front and sat in a pew.

"What are we going to do, Alistair?"

Alistair shook his head, "I don't know, Reka. Like Captain Sarros said, the law is clear. Cage murdered a man. A crime punishable by death."

She hardened her face, "he must have had a good reason."

"Agreed, let's just hope they will *listen* to reason."

"Maybe we can talk to the…what did they call him?"

"El Reconciliador," answered Alistair. "The Reconciler."

"Well, maybe we can talk to him. Maybe we can get him to listen?"

"I hope so. But we have to talk with Cage if we are going to speak on his behalf. I don't know him nearly as well as you do, but I just can't see him killing a man without a damned good reason."

"I bet he was defending someone. That has to be it," Reka said with hopeful eyes.

The church bells rang out.

"We'll know soon enough." Without realizing it, Alistair's hands folded as in prayer."

The bells rang together twelve times and then stopped. Reka looked over her shoulder toward the wooden doors. Minutes passed.

"Where's Cage? They said they were bringing him here for his trial."

"Give them time, Reka. It's a long walk from the beach."

The old women murmured louder and began to move slowly across the front of the church away from the altar dragging their beads behind them. The strands were perhaps twenty feet long, and unlike a rosary, they hung in a straight line. The women walked along the sides of the church to the back, positioning themselves on either side of the doors. The pastreco did not move. The doors opened, and sunlight poured in, spilling halfway up the aisle casting long shadows across the marble floor. Captain Sarros entered the church accompanied by Presidente Hernando Cristobal. The look on Sarros' face told Alistair all he wanted to know.

Sarros sat in the pew right behind Alistair and Reka.

"It's not good. Presidente Cristobal has spoken with the head of La Fuerza," he leaned in to whisper. "One of his men watched Cage butcher a man named Rancor Simms, captain of the Peccatum. The Peccatum was lost in the fire last night. She had a crew of twenty-four, all are assumed dead, and Cage will be made to answer for them."

"No!" Reka cried out.

"Our laws are clear in this matter, my dear," Hernando Cristobal said, resting a hand, likely intended as comforting, on her shoulder.

"Take your hand from my shoulder while it's still yours to take."

"Reka! You watch yourself, girl!" Sarros snapped.

Cristobal removed his hand, "I meant no disrespect señora."

"I'm sure none was taken El Presidente. She is understandably worried about her friend."

"I don't need you or anyone else to speak for me," Reka said with fire in her eyes.

"You are right to be worried, señora. There is no doubt that your friend will suffer the sea."

"You mean you are going to murder him." Reka snapped.

"Señora, please do not blame Orizaba for the actions of your friend. Our laws and the consequences of breaking them are clear to all who come here. Now I must go. I only came to prepare you, but I cannot be here when El Reconciliador arrives."

"Thank you for coming, my friend," Sarros extended a hand to Cristobal.

"I am only sorry that I am powerless to intervene."

Cristobal exited the pew, genuflected at the altar, and left the church.

"We have to get back to Serenity for our weapons," Reka was up on her feet, moving toward the aisle when Sarros stood and was about to speak.

Alistair waved a hand at him. "Reka, please sit."

Reka spun on her heels and glared at the Ranger.

"Please, Reka," he gestured with his hand at the pew.

Reka sat down and exhaled loudly.

"He's right, the law is clear, and if Cage can't offer an adequate explanation, he will be put to death."

Reka opened her mouth to speak just as the murmuring reached a fevered pitch. The doors parted, and an old and broken-looking man stepped into the doorway leaning heavily on a golden shepherd's staff. Four of the women broke from the group and accompanied the old man to the altar.

"Is he the reconciler?" Reka asked.

Sarros offered a nod of affirmation. The old man made his way up the aisle, having to step around the pastreco, who still hadn't moved.

"The next guy in will be El Acusador, the accuser. They must have at least one eyewitness to bring someone before the court. No sooner had he spoken than a young man in a policeman's uniform stepped through the door. He was followed by two other men, both wearing loose-fitting white shirts.

"They must be witnesses to the other crimes."

"Where's Cage?" Reka asked, craning her neck around, looking for her friend.

They sat and listened to the trials of the first two men, the larger man accused of being a thief, the smaller, a rapist. The proceedings were not at all what Alistair expected. The reconciler, old and frail-looking, was a lion in defense of the accused. Alistair listened to the men's stories and decided their guilt in a matter of minutes, but the reconciler dug and questioned until even their own mothers would have found them guilty. After each man was pronounced guilty, the reconciler would lift the sleeve of his robe and, using a seashell, cut a gash into his arm. Alistair watched as he dragged the shell repeatedly over scar tissue until his skin split. No sentencing was necessary because the penalty was always the same.

Three old women followed each man as he was escorted out of the church. They each dropped another wooden bead onto their lines, tied a knot, and began clicking bead after bead, praying at each. Several hours had passed since the first man, the thief, appeared before the reconciler. Now Cage stood before the sad old man.

"Habla Español?"

They waited, but Cage did not answer.

"He speaks English, Reconciliador," Alistair offered.

"Very well, though it sounded like *beddy well,* we will proceed in English. Blood ran from under his sleeves, and he turned his attention toward the policeman.

"Reconciliador, this man chopped a man named Rancor Simms to pieces in the jungle, using these," the policeman set the bearded axes on the altar in front of the reconciler. "I, Enrique Papado, of La Fuerza witnessed this with my own eyes." He touched his fingers to his eyes and continued. "Rancor Simms was capitan of the Peccatum. The Peccatum was burned in the harbor last night. It is believed that every soul aboard the ship was lost. This man stands accused of the murder of Capitan Rancor Simms as well as setting fire to the Peccatum and killing her crew of twenty-three."

"Do you have a witness to your accusations as they pertain to the Peccatum?"

"No, Reconciliador."

"I will not hear the charge. Speak only of what you have seen."

"Si' Reconciliador. As I ran into the clearing in the jungle, this man." He pointed at Cage. "Raised his axe and brought it down, taking Captain Simms' hand. My officers and I ordered him to stop, but he struck him again, removing the man's jaw as he begged for mercy. Before we could reach him, he buried both axes in the capitan's clavicles." The policeman made a chopping motion at the base of his neck with his hands. "Capitan Simms fell dead. Then he turned to face us and dropped his weapons."

The policeman stepped back, having spoken his piece. The reconciler studied the large black man before him. Unlike the other accused, Cage remained silent during the policeman's statement.

"Sir, may I have your statement?"

Cage did not speak. He fixed his gaze on the crucifix and would not engage the court.

"May I have your name?"

Nothing from the man facing death.

"His name is Cage Abrams, sir," Reka sprung from her seat.

"Thank you, señora. Were you present? Will you offer a defense for this man?"

"I was not, sir, but he is a good man."

"Thank you, señora, but we are not impugning his character. The court is only interested in what happened and why it happened. Were there perhaps circumstances that would justify his actions?"

"Cage!" Reka cried. "Please, say something."

Cage remained transfixed.

"Will you offer no defense, sir?" The reconciler asked. "Señora, is your friend deaf and dumb?"

"No sir," her voice quivered.

The reconciler rolled up his sleeve and slashed his arm.

"No!" Reka jumped over the pew and ran to Cage. "Say something!" She pounded her fists against his chest and slapped his face and had to be restrained by Alistair and Sarros.

"Sir, may I speak privately with the pastreco?"

The church fell silent as the accused spoke.

"You may, sir. See to it," he ordered the officer.

The officer bowed his head and led Cage out of the sanctuary; three old women followed behind with long-beaded ropes.

Pushing open the church's wooden doors, the heat hit them like a blast furnace. Reka watched as the pastreco followed Cage and the policeman to an area in the shade of a palm tree, and the officer stepped away. When Cage was done, he walked over to the policeman and was led away.

"Alistair, what are we going to do?" She paced back and forth. "We have to get him and get off this damned island."

The pastreco approached. "He does not want to be saved, Reka, and he wouldn't want you to do anything to free him. Cage Abrams is an honorable man. He understood the consequences and has accepted them."

A short scream through clenched teeth was all she could manage in her frustration.

"Did he tell you why he did it?" Alistair asked.

"He did."

"Well?" Alistair pressed.

"He said that I could tell you everything once we were off the island."

"You'll tell us now!" Reka lunged at the pastreco.

The pastreco didn't flinch, speaking in calm, even tones. "I will abide by the wishes of the man about to die."

Reka stomped furiously. She looked at Alistair, then at Sarros, and finally at the pasterco. No one said a word, and she hung her head in sorrow.

They followed their friend down the path toward the beach. Reka's mind was a menagerie of whirring gears and spiraling thoughts. Reality, as she knew it, was in the middle of a slow turn, and though she could watch it, she couldn't figure out how to stop it. Reka felt her stomach lurch, and she dropped to her knees and vomited. Alistair helped her to her feet and handed her his bandana.

By the time they reached the beach, the first two condemned men had been bound to their stones at the right ankle. The thief sat in the sand and wept while the rapist begged for his life.

"Amigos! Come on, you know how women are. They say no when they mean yes. My friends! Please, release me!"

In a large ring around the men, the old women in black walked, dragging their beads through the sand behind.

"Why are they doing that? I prayed all night, and God didn't answer."

"They offer prayers for their souls, señora."

Reka turned to face a young policeman standing at parade rest. Feet apart, hands behind his back.

"For theirs or for yours?"

He looked at her quizzically.

"You're murdering a good man," she said and spit on the sand in front of his feet.

"I am murdering no one, señora."

"No! You do not get to claim innocence. You may be using the sea to kill him, but the sea is the helpless accomplice, not you."

The young man held her gaze. "Our laws and the penalty for breaking them are very clear, señora. The only murderer here is *your* good man."

"What will happen now, officer," the pastreco interrupted.

"It is low tide; the guilty will be taken to the floating graveyard. You see how they are secured to their stones by the rope? The rope is just long enough to keep their heads above water. Their bodies will be kept afloat by cork vests, there, you see?" He pointed at the officer fitting the thief into his vest. "That will keep him floating until high tide when the water will slowly rise and drown them."

"Do you think we might have his body for a proper burial after the sentence is carried out?"

"I am sorry, but your friend, like all the others, will serve Pico de Orizaba as a deterrent to those who would violate her laws."

"You're an animal."

She sounded defeated as she watched an officer secure the shackle around Cage's right ankle. Heavy rope, knotted tightly and covered in tar to make it impossible to undo, connected the ankle shackle to the large rock. The rope was sectioned out to ensure that they would remain above the water line until the tide came in.

"Pick them up!"

A cat-o-nine-tails snapped in the air to drive the man's point. His long white beard made him look grandfatherly, but his black hooded cloak shattered any illusions of the kindly old patriarch. Four other hooded subjects joined him.

"Are they pastreco?" Alistair asked.

"No, they are not."

His tone was dire.

Cage plucked his stone from the ground like a child picking up a baseball. The other men lifted their stones with considerably more effort but managed. Trailed by the murmuring and now groaning old women, the three criminals walked down the pier to the dock. Midway down the wooden structure, the rapist dropped his stone and clung to one of the supports. Two hooded men grabbed hold of the sniveling mass and jerked him to his feet.

"Pick it up!"

Again, the cat snapped in the air. The rapist dropped to his knees, and with his hands held out, he begged for his life. The cat-of-nine whistled as it cut through the air and laid into his bare back, spilling blood from the tears it left in his flesh. The man dipped the cat into the saltwater, ensuring that the next lash would sting all the more. He snapped it once, and the rapist rose to his feet, lifted his stone, and trudged forward. The criminals were loaded onto a skiff which the hooded men piloted to the spot where their executions would be carried out.

"Perhaps we should leave," the pastreco suggested.

Reka watched as the little skiff moved farther and farther away. "You can go if you want, but I'm not leaving him to die alone."

The pastreco looked into her eyes, "We all die alone, Reka."

* * *

Cage sat facing the shore as the skiff moved slowly out of the harbor. He prayed silently for the safety of his friends and for success in their long and arduous mission. He watched the old women pounding their fists into the sand and crying out to the heavens in a language he did not understand and now could hardly hear. He considered his life and the joy and sorrow he had known. He would miss the boy. Stopping himself, mid-thought, he let the name crawl out from where he had hidden it in his mind; Ivan. He'd raised Ivan well, taught him about honor and integrity, about bravery and discretion. He was proud of his boy. He thought about Andalusia, her strength and beauty.

The skiff had entered the floating graveyard. Two robed men at the front of the little boat used poles to push their way through the dead that floated and bobbed on the ripples and waves. Each with its mouth agape as if it were calling out or perhaps surprised by its death. Some with eyes clouded over, some half-eaten, and some hollowed out and home to small crabs, like some macabre floating garden of the dead. Seeing their final resting place, the thief wept openly, and the rapist defecated and pissed on himself. Cage handed his stone to the man who would carry out his sentence, threw his legs over the edge, and slipped into the water among the corpses. The executioner dropped the stone in after, and Cage spoke.

"De profundis clamo ad te, Dominus."

"Muere bien señor, you die well."

The thief put up no struggle but had to be lifted and dropped into the water. The rapist fought, but unlike the young girl he had violated, he was no match for the executioner's men who quickly overpowered him. They deposited him in the water and shoved away a short distance to watch the sentence be carried out. The water slowly rose over the next six hours, and their lines became taut. Deliberately and with no consideration for the lives it was taking, the water crawled up their necks. A light breeze stirred the surface of the water and pushed the corpses into the men who would soon be joining them. Inch by inch, the briny water slid past their chins. The water filled their ears as they tilted their heads back to keep their mouths and noses in the air. They spat and clamped their mouths shut as the water spilled over their lower lips, trying to breathe through their noses. The thief and the rapist began flailing madly with death only moments away. Arms lunging, hands grasping, left legs kicking while their right legs served only as extensions to the anchor stones keeping them in place.

Cage drew in his final breath. With this life lived, he closed his eyes and opened his mouth, eager to see what the next life held for him.

Chapter 39

Morning broke over the mountain, spilling warm sunlight over Perseverance and the mighty Sherman tank that protected her through the long night. Randall threw open the hatch, and the crew welcomed the fresh air. Each man climbed from his hatch and slid off the tank.

"My brother-in-law said the Sherman wasn't worth the powder it would take to blow it to hell, but she's worth her weight in gold if you ask me."

Joe smiled, "My grandfather used to say that."

"He served on a Sherman?" Randall was the last one down.

"No, but he liked that expression. Not worth the powder it would take to blow this or that to hell. My dad picked it up too."

Randall and Mirk started the walk back toward town, and Joe ran after them. His feet were soaked in rainwater and blood and squished with each step.

"Where are we going, guys?"

"Bank building, gotta check on our families, son," Mirk answered.

"Shouldn't we park Sherman back in the barn?" Joe asked.

Randall looked up at the clear blue sky. "No. not just yet. We'll let her air out a bit."

Randall and Devlin's house had taken damage in the storm, part of the roof had been torn away, and all of the windows were broken.

"Randall, your house."

"Not to worry, Joe, we'll have her livable before nightfall."

"Do you think the girls are alright?"

"I'm sure they're fine. Devy knows the drill."

As the three warriors walked toward the bank building, they took in the devastation. Randall's house stood up well compared to others, while some sustained no damage at all.

"Thank goodness we stopped the docco. Can you imagine, Randall?" Colin Mirkwood said, picking up a hunk of wood in the middle of the road and tossing it to the side.

"You said it, Mirk."

As they approached the bank building, they were greeted with cheers and pats on the back. Mirk's wife Edith flew into his arms and smothered him with kisses."

"Mornin' Edith, have you seen Devy?"

"No, I haven't, but it was pretty chaotic. I would check inside."

Randall and Joe passed the tall steel gates, walked up the broken concrete stairs of the old bank building, and pushed past the tarnished brass doors. Joe thought the place looked more like a fortress or a prison than a bank.

"Carmen!"

Carmen Mata, the town's matriarch, was cracking eggs into a bowl in the kitchen just inside the doors. Randall was the mayor, but Carmen was the true voice of Perseverance. Carmen stood toe to toe with the men in defense of the town in the early days. She tended to the wounded and battled with the best of the men. In the end, they managed to chisel out the parcel of land they all called home.

"Have you seen Devy?"

"Mornin' Randall. No, can't say as I have."

Carmen added milk to the bowl and started whisking.

"Check the tunnel; I'm sure she's fine."

"I'll do that." Randall hurried over to what was once the bank's vault.

Joe could sense an urgency in the mayor. "What's going on, Randall? Where are we going? Where's Tine?"

Randall didn't answer. A ladder poked up out of the floor in the middle of the vault, and Randall climbed down. Joe followed.

"Randall, where is Tine?"

The ladder took them down into the tunnel system that ran beneath Perseverance. Oil lamps provided enough light to navigate, but most of the underground passage was left in shadow. Randall, still not answering Joe's question, pulled a canister lantern off the shelf and clicked it to life. The yellow beam stretched into the darkness. He handed it to Joe and grabbed another for himself.

"Are you going to answer me?" Joe demanded.

"I don't know where they are, son. That's my answer. But I pray they're okay."

They'd walked through the tunnels passing ladder after ladder.

"What's with all the ladders?"

"The ladders are how we access the tunnel to the bank building. Up those ladders are people's houses, or what's left of them. Ours is in the powder room. That's how Devy and Tine would have gotten to the bank building—if they had made it."

Randall's light began to flicker, and he gave it a smack.

"So, you think they're still at the house?"

"I hope not; you saw the damage."

The crying was thin and faint, more of a whimper. Randall and Joe stepped up the pace to a jog. The light beams bounced and flickered in the dark.

"Tine!"

Joe picked up speed leaving Randall to catch up when he could. At a full sprint, feet beating off the ground and heart thrumming in his ears, He barely heard Tine's pleading cry for help.

"Joe, we're over here."

Joe's flashlight swept toward her voice, and the beam caught her eyes. She put up her forearm to block the glare, and Joe saw the blood.

"She's not breathing, Joe," Tine said through tears.

Tine held the small object in her hands and offered it to Joe. A newborn, lifeless and silent. Joe took the baby by the ankles and swatted it on the behind. Nothing. He turned the baby in his hands and began infant CPR. Joe placed his mouth over the baby's nose and mouth and exhaled slowly. The baby still felt warm, which Joe took as a good sign, though he considered it might have been from Tine clutching it to her chest. He shoved the light into Tine's hands. "Point this at her chest, and let me know if it rises and falls."

She did as she was told, and Joe resumed breathing for the baby.

"It is! It is, Joe!"

Joe paused and began chest compressions.

"What are you doing, Joe?"

Joe didn't answer. He repeated the process several times as Tine did her best to keep the flashlight on the baby's chest. After a few moments, the shrill cry of a newborn infant echoed through the tunnel, and Joe handed it back to Tine.

"You did it!" Tine exclaimed.

"Are you hurt?"

"No, I'm fine," Tine answered. "You did it, Joe!" She wiped the tears from her eyes and rocked the baby to calm her.

"Where's the mother?"

Tine pointed to a girl lying on the dirt floor of the dark tunnel.

"Her name was Magdala. Mrs. Amari said she didn't make it."

Tine couldn't fight back the tears. Joe moved the light onto the body of a young girl lying, in a pool of blood just below her midsection.

"Mrs. Amari said it was a postpartum hemorrhage."

"Where is Mrs. Amari?"

Devlin Amari was coming down a ladder a few feet away.

"Right here, Joe had to go up for a blanket for Magdala's baby. I found a few women to help me carry her out."

Magdala was young. Joe guessed she was just a little older than Tine, 16 or so, but it was hard to tell for sure between the poor lighting and the dirt that covered her face. Joe handed Devlin the flashlight and scooped Magdala up into his arms.

"I've got her. You just help Tine."

He carried Magdala down the tunnel back toward the bank building. About halfway back, they met up with Randall, who had stopped for a breather.

"What happened? Where's Devy?"

"I'm right here, dear," she waved the lantern as a greeting. "Magdala went into labor."

"Is she okay? Is the baby okay?"

"The baby is going to be fine."

"Thanks to Joe," Tine added.

"Magdala didn't make it," Devy said somberly.

The air escaped Randall's lungs in a forceful blast.

"Poor child. Where are Theo and Dawn?"

Devlin lowered her voice. "They didn't make it either. Pinned under debris in their home."

Magdala weighed nothing in Joe's arms. "Were they her parents?"

Randall cleared his throat. "No, Magdala came to us about 6 months ago," Randall said. "She escaped the tickers, and Theo and Dawn Donacema took her in and cared for her."

"What's going to happen to the baby?" Tine asked as she cuddled the newborn in her arms.

"Well, I suppose we're gonna have to find someone to raise him up," Randall said.

"Her up," Tine corrected.

"Excuse me?"

"She's a her, you said raise him up, but she's a her, not a him."

"I suppose we could look after her till we can find a more permanent solution," Devy suggested.

"I think that's a fine idea, dear."

They reached the ladder leading up into the bank building.

"I'll go up and get some help," Randall scurried up the ladder.

In no time, helpers were coming down the ladder, and hands were reaching through the opening in the floor. Magdala's body was passed up first, followed by the newborn. The whole town gathered on and around the steps of the bank building to hear Randall's report.

"We haven't had a storm like that in some time, friends, and I pray we don't see another anytime soon. It has left our town and our bodies battered, but we shall persevere. It's who we are. It's what we have always done."

The people were tired, they'd been through so much in the previous twelve hours, but Randall's words struck a chord. Some clapped, others verbalized their agreement, but they were of one accord.

"We have lost some friends. Theodore and Dawn Donacema were among them, as was Magdala. Magdala died during childbirth, but thanks in part to my Devy and our new friends, Joe and Tine, her baby girl survived."

More applause.

"Now today is Sunday, the Lord's day, and we will have service and thank Him for all that we have as well as what we have lost. Then we will bury our dead and rebuild our homes, and we will persevere."

When the light applause died down, Carmen thanked him and invited everyone into the bank building, where breakfast was served, and mass was held. After service, Carmen spoke.

"As our mayor said, we have a lot of work to do. I'll need a few volunteers to stick around for clean-up and start on dinner. We'll all meet back here later tonight. For now, let's bury our dead and begin rebuilding our homes. Anyone whose home can't be rebuilt or repaired by nightfall will stay with neighbors. Whatever is left of the Donacema's house will be taken down and used to repair or rebuild the survivor's houses."

The citizens of Perseverance worked through dusk, and no one noticed the old man who entered from the north end of town. He walked, slightly hunched over, with the aid of a staff, in the dim light of the oil lamps that ran the length of the town. His waffled pale purple skin hidden by a long thin coat, he carried a saddlebag over his shoulder and strowed right down the middle of Main Street.

At the Amari's place, Randall and Joe managed to shore up the roof, repair the wall, and had begun shingling the new section of roof. Devlin took the baby and went down to the bank building to help prepare the community dinner. Tine sat leaning against the house, waiting for her next order from the men on the roof.

"What should we name her Joe?" She yelled up.

"Name who?"

"The baby, stupid."

"She's not ours to name."

It came out a little mumbled. Joe was holding nails between his lips. He took one, drove it through the roofing shingle, and repeated the process until he ran out of shingles.

"Well, she's still gonna need a name, and her mom isn't around to name her."

"No, I guess she's not. Tie off that next bundle."

Tine hopped to her feet and walked over to tie another bundle of shingles to the pulley. "All set; hoist away!"

"Will you send up another bucket of tar when you have a moment, dear?"

Randall's job was to follow behind Joe and tar over the nail holes.

"Sure thing, Mr. Amari."

Tine dipped the small bucket Randall had sent down into the cauldron of tar, hooked it back to the line, and got out of the way so she wouldn't get splashed. The old man stopped in front of the Amari's place and watched the proceedings with great interest. He seemed particularly interested in Tine. While Tine was distracted, the old man inched slowly toward her, hiding himself in a growth of sagebrush.

Randall pulled the tar bucket onto the roof and detached it from the line. As he turned, he lost his footing and slid toward the edge. Joe saw Randall slip from the corner of his eye and launched himself, hoping to catch hold of him before he went over the edge. Pushing off, Joe toppled the platform holding sixty pounds of roofing shingles. The bundles slid down the roof and over the edge toward Tine. She looked up as the first bundles came over the edge, but she couldn't move.

The old man shoulder tackled her at the mid-section, sending her tumbling out of the way, the tiles crashing harmlessly to the ground. Joe held Randall until he regained his footing and flew down the ladder to Tine.

"I'm sorry! Are you okay?"

Tine didn't say a word. She sat, knees up, hands back supporting her with a look of terror on her face.

"I think she's okay."

The old man stood brushing himself off.

"How can I thank you?"

Not the slightest indication of recognition from Joe. This man looked nothing like the man he battled in the cave only a few months back. That man was strong, a worthy adversary. This was a broken-down, deformed little man, no threat to anyone. Tine continued to stare.

Randall made his way down the ladder. "Is everyone okay?

"Yeah, I think so," Joe said as he extended a hand to Tine.

Tine got to her feet and clung to Joe like a shy child to her parent.

"Are you going to say thank you?"

Tine didn't answer. She just burrowed her face into Joe's back.

"Please excuse my sister. She's just a little shaken up, I think."

"No need for apologies, as long as your precious sister is alright."

"Joe, I think we're fine for the night. I'm getting a little tired, and I could use a bite. Mr...." Randall paused, allowing the old man to fill in the blank.

"Odium, Albert Odium."

"Well, Mr. Odium, what say we feed you? It's the least we can do. After all, you did save our Tine. Those shingles could have killed her."

Randall and Joe shot quick looks at one another. Joe thought he read blame on Randall's face, but that was absurd. Joe knew that if anyone was to blame, it was fat old Randall Amari. After all, if he hadn't fallen, Joe wouldn't have had to save him, and he wouldn't have kicked the support out from under the platform that held the shingles.

"Well, I am a bit famished." Odium turned and looked back at Tine. "Will you be joining us, dear?"

A devilish smile wormed its way through his lips.

Tine did not answer; she just pulled tighter into Joe.

"Come along, child, you're fine." Randall insisted.

"She's upset, Randall." Joe snapped defensively.

"Nonsense, she's fine, now come along."

"I think I know my sister, Mr. Amari."

Joe stood ramrod straight, chest expanded, hands balled into fists.

"Bah!" Randall waved a dismissive hand at Joe. "Let's go, Mr. Odium. Kids have no respect these days."

Randall began to walk off with the strange Mr. Odium.

Tine kept her face buried in Joe's back. "Is he gone?"

Joe peeled her off and held her at arms length. "What's wrong, Tine?"

"It's that man."

"Mr. Odium? He saved your life."

"I know, but there is just something about him. I've seen him before."

Joe's brow furrowed. "You mean like he's a ticker or something?"

"No, I mean yeah, maybe, I don't know."

Tine started shaking, her hands trembled, and she threw her arms around him.

"Hold me, Joe. I don't know what's wrong."

"Well, you *were* almost killed."

"I've been in scrapes before, Joe. That's not it."

"Was it the way he looked?" Joe could see a flicker in her eyes. "Cause I think he got burned or something. That doesn't make him a bad person." And just like that, the flicker was gone.

"Joe, did you notice how mean you were being to Mr. Amari?"

"Yeah, I guess he just got on my nerves. But he did have a good idea; I'm hungry too. Let's walk down to the bank building and see what's for supper."

Tine shook her head, "I'm not hungry."

"We haven't stopped since breakfast. You should eat something."

"I'm tired. I'm going to stay here. And Joe, I don't think you should go either, but if you do, please be careful and please, don't fight with Mr. Amari."

Joe got Tine settled in and walked down main to the bank building. Most of the activity along the road had come to a stop. Folks had set their hammers and saws down and followed Randall and the old man to the bank building for the big community dinner. A few stragglers, like Joe, were running a little behind, but for the most part, the streets were empty.

The amount of work the people of Perseverance had gotten done was nothing short of miraculous. In less than twelve hours, they managed to erase all signs of the damage caused by the storm. Two houses and the families that lived in them were gone, and all that remained were the foundations of the homes, just like the foundations Joe saw when he and Tine strolled into town the previous night. Besides the houses, Joe noticed something else conspicuous in its absence. The night sounds. The Katydids that were out in full force earlier had gone silent. Joe tried to take in a deep breath, but the air felt thick, and he couldn't manage more than shallow breathing. As he neared the bank building, he began picking up sounds.

The smile he hadn't realized he was sporting fell away from his face as bickering and discord replaced the eerie silence. Inside the bank building, there were raised voices and finger-pointing; bad behavior on full display, and in the middle of it all, Mr. Odium sat smiling and eating stew from a pot with his hands. Even the Amaris were having a heated exchange, though Joe couldn't hear what it was about. Mr. Odium beckoned with the crooking of a stew-covered finger, and Joe took a seat across the table.

"They have been going at it like this since we got here," Odium said. His voice was thin and weak, and Joe found his grin to be unsettling. "I suppose it's to be expected, though. You have all been through quite an ordeal."

Joe nodded his agreement. After all, hadn't he just had a disagreement with Randall Amari? *"Not that it was unjustified."* Joe thought. The guy all but blamed him for almost killing Tine. *"He's lucky I didn't knock him on his ass!"* The thoughts were firing one after another until Mr. Odium interrupted.

"How is that precious sister of yours? Did she not feel up to dinner? It sounded to me like Mayor Amari was blaming you for the accident."

The question fed into Joe's growing anger toward Randall. "My fault! How was it my fault? And I see the pompous little ass managed to work in the fact that he was the mayor of this shit hole of a town," Joe said.

"He did, and he also said that he had to save you and your sister from the docco last night."

Joe stood up so fast that he knocked his chair over. Albert Odium rocked back and forth in his seat, giggling like a child. Joe clenched his fists, the veins in his neck protruding like cords from under his skin, and he stormed off in Randall's direction. Three feet away, fist coiled back and ready to strike, and a shot rang out.

The whole place fell dead silent. A thin girl with long red hair and a smoking gun stood in the doorway.

"Tine!"

Joe spun in the direction of the shot and saw Albert Odium on the floor clutching his shoulder. He ran to the old man.

"Mr. Odium, let me look at that."

Joe ripped the old man's shirt open to find more of the honeycombed skin and a bullet wound that passed through Odium's shoulder.

"The bullet went through. We'll have to clean it up and…."

Albert Odium shoved Joe away, got to his feet, and addressed the crowd. "Let her go!"

Several of the town's folk had seized Tine and stripped her of her weapon.

"Dammit! I said release her!"

Odium helped Joe to his feet and whispered to him.

"Take your sister and go before they hurt her. You'll find my horse and buckboard about two miles up the road to the west. Take them and run. You can make Reverie in two days' time if you push hard."

"But you're hurt."

"Don't worry about me. These folks will see to me. You just take your precious sister and go."

Joe nodded and was on his feet quick as a flash. "Thank you, Mr. Odium."

Chapter 40

The executioner and his crew watched as the thief and the rapist joined Cage Abrams in the afterlife and raised a pole with a small, red, swallowtail flag, not unlike a military guidon, and waved it overhead. Seeing the flag, the old women ceased their pounding of the sand and chanting and walked off the beach. The executioner and his crew rowed the skiff back to the dock with the sentences carried out. Alistair, Reka, and the pastreco approached the boat even before they tied off.

"Did he have any last words?" Reka's eyes were large and pleading.

"Sí señora, he said, 'De profundis clamo ad te, Dominus' It means, from the depths I cry out to you oh Lord." The man cleared his throat. "Por favor disculpame," he said and followed the old women back toward the church.

Reka's eyes filled with tears.

"Let's get off this beach and off this damned island," Alistair said.

"You two go ahead; I need a moment."

Alistair and the pastreco honored her wish and started back for their camp to gather their belongings. Reka dug her heels into the sand and leaned back on her elbows. The sun chased away the chill that somehow managed to creep into her bones, and it felt good. She closed her eyes, inhaled deep, and held her breath as long as she could. She wondered what it would be like knowing that she had breathed her last. A violent coughing fit ended her experiment, and she broke down. Tears poured from her eyes, and like the old women, she found herself on her knees, slamming her fists into the sand. Clutching fists full of sand to her breast and collapsed on her back.

"Why God? Why?" She screamed at the sky. "What do you want from me? What do I have left to give you? You took our mother when Eva and I were still young and needed her most. You brought me, Joe, only to take him away. I have watched friends and their children die in battle, and now you have taken Cage. I have suffered pain and sorrow and so much loss. But you seem not to care. You continue to dump your seemingly inexhaustible supply of misery on *us*, the ones who call you father."

When she stopped screaming to catch her breath, she heard Cage's voice. 'From the depths, I cry out to You, O Lord,' and she repeated it softly.

"From the depths, I cry out to You, O Lord, and I really hope you can hear me. Why does life have to be so hard? Are you even there, or have you forgotten about us? Have you abandoned us like you abandoned your own son; to suffer and die in this fallen world?"

Tears ran down her cheeks and fell from her chin.

"You made us! You have no right to wash your hands of us. You have no right to ignore us! You have no right. You have no right!"

Her rage and her voice trailed off in ratcheted gasps. Waves lapped the shore in a soothing rhythmic rush, and Reka rested. Wrapped in a cocoon of sun that dripped from the sky like falling ribbons of gold, she drifted off to sleep and dreamt.

Cage Abrams walked out of the sea and sat next to her in the sand, and she sat up, still clutching her fists tightly, holding onto the sand. He took her hands in his and looked deeply into her eyes. He didn't speak, he just looked into her eyes, and she could not look away. His gaze penetrated deep into her soul and began to fill her, patching all of the damage she had suffered. And again, she heard his voice.

"You bear the sword because you are able, and you are willing."

He released her hands but not her gaze. Cradling her face in his right hand, Reka felt her mind expand beyond the soft shell that had encapsulated it. The hatred she had felt for the Reconciler, the executioner, and his men; for the faceless man that took Joe, for the freebooter who killed her mother, the anger she felt for God; all of it, it all melted away. In its place, no answers, just healing, filling her soul. The comfort of peace in understanding without knowing. The calming force of trust and acceptance.

"Reka!" Alistair screamed.

Cage opened his mouth, and the sea poured out.

"Reka!" She woke to Alistair shaking her and the wind and the rain slapping her face. The bells of La Iglesia de Cristo Redentor peeling their warning.

"We have to go! Captain Sarros wants to get Serenity out of the harbor before the storm hits!"

Reka was awake now, and Alistair lifted her to her feet.

The hot, bright afternoon was gone. In its place, a sky black as a cloud-filled night, though the sun hadn't yet set. Wet sand spun up in huge sand spouts that twisted and corkscrewed wildly across the beach as lightning spidered and crawled across the sky. In a few places, the sun managed to punch through the cloud canopy in shafts of light, one of which shone on Reka, which had allowed Alistair to find her in the brewing storm. They ran, holding hands so as not to get separated and lost. Reka was fast and strong, and she pulled Alistair along as she dodged sand devils and blowing debris. They reached the dock and sprinted for Serenity. Like a vast armada heading off to war, ships poured out of the harbor. Brave captains and their crews who preferred to take their chances battling the storm at sea rather than seeing their ships dashed to bits in the harbor. Captain Sarros managed to get Serenity sidled up to the dock and pointed out of the harbor. Tine and Alistair ran up the gangplank and pulled it up behind them as Serenity's crew cast off her lines. Her new storm jib filled and pulled her out of the harbor, headed for the massive thunderous storm clouds to the east. Sarros called out his orders, and every deck hand worked in hurried harmony to run up sails and bring Serenity about to make the run around the north end of the island of Pico de Orizaba. Sarros, with Serenity at full sail, fought to keep ahead of the storm. She danced across the waves heading west, moving ever closer to their destination.

When they had managed to put some distance between Serenity and the storm, Captain Sarros excused some of the crew. In their quarters and free of the commotion on deck, Alistair, Reka, and perhaps even the pastreco felt the absence of their friend. Alistair imagined his body tethered forever to the sea. They all peeled out of their wet clothes, laid them out on racks to dry, and sat quietly beneath heavy blankets. There was a knock at their cabin door.

"Yes?" Alistair called.

"It's Arben, Ranger."

Alistair looked at Reka, knowing that she, too, was naked under the blanket. She responded by rolling her eyes.

"Come in, Arben."

"I've brought you some hot spiced rum to warm your insides. Mr. Kohlhagen has sent these." Arben tossed clothing onto one of the bunks. "I'll take your wet things topside to lay out in the sun. Nothing will dry down here. Yourselves included. You should get dressed and get topside in the sun."

"Thank you, Arben. We will," Alistair said, and Arben excused himself.

"Before we do that," the pastreco said. "I would like to share Cage's words and thoughts with you if I may."

Reka and Alistair leaned forward in eager anticipation.

"Cage wanted you to know that his sentence was fair. He said that he did not speak because what he did, was between him and his God and that by not speaking, he took away the Reconciler's power to determine his fate. Cage had been to Orizaba before. He knew the island's swift justice. He told me that when he agreed to accompany us, it was with prayer and hope that he would be granted the opportunity to do exactly what he had done. Cage told me that he knew his prayer had been answered when he saw the Andalusia."

"The fire."

The words slipped in a whisper past Reka's lips, and the pastreco nodded.

"Cage named his ship after what he loved most in this world; his wife. She and their son Ivan were both aboard the Andalusia on the night of the mutiny. He had just finished his watch and returned to his quarters to find Rico Simms, the ship's first mate, and several other mutineers waiting for him. Simms had his blade to Cage's wife's throat. The edge was sharp, and it drew blood as it rested against her skin. Another of the mutineers held a pistol to the back of Ivan's head, and Cage knew that if he tried to save either, he would lose both. Simms told him that all he wanted was the ship and that he would set them adrift with a day's rations if he surrendered the Andalusia.

Cage agreed and allowed himself to be shackled. All through the night, Cage and Ivan were forced to watch the mutineers brutalize the woman they both loved. When they were finished with her, they tied her hands and shoved her to the deck next to her husband. He never closed his eyes that night. He said that he studied her face, the creases at the corners of her mouth, every fleck of brown and green in her hazel eyes. The memory, he said, would have to last him the rest of his life.

In the morning, the mutineers ripped Andalusia away from her family once again and made her kneel facing them. Simms slit her throat and dropped her to the deck, where she gasped and bled out and died. Cage watched her blood soak into the dry deck, his wife and his ship, one forevermore. Throughout the whole violent ordeal, she never cried out. Cage said that he would take her strength with him when it was his time to die and that he did." The Pastreco stopped and cleared his throat.

"Cage was still shackled when he was shoved overboard, and he began to sink as soon as he hit the water. Being a boy and no threat to the mutineers, Ivan was bound only with rope when they pitched him overboard along with his dead mother. He may have been a boy, but Cage and Andalusia Abrams boy was strong and fearless. Ivan managed to slip free of his bindings and drag his father and his mother's body to shore in the Barrens, over a mile away. Together, Cage and his son buried Andalusia on the island. He said that you knew the rest of his story but asked that you deliver these," he set the bearded axes on the floor, "to his son."

"The boy is his son?" Alistair finally made the connection. "But how did you get them?"

"The Reconciler was once pastreco. When I told him the story, he granted my request."

"But the Peccatum? He burned the whole crew alive?" Reka was stunned.

"Cage said that anyone who sailed with a pirate was a pirate and deserved death. Now let's get topside so we can warm up. Then we can come back here and rest. As bad as things have been, they are going to get much worse when we hit the Western Territories."

Chapter 41

The gunshot in the cavernous bank building made Joe's ears ring, but he heard Albert Odium loud and clear. Joe pushed his way through the crowd and pulled Tine away from the gathering mob. Randall Amari grabbed Joe by the shoulder and tried to hold him, and took a smash in the face for his troubles that sent him sprawling to the ground. Joe dragged Tine out the door.

"What about the baby, Joe?"

"Not now, Tine!"

He pulled her by the arm, took the stairs two at a time, and bolted for the edge of town. A few of the town's younger men gave halfhearted chase that ended upon reaching the street in front of the bank building. After clearing the wall at the west end of Perseverance and ensuring that they weren't being followed, Joe slowed to a walk. Tine pulled at him to stop.

"We have to go back for the baby!"

Ignoring her plea, Joe barked. "What the hell, Tine?"

She began exhaling hard and fast like she was trying not to cry, but the tears pouring down her cheeks betrayed her.

"Why did you shoot Mr. Odium?"

More huffing and puffing, more tears.

"You could have killed him!"

"I was trying to kill him!"

Her scream pierced the night and quieted the Katydids.

Joe hushed her. "Shh, keep it down. They might still be following us."

The new silence made Joe realize that the Katydids were back. Not a chirp from them in town, but out here, in the space in between one place and another, they were back.

Tine pulled her sling and dropped a stone in the pocket. "Good, let them come."

"What the hell has gotten into you, Tine? We're not going to hurt them."

"That man Joe, he's, well he's—I don't know who he is, but he's evil."

"He saved your life, Tine."

They continued down the road as they spoke.

"Those shingles would have killed you, but Mr. Odium saved you."

"I don't care. He's a bad person."

Joe exhaled hard and shook his head.

"And we left all of our supplies at the Amari's place."

He did nothing to try and hide his disappointment or displeasure.

"I'm sorry, Joe."

She sounded more exasperated than apologetic.

"Oh my god!" Joe slammed a palm against his forehead. "I think I knocked Mr. Amari out cold."

"And that's another thing!" Tine took on a motherly tone. "You two were acting like children. And from the sounds of things in the bank building, the whole town was being stupid."

They'd walked a little over an hour and were following a sharp curve in the road when they saw it. Bright green, Callaghan Stables and Farm stenciled in gold on the side. A chill passed through Joe's body, and he was sure Tine felt it too. Quickly, they unhitched the horse from the buckboard and rode bareback back to town. By the time they made it back, everything about the little town of Perseverance felt different. Moaning and wailing poured from the bank building. Joe ran in while Tine hitched the horse to the post out front. All around the bank building, the town's shelter, people sat holding their dead and dying. Spilled blood made the cracked marble floor slippery.

"What's wrong with her, Joe?

Randall knelt between Devlin's legs, her back propped against a wall, head lolling to one side. Over and over, he took her head in his hands and straightened her neck, and each time he let go, it dropped to the side.

"Joe, what's wrong with her? Why can't she hold her head up? Joe?"

"What happened here, Randall?"

"Devy can't hold her head up, Joe. What's wrong with her?" Lifting and letting it flop, lifting and letting it flop.

"Her neck is broken, Randall. Who did this?"

But he ignored him and continued his macabre game with his dead wife.

"Randall, Randall!" He knelt next to him, shook him, and slapped his chubby face. "Where is Taft?"

"Who, who's Taft?" He replied as if coming momentarily, out of a trance.

"Albert fucking Odium. Where is he?"

Randall looked around the room and shrugged his shoulders.

"Where's the baby?" Joe asked, as gently as he could.

"Joe, what's wrong with Devy?"

Joe stood up and looked around for the putrid-looking, skeletal figure of Hayward Taft, the man who called himself Albert Odium.

"Son of a bitch! Why didn't I see it?"

Tine appeared in the doorway, mouth hanging open momentarily before the huffing and puffing started again, and the tears fell. Joe ran to her, grabbed her hand, and dragged her out of the building.

"Joe?" Her volume rose. "Joe? What's going on? What's wrong with Mrs. Amari?"

"She's dead, Tine."

Joe ran hard for the Amari's house with Tine following. The front door stood open, and he braced himself for what he might find. The shingles still lay scattered in a heap where they fell, the hammer on the grass next to the pile. Joe picked up the hammer and armed himself. The house was dark, and Joe couldn't see beyond the threshold.

"Maybe I should wait outside, Joe."

He glanced over his shoulder. "You stay with me; I don't want you out of my sight." She clung to the back of his shirt.

Joe stepped out of the moonlit night into the pitch darkness of the Amari's house. He felt his way along in the dark like a blind man in a strange place.

Tine tugged his shirt to stop. She remembered Devlin showing her a small table near the front door with the candles and matches in the drawer. She placed two candles between her fingers, struck a match, and lit them.

"Here, Joe," he took one of the candles. "Do you think the baby's alright?"

"I don't know, Tine, I hope so."

Tine grabbed Joe's arm, and he shook her off. He had to be ready to swing his hammer. She clung again to his shirt, only this time, her grip was tighter. Together they moved slowly into the house, the candle dripping hot wax on his hand, the little stings staving off the tunnel vision that threatened to restrict his already narrowed focus. The floor creaked with every step they took. Clearing the living room, Joe and Tine moved left into the Amari's bedroom. The twin-sized beds were identically made, and a nightstand with a small oil lamp sat between them. Next to the oil lamp on either side was a Bible and a framed photo of Randall and Devlin on their wedding day. Randall looked lean and smart in his tux. Devlin was breathtaking, a rare beauty, hidden but still there all these years later. And now her time on this plane was over. All because of the man who had somehow followed him into the Western Territories.

Their bedroom was small. A quick look under the beds covered it. There was no closet and nothing large enough to hide behind. From the Amari's room back out into the living room and down the hall to their son's room, the space offered to Tine while they stayed with two of the kindest people Joe had ever known. There were bunk beds, a six-drawer dresser, and a toy chest; again, a quick and fruitless search. Across from the boy's room was a bathroom. A pedestal tub, a sink, and a high tank toilet. Back into the hall and into the wide-open kitchen. The only place left to check was the small powder room off the kitchen.

Joe pulled the door open and raised his hammer high overhead. A beam of light struck him in the eyes, momentarily blinding him, but not before he saw the twin barrels of the sawed-off side by side shotgun.

Chapter 42

Two large frigates flying Corsair colors sat in still waters less than a mile ahead of Serenity. The morning fog, which provided Serenity with some concealment, hid the Corsair ships from view until she was almost upon them. Too close to tack away safely, Sarros needed to find a way around them or concoct a viable plan of attack. The frigates could never out-maneuver Serenity, but they could match and even surpass her speed under full sail. Captain Sarros couldn't risk sailing between the frigates; that would open Serenity to attack from both sides. Trying to pass either on the outside would be disastrous as well. The frigate would train its broadside guns on her, and even if she turned, a hit in Serenity's stern could cripple her. With the idea of running put to rest, Captain Sarros needed a plan of attack. Sarros and his crew were veterans of numerous battles and had even taken their share of Corsair frigates, but never two at the same time. The plan with larger, faster ships was always the same. Nothing could be done about their size, so Serenity would take away their speed and maneuverability by targeting sails, masts, and rudder.

Sarros' plan would bring Serenity up behind the Corsair ships. They would come in slow, fire their port side cannons at one ship, then tack and fire her starboard cannons at the other. With a bit of luck, he could register two hits before the frigates could get underway. The frigates would then have to peel apart, and so long as they turned together in the same direction, Serenity could follow behind whichever ship was closer and inflict as much damage as possible while keeping the other out of the fight. They could also loose all sails and run. In which case, Serenity would lay back and slip into the fog and hide. But if they peeled off in opposite directions, or worse, toward each other, Serenity would be in for a battle she likely couldn't win. The ships would have to communicate by flying flags, and with any luck, the fog would hold and obscure them from view.

Sarros knew the maneuver was dangerous, but it was their best hope for survival. The order was whispered through the ranks; sails were set, and Serenity slid silently forward. Alistair and the pastreco on the mainsail and Reka with her long gun in the crow's-nest atop the foremast, the travelers, were set to do their part. Serenity got into position, tacked sixty degrees, and opened fire on the Corsair frigate Argent. The bells aboard the Argent and her sister ship Crucial rang, calling all to their battle stations. At Sarros' order, Alistair and the pastreco dropped Serenity's mainsails to slow her advance and tacked behind the frigates. Turning her starboard guns toward the Crucial, Serenity opened fire again. The plan was to destroy the Corsair's rudders, leaving them lame and allowing Serenity to escape.

As Serenity let loose her second volley, the Corsair ships returned fire with swivel cannons from their sterns. The swivel cannons were nothing more than anti-personnel guns, and they did no serious damage to Serenity. Still, Arben and Reka picked off the Corsair sailors as they attempted to man the small mounted cannons. Sarros turned Serenity's portside cannons once again on Argent and fired. From between the frigates, which, unfortunately, had begun peeling off in opposite directions, came a Corsair brigantine, which like Serenity, was small, fast, and maneuverable. The small ship tacked quickly, picking up all the speed she could. Black as tar with a vast white mainsail featuring a black bird, wings spread talons extended, she closed on Serenity.

"The Raven! It's the Raven!" Arben called down from the crow's nest.

Alistair felt a chill run up his spine.

"Stick close to her! The Argent and Crucial won't fire on us if they run the risk of hitting the Raven!"

Serenity pushed hard toward the Raven. The Crucial began to turn broadside at Serenity readying to fire. As the Corsair frigate settled into firing position, a small cutter flew out of the fog like a wasp, giving chase to the Raven, and fired small cannons at Crucial. The blasts were little more than distractions but were nonetheless successful. Behind the cutter came two massive galleons, Mystic and Defender, flying the crimson and black of the Maristo.

Sarros watched through his spyglass. "The Mystic and Defender and a cutter are chasing the Raven."

"May I?" Alistair looked through the captain's spyglass. "I'll be damned! It's the Ancora Imparo."

"Tobias Enzo's ship?"

Sarros took the glass back and looked for himself.

"The last time I saw them was when they pulled out of Armada. I didn't think they would have lasted this long."

The distraction from Ancora Imparo allowed the two massive galleons to block both the Argent and Crucial from firing on Serenity. The Mystic fired her thirty-six port side cannons smashing the Crucial's mainsail and several of her gun ports to splinters. Crucial fired what was left of her starboard-side battery registering several minor hits on the galleon. Raven found Defender's port side and fired her cannons but failed to cause any damage. Defender did not return fire with Serenity in the line. Serenity and the Raven were almost upon one another.

"Come alongside and prepare to board!" Sarros ordered.

Cheers went up aboard Serenity as she came against the Raven. Both ships fired grapeshot from anti-personnel cannons, and those not quick to take cover took the brunt of the blasts. Serenity's attack party readied to board the Raven as the small guns were being reloaded.

Raven's repelling party was like nothing the good Maristo of Serenity had ever seen. Hair and beards braided like whips swinging and snapping. Faces covered with tribal scarring and teeth filed to points. They screamed and howled and dragged the tips of their cutlasses or axes across their arms, legs, and torsos, drawing blood and working themselves into a frenzied state.

Serenity's crew froze, but the pastreco rose from the middle of the boarding party and launched himself onto the Raven. With Cage's bearded axes in hand, the pastreco took one and then another of the braided heads with single swipes sending them tumbling to the deck. The Raven's crew stormed the pastreco, who spun and slid like a dancer. Axes singing through the air as they split one then the next pirate in two. Shouts went up among Sarros' men as they poured over the rails firing short muskets and swinging boarding axes. From where he stood on Serenity's deck, Alistair could hear the sound of axes thudding into bodies, the wet slapping sounds of flesh splitting, the sound of metal splintering bone, and the cries of the dying. Some of Serenity's crew took to the rigging, hacking away at lines and setting fire to sails. Many of them sacrificing their lives for the job at hand.

And to his dismay, the Raven seemed to spawn Corsair pirates from below deck, like some horrible wooden womb. No matter how many fell in battle, more came crawling from below to join the fight. While the Mystic and Defender battered Argent and Crucial until they slipped below the sea, the Ancora Imparo came alongside Serenity, and Tobias Enzo sent Fallon Holton aboard with an urgent message. Sarros had a line lowered to assist the young man aboard.

"Captain Sarros! They won't stop coming, sir! No matter how many you kill, they won't stop coming! Please, you must call your men back."

Sarros cast a wary eye on the crewman of the Ancora Imparo, but Holton persisted.

"Please, captain, we have been chasing the Raven for months, and boarding parties, no matter the size, are slaughtered."

Sarros watched as pirate after pirate dropped in battle, only to be replaced by another from below.

"Ramsey, sound the retreat!"

Ramsey ran to the ship's bell and repeated the rapid three-strike pattern. Like Pavlov's dogs, the Maristo broke from the fight as quickly as possible and returned to Serenity. The pastreco, unaware of what the tolling of the bell meant, stood on Raven's deck covered in corsair blood, surrounded by her crew. Ramsey continued to beat the call while Alistair, Kohlhagen, and Villwock shouted for the pastreco to return. Weapons raised, sharpened teeth gnashing, they slowly closed in on him. The pastreco bowed his head and then looked to the heavens and spoke unheard words. Leveling his gaze at the approaching hoard, he spun like a dervish, blades, and blood flying through the air, and then he was gone. Engulfed by the swarming pirates. Reka and Arben, who had been firing into the mass, halted for fear that they would hit the pastreco, though both must have known their fear was pointless. Arben turned his attention toward the pirates moving across the deck toward Serenity. Reka stared in horror at the spot she last saw her friend.

"Reka! Wake up, girl!"

She snapped out of her daze and joined Arben, raining hot lead into Raven's pirate crew from above. But still, they came one after another. Holton tugged at the captain's sleeve as Raven's pirates began their assault on Serenity.

"Sir, you must break off before they take Serenity."

Sarros spun, enraged.

"We will not leave our man if there is a chance he is still alive!"

"Cut the line!"

The gore-soaked pastreco pulled himself out from a mound of dead pirates and ran for Serenity with the mass of pirates on his heels.

He called out again, "Cut the line!"

Villwock looked to his captain, and with his nod, the rope was cut, freeing Serenity from the Raven. Some of Raven's crew fell between the ships, either being crushed or left to drown. A few others made it aboard and were greeted with lead and steel. Alistair's Dragoons glowed red hot with round after round fired into the ghouls. Reka and Arben continued their assault from above while Ramsey pulled one of the swivel cannons from its mount and fired it like a shotgun, mowing down a charging hoard. Sarros, Kohlhagen, and Villwock repelled the remaining invaders as those remaining aboard the Raven threw out hooks in the hopes of snagging and dragging her back, but Serenity was free.

"Aloft and loose all sails!"

Aye, captain, came from all parts of the ship as the crew scurried the rigging.

"Set the sails!"

Serenity pulled fast away from the Raven, followed by the Ancora Imparo. Blood chilling screams of rage rose again from the Raven. Sarros broke out his spyglass and watched as Raven's crew went to work setting her sails.

The great white mainsail with the fierce black raven filled with wind snapped hard and broke loose. The Raven floundered as her crew flew up her mast like spiders hoping to repair her webbing.

Sarros began to come about to fire on her when the Mystic and Defender's cannons roared, and the Raven's main and mizzen masts fell. Their next volley tore into Raven's hull, splintering her and sending her to the bottom of the sea to rest forever with Argent and Crucial. Cheers went up on all four ships, but for the small Maristo armada, the fight was far from over.

Chapter 43

Joe shoved Tine back into the kitchen and lunged to his right to avoid as much of the blast as he could. The shotgun would still take a huge bite out of him, but if there was even the slightest chance that he could take Hayward Taft with him into the next world, he had to take it. The hammer felt good in his hand, and he could move it swiftly. Like a pitcher on the wind-up, Joe cocked his arm back and drew the hammer close to his ear.

"Joe, stop!" The voice came in a harsh whisper.

He halted his delivery.

"Carmen? What are you doing here?"

"Joe, where are you?" Tine called from somewhere in the dark kitchen, her candle having gone out when she hit the floor.

Carmen shined her light into the kitchen, careful to keep it low.

"Is he gone?"

"Yes, Carmen, I think he is, but I'm afraid he took the baby."

Carmen slid off the hatch and lifted it.

"No, she's fine. I lowered her down when I heard you come in." She pointed at the floor. "Squeaky floorboards." She hoisted the baby up and handed her to Tine, who had joined them in the small powder room.

"What happened to everyone?" Joe asked though he thought he knew.

"I've never seen anything like it, Joe; they all turned on one another. Even Randall and Devlin."

"I know, I saw," Joe said.

He broke her neck, Joe, and I think it had something to do with Odium fellow."

"His name isn't Odium, it's Taft, Hayward Taft, and he's the one who killed your shopkeeper."

"Sam, he killed Sam Halverson? But why, and why did he come back?"

"He killed him because he's evil, pure evil; why he came back is anyone's guess."

Tine rocked the baby in her arms. "What are you going to do now?"

"We're going to pray, and we are going to persevere."

Tine rolled her eyes and grunted in exasperation.

"Faith dear, it's a matter of faith."

"Is faith the reason you're hiding in the powder room?"

Joe turned toward the girl, "Tine!" he scolded.

"It's okay, Joe. Tine, faith sometimes calls for action rather than abeyance."

"What's that?" Tine asked earnestly.

"It means not sitting idly by and waiting for God to do things for you. It means using what God has given you, child. It means up rolling your sleeves instead of your eyes and getting to work."

Joe knew that if Tine hadn't been holding the baby, she would have crossed her arms, but as it was, she could only smirk and blast a puff of air out of her nose.

"Well, what are you going to do with her," she nodded down toward the baby. "While everyone is rolling up their sleeves, I mean."

"She is a natural-born citizen of Perseverance; she will be cared for and loved. And we would offer the same to you and your brother, born here or not."

"Thank you, Carmen, but we really have to go. We just stopped to check on... What's her name going to be?"

Carmen looked at Tine. "You are the only one left who was there when this little angel came into the world. Suppose you name her."

"Me? I can't name a baby! She'll be stuck with it her whole life!"

Carmen smiled. "Well, we're just supposing."

"Then I suppose I would name her Faith."

Carmen's smile widened.

"It's not why you think," Tine said defiantly. "Faith was my sister's name, and a lot of good it did her."

"It's a beautiful name Tine, thank you."

Tine couldn't hold back the smile.

"Well, I should take Faith and head back to the bank building. There is much to be done, and Faith will give us the strength to see it through."

They accompanied Carmen and Faith back to the bank building and said their goodbyes.

"Tine, we have to get to Reverie. I don't know what Taft is up to, but we have to find the Maristo and get back to Savista."

Joe climbed back onto the horse and offered his hand to Tine. She did not take it.

"You promised to take me to Dioj Volos."

"I know, and if that's what you really want, I'll get you to him. But I kind of thought we made a pretty good team."

"It's not that I want to, Joe. I need to. I can't explain it, but I can feel him calling to me."

"Like I said, I'll take you to him if that's what you really want." Joe offered his hand again, and this time Tine took it. "But my offer still stands. You can come back to Savista with me. There are kids your age there, and I really think you would like it."

Tine settled in on the blanket over the horse's back and grabbed Joe around the waist.

"So, how do you know that man?"

"He's from a place called the Barrens in the Midwestern Territories, and he makes the tickers look like cub scouts."

"What are cub scouts?"

"Cub scouts, you know," he paused. "No, I suppose you don't. Anyway, they're good guys."

"The tickers are not good guys, Joe."

"I know! That's the point." Clearly exasperated, Joe continued to explain. "Like Taft is so bad that he makes the tickers look good, you know, by comparison. It's a metaphor or something; I don't know. Look, forget it.

Let's just say that Taft is a very bad person."

"Well, why didn't you just say that?"

"I wish I would have."

She hugged him from behind. "Oh, don't be such a grump."

The sun rising in the east dragged their shadows out long on the road ahead. Tine held her hand with fingers splayed out behind Joe's head.

"Look, Joe, you have snakes coming out of your head."

Joe looked at the ground ahead and made scissors with his fingers.

"Look, I'm cutting your snakes up."

Tine wiggled her fingers wildly.

"No, you're not. They're getting away, see?"

Joe snipped here and there, and Tine wiggled and giggled, and they passed the time. Just past the point where the sun was directly overhead, the bright green buckboard with the gold lettering pulled by the ill-suited quarterhorse arrived at a shallow river. Joe unhitched Champion, Tine decided it was a fitting name, and walked him over to the cool, clear water. Together, he and the horse plunged their faces into the fast running water and drank deep. Tine busied herself setting out a little picnic just off the bank of the river under an expansive cottonwood. Joe walked Champion back and tied him off on a branch under the tree. He didn't want to spend too much time but knew that they all needed a rest.

Across the river, in the wavy heat of the midday sun, Joe spotted a large structure on the horizon.

"Do you see that?" Joe pointed at the object.

Tine squinted. "Sure, I'm not blind."

Joe rubbed his eyes. "Is that a roller coaster?"

"Could be, I guess. I've never seen one."

"Well, this might just be your lucky day; after we rest, of course."

Joe allowed for a two-hour break, and they were back at it. They crossed the river, which never got deeper than the middle of Joe's thigh, and started heading southwest toward Reverie, and the roller coaster Joe had spotted. The sun was ahead of them now, and the glare was blinding. Tine stopped and dug a small hole and began spitting in it. She jammed her fingers into the mud she created and swiped it under her eyes.

"Here, Joe, try this."

"I'd rather squint, thanks."

The farther they got from the river, the dryer and more cracked the ground became. Lush green grass and cottonwood trees gave way to parched red clay. Champion moved cautiously over some of the larger cracks that had opened up, but the buckboard fell victim to a particularly large gap. Joe climbed down off the rig and examined the damage.

"Well, that's it for the buckboard. We busted a wheel."

Tine tossed their gear down to Joe and hopped off and climbed down herself.

"We need to make piles, Joe. Stuff we need, then the stuff we want, and the rest is junk. Joe unhitched Champion from the buckboard and fit him with saddlebags. Together, he and Tine loaded all of the stuff from the need pile, fresh water, food, oil for lamps, weapons, and ammo. From the want pile, Joe kept a shirt and extra pair of pants. Tine selected a hair ribbon Devlin Amari gave her and the Holy Bible she swiped off the nightstand in the Amari's bedroom.

"That's a weird choice."

"I know, but if I ever learn to read, I'm going to figure out why you people go nuts over this thing. My sister told me that it's a book about love and sacrifice."

"I guess that's one way to describe it," Joe said with a smile.

She jammed it carelessly into the saddlebag.

"Don't worry, Champion, if it gets too heavy, we can toss it out."

"So, you never learned to read?"

Tine blew back a strand of hair dangling over her right eye and grabbed Champion's bridle.

"No, my dad said that women didn't need to know how to read."

"What the hell does that mean?"

Tine shrugged her shoulders and kept walking.

Eventually, the coaster came into focus. Sixty feet tall and over half a mile long. From their distance, it appeared that the old wooden coaster was covered in Cottonwood seedlings, and the setting sun made it look like it was burning. The sun played other tricks as well. Joe could have sworn that the roller coaster cars were moving over the tracks. The great attraction rose higher and higher into the reddening sky as they walked closer. They tied Champion to the fence. Joe pulled his repeater from his saddlebag, and he and Tine pushed through a rusted turnstile onto the carnival grounds. Passing the faded signs and burned-out bulbs of the midway. Stuffed animals and kewpie dolls hanging by their necks tied to pegboards. One booth featured Elvis novelty sunglasses; Joe grabbed two pairs. He put one on and gave the other to Tine. They looked at one another and laughed.

"You look stupid," Tine said.

"Not as stupid as you, I bet. Come on, we have to keep moving."

The closer they got, the surer he was that the ride was operating. By the looks of the rest of the amusement park, it made no sense, but he was sure the cars were moving across the tracks. He could even hear the excited patrons screaming.

"What the hell is that, Joe?"

"It's a roller coaster, and watch your mouth."

"Why? You said it before."

"That's beside the point."

"But really, is it killing something?"

The shrill screams rose to a crescendo.

"I might be crazy, but it almost sounds like people having fun!"

Tine scrunched her face and drew her head back. "I'm not sure what you call fun, but that sounds like a slaughter to me."

Tine had sharp eyes, much sharper than Joe's. As they cornered the corn dog concession, the coaster was dead ahead. Gray cigar-shaped cocoons hung like ornaments on a Christmas tree, some with faces, some without, and now the cars were moving across the supports.

"Spiders." Tine pushed the word out in a whisper the first time. She poked her companion in the side. "Joe… Spiders!"

She grabbed Joe's arm and pulled him away, quickening their pace. By the time they hit the midway, they were at a full run. Shrieking yowling spiders, like back in the fields near Espero, were closing in, clambering across the tin roofs of the bottle toss, balloon darts, and ring toss booths. Ahead, from around one of the fairway exhibits, on long stick-like legs supporting a black body, the spider crawled over the corner of the little tent and sprung at them. Spiders to the left, right, behind, and in front, they broke for the shelter of a nearby ticket booth.

"Champion!"

Tine tried to push past Joe, but he held her tightly and pulled her into the booth slamming the door behind them.

"Shh. They'll leave if they don't know we're here. Spiders hunt by movement and smell."

The metal roll-down shutter over the ticket window was still up, and they hid beneath it, under the counter. If a spider banged into the glass and broke it, the booth would quickly fill with the arachnid's black furry bodies.

"Stay put, and no matter what happens, don't move or make a sound."

Tine's eyes widened with fear, and she shook her head no. Joe pushed her head down.

"Close your eyes and cover your ears."

She did as she was told. Joe moved slowly, inch by painstakingly slow inch, hoping the spiders would sense him. He watched them move their thin black bodies over the glass, seeming not to register his presence. Unlike the spiders in Espero, fat, covered in thick black hair, these looked emaciated. Thin, hair growing in patches, with what looked like ribs punching through their gray leather-looking skin. But it couldn't be, and he knew it. Spiders didn't have ribs. They had exoskeletons. A shell on the outside of their bodies. And the way they moved was different too. Espero's spiders moved like jungle cats. Smooth, powerful with measured precision. These things looked like junkies; herky-jerky, jittery movements. Darting back and forth across the glass and over the grounds. Joe reached up slowly and grabbed the lip on the bottom of the shutter. The metal screeched in protest to its being forced to move after an unknown number of years of dormancy. The spider jerked its way across the glass, stopped dead in its tracks, and began vibrating violently. Joe thought the thing might shatter its own shell.

He pulled hard on the rolling shutter that squealed all the way down. The glass shattered and the shutter slammed shut with a bang plunging them into darkness again. Tine screamed, and Joe could hear the spiders racing over the little ticket booth, their only shelter from the horrid things. Joe pulled a small box of matches and a candle that he took from the Amari's place. In the soft candlelight, Joe found and secured the latch on the shutter. He set the candle on the counter and noticed that he'd inadvertently severed part of one of the spiders' legs when he slammed the shutter down. The acid in the spider's blood ate through the Formica countertop and right on through the wood dripping to the ground. It would have landed right on her if he had not pulled Tine out from under the counter. He pictured the aftermath of the bite of a brown recluse, flesh, and muscle eaten away down to the bone.

"If we stay quiet, they should go away. I just hope this shack holds up."

"Joe," Tine whispered. "What about Champion? Do you think he's alright?"

"I don't know."

He wanted to lie to her, make her feel better, and just give her some peace, but he couldn't do it. It was better, to be honest with her than to blow sunshine up her behind. Tine teared up but held herself together. Joe sat against the wall next to her and put an arm over her shoulder. Tine leaned her head against him and pressed her ear into his chest. She pressed her palm against her other ear and closed her eyes. They'd come a long way from the cellar.

They sat in total silence, but still, the spiders clicked and scraped and crawled over the shack. Back in the fields near Espero, the spiders lost track of him when he didn't move. And then it hit him. The spiders were picking up their heartbeats through the wall. As he pulled Tine away from the wall, he heard a spider screech, followed by the smell of burning hair filling the air. Then another screech and another.

"Joe, the smell; it's so bad, Joe."

"I think the spiders are burning."

The noise faded, and Joe stood up and raised the metal shutter a few inches. Except for the few that lay curled up and smoldering, the spiders were gone. Joe came out of the booth with his rifle at the ready. He scanned the area but saw no one. Half-burned arrows sticking out of the spider's bodies told Joe that their mysterious helper had to be no more than sixty yards away. He assumed that the archer had their best interest at heart, but he couldn't afford assumptions. Moving quickly from building to building, taking cover when they could, they had almost made it back to Champion when the screeching started again.

Chapter 44

About one hundred and fifty miles off the Assumption coast where the harbor town of Reverie lay, Kidwell, captain of the Mystic, called a meeting aboard his vessel. The captains and officers of Defender, Serenity and the Ancora Imparo gathered around the large table in Captain Kidwell's quarters.

"Thank you all for coming," Kidwell sat and motioned for his guests to do the same.

"Gentlemen, today we have rid the waters of the evilest ship on the open sea."

The men cheered.

"Too many of our brothers have fallen to the Raven, but no more!" Kidwell slammed his hand on the table.

"Because of you, the Raven will no longer haunt these waters."

His cabin steward poured rum for the captain's guests as he spoke.

"Raise a glass with me in honor of our fallen brothers, both today and in times past."

Everyone at the table lifted their glass. Alistair, whom Sarros included though he held no rank, raised his glass to his lips, but Ramsey placed a hand on his forearm, stopping him from drinking. With a slight nod, Ramsey called his attention to the rest of the men at the table, pouring their first drink onto the floor. Alistair followed suit, and the steward quickly set about refilling the glasses.

"And now to all of you, my honored guests. Brave men, every last one of you."

He raised his glass toward Sarros, and they all drank.

"Captain Sarros, we owe Serenity and her crew a special measure of thanks. Your men boarded the Raven, battled her unrelenting hoard, and crippled her, allowing Defender and Mystic to unleash hell and sink her like a stone."

All but Serenity's representatives roared and clapped, and Captain Sarros stood up.

"On behalf of our fallen, I accept your gratitude."

Sarros took his seat, and Kidwell continued.

"We have pursued that accursed ship for months, and in that time, we have lost over a dozen Maristo vessels to her. But no more. And now we will head for Pico de Orizaba and enjoy our well-earned respite from battle."

Again, all but the men from Serenity cheered.

"Aren't they coming with us?"

Sarros held a hand to Alistair, signaling him to hold his question. Kidwell was a mindful man and noticed the somber mood of Sarros and his men.

"Captain Sarros, I sense that there is something more than the loss of your men weighing on you."

"Aye, there is. We will not be joining you in Pico de Orizaba."

Kidwell wrinkled his brow. "Why not? You have certainly earned a break from battle."

Sarros looked around the table. "We have business in Assumption and the town of Reverie."

The table fell silent and then rose up in a clamor. Kidwell held his hands up and stilled the gathering.

"Why in God's name would you go there, my friend?"

Sarros stood up and invited Alistair to do the same.

"The reason we were here today, and able to lend whatever small hand we could in defeating Raven, is because of this man. This is Alistair Woodbridge, Ranger of Espero."

"Why is a Terren at the captain's table?" One of Defender's officers demanded.

Kidwell held his hands up again.

"What's a Terren?" Alistair shifted, unsure what to expect in answer to his question.

Sarros put a hand on his shoulder, "It's what the Maristo call people who live on dry land, terra firma."

Alistair nodded, satisfied that he had not just been insulted.

"He is," said Sarros, "and so is the man who butchered the Raven's pirates with no regard for his own life, and I am proud to call them, my good friends. If he is not welcome at this table, neither are my officers or I."

Kidwell ran a hand through his gray hair. "Of course, he is welcome. Besides, no one who could survive a battle like that could be all Terren." Laughter broke out among Kidwell's guests. After a moment, Kidwell held up a hand, silencing the group.

"Captain Sarros, the Maristo were driven out of the harbor at Reverie some time ago. In the time since then, I am sure the forces that drove them away have only dug themselves in deeper."

Alistair was unfamiliar with the stories of Reverie. "Who has dug in deeper?"

"Assumption is a brutal and vile place," Kidwell said. "A man who calls himself Dioj Volos has built an army of ravagers, like the crew of the Raven. The Maristo, who were lucky enough to escape, said that Dioj Volos turns men into those things you saw aboard the Raven, and they have made a home for themselves in Reverie. Whatever business you have there had better be worth your souls."

The room was silent as a tomb, then Sarros spoke up. "We are headed to Reverie to find the Ranger's friend and, with the help of our pastreco, to rid the dry part of the world of that evil."

More murmuring among the representatives of each ship. Captain Enzo spoke first.

"It is good to see you again, my friend," he nodded at Alistair. "Am I safe in assuming that you go in search of Joe Kott?"

"You are."

"Then the Ancora Imparo sails with you."

"It is not our fight," Daniel Sanchez, Defender's captain, said and slammed his hand on the table. "Why should the Maristo trouble themselves in land matters?"

Tobias Enzo stood and addressed the table. "I have sailed with the Ranger and his friend Joe. We transported them to a small island in the middle of the Midwestern Territories called The Barrens. I know of the evil of which Captain Kidwell speaks, and I know that it will spread to our seas. The crew of the Raven came from that island. Simple Corsair scum who turned into what we had been hunting for months. Turned into the flesh-eating wraiths who have taken a dozen Maristo ships. And this man emerged from that evil to be here today to fight a battle that was not his. He and his pastreco friend and the woman who fired from Serenity's crows-nest, it was not their fight, but they fought by our side, and by God, we sank that retched ship. Captain Sanchez, you ask why we should trouble ourselves in land matters? Well, maybe we shouldn't. But mark my words. When they have plundered the land, those things will board ships and bring the fight to us. The Maristo owe a debt for services rendered, and The Ancora Imparo, small as she may be, will see that debt paid. We are willing to show our gratitude with more than a toast to the dead and spilled rum."

The room fell silent as all waited for Daniel Sanchez to respond. He rose from his chair and walked over to Tobias Enzo. Sanchez had been called out, and Enzo was ready for whatever came. Sanchez stood nose to nose with Enzo and embraced his brother. 'Defender is with you."

Kidwell smiled at his guests, "Ahh, my brothers. It looks like our small armada is off on another adventure before we rest!"

Cheers went up all through the lower decks of Mystic and spread top side and all across the ship. Word was passed from ship to ship, and soon cheers and gunshots erupted across the water.

Kidwell allowed the celebration to settle on its own before continuing.

"We will need a battle plan. If Captains and Quartermasters will remain, we will begin our work."

Sarros and Ramsey stayed behind, as did the Ancora Imparo and Defender's captains and quartermasters. All the rest boarded their skiffs and returned to their ships to prepare for the battle ahead.

* * *

Back aboard Serenity, Alistair went below to Doc's quarters to check on the pastreco. He lay bleeding and battered on blood-soaked sheets.

"I have good news; the others are joining us on our quest." The pastreco tried to lift himself on his elbow but couldn't hold himself up.

Doc eased him back down.

"I told you to stay put. I got more stitching to do."

He passed thick thread through the eye of a needle used to sew canvas.

"And if you don't stay put, I'm gonna stitch you right to the mattress."

The pastreco laid still. Alistair looked at the man, who almost single-handedly vanquished what looked to be a hundred men. Battle-scarred and weary, the pastreco spoke.

"That is good news. We are going to need them."

Alistair pulled a chair next to his bed.

"I can't figure you out. I thought your kind had a strict rule against killing people."

"We do."

"Well, you sure killed a hell of a lot of them today."

"Those things weren't men, not anymore."

The pastreco coughed, and Doc cautioned him, but he continued.

"You can't kill something that's already dead, Ranger. I simply broke the jars to free the souls trapped inside."

Alistair squinted, wanting to make sure he paid close attention.

"What do you mean dead?"

Laying as still as he could, the pastreco drew in a deep breath.

"I mean dead. No longer among the living, like the wendigo in our world."

Alistair stood up. "That's just a legend."

"It's much more than a legend. You and your kind have the luxury of telling yourself that fallen angels aren't real. But the pastreco have battled to protect mankind from their evil since the beginning of time."

"What about Hayward Taft? Is he one of these fallen angels?"

The pastreco nodded his head. "Hayward is a man, an evil man for sure, but still just a man. Though he has sworn allegiance to Dioj Volos, and that makes him a very dangerous man." The pastreco coughed again as Doc pulled the last stitch and tied the knot.

"Ranger, he really needs to rest."

Alistair didn't register Doc's concern.

"What about this Dioj Volos? Can we kill him?"

The pastreco shook his head somberly. "It's not as easy as killing one man. Dioj Volos has transformed from a man into a collective. His followers are his windows to the world around them. He sees through their eyes, hears through their ears, and they do his bidding without the need of guidance."

"So, what; you're telling me that he's a seer?" Alistair thought of Thea.

"He is more than a seer. I am a seer. That's how I found you and Thea. He is a puppet master and a deceiver. The man you hunt, Taft, is a plaything for Dioj Volos. He has had control over him from the time he was a boy, although Taft never knew it."

Alistair's temper flared. "You mean to tell me that you have known about him all this time and are just now going to kill him?"

The pastreco sighed. "Alistair, time isn't what you think it is. It's not linear. It does not start and stop. There's no beginning, and there is no end. The true God is not subject to your limited understanding of time and space. What you call a year passes in the blink of an eye, a hundred years, in a whisper."

Alistair was dumbfounded.

"Are you familiar with the mayfly, Ranger?"

Alistair nodded, and the pasterco continued.

"The mayfly emerges from the water to live its whole life in one day, and to him, it's a lifetime. Man's understanding of time is even more limited than the mayflies. To everyone and everything, there is a time, and this is Dioj Volos' time. He has found his fire and make no mistake; if he gets her, he will scorch the earth."

"What do you mean, her, Thea?"

Alistair needed to understand what he had gotten himself and Reka into.

"Thea is in the safest place she can be. And as long as we stop Dioj Volos, she will remain safe."

Alistair slammed his fist against his leg. "Dammit! I should not be here! I belong in Savista where I could protect her."

The pastreco placed a hand on Alistair's forearm.

"Ranger, if you stayed in Savista, you would be powerless to save her. This is our best, our only hope of saving Thea, Siobhan, and the rest of our world."

"Then who are you talking about?"

"Your friend's traveling companion, the girl with the red hair. She's a seer, just like Thea, and like Thea, she is also a weapon. Dioj Volos has been calling her, and he is using your friend Joe to bring her to him."

"Wait, you're saying this Volos guy is controlling Joe? Bullshit!"

"Not physically controlling him, but he will use everything around Joe to see that his will is done. He will put the girl in danger from one direction to drive them in the other, and Joe will do anything to keep her safe. It's just his nature, and Dioj Volos knows it."

The pastreco took a deep breath and closed his eyes.

Doc had been listening intently and wanted to know more, but the pastreco needed rest. He stepped between Alistair and the pastreco.

"That's enough for now, Ranger."

Alistair nodded but hated the idea of leaving while he still had questions. "He's going to make it, right?"

Doc smiled, "I have no doubt."

***

The following day Alistair woke to find himself alone in the cabin he shared with Reka, the pastreco, and until recently, Cage. He reached over and turned up the wick on the oil lamp. On Cage's bed lay the bearded axes that had spilled more blood than Alistair's revolvers could have in ten lifetimes. They looked quiet, almost serene. Alistair leaned over and placed his hand on the blade of one of the axes. The steel was cold. He slid his hand down the handle, wrapped his fingers tight around the weapon, and lifted it. He found that he had to use two hands. The image of the pastreco handling them like conductors' batons seemed impossible, but he witnessed it with his own eyes. Alistair knew he was old and getting older by the minute, but he was still strong. He was willing to bet that he was as strong as any other man on Serenity, except for the pastreco and maybe Ramsey. But strong as he was, he couldn't wield the axe even with two hands, and he doubted Ramsey could either.

"What is the pastreco?" Alistair whispered, and the sound of his voice carried him away. He remembered the vanishing act at Siobhan's and again on the dock. Did he vanish again under the attack on the Raven when he disappeared from view? "What is the pastreco?" He whispered again, but this time a knock on his cabin door pulled him from thought.

"Yes?"

"Captain is requesting you on deck, sir."

Alistair set the axe down, stood up, got dressed, and joined the others on deck. The air was misty and smelled of salt and sea.

"Good morning, Mr. Alistair."

Alistair gave a half-assed salute touching his fingers to his forehead.

"Morning, Captain."

Sarros stood at the bridge and addressed the crew.

"Gentlemen! And Lady Reka, as you know, Ancora Imparo, Defender, and Mystic have agreed to accompany us to the Western Territories to fight alongside Serenity in whatever battle we may find. We are expecting heavy resistance. The word is that even the Corsair have been forced out of the harbor. There is some kind of demigod in power, and according to information garnered from Maristo tales, he commands a large and heavily armed militia."

Alistair recalled his conversation with the pastreco and muttered, "Dioj Volos," under his breath.

The captain sipped his coffee and continued.

"While we don't normally concern ourselves with the affairs on land, I am given to believe that if we lose this battle, all will be lost. We will sail in under cover of darkness. We are in the waxing crescent phase of the first quarter moon, and with a little help from God Almighty, we will have cloud cover. Our scouts will slip onto shore and report back to us. If we find what we are expecting, the plan will be as follows: we will load into lifeboats, leaving six men behind to pilot Serenity out to sea if the worst should happen. I will not ask for volunteers because I know that I will have none to choose from. Instead, we will load names into a bucket, and the first six drawn will stay aboard. The officers and I will refrain from inclusion in the drawing. I will appoint temporary command to a man of my choosing from the six names drawn."

"Captain," Arben said. "I pray that I am not one of the six, but I think I speak for all of your men in saying that we will not abandon you."

"And that is why you will not be named as the one in command. Maristo, I am your captain, and I am giving you a direct order. If and when the time has come, we will set fire to our lifeboats. When you see them burning on the beach, that will be your signal to sail for the open sea. We cannot risk these monsters taking control of Serenity. Kidwell, Sanchez, and Enzo are all instructing their crews likewise. If by some miracle the order is given, but we succeed in taking the harbor, a fire in the shape of the Holy cross of Jesus Christ will be lit on the beach, which you will be able to see a great distance from shore."

The crew grumbled at the thought of losing a fight but understood the need to keep Serenity safe from whatever they might find on land. Sarros took another sip and continued.

"Of the six who remain, five will need to make their way by rope over to the Mystic. They will need your help in loading and firing their cannons. Bombardment from Defender and Mystic will commence when we hit the shore. That will surely soften their defenses."

Sarros paused and lowered his voice.

"We are a day and a half out, and I suggest you all get your affairs in order. If you have loved ones on Pico de Orizaba or back on the mainland, write your letters, and say your farewells because most of us will not be returning to Serenity when this is over. Prepare your minds and bodies for battle and your souls for heaven. This will be a costly fight for a just cause. Men, it has been an honor."

Chapter 45

Joe turned, expecting to see a tidal wave of spiders rushing at them, but instead, from back in the direction of the rollercoaster, flames licked at the sky. It seemed to Joe that the unknown archer had turned his attention on the web-covered coaster. The chard and burning spiders tumbled down the sides of the coaster, disappearing in fountains of embers somewhere on the ground below. Joe and Tine used the distraction to get to Champion.

"He's okay, Joe!" Tine hugged the horse around the neck.

Joe mounted Champion, pulled Tine up behind him, and nudged the horse into motion. "Hang on tight."

Tine grabbed him tight around the waist, and they rode west as fast as Champion could carry them. After the first mile, and when Joe was sure they weren't being followed, he slowed the horse to a trot. Another hour put 15 miles between them and whatever was left of the spiders, and Joe hopped down and walked next to Champion, who now only bore Tine's very minimal load. When they reached a small creek, the trio stopped to rest. Tine gave Champion a good wipe down and made sure he didn't drink too fast. The last thing they needed was a sick horse. On their fourth day out of Perseverance, they came to a gray, weathered road post. Wooden planks shaved to a point at one end marked the distance to this place or that. None of the destinations mattered to them except the one that read Reverie, 25 miles. They were hungry and tired, and they had lost Champion just the day before. The horse turned an ankle in a gopher hole, and Joe had to spend a bullet putting their companion out of his misery. Joe figured that they had another 16 hours ahead of them at their current pace and decided to rest for the night. Joe felt exceedingly dull and slow in the head, and he wasn't sure it was a good idea to wander into a place that the Amari's said was so dangerous without his wits about him.

"Tine, let's get off the road and find some shelter for the night."

Since Champion died, she had been feeling down, and Joe had no idea how to bring her out of her funk. He hoped a good night's rest would do the trick. She didn't say a word; she just stopped walking and waited for Joe to tell her where to go. He led her off the path and into a gap between two large stones. She sat where he pointed without so much as a word. Joe sat next to her and lifted her chin.

"I'm so sorry, Tine; Champion was a great horse," he removed his glasses to rub his eyes, and Tine burst out laughing.

Joe was confused. "What?" Now he was starting to laugh. "Can I ask what is so funny?"

Tine pointed at his face. "Your eyes, look at your eyes!"

Joe rubbed at his eyes. "I don't get it; is there something on my face?"

She was holding her stomach. "You… you look like a…."

"Like a what?" Joe demanded lightly.

"Like a backward ra-ra-raccoon!"

She doubled over, took off her Elvis sunglasses, and brushed the tears from her eyes. When she sat up, Joe knew what she meant. They had both gotten good and burned on their journey west. Their faces were a deep dark red, except for the white skin hidden under the big novelty glasses. When she'd finally composed herself, she wrapped her arm around Joe and kissed his red cheek.

"I love you, Joe; I couldn't ask for a better big brother." She didn't let go but just settled into his arms and closed her eyes.

"I love you too, kid."

* * *

Morning came, and along with it, two dead bodies, both with arrows through their necks. Tickers by the looks of them, bolos hanging from their belts, customary leather pouch worn on a yellow strap across their bodies. Joe's head darted around, looking for the person who killed the tickers. Now he was sure they were being followed. He first felt it back when they reached Perseverance, but he'd shrugged it off as post-battle jitters. But now, there was no question. Whomever it was hadn't tried to harm them. On the contrary, it seemed he was their guardian angel…or maybe it was a she. Either way, they owed their lives to the archer. Somewhere out there, a person skilled with a bow had intervened and saved their lives on at least two separate occasions. But why? He hated to look a gift horse in the mouth, but he couldn't imagine why this person was looking out for them.

"Tine, do you have any other family out here? Anyone who would be looking out for you?"

Tine shook her head. "No, just you."

"Then how do you explain this?"

He stepped away from the opening between the boulders giving her a clear view of the two dead bodies on the ground. She took a quick peek at the bodies and turned her attention back to packing her things away.

"Dioj Volos, I told you already."

"Randall said it was nonsense."

She peered around Joe, looking at the dead tickers.

"Ask that guy if he thinks it's nonsense."

"That doesn't mean it's your hero."

"Joseph! You're jealous!"

"I'm not jealous, and don't call me Joseph."

Tine hugged him again. "I told you, Joe, you're like family to me. You're my big brother…stupid. Dioj Volos is like our father."

"I already have a father, even if he can't remember me."

He said that last part more to himself than to Tine.

"What?" She cocked her head.

"I said I already have a father."

"I know, I heard that part. What did you say after that?"

"Nothing, let's get going, huh?"

"Sure, Joe, I'm ready."

With the sun rising behind them, they started walking toward Reverie.

Chapter 46

Hayward was on the camp sentry before he had time to warn the other freebooters. The karambit sat nestled snugly below the ridge of the man's jaw, and Hayward pressed just hard enough to draw blood. His second trip through the Dead Zone was worse than the first, but it was over. Blazing sun blistered his already pocked and mottled skin, subzero cold claimed his ears and the three middle fingers from each hand. Hayward Taft was less whole than when he stepped back into the nuclear nightmare world but more complete. Laser-focused and clear about his purpose, for perhaps the first time in his life, and this was step one. He needed to recruit fighters; soldiers for the upcoming battle with Savista. Five hundred good men would do the trick, but he would have to sift through twice that number to find them. In his experience, most freebooters were soft, fat, and lazy. Merciless enough to kill any man, woman, or child you put in front of them, but only if they were too weak to defend themselves. The warriors of Savista were sure to be primed and ready for battle.

"Where is your chief?" Hayward's hot breath hissed and curled around from the back of the man's neck. The sentry raised his arm slowly and unrolled his finger at a tent with two sleeping guards out front. They would certainly not make the cut. Hayward pushed his human shield toward the tent where the camp commander lay asleep, no doubt confident in his men's protection. Hayward planned to have the sentry call out to his chief to draw him into a conversation, but his plan went awry as a bolt from a crossbow pierced his hostage's eye. Several more bolts flew from the tent to take the intruder down, but Hayward held fast to his shield and charged ahead. The guard's body collected the projectiles in soft thuds until Hayward sent it crashing hard into the camp's commander. Hayward slithered around behind the commander, just as the guards posted outside woke and charged into the tent.

"Order your men to lay down their arms."

The commander gave the order, with the tip of Hayward's blade a hair's breadth from his eye.

"If you kill me, my men will tear you to pieces with their bare hands." He did his best to sound menacing and unafraid.

"Had I wanted you dead, I wouldn't have used your man for a shield. I come to you with a proposal. I am here to make you a rich and powerful man."

"I am rich and powerful."

The tip of Hayward's karambit split the distance to the chief's eye.

"As I was saying, I am here to make you an offer. Refuse my offer, and you can watch with your one remaining eye as I slaughter every man in your camp."

The chief swallowed hard. "You have my attention."

"My name is Hayward Taft."

The mere mention of the name sent a stream of urine down the commander's leg.

"I've heard of you. Ask what you will, and it shall be done."

"Gather your men."

The commander called his camp to order, and they gathered in the light of the moon and growing flames of recently lit bonfires. Small by freebooter standards, perhaps 100 men. Some would be among the chosen few who would lay eyes on Hayward Taft and live to tell about it. The grotesque figure took the seat usually reserved for the camp commander and addressed the motley group.

"A great war is coming. The war between two worlds. The world of men and the world of gods! I have just returned from the Western Territories, where I have been charged with a great task by my father, The Fire King of the West. I crossed the Dead Zone not once, but twice."

"Bullshit," a voice from the crowd. The man spoke and then slunk back into the crowd, hoping to avoid detection. Hayward pointed into the crowd and made a sweeping motion that caused it to part.

"You!" He jabbed his finger at the man who spoke. "Come to me!"

The man, unable to disobey, walked heavy-legged and presented himself. Hayward grabbed the man by the jaw with the crab-like claw that was now his left hand and squeezed until the bone snapped and his mouth fell open. Then Hayward grabbed his tongue with his other pincer and tore it from the man's mouth. Unintelligible, even by screaming standards, the man yowled as blood sprayed while he worked at fitting his broken jaw back into place.

"Put this man on a pike and nail his tongue below his body. Place him in the middle of camp so that he may be of some use to our cause."

Several of the camp's men dragged him off, eager to please their new boss.

"Any other naysayers?" No one so much as cleared their throats. "I didn't think so. I am here to build an army. Most of you aren't worth a shit to me; you can stay, you can go, I don't care what you do, but you will not be a part of what I am building here."

The crowd murmured, but no one dared to speak.

"Who are your best men?"

The commander selected twenty men, "the rest aren't worth a tinker's damn."

Hayward looked them over. "Grab your gear; we are moving on."

Camp after camp, across the plains Hayward, built his army. Growing his numbers in the freebooter camps, sharpening their skills on the almost defenseless vagadi. Moving ever closer to Savista.

Chapter 47

Thea sat bolt upright in bed, screaming as Siobhan hugged her tightly. She hadn't slept through the night since Alistair left.

"It's okay, sweetheart, momma's here. What was it this time, burning or drowning?"

Her little body shook, and her eyes stared blankly into the soft glow cast by the fireplace from the next room. Siobhan squeezed tighter trying to stop the shaking.

"They're coming, momma."

"Who's coming?"

"Freebooters."

"We've dealt with freebooters before, Thea; we'll be fine."

"The bad man is with them."

"What bad man?"

Thea shuddered. "The man who tried to kill Joe."

She started breathing rapidly.

"We'll be alright; we have brave fighters and Jedrek to lead them. Now slow your breathing before you hyperventilate."

She placed her hand on her daughter's back to calm her, but Thea shook it away.

"We have to go tell him now. They're almost here!"

"I need you to try and calm yourself first, Thea," Siobhan said, surprised by her daughter's response.

"Please, mom," Thea worked to slow her breathing. "Can we go tell him?"

"Of course, get dressed, and we'll go."

Siobhan and Thea got dressed and grabbed jackets. They walked out the door to find Agermonte and Barrister, heads lowered, hackles raised, staring into the darkness.

"See, mom? They know it too."

Siobhan and Thea walked down the path toward Jedrek's place, Agermonte and Barrister flanking them. Thea's ability to look into other places was nothing new. She had been doing it since she was little, and many of Savista's residents owed their lives to her visions, but for whatever reason, Siobhan found this current situation to be unsettling.

Agermonte and Barrister moved more like jungle cats than dogs. For their size, they were remarkably quiet, and, in the stillness, Siobhan became increasingly aware of the absence of all sound. No chirping crickets, no croaking of frogs, not even the rustling of leaves in the breeze. In fact, there was no breeze.

The torches that marked the last twenty-five feet of the path that led to Jedrek's place burned arrow straight with no wind to disturb them. Two sentries standing guard at the bottom of the ramp that wound up to Jedrek's door greeted the visitors.

"Good evening Ms. Siobhan and Ms. Thea. Out for a stroll?"

No time for small talk, Siobhan skipped the exchange of greetings.

"We need to see Jedrek right away."

"May I ask…."

"Now, please," she demanded.

The guard jutted his chin, and his counterpart ran up the ramp and disappeared into the darkness above. After a moment, an unseen voice called down.

"Send them up."

Jedrek and Kallen met them at the door and invited them in. His place was laid out much like Siobhan's, except it had one extra room for his daughter and had been built into the crown of a long-dead Oak. Jedrek asked them in. They sat around his table, Thea and Kallen sharing a chair and holding onto one another as little girls sometimes do, and Siobhan started.

"Thea has been having nightmares, recurring nightmares."

Jedrek leaned forward. "Tell me what you've seen, Thea."

Thea rubbed the sleep from her eyes. "They're coming, the freebooters; they're coming."

Jedrek blinked, slightly taken aback.

"We've dealt with freebooters before. What's troubling you?"

"Jedrek, she said that they're being led by the man that killed Joe."

"Taft," he murmured.

Siobhan chose not to speak his name, as if doing so would stir evil spirits.

"How many men, Thea?" There was urgency in his voice.

"Hundreds and hundreds, and they keep growing."

"Can you see them now?"

"Yes, but I don't want to." Thea shook her head side to side, trying to shake the thoughts out, Kallen hugging her friend tighter.

"It's important, Thea. We need to know how close they are."

Thea stared out Jedrek's north window, raised her finger, and pointed. With winter quickly approaching, the trees around Savista had given up most of their leaves; Jedrek could see the fires out on the plains.

"Two days away at most," Jedrek said, making a mental note. "Are there any vagadi between them and us?"

Thea nodded.

"Can we reach them in time?"

Kallen began to rise, ready to get to work. Thea shook her head.

"No."

Kallen sat back down. Jedrek bolted from his seat, ran to his door, and threw it open.

"Men! Air raid sirens, north, now!

Savista maintained several World War 2 era hand crank air raid sirens to alert nearby vagadi to approaching danger. The tribes could then seek temporary shelter with Savista or brace to defend themselves.

"The screamers, mom." Thea looked up at her mother, who motioned to cover her ears. Thea clamped her hands over her ears just as the sirens whirred to life. Soon torches and bonfires appeared all around Savista as her citizens poured into the cold night and gathered near Jedrek's quarters.

Jedrek stepped out to address them. "Siobhan and Thea came to me tonight to warn us of a huge force moving toward Savista. They are less than two days out, and they are laying waste to everything in their path. So, let's start getting ready, people. We should start seeing our first vagadi seeking refuges by daybreak. They will be assigned to work crews as they arrive. Remember, all who wish to enter must surrender their weapons before bringing them up. The battle will likely start at our north face, but as always, we must defend all sides. I will keep you posted as best I can. In the meantime, prep weapons, gather food and water, and ready the medical tent."

* * *

The Bellich camp heard Savista's siren, but it was too late. Almost 600 strong after its merger with Mava, the largest of the freebooter camps, Taft's forces swarmed over Bellich and its ninety citizens. No quarter given. The men, young and old, were slaughtered, though some of the very old and weak were first armed with knives, purely for sport. Some of the women were violated; others, like the children, were murdered and butchered to feed Taft's army. If any from Taft's camp were shocked by the barbarism, none showed it. Hayward Taft himself delighted in it.

That night, while he slept in the bed of one he or his men had murdered, he was paid another visit by his Fire King. The Fire King took him by the hand and led him out of the tent in his vision. They walked through the sleeping camp.

"When we are done, you must kill these men."

Hayward didn't balk at the order, just listened intently.

"We can't build our new world with these vermin."

Hayward nodded his understanding.

The Fire King faced Hayward and blew into his face. Hayward inhaled his breath and fell into a trance-like state, and passed into another place. Standing in a room where a man, a woman, and two small girls sat at a table. The Fire King pointed at the girl with brown hair.

"She is our weapon Hayward. No harm can befall her. Do you understand?"

"I do, my king, I understand."

"Good, you may do as you please with the rest."

The girl with the brown hair stood up, looked at them, and screamed, and with that, Hayward was back in bed and alone.

* * *

Thea pointed into the corner of Jedrek's kitchen, where nothing looked to be out of the ordinary to anyone else. Siobhan rushed to Thea and stepped between her and the corner of the room.

"What is it?"

Thea worked to control her breathing. She huffed and puffed as if she'd just run a race. Seeing nothing in the corner, Siobhan turned toward Thea, brushed her hair away from her face with a mother's loving touch, and turned her child's face from the corner toward her own.

"What did you see, Thea?"

Her respiration slowed but were still catching and hitching. "They're coming for me."

Siobhan looked at Jedrek and then back at her daughter.

"Who's coming for you? What did you see?" Siobhan was frantic, though she did her best to hide it.

"Two men, standing right there," she pointed back at the corner. "They're coming for me, mom. They are going to kill everyone here to get me. We have to leave; now."

Siobhan had always taken Thea's predictions as gospel, but as right as she knew Thea was, she also knew that their only hope for survival was to stay in Savista. The tears were already falling. She turned toward Jedrek. He'd seen her upset before but never had he seen her look so helpless, and his heart broke. Her eyes glistened, her lips looked warm and moist, and he forgot himself. He reached out, took her in his arms, and pulled her close. He wanted to kiss her, but he caught himself and grasped her by her shoulders.

"You are part of Savista, and Savista will not turn her back on you in your hour of need. If they want Thea, they will have to go through every last one of us to get to her."

Siobhan sighed, and her knees went weak. Jedrek caught her and held her up.

"Siobhan, when you feel up to it, you will be needed in the medical tent, but I will leave Kallen and three of my best men here to guard Thea. If our defenses fail, Kallen will get her to safety."

Kallen jumped from her seat and clamped onto Thea's arm. "You can count on me, Ms. Siobhan, and you too, Thea," Kallen pressed her forehead against her friend's.

Siobhan took Jedrek's hands in her own, "thank you, Jedrek."

Chapter 48

The sign read, Reverie 10 Miles, a weathered strip of blacktop, baked gray by the sun stretched out and disappeared into a heat shimmer. Joe adjusted the saddlebag on his shoulder, took off his Elvis sunglasses, and rubbed his eyes. Tine copied the sunglasses move in the manner befitting a younger sibling.

"Ten miles to go, kid."

"I'm not a kid."

"Right, sorry."

Tine stopped and turned her face toward the sky. Joe walked on a few steps before he turned to see that she wasn't following.

"What are you looking at?" He asked and gazed up at the dead silver sky above.

"Are there clouds in Savista, Joe?"

He hadn't noticed the lack of clouds before. "Sure! I mean, I think so. You don't have clouds here?"

"Only before storms," she made a face. "Black, dirty-looking things."

Joe tried to recall if he'd seen clouds other than storm clouds in the Midwestern Territories.

"Hey Joe," she called. He pulled his eyes from the sky. "I saw a picture in a book once, and there were kids out playing, and the sky was filled with puffy white clouds. Those are the kind of clouds I want to see, Joe. Do they have those there?"

Joe remembered laying in the grass as a kid and finding different shapes in the clouds. "I can't believe you've never seen a sky full of white fluffy clouds."

"Just in the book. Hey, I bet that's where good dreams come from," Tine said as they began walking again.

"Yeah, maybe."

"I'd like to have a good dream."

"Are you telling me that you never have good dreams?"

"Not the sleeping kind. Do you have good dreams?"

Joe thought a moment and could not recall ever having a good dream himself. He remembered lots of bad dreams, some in vivid detail, but, at the moment, he couldn't recall a single good dream. "Sure, I mean, I think so."

"Tell me one of them."

"Well, I can't really remember any, not right now, anyway."

"Then how do you know you've had them?"

"Well, I've had bad dreams, and if there are bad ones, there have to be good ones too." Joe was still racking his brain, trying to remember a good dream. "I mean, I guess."

"But I've had lots of good daydreams. Those are the dreams you have while you're awake."

"Yeah, I'm familiar."

He thought about daydreams he'd had when he was a kid. Like the one about becoming a cop, or the one about one day owning a green 68 Mustang GT, like the one Steve McQueen drove in Bullitt. And both had come true. He'd had plenty of good daydreams. In fact, he couldn't remember any bad ones.

"Have you ever had a…"

He heard Tine mumble something, but he was already onto another daydream. He imagined Tine as a normal child, his child, having never been exposed to tickers or cannibals. Joe imagined them living back in Red Hook with Reka, taking them on picnics in Founder's Park, fishing in the Red Hook River, or to Gert's on Friday nights. He thought of her going to school and being in plays or on a sports team, and he and Reka watching her and then talking with other parents and bragging about her accomplishments. Joe thought about how happy they could all be, living in Red Hook. To his surprise, he found himself feeling a little homesick, and now he could never go home again. But if his choice was Reka or Red Hook, it was no contest. But both would sure be nice. He thought for a moment about Annie and how he cried like a baby when she left him. Now he could barely remember her face. When she left, he didn't even follow her down the driveway, for Reka, he'd followed her off the edge of the world he knew. And he had no problem picturing Reka. A smile crept onto his face.

"You're doing it right now, aren't you, Joe?"

Joe snapped out of it. "What? What are you talking about?"

"Ha! I asked if you ever had a daydream."

"Oh, well, everyone daydreams."

"So?" Tine wasn't about to let it go. "What was it about?"

"What was *what* about?"

"You were daydreaming!"

"Shut up," he said with a smile.

"Come on, Joe; what was it about?"

"If you really want to know, it was about you."

He stopped speaking and stared straight ahead.

"Me? What about me?" She stared at him. "Joe?"

She followed his stare.

About two hundred yards ahead and sprawling across the horizon, they stood like a blockade in the roadway. A field of corpses in various states of decay. Joe hadn't noticed them sooner, possibly because of the road glare, but there were hundreds, perhaps thousands of them mounted like scarecrows, crucifixion style on weathered wooden posts, as deep as the eye could see. Some disemboweled, others dismembered, missing limbs or extremities, some the entire lower half of their bodies, each with a burlap sack over their head.

Joe pulled Tine in close. "Reverie's dead ahead. It looks like we're going to have to go through."

All the color she'd gained since leaving the cellar on the Callaghan's farm faded into a pale green. Joe could see the wheels turning in Tine's head as she searched for a better plan and knew they had ground to a halt when her shoulders dropped and her breath escaped in a loud exhale. They entered the nightmarish human forest. And proceeded west, but with the random positioning of the bodies and the road no longer discernible, it wasn't long before they lost all sense of direction. Joe needed to find west. Looking up, Joe saw only the glaring silver sky. They'd walked for over and hour and still hadn't come out the other side.

"I think we're lost."

Tine placed her hands on her hips and mustered her most sarcastic tone, "Really, Joe? Do you really think we're lost?"

Joe ignored her tone, "Let's go back this way. We can try to retrace our steps and get back to where we started and try again."

She followed behind, and the two of them walked in silence, Joe feeling secure that they were going the right way until they came across two dead bodies. And while the whole place was dead bodies, these two were of particular interest. Not long dead and not mounted to T crosses, they sat slumped forward on the ground. One held a note, and Joe took it.

"What does it say?" Tine asked nervously.

"It says, 'Me and Beansy,' "Joe paused; "Beansy?"

"Go on, Joe, read it."

"Okay, sorry."

Me and Beansy been lost here, in this Hellhole for almost a month. We have walked in every direction there is, and there just ain't no way out. If you find this letter, you're as fucked as we were, so we invite you to join us. There's a pencil in my shirt pocket and a blade that I'm gonna try and stuff back in my boot just as soon as I slit my wrists. Kindly jot your name down on this here letter and return the pencil and the knife after you do the deed. Cut good and deep, so you don't suffer too long. See you on the other side.

Bernard

Joe folded the letter and stuck it back in Bernard's hand.

"Poor bastards."

"Them, what about us?" Tine started breathing rapidly.

"What about us? I didn't come all this way to just lay down and die. We'll get out."

He started looking around for natural direction indicators. I was still too bright to find the Northern Star or the tips of the crescent moon, and there were no trees that he could check for moss. It seemed that nature wouldn't offer any assistance. Holding his arm out, Joe looked for a shadow. It was faint, but it was there.

"I need a stick, about three feet long."

Tine looked around at the barren landscape.

"Where are we supposed to find a stick, Joe?"

The place was desolate aside from the dead bodies, hung as far as the eye could see. Then it hit him. He needed a stick.

"There are sticks all over the place. What do you think these guys are hanging on?"

Joe grabbed hold of a corpse and yanked it down off its cross.

"Joe!"

The nails used to hold the body to the cross passed effortlessly through flesh and only hung up on bone momentarily as the body dropped and crumpled to the ground.

"Sorry, buddy, but I need your cross."

He grabbed the arm support with both hands and pulled, and just like the body, the rotted wood offered no resistance sliding free of the nails.

"Come on, help me."

Tine looked confused, and a bit mortified.

"If whatever you're doing is going to help us get out of here, just tell me what to do."

"Help me dig a hole."

Using their blades, Joe and Tine stabbed at the parched and cracking ground and removed the loosened dirt by hand to make a post hole. Once it was deep enough, Joe jammed his makeshift stick into the hole.

"Now push the loose dirt around the base to keep it from falling over. I need to find a couple of rocks."

"What are you going to do with rocks?"

Unfortunately, rocks were even more sparse than sticks.

"You'll see, just keep packing that dirt around the base."

Among the things, Joe had taken from the Callaghan's house was the cleaver the old woman used to butcher Tine's father. Joe pulled the cleaver from his bag,

"You're not going to want to watch this Tine."

She turned her head, and Joe lopped off the feet of the corpse.

"Come on, Joe, you can't just go around chopping up dead bodies. What's next? Are you going to start ticking?"

"Do you want to get out of here or not?"

The sun was just bright enough. Joe took one of the severed feet and placed it at the tip of the shadow cast by the stick.

"We need them more than he does, Tine. We'll use one… um, rock to mark the end of the shadow cast by the stick and the other to mark it again as it moves from east to west as the sun sets. That will give us west. Reverie is to the west."

Tine watched for a couple of minutes. "It's not working, Joe."

"It takes more than a couple minutes. Why don't you give me the Amari's Bible? I'll read a little to you while we wait."

She reached into her bag and gave Joe the book.

"It says here that this is the Darby Bible."

Tine wrinkled her nose, "Maybe the Amaris stole it from the Darbys?"

Joe opened it and thumbed a few pages, "No, the Darby Bible is a version of the Bible, like the Saint James version."

Tine leaned forward. "Well? What does it say?"

Joe cleared his throat and began. "Genesis, Chapter 1, verse 1. In the beginning, God created the heavens and the earth."

"What did He make them out of?"

"I don't know, Tine. He's God. I think He can just think things into existence."

She looked around, "So he thought up all of this?"

"No."

"Then how did it get here?"

Joe scratched the top of his head, "I don't know, I don't have all the answers."

"But that book does?"

Joe heard the hope in her voice, "That's what they tell me."

"Who's they?"

"I don't know, people. My parents, my Sunday school teacher, just people. Now may I continue?"

Tine nodded and smiled.

"Verse 2. And the earth was waste and empty,"

Tine turned her head from side to side, taking in the landscape, "It sure is."

"No, I think it means that there was nothing here. Like it was all just a big empty rock. Let me finish verse 2." Tine nodded again, and Joe continued, "and darkness was on the face of the deep, and the Spirit of God was hovering over the face of the waters."

Tine slid in closer to Joe, "I don't like this book, Joe. It sounds scary."

Joe put an arm over her shoulder, "I bet it was, but listen to this, it says that God said, let there be light, and there was light!"

"I like that part."

Tine smiled and settled in, and Joe continued to read. He finished chapter 1 and got up to check the shadow.

"See?" He placed the second foot at the tip of the shadow dragged his blade between the two markers creating a line in the dirt. "That's west," he said, pointing the blade in the direction of the line. "Let's get moving. We are going to have to try and get another bearing reading before we lose the sun."

They gathered their belongings. Tine carried the stick but made Joe grab the feet, and they headed off west between the mounted bodies. They walked for another hour before Joe stopped them.

"Why are we stopping Joe?"

"We need to find west again."

"We've been walking west for an hour. Let's just keep going and get out of here."

"We thought we were going west last time, and you saw where that got us. Now help me dig."

Again, they dug a hole, set the stick in, marked the two points, and found that they were no longer going west.

"Your stick and feet method stinks, Joe. Are you sure this works?"

"It works where I'm from."

"Savista?"

"Red Hook," Joe looked at the marking he made in the ground and shook his head. "Maybe the sun is refracting or something."

"What does that mean?"

"I don't know; like the light is bouncing off something, I think."

"Bouncing off of what?"

"I don't know, Tine!" He snapped.

She hung her head, and Joe's shoulders dropped, and he exhaled hard.

"I'm sorry, Tine, I'm just feeling frustrated." He placed his hand on her shoulder. "We have to make a decision."

"What decision?"

"We have to decide if we should keep walking or, and I think this is the better option; camp here for the night."

Her eyes bugged.

"No, Joe. No way. Here? With all the dead bodies? Are you serious?"

The more she spoke, the louder she got.

"Tine, calm down. They're dead. They can't hurt you."

'That's what you think." She folded her arms in protest.

"Do you want to keep walking?"

"We might find our way out."

"We might also get hopelessly lost."

"Look around, Joe. It feels like we're there already."

"I just think that in the morning, with the sunrise, we will be able to find our way out. Walking in the dark seems risky."

"I'm not staying here, Joe." She grabbed her bag and started walking in the direction suggested by Joe's compass.

"Tine! Stop!"

The body on the cross next to her began making a croaking sound as it rolled its head in the direction of Tine's voice and jerked furiously to free itself. Joe ran to her and pulled her away. The nails through its wrists dripped red with fresh blood, but despite all the effort to break free, the nails held fast. Joe ripped the sack off the man's head. His tongue had been ripped out, his mouth and throat caked with dried blood. His upper eyelids had been stitched to his eyebrows so that he could not blink.

"Illee, illee, illee," he croaked over and over.

"He wants you to kill him, Joe."

Joe looked from the horrendous figure on the cross back at Tine. He had no words.

"Kill him, Joe, so he doesn't have to suffer."

Joe stared dumbly at her.

"I'll do it if you can't."

Tine pulled her knife from her belt and moved toward the suffering man. Joe grabbed her arm.

"No! Who did this to you?"

"Illee, illee, illee."

"Come on, Joe; would you want to live that way?"

"Who did this to you, to all of these men?"

The thing that was once a man croaked something in response, but Joe couldn't understand him. Tine launched herself at the unfortunate creature and stabbed him repeatedly in the chest and neck. The figure groaned and dropped his head. Tine collapsed, winded and angry.

"What the hell Tine? What was that about?" Joe wiped at the blood spattered on his face from the attack.

Tine growled a squeaky growl and lunged again, but Joe stopped her.

"He's a liar! A dirty liar!"

Joe grabbed her and took the knife out of her hand. "What did he say?"

Tine crossed her arms, "It doesn't matter."

Joe's brow furrowed, "Well, it does to me, and I bet it would have to him!"

Tine laid down and made a pillow of her bag, "I'm going to get some sleep."

Joe used his best fatherly tone, "We need to talk about what just happened, Tine." But she ignored him. "Tine, I'm talking to you."

Chapter 49

The moon slid behind a bank of clouds, giving Serenity and the other Maristo the advantage of darkness as they floated through the fog headed toward Reverie. Alistair could see the glow of bonfires on the beach and borrowed Villwock's spyglass to take a closer look. Activity seemed very light, and he made mention to Sarros, who signaled to the other ships to drop anchor.

From among the four ships, the two strongest swimmers, a man named Levitt from the Mystic and Finch from the Ancora Imparo, were chosen. Still a few hundred yards out, the captains couldn't risk moving in any closer without exposing their ships, especially if the cloud or fog cover lifted. Having been given their orders, the scouts slipped silently into the frigid water and swam to shore.

Alistair remembered the night aboard the Ancora Imparo; they were sailing from Gerrings to the Barrens, searching for Hayward Taft when the storm hit. Fallon Holton had gone overboard, and it was Joe who, with no consideration for his own safety, dove in and saved his life. That was the night that cemented their kinship with the crew of the Ancora Imparo and one of the last nights he would spend with the young man he'd come to think of as a son.

"They've made it to shore," Sarros said.

"Where? I don't see them."

"Just to the right of the dock, about ten feet up the beach."

Alistair, still using Villwock's glass, spotted Levitt and Finch as they crept up the beach, getting a little closer to the first of the bonfires.

* * *

Headlights bounced in their direction as a blunt-nosed, seafoam green, flatbed truck pulled up and dumped a pile of bodies in the sand. Men wearing yellow sashes loaded the bodies, most of whom wore identical yellow sashes, onto hand carts and labored to push them through the sand toward the fire pits.

"They're burning the bodies," Finch said.

"Levitt covered his nose and mouth with his wet shirt. "Disease?"

"Finch pulled his shirt up over his nose and mouth as well. "Who the hell knows, seems likely, though."

The bodies were then tossed into fire pits where they blistered, popped, and hissed as the fire consumed them.

Levitt cocked his ear. "Do you hear that?"

Finch concentrated. "The ticking sounds?"

"Yeah," Levitt said.

"I think it's coming from the tossers," Finch said and laughed.

"What's funny about any of this?"

Not wanting to waste time explaining the slang of the word tosser, Finch just shook his head. "Nothing," he said and pointed at the truck, making a U-turn to start back down the beach. "Let's see where it's going."

Finch and Levitt hurried along behind the truck as it dipped and bobbed across the uneven sand toward a colossal wall about a mile away. They quickly lost ground on the vehicle and had to make their way without the aid of the cover provided by the size and noise of the truck. They moved up the ridge for a better look at the wall. They crawled on their bellies up the ridge and saw a row of tanks flanking a bridge that ran over what Finch estimated to be a thirty-foot wide trench. Across the bridge on the other side of the trench stood a phalanx of armed men protecting the opening in a twenty-foot-tall wall that looked to have been made of railroad ties and concrete. Beyond the wall sat a towering red building that seemed to stretch on forever. Neither Finch nor Levitt could see the top or end of the building. There was writing on the wall, but neither man could read. They had found a fortress but had no way of knowing what lay inside.

Both men agreed that they had to see what was on the other side of the wall before making their report. There was no way to tell if the tanks were manned or where the fortress' lookouts were stationed. They had to find a way over the bridge without being seen.

Finch was the older of the two and naturally assumed command.

"We could try going under the bridge."

Levitt considered the idea, "But how do we get to the bridge to go under it?"

Finch stroked his chin, "What about a distraction?"

Levitt looked around; there was nothing to create a distraction. While they pondered their dilemma, another body truck emerged from behind the wall.

"There's our way in."

Finch elbowed Levitt.

"We'll wait for it to come back and hop on before it gets to the bridge."

The scouts moved back away from the wall until the tanks were obscured by a small sand dune. As the taillights faded into the distance, Finch and Levitt moved close to the path taken by the truck and buried themselves in the loose sand. They kept their heads above the sand but built mounds so that the driver could not see them on his return trip. Before long, the two dim headlights of the flatbed came wobbling back over the sand toward them. As it passed, both men emerged from their hiding places and ran for the back of the truck. Levitt reached it first and set his feet on the rear step offering a hand to Finch. Finch swatted it away and dove, catching the bottom step and a face full of sand for pride's sake.

The men laid in body fluid and chunks of flesh as the truck rolled over the bridge and through the gate. Just inside the entrance, small fire-pots spread out around the grounds provided just enough light to see. Passing through a patch of darkness, the men rolled off the truck as it slowed between two piles of bodies to reload for its next trip to the fire pits. Roving groups of three to five men, all armed and wearing dark-colored clothes, patrolled the grounds moving silently over the sand. Two of the patrols, one from the north, the other from the south, were closing on Finch and Levitt's position.

Levitt's eyes were sharp, and even in the low light, he could see the men coming toward them. "Finch, men," he whispered as he nudged his partner.

Finch squinted in the darkness, barely making out the forms.

"Quick, under the bodies."

Levitt's eyes bugged. "What about the plague?"

Finch grabbed his shirt and pushed him toward the pile of corpses.

"You want to die now or later? Get in there!"

The scouts burrowed into the mound and waited for the patrols to pass. Here the smell of piss and shit mingled with the general sickening aroma of decomposition. As Levitt lay there waiting for the patrols to pass by, he noticed that the bodies around him were squirming. A chill ran up his spine, but he didn't make a sound. The truck, loaded back up, drove around the pile of bodies to the north and back out the gate, taking the racket made by its old diesel engine when it left. In the absence of the engine noise, a new sound emerged. A deep groaning rose from the piles of bodies. The patrols responded by pushing long pointed poles into the piles. One of the dying who lay near Levitt began to moan as the pikemen approached. Levitt slowly reached his hands around the man's throat and squeezed until the noise stopped.

All around the scouts, blood spilled, lungs and bloated bellies hissed, but mercifully, neither was run through. When the patrols passed, Finch and Levitt crawled gore-soaked from the piles and made their way closer to the big red building. They saw a vast tent city and the hub of activity inside the fortress. Men, women, and children, all wearing the yellow sashes, were being forced at gun and spear point to work at breaching the wall to the red building. As they fell from exhaustion, their bodies were tossed onto a pile where another crew of men in yellow sashes collected them and threw them on one of the piles to later be taken off to the fire pit and burned.

"What do you think is in that big red barn?"

Finch looked at Levitt and shrugged his shoulders, "Beats me, but that man," Finch pointed at a large man seated at a place of honor overlooking the work being done. Broad-shouldered, thick neck and arms larger than either Finch or Levitt's. "That guy wants in there."

The roving parties near the tent city were more like platoons. Fifteen to twenty heavily armed men marching in formation. They didn't wear typical military uniforms. They looked more like well-trained guerrilla fighters. Along the wall in the area's not being drilled, blasted, and banged on with pickaxes were rows of M2 9mm anti-aircraft guns.

"What are we going to do, Finch? We can't go up against this place."

Finch looked disgusted. "We are the Maristo! There is nothing that can stand up to Defender and Mystic in an all-out assault. Besides, it's not for us to decide what to do. That's for the captains. We just report back."

They made their way back to the body pile and waited to be loaded onto the flatbed. When they made it out of the compound, they jumped off in the shadows and made their way back to the dock. The wind was at their backs, and with it, the smell of burning flesh. They entered the water and waded out as far as possible before starting their swim. They had just pushed off the sandy bottom to begin their swim when Finch disappeared beneath the surface of the water.

* * *

Dioj Volos bolted upright in his throne, and his eyes rolled back into his head. He watched two men wade into the water through his eyes in the sea. Looking farther out, he could make out ships. He darted from vessel to vessel, wanting a better look at his uninvited guests. He sniffed at the air like a bear scenting a carcass.

"They were here!"

Dioj Volos shot out of his chair and flung back his head, threw out his massive chest, and roared, angry that his men had allowed intruders to get so close to their lord. He stayed in that position, eyes still rolled, and watched as the men pushed off the seafloor to begin their swim. Dioj Volos opened his eyes, and with them, the floodlights set along the top of the wall illuminated shining brightly but were unable to penetrate the fog that hung heavy over the water.

* * *

Levitt heard the splash and turned to look for Finch but saw only red foam on the water. He swam back, reached down, and pulled Finch up so his head was above the water.

"Swim! Finish our mission!" Finch yelled before being dragged back under.

The Raven's Corsair pirates were on him, sinking their jagged teeth into his flesh and dragging him under. Levitt turned and swam hard. He had to tell the Maristo what he and poor Finch had seen. He could hear the screams and gurgles of his fellow scout fade and then stop. Terror gripped him.

* * *

The crews aboard their ships could see the light behind the fog bank that hung between them and the shoreline, but it could not penetrate. Thrashing at the waterline near Serenity's bow alerted Alistair to Levitt struggling to keep from drowning.

"Someone give me a hand!"

With Villwock's help, they pulled Levitt aboard and searched the water for Finch.

"Where is he? Where's Finch?" Villwock demanded.

Levitt lay on the deck of Serenity, coughing and spitting up seawater. Serenity's flagman signaled to the Mystic that her scout had returned. Enzo, aboard the Ancora Imparo, would not receive the same message.

Sarros wanted to get him to the Mystic as quickly as possible.

"Load him into the lifeboat, Ramsey, join me. We have to reconvene the captains."

Ramsey climbed down the ladder to the lifeboat and accepted Levitt's exhausted body as it was lowered to him. Sarros began his climb down when Alistair stopped him.

"Captain, I believe the pastreco and I may be of some assistance."

Sarros looked him over and nodded, and the five men rowed out to the Mystic. Once captains and quartermasters from the other ships were present and accounted for, condolences were expressed to Enzo and Salazar for the loss of their shipmate, and the information he'd lost his life to obtain was given.

Enzo stood and addressed Levitt. "Can you tell me what happened to Finch?"

Terror showed on Levitt's face. "The crew from the Raven got him."

"Bullshit!" Sanchez boomed."

Levitt shook his head with a vacant look in his eyes. "It's not bullshit."

Sanchez challenged him, "They all went down with the Raven."

"I know that captain, but I know what I saw."

Kidwell held up his hand and took the room back. "Tell us what you learned."

The captains listened intently as Levitt described the burning bodies, the pit, the tanks, and the fortress-like wall surrounding the grounds. He told of the well-armed militia and the large mounted guns, which like the tanks, were leftovers from World War 2. Then he told of the great red barn that the slaves, for lack of any other suitable word, were being forced to try and breach.

Alistair slumped back in his chair. "Diastole." He said it softly, and though there was much talking, Kidwell caught it.

"What is diastole?"

The pastreco answered before Alistair could open his mouth.

"It is a ship larger than any that sails. It is a cemetery, the space between heartbeats and the gateway between worlds."

"You're not making sense," Sarros said.

"Because it is not for us to understand," the pastreco said.

"So this big red building is a—what did you call it, a diastole?" Sanchez asked.

"Diastole is a state, but you may call it that if it helps."

"So, how do we get in it?" Enzo asked.

"We don't! We must keep Dioj Volos from breaching the wall," the pastreco answered.

"Then let's get started!" Sanchez was on his feet. "Defender is ready to do her part."

"Captain Kidwell," the pastreco said. "An all-out assault on Dioj Volos would be disastrous. We must stop Joe and the child he is traveling with."

Alistair flew to his feet. "What the hell are you talking about? You said we were going to rescue Joe!"

Sarros and Ramsey held Alistair back.

"I said that I would take you to him. But we cannot let him reach Reverie." The pastreco turned his attention back toward Kidwell. "We knew about the gateways in Espero, Reverie, and the Barrens, but it seems that Joe has found another near the Dead Zone. Or perhaps, and this is our greatest fear, he is able to open them where he wants. We aren't exactly sure, but we know that Joe is a key that unlocks the gateways, and he is headed right for Reverie. If Dioj Volos has Joe and the girl, he will destroy this world and set the dead free to take what's left."

Kidwell stood and addressed the man.

"And who are you, sir?"

The pastreco dropped his head apologetically, "Please forgive me, captain, I am pastreco."

"The pastreco are old, robe-clad ghouls who take vows of silence. But it seems that you, young man, have no idea what silent means.

"And I shall suffer for it, but this is a matter of mankind's salvation and not a time to remain mute."

"Do you have a name?"

"No, captain, I have no name. I have been tasked with stopping Dioj Volos, and I am afraid that to do that, we must stop Joe."

Alistair raged. "You son of a bitch! I'll kill you myself, and then I'll kill your brother!"

"Ancora Imparo and her crew will not aid in a quest to kill Joe Kott," Enzo said. "And we will stand with the ranger in his defense."

Kidwell held his hands up in a calming gesture. "Gentlemen, please. What more can you tell us about Dioj Volos, pastreco?"

"He can see and hear everything through his crusaders and the people he possesses. They are a conduit for information, and if I am going to have any hope of killing him and saving Joe and the girl, I need someone to break that connection."

Sarros stood up.

"When we start firing cannonballs into his camp, I doubt he'll be thinking about his conduits. We'll need to go ashore at different points on the beach. We'll be sitting ducks if we bunch up. And if those things from the Raven are there waiting, we'll need the pastreco front and center with heavy support from our best men."

"Then it's decided. We will launch an attack and spare the ranger's friend and the child. The officers firmed up their plan of attack and then moved topside to return to their ships. Up on deck, a sailor from the Mystic turned the crank on a well-worn hurdy-gurdy filling the night with music intended to stir men's souls.

Chapter 50

Sleep took her fast, and that concerned Joe almost as much as the brutality of the attack he'd just witnessed. There were times when she seemed like a normal child; helping Mrs. Amari prepare lunch came to his mind. He thought about how quickly, maybe even naturally, she took to helping Devlin Amari in the kitchen. How proud she was to have helped make lunch and how happy she seemed to have a mother figure so willing to share her knowledge. But then there were times like now. Times when she seemed—he didn't know how to finish that thought.

Joe stared at her as she rested, and he wondered about the life she had lived. Only twelve years old, orphaned, and held prisoner in a cellar by a family of cannibals. In his short time with her, she had been through more than anyone he had ever known. She had taken life and helped deliver new life. He had seen her laughing and happy, and he had seen her angry and raging with all the force of a storm. And he'd seen her weep like a baby when she told him about her mother.

Had Tine ever played with dolls or had a tea party with her mom and sister, or had her whole life been turmoil? Joe sat down next to her, and she, perhaps sensing his presence, leaned into him. Joe put an arm around her and closed his eyes. There, with the dead mounted on sticks all around them and with thoughts of Tine swirling in his head, Joe drifted off to sleep, only to be woken a short time later by the sound of explosions and a strange pulsing glow in the distance.

"Tine, wake up."

She stirred from her deep sleep.

"Jeez, Joe, let me sleep."

The explosions continued.

"Tine, wake up. Can't you hear that?"

Tine rubbed her sleepy eyes and yawned. There was another series of thundering booms.

"Yeah, what is it?"

"I'm not sure."

Tine came alive with excitement and grabbed Joe's arm. "Reverie! It has to be coming from Reverie."

"That's what I was thinking, and as long as the sound keeps coming, we can follow it out of this place."

Tine grabbed up Joe's gear, shoved it at him, and grabbed her own. "Let's go, Joe."

She started pushing past the bodies almost at a sprint, and Joe had all he could do to keep up. Nearing the edge, Joe could see open space just ahead. "Tine, wait, slow down."

But she either ignored him or didn't hear him because she burst past the last row of bodies back onto the open road.

"Dammit, Tine! Wait for me!" Joe emerged from the field of mounted corpses to find her being held captive by a large, thick man with a yellow beard and fingernails. He stood behind Tine, holding a knife to her temple, as he dug his long dirty nails into her throat and gave her a sniff.

"She belong to you?" He ran the blade from her temple down to her throat.

"Let her go, asshole, or so help me, I'll fucking kill you!"

Joe inched forward, and the man pressed the blade drawing a trickle of blood.

"Lookie what we got here, boys, a two-fer-one deal."

Two more men stepped into view. They'd been there the whole time, but Joe's vision tunneled on the man with the knife.

Joe's hand dropped to where his service weapon would have been, had he been in uniform, but instead found the grip of his blade.

"Easy boy, you don't want me to slit her pretty throat now, do ya?"

Joe's eyes locked on the man doing the talking.

"You hurt her, and I promise you'll all die here today."

Calling his bluff, the highwayman pressed the blade harder, drawing more blood and eliciting a cry from Tine.

"You mean like this? Now whatcha gonna do?"

A loud crack from a rifle answered, and a hole opened in the man's face at the point where the bridge of his nose met his eyebrows. The man fell dead to the ground. Tine screamed and ran to Joe's side. Joe pushed her behind him just as another shot rang out and another highwayman fell dead. Joe pulled his blade and threw it; the razor-sharp steel pierced the last highwayman's throat, who fell clutching at the gushing wound.

Even over the explosions that continued in the distance, Joe could hear a whistling sound coming from the man's neck until he took his final breath. Joe spun, shielding Tine with his body. The shots definitely came from behind them, back in the forest of the dead, but he couldn't see the shooter. They backed down the road, away from the dead and the source of their salvation.

"Dioj Volos sent that man to protect us, Joe, I know it."

Joe was feeling a little less skeptical.

"Well, if you're right, we owe him a thank you."

"I'm right. I know I am. He's a great man Joe, you'll see."

The explosions grew louder as they walked, and the pulsing lights also came into focus.

"Searchlights," Joe said, pointing. "Coming from up on that wall."

* * *

A dozen lifeboats dotted the shore where the Maristo landed, and they were immediately welcomed by bullets and exploding shells. Defender and Mystic responded with heavy cannon fire, which tore through everything they hit. In the opening minute of the battle, ten Maristo fell. Then came the soulless crew of the Raven from up out of the ocean, followed by the tickers assigned to the burning pits who charged across the beach. Making no distinction between Ticker and Maristo, Raven's crew devoured the tickers the instant they had joined their ranks. The pastreco, having made a truly miraculous recovery, jumped into the fray, spinning and chopping his way through the soulless pirates. The few remaining tickers were cut down by Alistair and the Maristo. But behind them came another swarm of the yellow sashed ineffectual bastards swinging bolos overhead.

Where the tickers failed, the shelling from the tanks and the camp's big guns dragged the Maristo's numbers down. The only positive was that the shells killed more tickers than Maristo, but still, they came. Alistair loaded, fired, reloaded, and fired again until the barrels of his deadly Dragoons were too hot to touch, and then finally, a lull.

***

The Maristo on the Great Lake back in the Midwestern Territories concentrated their forces near Savista's Straits freeing Ivan to head to the front line. The attack was focused almost entirely on Savista's eastern wall creating a target-rich environment for Savista's rifle companies. Dragging Cage's long gun, Ivan set up at the edge and delivered shot after shot with deadly accuracy, but the freebooters still came. They came in numbers that even they likely had no idea they could muster. Grappling hooks by the hundreds found purchase in the trees and boulders near the front edge of the plateau. Kite crews launched assault after assault dropping flechettes and bombs and killing as many as they could hit, but the freebooters kept coming.

The first wave of freebooters cleared the ridge and began their assault. Savista's fighters met them head-on in battle, dropping no less than six freebooters to every man, but still, more came. The field medics dragged the wounded into the medical tent as quickly as possible and then hurried back out to collect more injured. Siobhan was overwhelmed and called for more help, but no one was available. She and her four nurses would have to see this through on their own. Bleeding, wounded, and dying men choked the entrance to the medical tent. Women and even children filled the hospital's beds, and the new arrivals were made to find space on the floor.

Back on the line, Jedrek missed Alistair. Many of Savista's fighters thought his shooting freebooters who were trying to collect their fallen comrades was beyond the pale, they had no stomach for warfare, not real warfare, and it showed. Jedrek wasn't sure he had what it took to massacre men wholesale, but he knew it needed to be done. As he watched Ivan take shot after shot at the ground under a boulder to send it down the mountain to kill whomever it hit, Jedrek knew he had found his new commander.

"Boy, I need to speak with you!" Jedrek yelled.

With the boulder freed to do its work, he ran over to Jedrek.

"Names Ivan Abrams, sir, not boy."

Jedrek extended a hand, "Good to meet you, Ivan. Will you help me with something?"

Ivan smiled. It was good to hear someone say his name again. "My father told me that I was to serve Savista. Just tell me what you need."

"We need your leadership out there, Ivan, and I can't think of anyone better than Cage's son. Can Savista count on you?"

Ivan gripped his father's rifle and nodded.

"Well, Ivan Abrams, you are now Savista's field commander. I'll get word to all of the command staff. Now repel these freebooting sonsofbitches!"

"Aye, sir," Ivan said and moved toward the ridge. "Set fire to every line that reaches the ridge," he ordered.

The torchmen ran along, setting fire every rope that reached the plateau, sending the climbers back down into the gorge below. The freebooters responded by loading cables into grappling guns and resumed their assault. The freebooters greatly outnumbered Savista, but so long as they could keep them off their mountain, Savista stood a chance.

* * *

The phone at the nurses' station on the second floor rang, and Chris picked it up. She was about to say hello when a gruff voice cut her off.

"This is Dr. Belter. Tell Chris that I want Lucas transferred up to three."

Chris rolled her eyes. Perhaps she should ask Bob to have a talk with Dr. Belter as well. "This is Chris. Are you sure it's safe?"

The words came out, and Chris braced for another lecture, but it didn't come. Instead, the doctor addressed her concern calmly and logically.

"I think it's okay. I checked with maintenance, and they said that the elevators and operating room all run on separate generators. I'll come down and ride up with him if you can just get him ready for me."

Chris was taken aback. In all the years she'd worked with Dr. Belter, he had never treated her with such kindness and respect. "I'll have him ready to move in five minutes, doctor."

"Thank you, Chris," Belter said and hung up.

Chris stood with the phone to her ear for a few seconds staring at the wall.

"Are you okay?" Terri asked.

"Yeah, it was Dr. Belter."

Terri chuffed air out of her nose and slammed her hands on her hips.

"No, nothing like that," Chris said. "On the contrary. He was actually very sweet."

Terri looked at the flashing call lights above the patients' doors and the emergency lights throwing soft yellow light and shadows across the floors and walls. "I don't need any more weird shit today."

Chris excused herself and prepped Lucas for the move. Five minutes later, the elevator doors opened. Chris was already waiting with a comatose Lucas Travidi as Belter stepped out.

"So far, so good," he said and pulled Lucas' bed into the elevator. "I'll meet you up there," he said.

Chris chewed her lip and stuck out her hand to stop the closing door.

"What are you doing?" Travidi asked.

"I'll ride up with you."

They hit the button for the third floor, and other than seeming a little more sluggish than usual, it seemed to be working fine.

"Now's probably not the best time to mention it," Belter began. "But I tried to go up to six a little while ago, but the damned thing wouldn't go past five."

"Now you tell me? After I'm already trapped in here."

There was a ding, and the door slid open. Chris hurried out, pushing Lucas ahead of her. Belter walked out flipping through a medical chart, not seeming to be bothered by the strange malfunction. He walked over to the phone at the nurses' station and dialed the line up on six. The phone rang twice and went dead. He dialed again, and the same thing happened. "Chris, find Terri and tell her to meet me up to six. Something weird is going on up there," Belter said. "The elevator won't go to six, and when I tried the stairwell, the door was locked."

"The door is always locked on six," Chris said.

"Not going onto the floor it's not. Only to leave, and I've tried at least a half dozen times to call, and every time it's the same. It rings a few times, and the line goes dead. I'm telling you, something's not right. I grabbed a master-key from maintenance." Belter held it up. "The guys said it will unlock any door in the hospital."

Belter walked out from behind the reception desk and had started for the stairwell when Chris called to him. "Um, Dr. Belter. I think you should see this.

* * *

Joe and Tine entered the town of Reverie. Rotted wooden structures, lean-tos, some made of human flesh stitched together and some made of canvass, were laid out in a totally random pattern and filled the mud and filth-covered streets. A man squatted on his haunches and shit right in the middle of the road, not bothering to wipe his ass when he'd finished. Women beat up, used up, laid on heaps where slovenly men came to drag them off and use up what was left. The stench of death and disease filled Joe's nostrils. Passing a dark corner, a man reached out and grabbed Tine by the hair.

"Come here, little whore," he muttered, sounding drunk, globs of saliva dripping from his slack mouth.

Tine spun under his arm and kicked him square in the balls. As he fell, her blade found the soft part under his jaw, and she drove it deep into the bastard's head. Joe grabbed her arm, and they ran a good mile past the shantytown. Now they could clearly see the battle raging before them. They crept unseen near the north end of the compound, where the huge wall disappeared into the side of a mountain that climbed up and out of view.

Joe paused. "Tine, tell me what that man said."

"What man?"

"The man you—helped die, back at the body field."

"He was a liar, Joe." Her eyes narrowed.

"I'm sure he was, Tine. But please, tell me what he said."

"He was a liar, Joe, but he won't be telling no more lies."

Joe shook his head. "I suppose not," he said, still unsure what to think.

The fighting was well to the south, and they were able to sneak along the edge of the moat that separated them from the wall. As they continued south, the line of tanks roared and fired into the night sky. Searchlights swept the beach and swung out over the ocean, scanning the water. The fighters inside the tanks hadn't noticed them as they reached the bridge and took shelter behind a flat-bed truck that sat disabled before it could make it back across the bridge.

"We have to help him, Joe!"

Joe looked around. "Help who?"

"Dioj Volos! They're attacking him!"

"Who is?" Joe still wasn't sure which side he was supposed to be on.

"The bad men, I don't know, I just know we have to find him!"

"Well, if you have a plan on how to do that, just let me know."

"Hey, Joe, what does that say?" Tine asked, pointing to the words over the entrance in the wall.

Joe stared, and the words came out as if he were merely a radio. "There must be some kind of way out of here, said the joker to the thief." It was signed B. Dylan.

"What is that supposed to mean?"

Joe stared in wonder, "I'm not sure."

A barrage of shells fired from somewhere in the darkness over the water struck the wall not far from their position. One landed unexploded in the sand, not twenty feet away. Expecting it to explode, Joe shoved Tine into the sand and threw his body on top of hers.

"Would you get off of me? What are you doing?"

Joe looked at the projectile. It was a cast-iron ball. "Cannonballs."

"Yeah? So that's a reason to knock me down and jump on me?"

"I thought it was going to blow up."

"Really, Joe?" Her eyes softened. You would risk your own life to save me?"

"Of course, I would, Tine, you're like family to me. Heck, you're the only person I know in this whole crazy place…well, not counting the Amaris, well Mr. Amari anyway."

"I love you, Joe," she said as she hugged him.

Joe grabbed her behind the neck and pulled her close. "I love you too, Tine. Listen, we have to find your guy and get out of this place."

Tine pointed at the wall, "Hey! Like the words up there."

Joe re-read the words and shook his head. He preferred the Hendrix version, but still, could Bob Dylan have been here? Maybe it was just another guy like himself who found himself in this strange place and just happened to be a Dylan fan. Either way, Joe now knew he wasn't the only person to visit the territories. Maybe, whoever this guy was, made it back to the world and called the Todd Zeelander show. And if he had, that meant there was another gateway back, back to Red Hook. He just needed to find it. Then he could leave with Tine and give her a fighting chance at a normal life. But what about Reka? He couldn't go without her. Could he?

* * *

The freebooters came crawling up and over the edge like spiders. Savista's forces fought hard, but they were losing ground. One of Savista's fighters called for a retreat. An order not given by Ivan.

"Hold the line!" Ivan stood on a fallen tree and screamed at the top of his lungs, but Savista was farmers and carpenters, not soldiers, and the line was failing. Jedrek stood on the ramp leading up to his cabin and felt his heart sink. He considered giving Thea to them, but he dismissed it just as fast as the thought entered his head. Spotting Ivan, he yelled to him.

"Get Siobhan from the medical tent and meet me at the bottom!"

Jedrek ran up the ramp to his cabin. The three men he posted were standing ready to fight whoever came up the ramp. Jedrek announced himself before he rounded the final turn for the cabin. The men let him pass, and Jedrek entered his home for what would be the last time. Agermonte and Barrister, who had found their way up to Thea, lowered their heads and began to growl at the turning of the doorknob. Seeing Jedrek, they calmed a bit but were still on edge. Kallen and Thea hid when they heard someone coming.

"Kallen, where are you?"

She popped out from under her bed with Thea in tow.

"Right here, daddy."

Jedrek knelt down and spoke as softly as he could.

"We have to leave Savista. She has been overrun. Grab your things."

* * *

The lull was short-lived. The tanks began rolling toward the bridge to head out into the battle, firing as they moved, and more Maristo fell. Behind the tanks came the crusaders and Dioj Volos himself.

"Find her! She is here. I can feel her."

Tine was overjoyed. She knew he must be talking about her. She tried to get out from under the truck, but Joe held fast to her.

"What are you doing, Joe? That's him! That's Dioj Volos! I have to go to him."

She said I, not we, and Joe's heart sank. He cared for this child, and he had hoped, perhaps foolishly, that she would go back to Savista with him, and he and Reka could raise her as their own. Suddenly, Joe understood what was missing. He was a square peg, and the world was full of round holes, and he was being stupid. He didn't fit here any better than he did back in Red Hook. He felt so lost and alone. His world or this world, it made no difference because he didn't belong anywhere. He'd never had a relationship that was worth a damn. He was a decent cop, but big fucking deal. There were plenty of decent cops out there. He wouldn't be missed. Hell, Reka had probably found some new guy anyway. His eyes glazed over, and he'd gone almost catatonic.

"Joe? Are you okay? You're scaring me. You look like my dad did after I killed my mother." Tine was holding his face in her hands like a child holding their puppy's face when trying to have a serious conversation.

"Joe, please, you're scaring me. I don't know what I would do if I lost you too."

It was her voice that snapped him out of his despair, and he grabbed her tightly and whispered. "He's not what you think, Tine."

"What are you talking about?"

"It's just like in the Barrens."

Tine looked confused, "What's the Barrens?"

"Tine, I love you, and you are going to listen to me, do you understand?"

He had gone into full father mode, and Tine responded with a nod of her head.

"Good, now you are going to stay put. That man is not what you think he is."

Tine began to cry and buried her face in Joe's chest.

"The man on the cross," she sputtered out the words through her sobbing. "He, he, he said that Dioj Volos put all of those men on those crosses. Why would he do that, Joe?"

He saw the sadness in her eyes, the sadness of broken dreams and lost hope.

"Because he is an evil man."

As if helping Joe prove the point, Dioj Volos bellowed again.

"Find her, bring her to me, and kill her traveling companion."

Tine went from tears to rage, and Joe didn't like what he saw in her eyes.

"Easy Tine, he's not going to get you."

"He's not going to get you either, Joe."

Her body stiffened and began to shake. Her green eyes turned a smoky gray.

"Tine, listen to me. We will find another way. Just calm down."

From somewhere back on the beach came the sound of screaming, like animals being slaughtered. The sound was so jarring that it made both Joe and Tine jump. Joe couldn't believe his eyes, the Maristo! Enzo, the Holtons, and Alistair were led by a whirling spinning machine that chopped through the crusaders that flooded from behind the wall. The tanks moved but slowly in the soft sand. Firing as they went. Shells exploded all around the charging Maristo.

***

Sanchez was the first of the captains to fall. His men, enraged by the death of their captain, picked up speed and slammed into the crusaders, pushing them back toward the fortress. And still, they came by the hundreds. Kidwell saw the numbers pouring from behind the tanks and gave the order.

"Burn the lifeboats!"

The few Maristo ordered to stand by the lifeboats, dragged them onto the sand, set them ablaze, and then joined their brothers in battle. Defender and Mystic fired fast and hard, determined to do all the damage they could before they followed their captain's orders and pushed out to sea. Cannonballs turned the wall to dust, knocking out the searchlights and crippling most of the tanks. Another volley and the ships weighed anchor and moved to deeper waters.

* * *

When the smoke and dust cleared, Joe saw what lay beyond the wall, and his blood froze. A Massive red barn rose up before him.

"Joe," Tine said, tugging at his arm.

"What?"

"I asked what that thing is."

"Diastole."

"What's Diastole?"

"I'll tell you later."

"If there is a later," she said.

The battle on the beach continued. Alistair fired relentlessly into the approaching fighters dropping one after another. The remaining tickers under Dioj Volos' command fled amid the last barrage, not knowing that it would be the last. But the Maristo were still vastly outnumbered. Joe and Tine watched from under the truck as the Maristo, and the crusaders were locked in battle, and then he saw her. Reka was standing, backlit by the burning lifeboats, firing her rifle into the fast-approaching zealots.

"Reka!"

No one but Tine could hear him over the chaos.

"Where, Joe?"

Joe pointed as he stood up. "There! I have to get to her Tine. You stay here. I'll come back for you."

Tine grabbed Joe's arm. "No, Joe, I go where you go."

"It's too dangerous, Tine."

"I go where you go!"

Joe could see that there was no winning the argument, so he took her by the hand, and they kept low. The last thing he wanted was to find Reka but lose Tine in the process. They carved their way through the sand, keeping out of sight, and they had just about made it when Reka's rifle swung in his direction and stopped. He shoved Tine behind him and waited for the shot, but it didn't come.

"Joe?"

She ran to him, and the two met in an embrace and fell to the sand.

"Oh my god, Joe! I can't believe it! It's really you!"

"Reka, what are you doing here?"

"Looking for you. The pastreco said that you would be here and that we had to kill this Dioj—" It seemed Reka couldn't recall the last name.

"Volos," said Tine.

Reka looked at the thin child.

"Who is this?"

Tine, possibly feeling a little jealous, crossed her arms and answered.

"This," she said. "Is Tine. I'm Joe's best friend."

Reka knelt down and hugged her.

"She doesn't like to be touched," Joe warned.

But Tine wrapped her arms around Reka, "I've heard so much about you."

"You have?" Reka smiled.

"Yes, and you're very beautiful."

"We have to get out of here," Joe said.

All around them, the Maristo were falling. It seemed that defeat was at hand.

"Reka, I think I have a way to get us out of here, and I don't know if it will land us back in Espero or back in my world, but I think it's the only way out."

He pointed at the red barn.

"Remember how I told you that I came from another place and I would explain it all one day?"

Reka reached into her pocket and pulled out the RHPD collar pin he'd given to her before he left for the Barrens with Alistair.

"That's right, well, the doorway might take us back to Espero and Savista, or it might take us back there," he pointed at the pin.

Reka clutched the pin in her hand. "As long as I am with you, it doesn't matter."

"Then let's get Alistair and get the hell out of this place," he thought again of the words on the wall, now blasted into oblivion.

Reka looked at the thin little girl with red hair.

"Are you okay with this plan?"

Tine smiled, "I go where Joe goes."

Death whistles screamed as shells passed overhead. The three made their way toward Alistair, still firing his Dragoons at the approaching hoard. Next to him in battle was a short, stocky man with a great white head of hair and beard to match, a massive bear of man, and two others.

"Who are those guys with Alistair? Are they going to be a problem?"

Reka looked sad, "No," she said. "They won't be a problem."

"What's wrong?"

"Nothing," she answered, though deep in her soul, she must have known that they were destined to die on that beach.

Joe topped off his repeater, and Reka loaded another magazine into her rifle. They ran and fired and took out more crusaders as they moved closer to Alistair. With the pastreco swinging Cage's bearded axes, the tide seemed to turn, and Alistair, along with the rest of the Maristo, moved closer to the crumbled wall.

* * *

Jedrek came down the ramp fast with both girls in his arms and Agermonte and Barrister leading the way. The men assigned to guard the girls followed close behind. Ivan and Siobhan met them at the bottom of the ramp. Savista was overrun. As they turned to make their way toward the straits to escape, Kallen tried to stop him, but Jedrek didn't listen.

"That's the wrong way!" she cried.

But Jedrek kept going. They made it to the drop, and Jedrek lowered the guards down first, then the kids and Siobhan. When it came time for Ivan to descend, he refused.

"You go, Jedrek; I'll stay at my post."

"Ivan, there is nothing left to defend."

Ivan shook Jedrek's hand. "You gave my father and me a home, and we can never repay you. You take care of the girls, and I will stay and defend Savista. If there is anything left when this is over, you can return and rebuild."

Ivan turned and ran back toward the fight, and Jedrek lowered himself down into the strait.

* * *

Defender and Mystic returned and entered the harbor, disobeying their orders. With Dioj Volos' defenses crumbling, the Maristo ships turned their cannons, seventy-two in all, on the compound. Small munition dumps exploded, sending flaming shrapnel tearing through the air, cutting down crusaders and Maristo alike. Debris from the blasts ignited the camp's diesel depots. The viscus fuel clung, burning to everyone and everything in its path. Still, neither side would retreat. The pastreco charged out of the smoke and debris toward Dioj Volos in the midst of it all.

"I have been sent for you," the pastreco said.

Dioj Volos was even larger than the pastreco. He held a long broadsword in his hand and wielded it with fluid dexterity.

"Gabriel, my brother. Join me, and we can rule this land. We owe nothing to these men, and we owe nothing to God." Dioj Volos spoke in calm, controlled tones. "He has abandoned us, brother. We owe him nothing."

The pastreco moved cat-like around Dioj Volos. Cage Abrams' bearded axes glinting in the light of the fires burning all around them. "You're wrong, Moloch. We owe them everything. The pastreco were sent here to serve, but you! You murdered our brothers and enslaved men. You are a disgrace, and you will be judged."

The broad sword and axes clashed, sending sparks into the sky and rang out like the bells of La Iglesia de Cristo Redentor. Moloch, who called himself Dioj Volos, raised the broadsword again and struck at Gabriel. Gabriel caught the blade with one axe and swung the other at Moloch's midsection. The edge passed close, drawing blood but causing no real damage. Moloch drew back his sword and pierced Gabriel's side. Blood poured from the open wound just above his hip.

"Join me, Gabriel. It's not too late. I will forgive your trespasses if you only lay down your weapons and kneel before me.

Gabriel lunged at Moloch and caught the broadsword in his left breast. The blow staggard him.

"Brother, please. Kneel before me and take my hand. I will destroy these fools, and we will build our empire."

The world was spinning, and Gabriel had all he could do to remain standing. Cage's axes suddenly felt heavy in his hands. He swung wildly, missing Moloch and losing his grip on the axe sending it harmlessly into the sand. Moloch spun with his blade and split the flesh across Gabriel's forehead. Blood poured into his eyes.

"Why die for these animals? There is no one here to bring you to Diastole. You will die in the sand like—" He waved a contemptuous hand. "Like one of them. That is no way for an archangel to die. Join me, sit at my right hand. It is where you belong. We have both killed men. We are both of us fallen, so, if this world is our punishment, our inheritance, let's make it truly ours."

Gabriel fell to one knee and steadied himself on his remaining axe. Moloch hung his head and took a position behind Gabriel.

"You are on your knee, just drop the axe, and all will be forgiven, brother. Please, take your place beside me."

Gabriel held tight to the axe, and Moloch grabbed Gabriel by the hair and raised his sword. Alistair charged, unloading his Dragoons into Moloch, but the bullets struck with no more effect than wasp stings. Moloch spun and hurled his broadsword at Alistair. The blade nearly cut his body in two, and Joe watched as the man he'd come to think of as a father passed from this world.

Joe screamed and emptied his repeater into Moloch. Moloch looked down as if wondering if any of Joe's shots landed, released Gabriel, and took a step toward Joe. As he did, Gabriel summoned what strength he had left, picked up Cage's axe, and brought it down between Moloch's shoulder blades. The axe sliced down the middle of Moloch's back, severing his spinal column, and Moloch fell, unable to move. He lay grunting, face down in the sand.

"This is Dioj Volos!" Gabriel shouted. "This is God's Will!"

Gabriel lifted the axe again and brought it down across the back of Moloch's neck, freeing his head from his body. Gabriel fell dead in the sand, next to his brother.

* * *

Siobhan reached the bottom of the strait and pulled her daughter and Kallen to her. It was almost too dark to see.

"Thea, where are the guards?"

"I don't know, mom; I think they're gone."

Siobhan's squinted, trying to adjust to the darkness. Jedrek lowered himself down. And Kallen ran to him.

"Siobhan, Thea, are you okay?"

"We're fine, but the guards are gone."

Suddenly the putrid smell of festering wounds filled the air, and Hayward Taft slithered up behind Siobhan in the darkness and grabbed her. One hand around her midsection and the other pressing the tip of his terrible karambit into her back. Jedrek pushed both girls behind him and moved toward Taft.

"Let her go!"

And he did; he slid the blade into her back and sliced her open. She fell helplessly to the ground and died.

Jedrek lunged for him, and Taft dragged his blade across his throat. Jedrek fell alongside Siobhan.

"Come to me, child."

Thea began to tremble with rage. She looked down at her mother and back at Taft, and she flashed.

The light expanded a few feet away from her body and collapsed back into her. Hayward Taft's eyes filled with tears.

"At last, I am free."

The light exploded from Thea's tiny body, and the world was bright as day. Her light flew out across the entire territory. It flashed over the Great Lake, through the Barrens, and clear past the Columbias, to all points north to south and east to west in the world. It boiled the seas, leveled the mountains, and consumed every living thing, even the mighty docco.

Chapter 51

Tine felt the flash even before it had happened. She saw one of Joe's bullets as it entered Moloch's neck and stopped. Tine saw Gabriel's blade in Moloch's back, and she plucked a grain of sand out of the air in front of her face and rolled it between her fingers. Everything around her had frozen in time, and she walked through the living display like a curator. As she walked, Tine glanced to the east and saw it coming. The blinding white light, like her own that had killed her mother, but on a much larger scale.

"Joe!" Tine cried out, but if he heard her, he didn't respond.

Tine rushed to him, releasing the grain of sand from between her fingers. Instead of hanging in mid-air, the sand fell back to earth as her touch had reanimated it. She grabbed Joe by the hand, and he, too, came alive. He looked around at the stillness.

"What the hell is going on?"

"We have to go, Joe," Tine said.

"What? We can't leave."

"We have to, Joe. There's no time!"

Joe turned to find Reka standing as motionless as a statue, her mouth opened wide in a scream. Joe grabbed her by the shoulder, but he couldn't move her. "Reka!"

"Leave her, Joe!" Tine looked east again. The flash was getting closer by the second.

"I'm not leaving her, Tine."

Tine scratched madly at her head, and an idea came to her. Touching Joe seemed to bring him out of his trance-like state. Maybe it would work for Reka as well. Tine grabbed Reka's hand, and Reka drew in a great breath of air.

"What happened, Joe?"

"I'm not—"

"There's no time for that! We have to go!"

Joe looked at Alistair lying on the ground, and he looked at Gabriel and Enzo and the men of Ancora Imparo, and he knew they were all dead.

"Come on, Joe!"

Tine was running toward the red barn. Joe grabbed Reka's hand, and together, they ran after her; all the while, the air was heating up as the flash drew nearer. They reached the barn, and Joe searched frantically for a knob or handle, but there were none to be found.

Tine kept one eye on Joe and one on the approaching flash. "Open it, Joe!"

"I can't. I don't know how!"

Tine watched as the light reached the far end of the beach, vaporizing everything in its path. Reka took Joe's hands in hers and looked into his eyes.

"Yes, you do, Joe. I heard Alistair tell the pastreco that you are the key. You can do this, Joe." Reka touched a hand to his cheek.

Joe looked at the wall, "I am the key? What does that mean? How am I the key?"

The heat was almost unbearable. Tine began to tremble, and her eyes clouded over.

"Joe, something is happening to Tine!"

He felt helpless and leaned his forehead against the wall. The wall flew open Joe fell forward. Reka grabbed Tine and pulled her inside as the wall slammed shut, stopping the light. Just as he had in the barn in Espero, Joe smelled the warm, inviting scent of wood and oil.

"We made it," Joe said.

Reka held Tine in her arms and hushed the trembling little girl. "Shh, it's okay, Tine, we're safe now."

The three sat on the floor inside the red barn clinging to one another.

* * *

Belter walked back toward the reception desk across from the elevator bank. Chris didn't say a word; she didn't have to. Belter followed her gaze. The number six glowed bright red above the elevator door.

"Am I crazy, or did those numbers used to be green?" One of the floor nurses said.

"Looks like it's on six, doctor," Chris said.

"It would appear so," he agreed.

They stood staring at the number for what seemed like an eternity. Chris gasped when it finally blipped off and then back on reading five, then four, and stopped on three. Everyone held their breath as the chrome doors separated. Vicki Loerzel, head nurse from the sixth floor, stood with her back pressed against the far wall. The group let out a collective sigh of relief.

"Vicki, is everything okay?" Belter asked as the doors began to close.

"Chris stuck her arm in the door to keep it from closing, and Belter stepped onto the elevator to help the nervous-looking psych nurse off.

"Why didn't you answer the phone when I called?" Belter asked, holding her hand just a little too long.

"I tried," she said. "But every time I picked it up, it started ringing, like I made the call and then disconnected."

"What's going on up there, Vicki?" Chris asked.

Vicki didn't make eye contact with anyone. She just stared at the wall as she answered. "Every patient in my ward went comatose right after the power went down."

"Same with most of our patients," said a floor nurse who'd come up from the second floor.

Vicki blinked slowly and continued. "Then there was the second power surge, and they all woke up. Only for a second, only long enough for them all to say—"

"Reverie?" Terri asked.

"How did you know?" Vicki asked.

"Same thing happened in Joe's room."

"But what does it mean?" Vicki asked.

"I don't know," Terri said. "I sent one of the girls to the hospital's library and grab the dictionary."

The candy striper who'd been sitting at the reception desk rolled her eyes. "Why don't you use the computer? Webster's dictionary is on the world wide web now."

"I tried; I couldn't even open AOL."

"AOL is down?" The candy striper sounded absolutely panicked.

"Here she comes now," Terri said.

A tiny figure in white shoes sprinted toward them with a book that looked absurdly large in her small hands. She tossed the dictionary on the counter with a thud, and Vicki flipped it open to the R section and started flipping through page after page of *ra* words, then *re* words. Reaching rev, she ran her finger down the page, reverend, reverent, reverential, reverentially, reverently. "Reverie, a state of dreamlike meditation, a fanciful vision too unrealistic to come to pass."

"But what does that have to do with being comatose?" Vicki asked. "Catatonic," Belter corrected. "They aren't unconscious; at least Joe and Lucas aren't." Belter rubbed his jaw. "The patients up on six and Lucas and Joe." He shook his head. "I'll be damned if I know what to make of it."

Suddenly everyone froze.

"Chris placed a hand on the counter to stabilize herself.

"Did you feel that?"

Doctor Belter looked around, "I think everyone felt it."

A second shudder bigger than the first, and the hospital was plunged into darkness. No emergency lights, no backup generator, no more blinking call lights above the patient's doors. Belter pulled his penlight from his pocket and clicked it, but it didn't work. He pulled his pager from his belt and hit the button, expecting to see the display light up, but again, nothing.

"What the hell? Does anyone have a lighter?" Belter asked.

One of the nurses pulled her Bic lighter from her pocket and rolled the striker with her thumb. A blinding flash lit up the whole floor, but it hadn't come from the Bic. It came from 306, Joe's room. When the flash faded, they were left with only the flickering flame from the Bic to provide light. Chris took the lighter from the stunned nurse and made her way to Joe's room, followed by Belter and Terri. Chris touched the door to feel for heat. She had learned a lot from the movie Backdraft, and feeling only the smooth, cool wood, pushed it open. She looked around in the glow of the little plastic lighter at an empty room. Empty except for Bob, who was sleeping in the chair in the corner.

"Bob, Bob, wake up. Have you seen Joe?"

"Joe?" Bob had been in the deepest sleep he'd had in days. "He's right there, in his—" But Joe wasn't in his bed.

Chris walked over and patted the covers even though she knew it was pointless. Joe was gone.

Belter cleared his throat, "He could have snuck out in the blackout."

"I'm going down to the second floor," Chris said.

"I'll come with," Bob added.

Just as they turned to leave the room, Chris lost her grip on the fuel lever, and the lighter went out, only the room wasn't dark. The television screen flickered to life as power to the hospital was restored.

"We interrupt our regularly scheduled programming for a special message from the President of the United States of America."

* * *

Joe, Reka, and Tine got to their feet. Joe knew the drill, and he knew they had a lot of walking to do before they reached the other end of this trip. Hand-in-hand they walked past the rows and rows of crates stacked floor to ceiling in all directions as far as the eye could see. As they walked, Joe told them about the first time he had come to their world, how he walked through the darkness, how the acid rain burned his skin, how when he finally reached the end, he stepped out into Espero.

"There is no more Espero."

Joe looked at Tine. "What do you mean, no more Espero?"

"The flash, someone flashed, big Joe, they flashed really big."

"What do you mean, flashed?"

"Remember when I told you about my flash and how it killed my mom and the docco?"

"Of course, I remember."

"Well, mine was a baby flash compared to that one. There's no more Espero, Joe. Or anything else."

Joe remembered the films he'd watched in school about the atom bomb explosion and how everything around it burned up in a white flash. "Who did it?"

Tine looked at him. "How should I know; I was with you when it happened, remember?"

Reka looked at Joe, "Eva."

He squeezed her hand. "I'm sorry, Reka."

She cried, and he held her. He let her cry herself out. They were in no hurry. When she regained her composure, they walked on in silence, and slowly, the light faded until they were in complete darkness.

"Joe, where are we?"

"It's okay, Tine, just hold on tight to Reka's hand, Reka, you hold onto mine."

He squeezed, and she squeezed back. They walked in the darkness holding hands and hopeful. Finally, Joe stopped.

"Okay, this is it. I'll go up first. You two follow."

Joe set his foot on the bottom rung, climbed up, and pushed the heavy steel door open. Joe climbed out and helped Reka and Tine. They found themselves standing in a tunnel with faint yellow and green lights along the walls. From ahead of them came a rumbling and then a light in the darkness.

"Train!" Joe screamed.

"What's a—"

Tine was about to say train when Joe grabbed the girls and pressed them up against the wall just as the EL train screamed by.

"What the hell was that?" Reka was shaking.

"That was a train, an EL train."

"What's an El train?" Tine's little voice squeaked.

"It's an electric train that runs through the city."

Reka looked beautiful in the soft light, beautiful and confused.

"Electric train?"

"Yeah, it runs on electricity. Oh! And speaking of electricity, you see that rail?" He pointed to the third rail on the track. "Stay away from it. That is how the electricity flows to the train. If you touch it, it will kill you." He was speaking more to Tine. "Am I clear?"

"Clear," said Tine.

"Good, now these things run like clockwork, so let's get out of here."

The three hurried down the tracks and finally reached the platform. The crowd gathered to await the approaching train gasped, and two men in suits dropped down to their knees and waved them over.

"Come on! Get over here! The train is coming!" one of the men said.

Another rumble and the bright light of an approaching train came screeching down the rails. Reka lifted Tine up to the men and extended her hand. Joe jumped up, caught the platform with his stomach, and swung his legs up just as the train came into the station. The crowd erupted in applause.

"What the hell is wrong with you people! Are you trying to get yourselves killed?" scolded the man who had pulled Reka to safety.

Joe ignored the man and read the sign on the wall. "Washington Station. Holy shit, we made it. We're home."

He gathered the girls and rushed up the stairway out of the subway. When they popped out onto State Street, Reka and Tine stared dumbfounded at the traffic, people, and tall buildings.

"Where are we, Joe?" Reka clung to his arm.

"Ladies, I give you Chicago! Home of the Bears."

"Bears?" Tine looked around. "I don't see any bears."

A bus rolled by belching smoke and stinking of diesel fumes.

"They're a sports team, football. Man, I have so much to show you guys! Like right there," Joe pointed at a large building with a clock mounted on the corner. "That's Marshal Fields. You guys are going to love that place once we get settled in."

Reka smiled; Joe seemed so happy. He grabbed their hands and hurried across State Street. Drivers hit their brakes and honked. He dragged the girls into The Ferris Wheel restaurant forgetting that he had no money. A crowd had gathered around the counter and stood silent, staring at the small television mounted above the cash register.

On the television, the president stood behind a podium. In the caption below, the copy crawled across the screen: *Reports of earthquakes and fires coming in from Russia, China, Argentina, Canada...,* names of countries, some Joe had never heard of, crawled across the bottom of the screen.

* * *

Chris grabbed the television remote attached to the bedrail and raised the volume.

"Good evening, my fellow Americans. Today, Friday, December 8th, 1995, at approximately 3:00 pm, our scientists detected unusually high radiation levels in the atmosphere. We have reports from as far away as the Pechengsky District on the Kola Peninsula in Murmansk Oblast in Russia. Scientists at the sight of the Kola Superdeep Borehole reported an explosion some forty-thousand feet below the surface. Our neighbors across the globe have been reporting earthquakes and typhoons. Israel has reported a wall of fire that has risen from the Dead Sea Depression, as have China in the Turfan Depression and Argentina in San Julian's Great Depression. We also have reports from our own Death Valley of fires spinning up in dust devils and breaking out in various spots across the land."

Chris felt Bob's arm wrap around her as he pulled her close. On the television, the president continued.

"Initial reports from Moscow estimate the quake at 9.5 magnitude, equal to the Valdivia Earthquake in Valdivia Chile on May 22nd, 1960. The largest earthquake ever recorded. As I have said, similar quakes have been felt across the globe. At this time, we have no reason to believe that this is anything other than a natural occurrence, and our scientists are working to determine the best course of action."

***

The crowd in the diner shifted and murmured.

"Our scientists are reporting seismic activity near Alamogordo, New Mexico. Initial readings indicate that the quake registered a magnitude of 9.3, making it the most powerful quake in US history, surpassing the Alaskan earthquake in 1964. The Alamogordo quake has caused a number of explosions in the area, and with it, an unknown number of casualties. In time we hope to determine the cause of all of this activity, but for now, we need to focus on self-preservation."

The president wiped his brow and cleared his throat before continuing. "Additionally, power has been disrupted to a number of nuclear facilities, and work is underway to restore power to keep the cores from melting down."

Some people in the restaurant pushed their way out the door, some sat and cried, but Joe was glued to the report.

"The American Red Cross and the CDC are out in full force as I speak delivering iodine pills to local hospitals for distribution to aid in fending off some of the effects should the worst happen. But an even more immediate danger exists. We have received numerous reports of tidal waves on the Atlantic and Pacific oceans bearing down on our coastal states. If you can hear my voice and you are in a coastal state, move. Move now, move as far inland as you are able. As I speak, the evacuation of all east and west coast states is underway. Early models are telling us that even the Great Lakes will be affected by the seismic activity caused by the quakes."

The president paused again and took a sip of water.

"I don't need to tell you all that we are in serious danger. It saddens me.

No, it crushes my soul to say that most of us will not survive this. Those of us that do will need to rely on one another and on the things that make our nation great. Our commonalities, our love for our fellow man, our thirst for freedom. Our great republic will remain intact, and our nation's leadership will remain intact so that when the worst has passed, we can assist the American people in rebuilding. We have relocated White House operations to an undisclosed location, and this will be the launching pad from which we will begin our resurrection once this threat has passed. And rest assured that it will pass."

He slammed his fist on the podium.

"In the days ahead, we intend to continue to keep you updated with the latest information available over every available means of communication at our disposal. The government has locked down all television and radio communications to ensure the most saturated coverage imaginable. In the event that fails, we will broadcast over shortwave for as long as we can. We will provide daily briefings at 6:00 pm Central Standard Time. We have named our stronghold Columbia, a name that embodies liberty and manifest destiny. The very things our great republic was founded on. My fellow Americans, Children of Columbia, I beseech you, watch over one another, be strong, and may Almighty God have mercy on us all.

About the Author

PAUL VANDORN is a retired police officer and the author of 4 novels. These include Hiraeth, Inaki, Challenging Entropy, and Diastole, as well as several short stories, including The Van Meter Incident, Obdach and Yellow Bird.

You can connect with me on:

🌐 https://coldfrontpublishing.com

🐦 https://twitter.com/ColdFrontPub

Also by Paul VanDorn

HIRAETH

Officer Joe Kott settled into his cruiser prepared for another long midnight shift in rural Red Hook, Illinois. He planned on spending this night as he spent most. Listening to Todd Zeelander's weird radio show, smoking cigarettes, and drinking coffee to try and stay awake. But the driver of a dark blue 1970 Mustang Boss 302 disrupts his plans, and before day breaks, Officer Kott's cruiser is discovered abandoned, and he is left to find his way through a world that even Zeelander wouldn't believe.

INAKI

The small Midwestern farming town of Chesapeake Station in southern Illinois has a dark secret. For nearly 300 years, a creature known as the Inaki has fed on the blood of the innocent. Those with the power to stop it have chosen not to, placing their power and wealth above all else.

Now it is up to anthropologist Nick Ryan who is visiting Chesapeake Station to study the Native American Nation of the Mooka'am who vanished in the 1700s, to dig deeper and unlock the mystery surrounding the legend of the Inaki. Along the way, Nick must face the demons of his past and come face to face with the monster that drove his father to madness.

CHALLENGING ENTROPY

Detective Charlotte Rittenhouse of the Northeastern Major Crimes Task Force has been assigned to investigate the brutal murders of four women in northern Iowa. While it's apparent that the murders are connected, it isn't clear until a fifth woman is taken that they are tied to a series of murders that occurred in Chicago almost ten years earlier. Now Rittenhouse must enlist the aid of a disgraced US Marshal and a campus security guard if there is any hope of finding the missing woman before she becomes the next victim of the infamous Tooth Fairy.